The Color of Light

William Goldman

WARNER BOOKS

A Warner Communications Company

WARNER BOOKS EDITION

Warner Books, Inc.
666 Fifth Avenue
New York, NY 10103

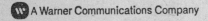 A Warner Communications Company

Printed in the United States of America

This book was originally published in hardcover by Warner Books.
First paperback printing: May, 1985

10 9 8 7 6 5 4 3 2 1

<u>THE COLOR OF LIGHT</u> SHINES!

"Arresting . . . Goldman is a compelling writer."
—*Cosmopolitan*

"One of the most engrossing and moving novels you're likely to read this year. It is subtle, multi-layered, and it may be the best thing Goldman has ever written."   —*Fort Worth Star-Telegram*

"Engrossing . . . a godsend . . . not only fresh but compelling. This is the kind of book that can make you forget you are doomed to six hours wedged into the center of ten seats on a 747."
—*Atlanta Journal-Constitution*

"Goldman writes with a speedy grace, creating a smooth readability while staying close to the spine of his story . . . a novel that is as unique as anything Goldman has ever written. It is an honest story written by an author who believes in honest passions, honest fears and an honest sense of humanity."   —*Richmond Times-Dispatch*

"Captures the reader's interest immediately . . . the first part of the book is so innovative and riveting that the reader is compelled to stay with it. . . ."
—*Tulsa Daily World*

"Masterful and fascinating Goldman."
—*West Coast Review of Books*

"Goldman's story of the making of a writer and a man . . . wins and holds our respect as he goes after the truth of Chub's life and renders it skillfully and movingly."   —*Publishers Weekly*

I'll go see Del tonight after work

ALSO BY WILLIAM GOLDMAN

FICTION
The Temple of Gold (1957)
Your Turn to Curtsy, My Turn to Bow (1958)
Soldier in the Rain (1960)
Boys and Girls Together (1964)
No Way to Treat a Lady (1964)
The Thing of It Is . . . (1967)
Father's Day (1971)
The Princess Bride (1973)
Marathon Man (1974)
Magic (1976)
Tinsel (1979)
Control (1982)

NONFICTION
The Season: A Candid Look at Broadway (1969)
The Making of "A Bridge Too Far" (1977)
**Adventures in the Screen Trade: A Personal View
of Hollywood and Screenwriting* (1983)

SCREENPLAYS
Masquerade (1965)
(with Michael Relph)
Harper (1966)
Butch Cassidy and the Sundance Kid (1969)
The Hot Rock (1972)
The Great Waldo Pepper (1975)
The Stepford Wives (1975)
All the President's Men (1976)
Marathon Man (1976)
A Bridge Too Far (1977)
Magic (1978)
Mr. Horn (1979)

PLAYS
Blood, Sweat, and Stanley Poole (1961)
(with James Goldman)
A Family Affair (1962)
(with James Goldman and John Kander)

FOR CHILDREN
Wigger
(1974)

*Published by Warner Books

This book is for John Newey

PART I

Under
the
Weather

CHAPTER 1

The Girl(s)
of My Dreams

Late on a late spring afternoon, Chub, ambling across the Oberlin campus, was astonished to see the girl of his dreams break into tears.

He had fallen—quite literally—for B. J. Peacock twenty months before, his first day of Orientation week freshman year. Chub was dashing toward the steps to Peters Hall when she began coming down. He reached the stairs, glanced at her, then away, then back, and was so stunned by what he saw that he actually fell *up* the stairs and landed hard, sending the books he was carrying all the hell over and severely bruising his hip.

She knelt quickly beside him, gathered up his books. "You okay?"

Prone, he kept his head away from her and managed a mortified nod.

"First day?"

He nodded again, took his books, stood, took a step, or tried to, but the pain in his hip made him limp around like Quasimodo. "Very first. I'm majoring in ballet—either that or gymnastics, I haven't decided yet."

She came close to laughing, settled on a smile, and moved down the steps, hurrying away. Chub watched her till a building corner took her from his sight. Trying to salvage something from the encounter wasn't easy. Finally he told himself, "What the hell, I almost made her laugh."

(Chub had known and dated a lot of girls during high

3

school, late on hot nights after his many endless summer jobs, but it would be a dozen years before he could crystallize what was so special about B.J.

(He and The Bone were walking out after a screening of *Tootsie* in New York and Chub, like most of the rest of the audience, immediately wanted to run away with Jessica Lange, and he was going on about how pretty she was when The Bone, gaunt and dark, lit one of the hundred unfiltered English Ovals she consumed each day, interrupted him, speaking as she always did, fast and factually. "She's not pretty," The Bone said. "*I* was pretty, Lange's *movie* pretty, there's a difference," but as she went on to explain the difference, Chub wasn't there. He was back again, lying humiliated on the steps of Peters Hall, with B. J. Peacock kneeling above him, her green eyes bright, her pale red hair tumbling down well below her shoulders, wondering if he was okay.)

The day after the Peters Hall debacle, Chub spotted B.J. again. He was walking across Tappan Square, the rectangular park that served to separate Oberlin College from the town. His arms were full of books again and he was heading toward his dorm while she was coming in the opposite direction, toward him. Whether she saw him or not he couldn't know, because he averted his eyes, hurrying along until they were close, and then he did something either brave or stupid, he wasn't sure at the time, he just did it—

—tripped again, this time intentionally, sending his books all the hell over, as he lay there groaning theatrically at her feet.

This time she *did* laugh.

And they gathered up his books together. And then had coffee. Which was how their friendship began.

B. J. Peacock—the initials did not stand for Betty Jane or any words at all, they were just initials; she was from Texas, they did that there—was a junior, and the leading actress at school.

There were those unfriendly to her cause, who said the only reason she got main parts was because one of the men who ran the Dramat had the hots for her, but Chub put that down to jealousy. Especially when he saw her be wonderful later that fall, playing Helen of Troy in *Tiger at the Gates*. She was almost as good in the spring musical, *Kiss Me Kate*—she had a lovely, small, soprano voice, even though some of the spitfire elements of the comedy were a bit strained.

Her senior fall she played the Katharine Hepburn part in *The Philadelphia Story* and even Chub was hard put to admit that her performance wasn't being carried by the quality of her lines. Alas, not even the quality of the Bard's lines could get her through her last play in school, where she was cast as Lady Macbeth. The idea of putting someone with her beauty in that role wasn't totally original—Olivier had wanted to make a movie of the play with Vivien Leigh. And B.J. truly never looked better. And she moved with natural grace. And her Texas accent, which she had slaved to lose, was indeed totally gone.

Which did not stop some of the audience from laughing in the wrong places. Actually, there are very few *right* places for guffawing in that play and Chub knew, as he sat through the opening performance, that every one was knifing her. Afterward, he concentrated on all the wonderful choices she had made, and she seemed grateful for his words.

But the truth, Chub had to admit, was that, as an actress, B.J. had a flaw: She wasn't overwhelmingly gifted; Duse need not spin.

She also had one other flaw: She was engaged.

At least Chub assumed it was a flaw. But that was before he met Del Hilton. Until their initial handshake in the No-Name Pizza/Bar, Chub assumed Hilton would have to be one of the following:

(a) rich

(b) brilliant, or

(c) a ringer for Rudolph Valentino.

In truth, he was (d) none of the above. Del was a scholarship student who bartended nights to accumulate income; he studied endlessly for his "*A*"s—he was willing to outwork anyone; and although he was tall, he was also pale and balding and wore old-fashioned rimless glasses.

What he had was strength, quiet strength. Mental and moral. B.J. was emotional, and when she took off on a flyer, he was always there to ground her. He was her foundation.

It was unusual that a junior would be allowed to bartend (even though the only alcoholic beverage legal in the town was 3.2 beer; you could get buzzed on it, but it required imagination and hard labor). But then, Del was not your normal junior. He was twenty-five years old, having spent many years in the Army, saving money for college. He had served in Viet Nam, unusual on campus at that time, and there were rumors that he had been fired upon, been wounded, had killed. Whatever the truth, the subject of military service was not one he ever brought up.

Chub became first their mascot, eventually a confidant, and they double-dated more than a little, sometimes driving in Del's car to Cleveland when there was a road company of a musical that B.J. was desperate to see, like *Hair,* the first one they went to together.

They had been engaged for six months when Chub met them, and in all the hours that were to come, they argued only occasionally and never fought. There was no situation Chub could think of that would be sufficient to make Del lose control.

If they had a problem, it was not whether they were going to get married—after graduation, no argument there. But, Chub realized, it was this: Would they be second-raters when they did?

B.J. wanted one thing in her life—to act in the theatre, but not regional. She didn't care if it was off Broadway or on; for her it was to be New York or nothing. Except she felt she wasn't ready, needed seasoning, and that meant grad school. Iowa was all right and Northwestern was, too, but nothing to her compared to Yale. Julie Harris had gone there, Paul Newman had gone there, it was the best—and it was near New York. If you went to North-western, you were almost in a desert, and if you studied in Iowa, you were in a desert. Yale. It had to be Yale.

Del, dirt poor always, had his own ambition, too—the law. But not John Jay at night, thank you. He wanted Harvard or he wanted Yale.

All through their junior year, B.J. and Del ran colleges around in their heads, Chub sitting beside her at the No-Name, Del joining them when his duties allowed. The first decision they reached was only to apply to the same schools, which meant Del decided not to try for Harvard; he was not being magnanimous, he explained: Reality told him he didn't stand all that great a chance.

Then they agreed that just the three schools—Iowa, Northwestern and Yale—was cutting it too fine. So they went over catalogs and listened to scuttlebutt and added Indiana and Ohio State.

Five schools. Five graduate schools. It all made sense; they both felt that.

But Chub, listening to them, soon realized that really there was only Yale. They started making little down-putting jokes about the other four. B.J. promised, since she'd managed to lose her Texas accent, to work equally hard so she could pass for a native Iowan. Del kept coming up with lawyers he "discovered" had attended Northwestern—Darrow, Cardozo, Learned Hand.

Chub had no doubt that one of the five schools would undoubtedly take them both. But Yale? Del got wonderful grades, but he wasn't quick; he had to slave, and he needed a scholarship to get him through. And B.J.? A glory to look at onstage, no question. And she was willing to work like a tank. But there was no fire.

And there was no way, he knew, it was going to happen. It was madness, their fantasy. And when it fragmented he knew one thing: Forever and always, they would carry inside the stigma—they were second-raters.

It wasn't true, of course; not to him. But their hopes had slipped beyond control. They seemed, to themselves, at least, on top of the situation. They even discussed what would happen if one of them got into Yale but not the other, and they were casual about it. No big deal. They'd simply forget about New Haven and study someplace together.

Chub wondered about the anger that the one who gave up Yale would feel. How deep and how long before it would surface and what would happen when it did?

And then, late on that late spring afternoon, Chub, ambling along, spotted them in the shadows of Tappan Square. He started toward them, suddenly stopped—

—because as he watched, Del was grabbing her, hands on shoulders, and shaking her.

B.J. slipped free. Del went for her again, but as he did she swiped out with her left hand, slapped at his face, connected, and his rimless glasses balanced askew for a moment, then fell and shattered on the sidewalk. She tried another swing but this time he was too quick, and again he was rippling her body, shaking her off balance.

Which was when she broke into tears.

Del released his hold, picked up his broken glasses, started away, stopped, turned back, said something, and whatever it was, it made her bend forward, her arms across her stomach, and she turned and he turned, hurried away, leaving her.

Chub watched it all, standing frozen in the nearing dusk, standing too far to hear it but close enough that what he saw was seared—"through a glass, darkly" was the phrase that seemed to fit, who said that, where was it from, the Bible? Corinthians, probably, First or Second, he couldn't quite get it and he couldn't quite get what to do now, how to act, should he turn and walk away and pretend he had seen nothing; he only knew that he understood nothing, and then his choice was removed because B.J. spotted him and came toward him quickly, her arms down now, whipped, the tears pouring unencumbered from her reddening green eyes.

He waited, took her in his arms, held on easily; she was a weight he could bear. When she seemed better he asked if she wanted to talk and she first shook her head, then nodded, then wept again, so he took a handkerchief from his jeans pocket, gave it to her and they sat close together at the base of one of the giant elms that dotted the square.

Eventually they were both quiet. "Naturally, I'll challenge him to a duel," Chub tried.

She didn't smile, but probably she appreciated his effort.

"You don't have to say anything, y'know."

From her smudged face he saw that she wanted to.

Chub waited.

"It doesn't make any sense, no sense at all," B.J. said. "Not a bit."

"What was the argument about?"

Now she was crying again, but this time talking through the spasms. "Pep—pep—pepperoni pizza."

"That makes a great deal of sense," Chub began. "There are few more explosive topics than pepperoni pizza; why, I personally have had more than several fights on that very subject," and he was about to go on, trying to soothe, but it wasn't working so he shut up fast.

When she spoke again, the spasms were gone, replaced now by less dramatic pauses. "I said . . . 'Let's go to Cleveland,' and he said, 'Fine,' and I said . . . 'Let's have the most expensive meal in all of Cleveland, Ohio,' and he said, 'Fine,' again, but then he shook his head and said, 'I can't,' and I said, I said, 'Why not?' and . . . and he said, 'Got to work at the No-Name.' . . . I couldn't believe it, I said, 'Get a sub,' and he said, 'It's too late to get anybody,' and . . . and I told him, I said, 'Del, it's crazy, you got accepted by Yale Law, you've got to celebrate, you can't tend bar.' . . ."

And in the pause, Chub, who understood nothing while he watched them, now understood it all. He had gotten in, she had not, reality had struck them down.

" 'I work there, it's my job, I need the money,' he said then, 'and I can't help it if it's crazy, there it is,' and I said, 'I'll pay for a substitute, you could at least try and find someone,' and he said, 'I've never missed a minute on a job in my life, we don't have to go to Cleveland to celebrate, let's celebrate now, I'm starved, let's get a pizza,' and I said the truth, it was just afternoon, I wasn't hungry and he said, well, couldn't I come along with him while he ate, and maybe I made a face or something, I don't know, but he said, 'Forget it' ... and I thought maybe I was being bitchy, so I told him I'd come along and watch and he said, 'It's not worth it, forget the whole thing,' but I could tell he didn't mean it so I said, trying to make it fun, 'I love watching you eat, I've told you that often enough, the cute way your jaws go up and down,' and then he was having fun, too, because he said, 'Don't complain, it's better than if they went sideways,' and we were okay, and we started to walk and I said, 'As a matter of fact, all this talking has made me a little bit hungry,' and he said that was good and I said I'd have part of his pizza and he said that was good, too, and I said, 'But no pepperoni,' and he said—well, he didn't say a word for a while and then he asked quietly did I remember that the No-Name only made whole pizzas, you couldn't have a slice, they didn't do the business for that, and you couldn't have half and half like you can at most places back home and I said 'course I remembered and he said, 'I thought you did,' but there was an edge and I asked what was *that* supposed to mean and he said, 'I only like pizza with pepperoni, you know that, it's my favorite thing,' and now the edge was worse and he said, 'Why are you trying to zap me?' and ... I didn't know what he meant, I told him I didn't and he said, 'Oh sure,' and I said, *'What's that supposed to mean?'* and now there was, I guess, my voice had taken on an edge, too, and he accused me of always ruining things and I said never, never, that was what he did, ruin things, and then it got nasty, very quick ... he called me a spoiled bitch and I called him a humorless bastard and he said why did I have to insist on the most expensive meal in Cleveland when I knew he couldn't pay for it and I said to hell with that, I'd pay for it and he said I don't take your money and I told him I was goddamn sick and tired of him trying to rule the world with his poverty and ... and then we both got real mean. . . ." B.J. swiped at her eyes with the now sopping handkerchief and stared at the darkening sky. "On the day Del got into Yale," she added finally.

"It'll all work out," Chub told her.

She shrugged.

Carefully Chub waited, then asked in as offhand a way as he could: "When do you think you might hear?"

Now the tears were covering her green eyes again. "We both got envelopes in the same mail delivery, an hour ago; Yale took me too. . . ."

Chub managed a "Wonderful" and it was, and he wanted to enthuse but he needed to take refuge in silence—because watching them fight he had understood nothing; then, with Del's news, he understood it all. Now he understood nothing again. No. Less than that.

"Sure feels wonderful," B.J. said, and then they both watched the sky, and after a while Chub walked her to her dorm and certainly they talked, but he had no memory later of any of what it might have been about. He went to his dorm, tried to study, went down for dinner, ate alone, or rather sat alone, he had no hunger, and then he went to his evening job at the college library, and later he had no memory of anything that happened there either.

He was in bed in his single by half past twelve, and through his growing up years sleep had always been a willing companion, there and waiting for his embrace.

Not this night.

He was surprised at how tense he obviously was. From dinner on, he'd gotten through hours by rote, his mind not on anything much in particular.

It still wasn't.

But he could feel, somewhere inside, what? Chub found no word. "Something" was the best he could come up with, not a whole lot to go on. At one he switched on his bed lamp and took *The Goodbye Look* from his bookshelf. It was the paperback edition of the newest Ross Macdonald, and he loved Ross Macdonald more than any American now writing, except for Irwin Shaw.

He couldn't focus on the novel. Chub dropped the book to his chest and wondered what the hell was going on. He put the book back, turned out the lamp, closed his eyes, forced himself to relax, or tried to, but he must have failed because at one-thirty he was dressed again and wandering around the dark campus, aimlessly crossing and recrossing Tappan Square, detouring out to the athletic field. He ran a quarter of a mile, thought about running another, decided against it. The night was growing cold. What was strange about that was while he was walking he'd felt warm, and now, after exercise, when he should have felt warm, he was shivering.

Must be getting something, he decided; one of those glorious springtime viruses that waylay the campus constantly. He returned to his room and his bed.

And lay there. More tense than ever, wondering again about the virus and did he have a fever?—no, he felt cool, and his joints didn't ache, no sick symptoms, and the longer he lay there the more he knew it was no virus but still this strange "something" that was pressing, harder now than ever, pressing for escape, and at a little before three in the morning Chub went "unh" and rolled into a fetal ball and covered his eyes with his thumbs and pushed till pain because his memory was clear now, he couldn't fight it anymore—

—and he was six—

—and in Fort Lauderdale, on vacation with his parents—

—and it was the day he learned to swim.

His mother's folks had a house in Lauderdale, a small one with a small backyard, and they had built a pool in the yard, but the bugs were murder there in the summer so the entire pool was screened in, roof and all, and connected with the house. It wasn't big, really more for cooling off in than for exercise—

—but it was deep enough for drowning.

Chub and his parents visited each summer, and what he remembered most was the constant fretting—"Where is he?—he out near the pool?—*can you see him?*—Chub-don't-you-dare-go-near-that-water-without-one-of-us-with-you—DO YOU UNDERSTAND THAT?"

He understood it but he didn't see the reason for their constant worry. He was frightened of the water, he would never dream of going near it alone.

At least, not for the first couple of years. But when he was six, as he waded in with his mother right beside him and his father standing near, he realized something: He could do it now, if he wanted to. He could put his face underwater without fear.

That is, he thought he could.

Each day he came closer and closer to actually doing it, but he never told them, because if he was fooling himself, if he was still afraid, he did not want their disappointment.

He adored his parents then. His father, Michael, seemed so gentle, his skin ruddy and smooth (this was before the bottles). His mother, Gretchen, seemed so kind (this was before the moods).

Suddenly he let go of his mother's hand, ducked under the water, closed his eyes, pushed off hard with his legs and kicked, holding his breath, kicked and kept on kicking until he felt the other side of the pool and then he surfaced and blinked and stared around at them.

His mother was already coming for him and his father jumped alongside and then they were both hugging him, fighting for possession, and they were so happy, so happy, and his father said, "I knew you could do it," and his mother echoed that and then Chub, to show it wasn't a fluke, scooted back all the way across the pool underwater again, and this time he used his arms a little and when he came up again they stood there, across from him, clapping and smiling, and the first trip was courage but this second one he enjoyed, so he made a third—he liked it down there and as he felt the far side of the pool approaching he opened his eyes as he began to surface and was amazed at how the world altered—sizes, shapes, the color of light—everything changed when you came up from under. He should have been tired but he wasn't, so, grabbing a deep breath, he began another successful journey through the silence—

—only this time when he came up for air he heard a sound.

He swam another time through the silent pool, and when he came up again, the sound was worse.

Chub was tiring now, but he didn't think of stopping, and down he went and across he went and up he came—

—and the sound, the terrible sound, was much worse now, much louder—

—his parents were fighting with each other.

Breathing hard, he sank down to where he couldn't hear and he pushed off and kicked and when he came up they were shouting. Kind Gretchen and gentle Mike with such smooth skin—they were saying such terrible things—

—such terrible screaming things—

—the screaming wouldn't stop, he could only make it stop in the silence, and he crossed again but only got halfway before he needed air and now his grandparents were running toward the pool and—

—and Chub, twenty, an Oberlin sophomore, lay on his bed, hearing it all. He heard it once and then, against his wishes, it instant-replayed and then, quickly, he got up, turned on the overhead light, sat at his desk and put a piece of scratch paper into his Olympia.

He had, at least since the start of high school, held tight the secret fancy of someday being a writer. And he had written—fragments, little ditzy stories—there was one about the totally unexpected results that happened when the country of Venezuela, in an effort to cut down on victimless crime, had legalized revenge; another about an astronomer who discovered that Heaven was located just behind Pluto and that was good news for the world until a second astronomer proved that that wasn't Heaven behind Pluto, there was no Heaven, that was Hell—a bunch of stuff along those lines, but few had seen them, and of those, fewer still had cared. This, though, was different—

—the *impulse* was different.

Always, before he wrote, Chub doodled notes, at first in his illegible scrawl, later, when he learned to type, on his machine. He touched his fingers to the keys, took them off, not ready, not sure where to begin. He went out of his room down the hall to the john and threw some water on his face, waited till the water chilled as much as was possible, filled the sink, stuck his face down, held it there, eyes tightly shut. He did that several times, pushing his face back into the cold, then paced around, then returned to his room, paced some more before sitting down again at his desk, starting to fiddle.

```
maybe the moral is--never learn to swim.
jesus, jesus--

what a bad day, what a bad bad day--
--the things you choose not to remember.
fifteen years ago I'll bet that was.
and five since I've thought of it--
no
no
more than five--
at least ten.

question--crucial question--

WHY IS IT TROUBLING THE SPIRIT OF YOUR DREAMS?

wait--wait--
it must have been their worst fight--

no
no
christ, they had a million worse than that--
wait--wait--

maybe if it wasn't their worst it was their
  first.

i think.
first around me anyway.
and them's the ones that matter.
(self-centered prick)
```

```
it was so hot down there--
the way my grandmother used to sweat--
drenched and fat--
and she had that lemon tree--
she loved it, how she fussed--
the lemons were as big as oranges--

YOU'RE DRIFTING, THE SUBJECT UNDER DISCUSSION
  IS NOT YOUR GRANDMOTHER'S GODDAMN LEMONS.


 BACK TO IT, GET BACK
 TO IT, BACK TO THE CRUCIAL QUESTION.

no
no
wrong--
not the crucial question--

here's the real one--
not, why is that memory troubling the
  spirit of your dreams

crucial question is this:
why is it troubling the spirit of your
  dreams now?

why
why
why on this day?------
```

At close to four in the morning an answer came to him, so he took out the scratch paper, reached for his Eaton's Corrasable and a carbon set, and began to write about B.J. and Del.

Except of course he couldn't call them that. Chub was never good with character names, so he took out his beloved *Mixed Company* by Irwin Shaw; it was the book that finally made him admit he wanted to be a writer. And flicked through the pages. The hero of "The Eighty-Yard Run," one of his favorites, was Christian Darling, so Del became Chris. And Darling's wife was Louise. Chris and Louise would be the names.

Chris and Louise were young, early twenties, and engaged; they had met at acting school and now they were both up for the final audition of a touring company of *Hair*. They shared a crummy apartment in New York— (Chub had never been to New York, so he kept the city details skimpy. He had seen lots of movies about the place, though, knew what Times Square looked like, knew that that was where the theatres were.) They shared a crummy apartment near Times Square and if *Hair* took them both, they would get married. If only one got in, they would stay engaged, but the tour was for a year and a year can do things to people.

Louise was from Oklahoma, a blonde with green eyes (Chub couldn't bring himself to lose B.J.'s eyes), and Del was from . . .

(Chub stopped writing. What he was putting down was from Del's point of view, so while B.J.'s point of origin was of little moment, Del's was. His childhood mattered. Chub was from Athens, Illinois, the smallest and least valued of the commuter towns that spread north from Chicago along Lake Michigan.)

Louise was from Oklahoma, a blonde with green eyes, and Chris came to New York from Athens, a small commuter town outside Chicago. She was beautiful, he was not, people pursued her, he was alone, and as he watched her in class those first days, he daydreamed about her, but he knew that was going to be that. Then they were given a scene to do together, a short adaptation of "Return to Kansas City," a wonderful story by Irwin Shaw.

And as they worked on the scene, as the characters they were playing ripened, real life went parallel. Within six months they were (a) in love, (b) living together, (c) engaged. But money was a problem; although Louise had some, Chris didn't, which was why, when they both were called back for the final auditions, though they decided not to talk about it much because it didn't really matter, not in the long run, they both knew, or at least Chris did, that more than likely it *was* the long run.

Then the day of the *Hair* auditions. (Chub was tempted to skimp here; he didn't know that much about auditions, how they worked. B.J. had snuck him into several of the shows she had been cast for, and he had tried out for a couple of plays in school—who could forget his Friar Tuck in a sixth-grade short musical production done one disaster-prone day in assembly? But he decided he needed the tension, so he went inside the theatre when Chris sang and danced, stayed outside with Chris while Louise went in for her turn.)

And then when the good news was theirs—when they both were accepted—on a hot street in mid-afternoon with people scudding by, Chris and Louise began to talk about celebrating. (Chub built the scene his own way, but he kept the pepperoni pizza as catalyst. He knew nothing he might invent would be as insignificant and therefore right as a life-changing event begun by arguing over pepperoni pizza.) As their voices rose, as the temperature on the street became less and less bearable, Chris and Louise demeaned each other, and people were stopping now, watching now, and they tried to stop but each time they did another bubble of anger burst and now there was a crowd but it didn't matter, they could not help their wounding, and as Louise began reaching with her one hand for the engagement ring on the other, Chris yelled, "Let me! Give me the goddamn thing," and he ripped the ring off, or tried to, but it wasn't easy and now Louise was in pain but Chris kept at it until he had it in his hand and she swiped at his face, shattering his rimless glasses on the sidewalk, and then she ran, burst through the crowd, and he picked up his glasses, spun into the nearest bar, ordered a shot of Wild Turkey. (Chub's father had used Wild Turkey, when he could afford it, in the beginning, before the money ran out.)

Several drinks later, Chris left the bar, bought a bottle of Wild Turkey, returned to their place, found Louise's clothes gone, the closets empty. He opened the bottle, took a long pull. He knew where she was. Down the block, bunking in with another girl, a friend from their acting class.

Chris didn't even think of reaching for the phone.

He drank some more, lay down, got up, scrambled himself some eggs, picked at them, drank some more, then pulled the curtains and turned out the lights and closed his eyes—

—and suddenly he was six, and in Fort Lauderdale, remembering the day he first learned how to swim. (Chub was never tempted to switch the swimming to something else: learning how to cross the street or along those lines. The main thing, the best thing, about the swimming was the silence underwater, followed by the sound of his parents, then silence, then building sound, the alternation, the silence always the same, the sound increasingly deadly.)

Chris lay there, half drunk and blinking, thinking of his parents and the way they fretted over him. They weren't supposed to be able to have children, he arrived late in their lives, a Christmas gift that came in deep September. And as he lay there, Chris realized the connective tissue between that Lauderdale day and what had happened with Louise a few hours before.

His parents had worried so about him and now, somehow, his freedom in the water freed them to face something else—

—each other.

And it was not pleasing, what they saw. Perhaps they should have never been together; certainly they should have never stayed together, but he had glued them, and now, released, not young, they would begin their battle that led, eventually, to death.

Both fights, Chris realized, were simply this: harbingers of affliction. Louise, then, was really two girls: The one whom he had courted had raised him up so high; the one whom he was to marry would surely bring him down.

Yet, knowing this, he could not blot out her green eyes. So he filled the sink with cold, cold water, and buried his face again and again until he felt nearly sober. Then he took the engagement ring and went to where Louise was staying, and at first she would not see him, but he persisted, and then she would not marry him, but he persisted, and as he slid the ring back onto her perfect finger, Chris knew his future: only agony, if his luck held. . . .

Eighteen hours after he sat down to write, Chub held the finished *thing* in his hands. Whatever it was, it was twenty-three pages long, more than triple anything he'd ever done before; the one about legalizing revenge had barely made seven, and that with very wide margins.

Incredible.

He lifted the original several times. It actually had weight.

Amazing.

It didn't have a title and he didn't know what the hell to do with it, but at the very least, it was in existence.

Then he thought of calling it "Dreamgirl" but that stank. "The Girl of My Dreams" wasn't better, only longer, and just as cornball.

Then he remembered the passage where Chris realized that there were two Louises, and they were so very different and he got the notion that maybe parentheses would help the demarkation. He decided to go with that and typed a title page and looked at it.

''THE GIRL(S) OF MY DREAMS''

by

Charles Fuller

At least it had a title now, but he still didn't know what the hell to do with it, stick it in his drawer, show it to somebody and if so, who?

Chub rubbed his eyes, half nodding to himself, because there was a "who." And so, carefully putting a paper clip on the carbon, he took it with him and went searching for none other than Two-Brew Kitchel, the one and only. . . .

CHAPTER 2

The Half-Empty House

Stanley Kitchel, a classmate of Chub's, was easily the most famous figure on the Oberlin campus.

If what the English loved most was their disasters, and they do—viz., Arnhem, Dunkirk—then Oberlin cherished its oddballs. (Jocks rated not at all; the football team's greatest moment was when they supposedly came close to upsetting Ohio State, this in the early 1900's, and they had rarely had a winning season since. It was a known fact that Oberlin's cheerleaders really only had to have two cheers down pat, those being "Push 'em back, push 'em back, waaaaaaay back" and "Block that kick.")

Kitchel had a natural advantage in that he *looked* odd. His great mass of black curly hair rose inches above his head—from a distance he resembled Franz Schubert. He was also a good forty pounds overweight and he always seemed to be wearing the same black and red lumberjack shirt.

Plus he was crippled. Both of his legs were pretty much useless, and he made his way around campus with the aid of wooden crutches, which he decorated with as many obscene decals as he could find room for.

Chub saw him a couple of times during Orientation week, didn't think much one way or the other; B.J. was filling his mind then. No one paid much attention to Kitchel those early days, and if you had said that within a month he would be famous, you could have gotten excellent odds. Chub, in a minor way, contributed to the incident that brought sudden and lasting celebrity. They met, for the first time, toward the end of September, quite naturally, in the library.

Chub was good at libraries. Odd, but there it was. He loved their silences, the occasional squeak of shoe on linoleum floor. His aunt had worked in the Athens library. And of course he read compulsively. None of that, though, explained why he decided, when he was fourteen, to find out how they worked. It just happened and it was helpful when it came to term papers.

That it might be helpful to others didn't cross his mind until his second week at Oberlin. His campus job was basically to load up carts and put books back into their proper positions in the stacks. He was loading up a cart that second week, near to Mr. Durning, the librarian who, in the insane logic of Oberlin, had once been their best basketball player, even though he stood less than five feet eight. Mr. Durning was going over some papers at his desk when a slender girl rushed up and said, "There's nothing on guns."

Mr. Durning held up his hand for her to be silent and went back to his papers.

"But it's im*por*tant," the slender girl said.

"Hush," Mr. Durning said, "up."

"*Croo*-shull."

This time he ignored her, read silently on.

Chub, his arms full, said, "Mr. Durning will be with you when he can."

The girl came to Chub now, going, "Do you know where guns would be?—I've got this paper, this asshole assignment comparing the quality of guns between the North and the South, and it was only due yesterday and I'm only a history major, and naturally I've got my period and my boyfriend's old girl friend has selected today to visit him and . . ." she caught herself, started to turn away.

Chub put his books down, called her back. "I'm just kind of spitballing this, but maybe 'G' for 'Guns' isn't quite the main topic you need. You might try 'U.S.—

History—Civil War' and then, under that, check out a couple of subject headings. Personally, I'd give 'A' a shot."

" 'A' for what?"

" 'Armaments,' " Chub told her. "And as long as you're in the vicinity, 'F' for 'Firearms' might be worth a look—"

She had a notebook out now, was writing as he talked on.

"—and I don't know if you want handguns or rifles but both might be worth something and 'W' for 'Weaponry.' All this under 'U.S.—History—Civil War,' understand."

She nodded.

"But before any of that, you might save yourself a lot of time by just checking Sheehy."

"She-who?"

"Just like it sounds. S-h-e-e-h-y. It's *the* guide to all major reference and bibliographical stuff. Just over there." He pointed across the main reading room he was standing in. "Kind of an ugly gray binding." Chub was aware that Mr. Durning was staring at him now and he knew he ought to get back to his job but as he half turned he said, "And personally I like Walford—same shelf as Sheehy, only Walford covers anything written in international periodicals, 'bye," and he completed the turn now, worked hard at loading up his cart.

And Mr. Durning was still staring at him.

Chub was about to start pushing the cart toward the stacks when "Fuller, come here" came from the librarian.

Chub, very nervous now, obeyed.

"You're new."

Chub nodded.

"Freshman or transfer student?"

"Freshman."

"And this is the job you've been given?"

"I requested the library, yessir."

"Then you'll be working here four years?"

"Yessir, I hope."

"Grace," Mr. Durning called out then to a youngish librarian passing by. She stopped, came over. "Mrs. Mahnken, this is Charles Fuller, a freshman, and I want you to believe me, Grace, when I tell you I have not been drinking—Fuller here not only has heard of Sheehy, *he knows of Walford.* Do you realize the ramifications?"

Chub didn't, but obviously Mrs. Mahnken did, from the way she nodded.

"Go about your business, Fuller," Mr. Durning said then, making a flicking gesture with his hand. "I make you this promise: I shall weep on your graduation day."

Less than an hour later it all began making sense, as Chub, standing on a ladder, returning books to their proper places in the stacks, was accosted by an anxious senior who said, "Mr. Durning told me you could help me on this paper I'm writing about Paris street life at the turn of the century." The anxious senior was to be the first of an endless parade—whenever the librarians were too busy or on the verge of going mad with the inability of college students to defeat the Dewey Decimal System, they shipped them off to Chub. He became a librarian without portfolio, suggesting to some Klein's *Guide* or the *Index of Business Periodicals* or the *National Directory of Newsletters and Reporting Sources.* He was always patient, almost always helpful. There were times, in fact, when he wondered if he wasn't better at libraries than people.

He was standing on a very tall ladder when Kitchel found him.

Chub heard him coming a good distance away. So did a lot of people—the stacks were lined with carrels and many of the students studying in them looked up as the voice grew nearer. "Where is this Fuller fellow lurking? Where is young Fuller?"

Chub put a few more books away, listened to the sound, then heard the accompanying sound of the crutches thudding against the floor. Then Kitchel turned a corner and spotted him. "Ah, my quest is ended."

Kitchel was wearing his standard black and red lumber-jack shirt and his stomach bulged decisively over his belt.

"What's up," Chub said.

"Quite obviously, *you* are. Leave your perch at once. An assignation is needed, and like Chaplin in the Hitler film, I detest people whose heads are higher than mine."

Kitchel's voice boomed and Chub was aware of growing agitation from those in the carrels, so he hurried down the ladder and moved up beside Kitchel; at least that way he wouldn't be so loud.

"Good, obedient lad," Kitchel said then—and his voice was louder.

Chub told him to keep it down.

"Would you tell Oscar Wilde to keep it down, Fuller? Would you instruct George S. Kaufman to shush? You would not. Probably you would keep a notebook handy to remember their sparkling dialog. I suggest you get a notebook, Fuller; the *bon mot* is but a small part of my arsenal."

"Knock it the fuck off" came from a nearby carrel.

"Clearly an English major," Kitchel said, unfazed.

Chub led him to an isolated part of the floor and stopped, gestured for Kitchel to speak.

"I need your help," Kitchel told him.

Chub was, frankly, surprised. Kitchel did not seem the type who couldn't find his way around a library. Anyway, the word on him was this: brilliant. Part of that was based on the supposition that anyone who looked as buffoonlike as Kitchel had to be brilliant. But it was more, he couldn't be ordinary—there was too much going on behind his eyes.

Chub gestured again for Kitchel to go on.

Instead, Kitchel studied him a moment. "Why do they call you 'Chub'? You're not fat at all; *I* might be termed 'Chub' but you're actually quite comely."

Although he had never been called "comely" before, Chub realized a certain justification to Kitchel's questioning. As a kid, Chub had been a fanatic about sports, and he still maintained an athlete's body. He stood a little over five nine and had never weighed as much as a hundred and sixty. His eyes were light brown, and so was his hair, and he kept it at almost crew-cut length, but it was so fine it parted evenly and was always neat, even when he awoke. He smiled often and people seemed to find him reassuring. His face was round, less so now than when he was younger, but that was where the name came from. "It's short for 'Chubby-Cheeks,' " he explained.

"Most unappetizing."

Chub nodded. "I was tweaked a lot when I was growing up. And I'm also being paid to work, so how can I help you?"

"I have chosen you to be my second. An adventure is upon us, Fuller, and I trust you feel honored at the inclusion. Are you aware of the business of drinking a shot glass of beer a minute?"

Chub thought back. In high school there had been a lot of talk about it. A couple of his classmates had tried and failed, or at least they said they'd tried, he was never sure. The main thing was it couldn't be done. The amount of beer—sixty ounces in an hour—was nothing by itself. But when your intake was shot glass by shot glass, the amount of air that entered did something to your stomach. "It's the air that makes it impossible, isn't that it? Bloats your stomach, so there's not enough room."

"Such is indeed the common wisdom, Fuller, but like much common wisdom it is false, elephant shit, pure and simple."

"Have you done it?"

"No, but I'm going to—that's the adventure. A half hour ago I was in the coffee shop and at the next table Armbruster was going on about it—you know of Armbruster, our fumbling senior fullback, the one with fingers of stone who is called 'Clang' behind his back? He said it was impossible and I—politely, I assure you—assured him he was an asshole. One thing led to another culminating in this: We have made a bet—he said fifty dollars and that, I need not tell you, is a lot of money, but when he challenged me to prove my point I agreed to scrounge up fifty from someplace. That is the adventure I have undertaken—with, of course, your noble assistance."

"What am I supposed to be, your shot glass lifter?"

"Smartass repartee does not become your sweet visage, Fuller; plus you're not clever enough by half. Now close your hole while I explicate." Kitchel rocked back and forth on his crutches then. "This wager will become, I promise you, legendary in the history of this very small tower of learning. In the next century, when they speak of Oberlin, they will speak of the Underground Railroad, and they will speak of Charles Martin Hall inventing a way to make aluminum cheaply, and along with those will come the mention of the Kitchel Triumph. It must be done with professional finesse. There is only one place to hold it, and that is the only bar in town, namely the No-Name. Word reaches me that you are intimate with the bartender."

"Sure, I know Del."

"I know you know him, twit. Which of us has not seen you down there these past weeks, panting after his nubile fiancée? Armbruster wants me to do it in his room, but that would be unfair to my cause. He might put piss in the fortieth shot, to throw me off my game. What you must do is get this Del to agree to let us use the No-Name, and to carefully watch the contents I imbibe, to pour it himself, et cetera. And you will be beside me on the designated night to hold the money, to ward off arguments, to keep an eye on Clang so that nothing nefarious happens. When I said a second, that is precisely what I need, someone to aid, to abet, to support. Do I have your acceptance?"

"You're going to blow fifty bucks, Kitchel."

"Telling me I'm going to lose does not precisely fall in the realm of support, Fuller."

"Right, right, sorry, I won't do it again."

"I take it then that we are joined?"

"I'll go see Del tonight after work."

"Blessings on thee, little man," Kitchel said, and he manipulated his crutches, swung around and made his slow way out of the stacks.

Del had heard of the shot-glass-a-minute business, had never seen it attempted. This was a Wednesday and he agreed, since Mondays were slow, to allow the bet to take place in five nights. He thought it might be good for trade, and he seemed more than a little interested in the outcome, which surprised Chub.

If Del was interested, Dr. Wallinsky, who overheard their conversation, was fired up by the possibilities. Again, in the insane logic of Oberlin, Felix Wallinsky, the town rummy, had graduated with honors in languages some forty years before, earned a Ph.D. from Yale. He lived more or less at the No-Name, spoke German, French, Italian, Polish and Russian when sober, when drunk, a very slurred patois that was occasionally English. "Izzy fat?" Dr. Wallinsky asked Chub, butting in on the Del conversation. "Fat's gotta chance."

Chub assured him that Kitchel was considerably overweight.

"Hazzy got tits?"

Chub said he had not yet seen Kitchel unclothed.

"A man ain't got tits ain't fat," Dr. Wallinsky proclaimed. "Fine-dout."

Chub promised to do some heavy investigation and, setting the starting time at half past nine next Monday, he went off in search of Kitchel to give the news.

Kitchel's room, down the corridor from Chub's, was even sloppier than Kitchel. Chub knocked, was told to enter, went in. Kitchel was lying on his bed in his underwear shorts, his crutches angled on a nearby chair, reading *Everything You Wanted to Know About Sex but Were Afraid to Ask*. He told Chub to stand and report. Chub did.

"Five days is more than enough for training; good work, Fuller. Anything else?"

"Dr. Wallinsky was interested in your cup size," Chub said.

"Tell him I put Annette Funicello to shame," Kitchel replied, obviously in a fine frame of mind.

He was anything but when Chub saw him again, the next noon, in front of Peters Hall. "The bet is now seventy-five dollars, Fuller, and I'm up to ninety shots in ninety minutes. But I had to do something."

"Why?"

"Clang was snickering at me during breakfast and I had to put a halt to that. So I upped the stakes."

"Can you do ninety?"

Kitchel shrugged. "At least I shut him up. I told him, with triumph in my voice, that what he didn't know was that I had snookered him royally, since years ago in the Orient I had learned the secrets of Indian stomach control. He was dumb enough, I suspect, to believe me." He rocked on his crutches. "I had to make him stop mocking, and it was the best I could come up with—I figured if the Orient was good enough for Lamont Cranston in *The Shadow,* it was good enough for me." He started off. "I'll have to redouble my training."

Whether it was the extra thirty minutes that raised interest in the bet or Kitchel's training methods, Chub was never quite sure. But the following morning, Friday, an empty six-pack of beer was found in the hall outside Kitchel's room. On Saturday, an empty *case* resided there.

Then there was the business of the sounds. Anyone passing Kitchel's room could not fail to hear strange wheezes coming rhythmically from inside. And when he was alone in the john, odd gargling noises came again and again—always stopping immediately whenever anyone else entered to use the facilities.

Chub began getting pestered with questions as to what Kitchel was doing. "Indian breathing exercises" was all he ever replied.

Another empty case was outside Sunday, and by Monday afternoon Chub was aware that they were certainly into something. But he was stunned when he and Kitchel entered the No-Name at shortly after nine that evening.

There was simply no extra room inside. The crowd had to be close to two hundred people and the bar was swamped with business.

Clang Armbruster and a dozen or so other footballers waited by a reserved chair at the center of the bar near the beer taps. Kitchel wore an oversized pair of sweat pants, the customary black and red lumberjack shirt. The noise level, high to begin with, went up several notches when Kitchel, seating himself in the chair of honor, ordered a large glass of water to begin with and chugged it down. He and Chub had come up with the ploy that morning, and from the uncertain look on Clang Armbruster's face, it worked.

Then Dr. Wallinsky elbowed his way alongside, crying exultantly, "He's a crip, I knew a crip in Akron could drink all night; they got extra room in their legs is why, I'll bet three bucks he makes it all the way."

That began a fairly intense period of side betting, the odds ten to one against Kitchel, Chub holding Kitchel's money. Then ensued a brief rehashing of the rules—one shot per minute, any time within that minute. Loser bought all beer. Five shots to be drawn at a time so that Del could top each off, getting rid of excess foam.

"You want the beer cold, I guess," Del said.

"Luke," Chub told him. And then he turned to Armbruster. "The *Britannica* explains there are fewer bubbles in lukewarm beer." The rules took up a bit more time—

—during which Kitchel, eyes gazing at the ceiling, practiced his Indian breathing, the wheezes coming loud and evenly. The room quieted slowly, everyone watching and listening.

"No pissing in between shots," Armbruster said.

Kitchel grew silent, stared at the fullback. "I have known men in Calcutta who survived three days without urination. Don't bother me with trifles."

Chub watched this exchange, wondering if Kitchel had actually come to believe that, he said it with such authority. And he wondered if somehow Kitchel could pull it off, the whole hour and a half. Forty minutes he had no doubts about; Kitchel had sufficient bulk for that. But longer? He just didn't know.

He also didn't know about the large box of Morton salt that Kitchel produced from a pocket in his sweat pants and set on the bar. He opened the spout, poured his left hand full.

The time was 9:26 according to the clock behind the bar, and Armbruster exploded, "No fair using salt," and Chub said, into Kitchel's ear, "Why the hell didn't you tell me?" to which Kitchel replied, "I make it a practice to keep everyone on his or her toes," and Armbruster was reaching for the salt container now, yelling that salt made you artificially thirsty and if Kitchel used it, the bet was off.

Kitchel raised his hands and the room quieted. In a voice much like Orson Welles's he said, "There was never any intention to use the salt—I just wanted to judge your character, you chickenshit poltroon."

The odds on Kitchel suddenly dropped to five to one.

And the time was 9:28.

Chub realized he had underestimated his man—forty minutes would be nothing.

Del had the first shot glasses filled without foam now, and he moved them carefully to directly in front of Kitchel.

9:29.

Kitchel gargled. Again. Chub stared around the crammed room, heard the odds down to three to one.

The clock on the wall hit 9:30.

Kitchel took his time, pulled one shot glass toward him, looked down at it, lifted it, held it high, peered up at it. Then he chugged it down as a cheer went up in the room. Everyone was crowding in, and those who couldn't were standing on tables and chairs against the wall, watching. Chub gave Kitchel a quick shoulder massage, as if they were in a prize ring, which in a sense they were; a ninety-rounder was taking place and there were eighty-nine left to go.

9:31.

Kitchel reached for the second shot glass and this time he brought it to his nose, sniffing it daintily, as if it were a fine red wine and he was checking the bouquet. He turned to Chub. "Nineteen seventy was an excellent vintage for 3.2," he said. "Fabulous deep color, clearly has years of development ahead."

Chub smiled.

Kitchel drained the second glass, and another cheer came from the assembled. Armbruster and the other football players were clearly ticked that the crowd was with Kitchel, and they muttered to each other quietly.

9:33.

Kitchel stood and Chub watched as his man, he assumed, was about to stretch and get more comfortable, and as he watched, Kitchel grabbed for his crutches, shoved them under his shoulders and without a word, his head down, forced his way through the crowd to the door and when he was gone there was this incredible stunned silence in the bar—years later, when he and The Bone watched Duran quit on Leonard in the *"no más"* encounter, Chub was aware of a similar wordless astonishment, and—

—and then the No-Name came alive, because it was over, and first there were mutters, and then shouts and then came the first waves of laughter and in that first wave someone, maybe Clang, cried out that Kitchel's name shouldn't be Stanley, "Two-Brew" was more fitting and the nickname swept the bar and the laughter built and Chub had not moved when Armbruster was on him, grabbing the money, insisting that Chub pay for the beer, which Chub did, handing a few bills to Del, and as he did it he was ticked, but that didn't last long, because whatever embarrassment he was feeling was nothing to the humiliation that would surely haunt Kitchel for the rest of his Oberlin days—

—only it didn't work that way.

Kitchel's door was locked and he didn't answer Chub's voice half an hour later, but the next morning, when he left for classes, Kitchel wore his standard lumberjack shirt and a different pair of sweat pants, but over them he had on a kimono that he had somehow belted to resemble a fighter's robe and on his back was a hand-drawn sign that said, "I couldda been a contender," Brando's famous words to his brother from *On the Waterfront*.

As he made his way through the day, whenever anyone shouted, "Hey, fink, hey, Two-Brew," Kitchel would reply with a nod and then flash Churchill's "V for Victory," only it was clear that the two fingers he held up stood for the number of beers he had gotten through.

His costume the next day was different—in place of his usual red and black job, he wore a T-shirt on which he had had the words "Two-Brew" printed, and more than likely that was what put him over the top, because it was clear that Kitchel was mocking his own humiliation, but more than that, he was doing it with style and everything was more than forgiven.

A "Two-Brew" T-shirt fad began shortly thereafter, dozens and dozens of them appearing on campus, worn by both sexes, and within a month the clothing store that stamped them claimed it was their hottest-selling item.

The fad didn't last, of course, but Kitchel did. He was famous now, associating with upperclassmen, sought out for gatherings. For here was as odd a creature as had come to Ohio in decades. Plus, of course, he was funny. And there was always the clear brilliance he could never shield that emanated from his dark eyes.

He came to Chub briefly one night in the library the week following the No-Name, and thanked him for his help, and Chub said he wouldn't have missed it, which was true. They shook hands, perhaps even warmly, but they were not yet friends.

Nor were they friends a year later, the first days of September of sophomore year, when Chub made his move to gain admittance to Cheyney's class in creative writing.

Individually, the Oberlin faculty was not famous, but Andrew Cheyney was. Just as John Crowe Ransom had spent his years in Ohio at Kenyon, Cheyney was an

Oberlin fixture. A leading critic of contemporary fiction, he was frequently quoted in *The New York Times*, wrote endless articles for learned journals, had written many books, including the definitive biography of Kafka.

Cheyney's class was normally only open to juniors and seniors, so Chub was aware his chances were slim. But it meant so much to him that he sucked it up and knocked on the door to Cheyney's office. He had seen him around campus—a little man, a dynamo, who looked no more than forty-five but must have been edging in on sixty.

"Who is it, come in?"

Chub entered, stood across the room from Cheyney who was seated at his desk, writing with an old-fashioned pen—there was an open inkwell near his papers. Chub had a whole speech prepared, but it was gone the instant Cheyney looked up at him. "Fuller, sir," he managed finally.

"I won't bite you, Fuller," Andrew Cheyney said. He studied Chub awhile. "I take that back. I might, in point of fact, bite you, but not here and now, what's on your mind?"

"Writing class?"

"It's very limited in number."

"I know. And I'm just a sophomore—"

"—then you know I don't like to admit them. Besides, I've already admitted Kitchel for this semester and I think that more than fills my quota for underclassmen."

I'm as good as Kitchel, Chub thought—maybe not as good but I'll shut up and I'll work harder—I'll work harder than anyone. Chub made a smile. "Understood. Maybe next year." He almost didn't get those words out, his throat was drying on him.

"You want to be a writer?"

More than anything, Chub thought, and it was the truth, of course, but he had never said that to anyone. He shrugged. Made another smile. Turned.

" 'Fuller,' you said?" he heard from behind him. "Are you the library Fuller, the one old Durning's always talking about? Look at me, Fuller."

Chub did. "I work there, yessir. Nights I do."

"I believe old Durning referred to you as being better than a health spa for him. And he's not given to flattery. I owe him a favor, you wouldn't mind if it turned out to be you, would you, Fuller?"

Chub shook his head. Cheyney and Durning lived together; Chub didn't know that then, but if he had, he wouldn't have minded. They could have been The Purple Gang and he wouldn't have minded.

"First class is Friday, I've given the others the initial assignment. It's to be a description. Of anything. But it must run less than a page and there may be no character, no dialog, nothing but a description and you will have it *typed neatly* and in my box outside by Thursday noon, good-bye, Fuller." He dipped his pen into the inkwell, went back to work.

Chub hesitated, then said, "I'm in the class, then, for sure?"

Andrew Cheyney sighed, looked up at him. "That was, I hope, one of the less astute questions you will direct my way. Generally, when I give someone an assignment, it means they are in my class. Be gone before I change my mind."

Idiot, Chub berated himself as he backed from the room, looking, he realized, like a servant leaving the presence of a potentate.

Outside, he moved into the autumn of Tappan Square, paying no attention to much of anything. Because somehow, from somewhere, came the thought that his life had just changed.

It had, of course, but not in the way he imagined.

What to write, though?

This was only Tuesday and the assignment was just a single page, so time wasn't a problem. The problem was quality, for Cheyney had given him a break and Chub didn't just have to put words on paper, they had to be so good, so fucking *right,* that Cheyney would know that he, Charles Fuller, was Someone, Someone Special, Someone Special On The Come.

What to write, though?

Chub went to work at the library and thanked Mr. Durning, recounting the Cheyney talk that had happened earlier in the day and Durning, he thought, smiled kind of oddly, didn't say anything other than he was glad to be of service and get busy. Chub did, and he put a ton of stuff away, and he answered a number of questions from distraught students but it was all by rote.

Back in his room, later, he came alive, grabbing for his notebooks. When he first began to get notions, Chub took to jotting them into standard spiral school notebooks, and he did his first stories in them, too, in pencil. He'd filled a bunch of them but when he glanced through them now, trying to find something to spark him, his early stuff, the high school stuff, was embarrassing and more than that, his handwriting was so shitty and the pencil markings had smudged so much that he soon realized the cause was lost. He shoved them back into his top desk drawer, hesitated, then opened the bottom drawer and reached way into the back.

Nervous now, he brought out his Journal.

He always thought of it that way, the "J" capitalized, and perhaps there were items in his possession he cared about more deeply, but he couldn't think what. He had gotten it Christmas day of his junior year in high school, not a good day, because his father hadn't been able to get out of bed and come down to the tree so Chub and his mother, Gretchen, had exchanged gifts alone, with little talk, and then his mother had to get busy seeing to the turkey and they ate it at dinner, just the two of them again, alone, because his father was unable to make it.

That night, Michael was suddenly in his doorway. "Those notebooks you got?"

Chub glanced, startled at his weaving, pajama-clad father. "Yessir?"

"They're crap, is what I think."

"They're okay."

"Nah." His father shook his head, but the movement must have dizzied him, because he was grabbing at the doorframe next. Chub got out of his desk chair, started across when the loud "I'm fine, stay there" stopped him.

Chub waited, watched as his father suddenly was thrusting a package at him.

"Maybe you better come take it," his father said then.

Chub took it, unwrapped it, and inside was a large brown book with a beautiful leather cover and the words "Charles Fuller, His Journal" embossed on the front. Inside were maybe a hundred or more blank pages, thick textured golden paper. "Now that's not crap," his father said.

"No," Chub said. "Nossir," and he was about to start thanking when he could see his father's grip starting to loosen on the doorframe and he grabbed him before he fell, helped him down along the hall to the spare room where he lived now, laid him down. His father was out of it by then, but Chub said, "Thank you, Michael," even though he knew the words weren't getting through.

Then he went back to his room, got on his bed and looked at his gift. In a minute he was reaching for not a pencil—this was not a place for pencil scrawlings—but a ball point and began jotting down a notion that had just come to him, about a kid who is given a Gilbert chemistry set for his birthday and he fiddles with it, makes a potion and before his eyes a figure appears—it's the Devil, and the kid is afraid until he discovers the Gilbert people had made an error: All the new sets could do the same thing, and the Devil, materializing against his will in rooms all across the country, was pooped.

Chub filled three pages with "Raising the Devil" before he was horrified because if he did that kind of thing, the book would be used up in no time and that must never happen, the book must never be done.

So from then on, he put in his Journal only his very best stuff—first lines, titles, story ideas. Carefully and clearly written in ink. He almost never glanced through the pages of what he'd put down though—it was too risky, what if it was terrible, childlike, devoid of anything resembling quality?

Now he lay on his bed at Oberlin, skipped past the Devil pages and immediately realized his panic was unnecessary because there it was, what he was looking for, all contained in one of the first titles he saw: "The Arbor Day Tree."

In kindergarten, on Arbor Day, everyone was given a tiny tree to take home and plant. Chub did it dutifully, as he did everything, though he wasn't nuts about nature, and it came as a shock that he began connecting somehow to this little thing in the ground in the backyard of his house, took to nurturing it as a horticulturist might treasure an orchid. They were in a sprouting race, and in the beginning he was much the taller, but by third grade they were even and the last time he saw the tree, when he left for Oberlin freshman year, the house sold, strangers inhabiting, it must have been fifteen feet high.

Chub sat at his typewriter then and worked till three, detailing the look of the tree that last day. He went to sleep, got up for breakfast, had coffee until he was awake, reread his previous night's efforts.

Gahr-bagh.

It really sucked. Dull and stupid and flat. It was just this *tree,* for Chrissakes. Fug, Chub thought, no way Cheyney was going to find it Special.

Back to the Journal, flipping through, and there, on a page titled "Things Seen," he came across these words: "black man with white face."

He remembered the guy so clearly. Chub had been maybe twelve, and walking State Street with his mother, when coming toward them was this husk of a Negro, massive and old with a face still very much alive. But what made the face memorable was the entire right half was covered with white skin. Maybe it had been from birth, Chub never knew; he only was sure he had never seen anything close to it before—

—only that wasn't the kicker.

Because the guy was walking a dog, an old dog, old and black— except the dog had the identical white marking on the right half of its face too.

Chub sat quickly and ripped the description off. He'd rarely had anything unspool as easily; the problem wasn't making it interesting but keeping it to under a page. He reread it, was pleased, rewrote it again, smoothing some of the language, then took off for classes.

He returned just before dinner and gave the piece one final read-through. And this was sure as hell not gahr-bagh. It was just as well written now as it had been when he'd read it the first time, so he was terribly pleased.

And remained that way till halfway through the evening meal when he realized that what he'd done didn't come close to fulfilling Cheyney's assignment. It was a description, sure, but Cheyney had said *no characters* and all he had done in his own inimitable assholeish way was write a description totally of characters.

Christ!

It was Wednesday night now and the assignment was due by noon tomorrow and he had his job to get through and he thought about lying to Durning about being sick only Durning knew Cheyney and what if they talked and Cheyney found out and—and *shit.*

He was back in his room by eleven, going through the Journal, but it all seemed useless for him, nothing jumped out, and then he thought maybe in some of his earlier stories there might be a description he could use so he read a couple of them but they embarrassed him, they were kid stuff and he'd always relied on dialog anyway, dialog and plot, that was what he felt comfortable with.

I'll have to hand in the tree, Chub thought, and it was after midnight when he reread it and it was worse than he remembered, but at least it fitted the assignment, and maybe he could make it up to Cheyney the next time, Cheyney didn't seem like a forgiving guy but who could tell for sure.

He put the tree description down, picked up the Journal, held it closed between his hands, thought of his father, of the giving of the gift, how it was the last gift he had even gotten from him because before the end of spring he was gone. And once begun, once Chub entered those last killing months he couldn't stop tripping off, going from bad time to bad time to worse and usually when he did it, it was hateful, only this time was different: It was still hateful, but now it gave him his answer.

He would write about the men's room in Melchiorre's.

Melchiorre's was a bar in Highwood, a town not too many miles from Athens, and one night Mr. Melchiorre called and Chub took it and heard Mr. Melchiorre saying that his father was there and in no shape to do anything, much less drive, and to come get him before he hurt himself.

Chub told Gretchen and she got up from watching the tube, got her purse and gestured for him to come along. "You'll have to help me lift him" was all she said and then they got in her beat-up car and drove to the place.

They walked in and Gretchen said to the bartender, "I'm Mrs. Fuller," and the bartender said he was Mr. Melchiorre and was about to apologize about all this when Gretchen cut him off with "Where is he?" and Mr. Melchiorre pointed back toward the men's room sign and looked at Chub, asking if Chub wanted help and Chub said no, he didn't, he could do it alone and then, so scared, petrified really of what was beyond, he opened the door to the men's room and stepped inside.

His father was kneeling over the toilet, the stall door half open, and Chub said, "It's me, Daddy," but his father went on vomiting so Chub waited, looking around—

—and then the power of the room hit him.

The ceiling was very low, and it wasn't the dirt or the stink that shocked him and it wasn't the urinal that flowed continuously and it wasn't the bugs that skittered across the walls—

—it was the walls themselves. Because every available inch was taken up with something foul. Virulent graffiti, not the kind at the No-Name where what you might see written was "Nietzsche is pietsche" with an answering "But Sartre is smarter" printed underneath. These were mindless growls from the darkness but they weren't as

malignant as the hundreds of drawings, of gigantic penis-
es dripping sperm and vaginas with spiders crawling out
of them and breasts with gigantic nipples slashed off and
lying nearby. Chub wanted to get the hell out but his
father wasn't done yet and he stared away from the walls,
up to the low ceiling, and they were up there, too, the
drawings and the rest, and Chub was totally surrounded,
enveloped in this putrescent cell, and he didn't know
what level he was on, but surely Mr. Alighieri would
have been able to tell him.

Chub put the Journal down. There was never any
mention of any of this kind of thing on those pages. The
material was too fiery for him, he never thought he
would be able to write it.

But he wrote it now. And if the page about the man
and the dog wrote easily, this was easier still. He let it
pour out, censoring whatever he felt might prove taste-
less, using euphemisms as often as he needed. He had no
need to be overly·specific—he knew the power of the
room was there, and when he put the paper in Professor
Cheyney's box the next morning, he felt, no point denying it, elation. . . .

There were a dozen in the class.

Chub didn't know any of them; they all looked
bright—none of them needed to be helped in the ways of
the library. They met in a seminar room the floor above
Cheyney's office. Chub arrived early, but there were still
half a dozen ahead of him. The table was round and
Chub sat quickly. A few more straggled in, then last
came Kitchel, who seemed to know them all. He nodded
at Chub and Chub thought he looked surprised. Then
Kitchel looked at the others, shook his head. "I see few
Fitzgeralds here and fewer Faulkners." The girls smiled
and one of the senior boys told him to blow it out.
"Clearly a man with a poetic turn of phrase," Kitchel
said, and this time the girls giggled. Kitchel sat. It was
time to begin. Everyone grew quiet. Chub sensed the
tension.

Cheyney swept in late, pulled a chair from the corner.

It was taller than the others and his head was above theirs. He carried a folder, opened it, closed it, studied them all in turn.

"I can and will make you better writers," he began. "And the reason I promise you that is this: We will work on basics. No one works on basics today—young people are taught to write their 'feelings' with total disregard of the skills required to make their emotions clear. Your next assignment, due Tuesday, will be this: Characterize an individual totally and only through dialog. Clear?"

Everyone nodded, wrote down the assignment.

Chub didn't. He knew he wouldn't forget it and moreover, dialog was what he was best at. No problem getting ready for Tuesday.

"The procedure in class will be simple: I shall read aloud your various attempts at writings, but I shall never name the author. That way we can all feel freer to criticize. Clear?"

Everyone nodded again.

"Although this is termed a course in creative writing, I don't think of it that way—it is a course in *literature*. Any of you who want to be Jacqueline Susann should leave now. Clear?"

No one left.

Then Cheyney began to talk extemporaneously about what they should all strive for, and that was the uplift of the human spirit. Yes, you could make a murderer your main character—*Crime and Punishment* was one of the masterpieces; yes, you could make your main character a bug—*Metamorphosis* was another of the masterpieces. Cheyney's discourse went acutely on, and Chub listened, agreeing.

But then, as it was clear that the half hour talk was climaxing, he began to get nervous. Because Cheyney was going to read something out loud soon, and Chub desperately wanted it to be his. There was no way Cheyney would begin with something rotten.

Or was there?

Would he want to set an example? Yes, Chub decided,

that was possible, Cheyney was a sadistic type, witty, and his reputation was tougher than hell.

Chub decided he desperately didn't want Cheyney to read his. Not first.

But it's good, he told himself. Let the fucker read it.

Then he told himself that Cheyney's opinion might not coincide with his. Let him attack somebody else, please. Chub was aware of a surprising thing: Sitting there, listening, or not listening really, he was beginning to perspire. Not heavily or anything like that. But there was moisture on his face. He got out a handkerchief, turned away from the table, faked blowing his nose and quickly mopped his skin dry.

Ridiculous, you ass. What can he do to you? Chub had written something as well as he'd ever written anything, and that showed. He knew that. It was on paper, and then Cheyney had a paper in his hands, muttered, "Perhaps we'll have time for this," and he was reading aloud, reading about the men's room at Melchiorre's, and at first Chub felt panic, but that went fast, pride followed it, but then—

—then he realized, it was so obvious from Cheyney's voice, he realized that Cheyney didn't like it. He accented certain syllables strangely and he paused for emphasis where Chub had been trying for a faster rhythm—

—and now the others in the class were glancing quickly at each other, some of them shaking their heads, meaning "It isn't mine," and now they were all querying each other in silence as Cheyney read on, his eyes to the paper, and Chub tried not to notice them but he was flushed now, and soon he was aware how the others at the round table were eyeing him, looking fast away, and had he ever felt such quick humiliation and if so when and—

—and now it got worse, because as Chub concentrated all he could on his words, he realized something so terrible: Cheyney just didn't not like it, he was reading it with *scorn*. Chub locked his hands tightly together and stared down at the table because this couldn't be happening, if the best thing he could do was shit and if more than anything what he wanted was to write, where did that leave him?

Long silence when Cheyney was done.

Chub noticed some initials carved in the table but they were old and he couldn't quite figure what they were, originally, "I.M."? or "J.M."? or was the "M" an "M" after all or maybe a crappily done "W" and then Cheyney was speaking: "Clearly, this just won't do," he said.

No reply from around the table.

"Ordinarily," Cheyney said then, "I would ask your opinions, and I would do my best to refrain from speaking, but since this is our first outing and I took up so much time at the start and we have so little time left, forgive me if I explicate."

Chub lifted his eyes now. Cheyney was not looking at him but he was the only person in the room that wasn't.

"Forget the difficulty of having a major scene take place in such a lavatory. I've thought a bit, and I can come up with no novel or story that contains such a setting, but you're all young and ingenious, perhaps you might. It's a problem, certainly, a locale like this, and I would argue, were there time, that it is a major problem, but that is *not* the most severe one."

Pause for emphasis. "What did I say this course was?"

"Literature," one of the bright senior girls replied immediately.

"Yes. And what did I say literature was about?"

"Uplift of the spirit," the girl answered again.

"Not quite. Of the *human* spirit."

"Sorry," the girl said, and she seemed, momentarily, downcast.

Sorry? Chub thought. You didn't write it—what have you got to be sorry about?

"All right, we're running out of class time, hear me now: This will not do for one simple reason: I-do-not-want-to-know-anybody-who-frequents-such-a-place."

That was my father in there.

"My reading time I cherish," Andrew Cheyney said. "I want to discover glory. And there is no glory here. It deals with scum, and I do not want that in my literature, there is plenty on street corners."

My father wasn't scum. You didn't know, I knew, and he was a better man than you'll ever be, *he was.*

The bell rang.

"I don't think you can say that," Chub managed.

No one got up to leave.

Cheyney studied him. "Come again, Fuller?"

"I just don't think you can say that, limit everything."

"I love disagreements, Fuller." He looked at the group. "Any of you, feel free to leave."

No one budged.

"You find glory here, Fuller?"

"I don't know what 'glory' means."

"I suggest you look it up in the library. It has yet to damage an artwork, at least to my knowledge. But let me ask you about your knowledge, Fuller. Answer this please: *Today,* name me a writer you admire."

"Shaw."

"Excellent choice—Bernard Shaw was a brilliant dramatist and a far greater essayist, but this is not a course in play construction, so you didn't answer what I asked you."

Chub's voice was going increasingly dry and his stomach was tight and he couldn't help the way he was perspiring, didn't try to wipe it away, they would have all seen, because none of them would stop staring. "I meant Shaw. Irwin Shaw."

"Ahhh yes, well, that explains a great deal, Fuller. Here I ask a question to which the answer could have been Poe or Tolstoi or Kafka or Chekhov—and you come up with Irwin Shaw, who at his infrequent best is nothing more than a common popularizer."

Helpless now, Chub sat there. So did they all. The silence lasting until from across the table Kitchel boomed in. "Your question was confusingly put."

"Come again, Kitchel? I'm told I tend to speak more coherently than most."

"Not this time—you asked, 'Today, name me a writer you admire,' and you emphasized *today,* and I thought, and I'm sure Fuller did, too, that when you used that word you meant living, contemporary, not a figure from the past. Personally, I might have mentioned Shaw or I might have said Graham Greene, but I would have answered someone alive."

"Is that what you thought, Fuller?" Cheyney asked.

And then Chub went out of control, shouting, *"It doesn't matter what I thought, what I thought is on that paper you read,"* and he grabbed for his books and ripped them from the table and shoved his shoulder into the door that led outside and he ran down the stairs and out across Tappan Square and within an hour he had dropped the Cheyney, substituted a course in the Intellectual History of Europe that was supposed to be terrific. The following Wednesday afternoon there was a thumping at his door and Kitchel's voice blasting, "Is this where young Fuller abides, open up, you slugabed."

"Unlocked," Chub replied. He was, indeed, lying in bed when Kitchel filled the doorway.

"Your countenance was notably absent from Cheyney's," Kitchel said.

"You'll have to struggle along without me."

"You dropped the course, I suspected as much." He clomped in on his crutches and dropped into Chub's desk chair. "We share a certain mutual skill—we both flee magnificently."

Chub thought back to Kitchel's exit from the No-Name, a year before, the night he got famous.

"I was thinking of maybe majoring in departures in graduate school." He looked at Kitchel, who was busy scratching his red and black lumberjack shirt. "Thank you," Chub said then. "For coming to my defense like that with Cheyney."

Kitchel held out one hand. "You may kiss my ring." Then he went back to his scratching. "I was not coming to your defense. The oaf had phrased a question incorrectly and I was trying to help him along the way to literacy."

"Whatever," Chub said.

"And I had to say something—my God, Fuller, the whipped kitten look you were wearing—Himmler would have had to say something."

"Do you intentionally piss people off, or is it kind of a natural gift?"

"It's a natural gift, but I work at it."

Chub held up the book he'd been reading. "Kant," he said. "We whipped kittens need our concentration."

"You are a great ass, Fuller."

"For trying to make sense of Immanuel Kant? Agreed."

"No. And you know full and well what I mean—you are a great cowardly dolt for dropping Cheyney."

Chub picked up the Kant, opened it to his place.

Kitchel grabbed a crutch, thrust it forward hard, knocked the book flying. "*You listen to me, Fuller*—you do not read in my presence."

Chub, surprised by the blow, half sat.

Kitchel rose now, put the crutches under his arms, moved closer. He seemed, as he stared down, almost angry. "Cheyney was wrong, pedantic and wrong, and we both know it. You have a voice, Fuller. It's there. I felt that slimy men's room and I'll tell you what else I felt—you weren't alone in there. Say I'm right."

Chub nodded.

"That was your father in there with you."

Chub stared up, stunned, because there had been no personal description in what he'd done—just the walls and the ceiling and despair.

Kitchel was bending close now, his shaggy hair inches from Chub's face. "Say I'm right."

"How did you guess that?"

Kitchel erupted—"*Guess?* A person enters and tells you a startling fact and you insult him with the word 'guess'?"

"How did you know?"

Kitchel shook his head. "Part of genius is mystery, Fuller; allow me to keep my mystery." He seemed terribly pleased with himself as he turned his body on his crutches, made his way to the doorway, stopped, looked back. "You have the gift, you chickenshit nit, but probably not the courage to capitalize. You want to be a writer, don't you, Fuller?"

"More than anything," Chub heard himself reply.

Kitchel left on that.

Chub stared at the empty doorway, wondering why he had told the truth to someone he didn't know really at all. Probably because of what Kitchel had just said: Chub didn't know exactly what "the gift" was, but whatever it was, it had to be something good and besides that, no one had ever told him he had it before. . . .

Now, half a year and more later, exhausted from eighteen straight hours of writing, Chub, the carbon of "The Girl(s) of My Dreams" in his hands, walked up the flight of steps from his dorm room to where Kitchel lived.

Kitchel was, while still a sophomore, the unquestioned literary star on campus. He wrote numberless satiric letters to the biweekly college newspaper in which he blamed the evils of the country on President Hubert Humphrey who had defeated Richard Nixon in the '68 election.

And he caused a stir outside Finney Chapel one night where a professor from Pitt was giving a speech explaining that Marlowe had authored Shakespeare. Kitchel stood outside, hawking a Xerox of an essay he'd written, the point of it being the heretical notion that *Shakespeare* had written Shakespeare's plays.

Plus, he was Cheyney's pet by now. This happened the first month of class when Cheyney read an assignment in which the student was to write the same brief scene but from two different points of view, first person and third. Kitchel, when Cheyney was finished, ripped the attempt brutally. He vilified the unnamed author as a fraud and an illiterate and then he really warmed up. Such was his attack that several senior girls were forced to defend the writer, at which point Kitchel ripped them as being frauds and illiterates and one girl actually wept. Cheyney watched all, saying not a word, and it wasn't till class was over that the other students realized that the author Kitchel had been slaughtering was Kitchel himself.

Chub approached his room. The door was open. Inside, Kitchel sat on the floor in his underwear, putting fresh dirty decals on his crutches.

When he saw Chub, Kitchel went quickly into a Butterfly McQueen imitation: "Miz Scarlett, Miz Scarlett, look, it's that handsome Fuller boy come coatin'."

"Busy?"

"Shit, Fuller, if I were painting the Sistine Chapel or writing the Brandenburgs, it might make sense, but how can this"—he licked another decal, smoothed it on— "qualify as being busy?"

"I just didn't want to bother you."

"Of course you wanted to bother me, why the hell else would you be here, now what the fuck is it, can't you see I'm busy?"

"I'm kind of tired and I don't feel like doing battle, okay?"

"Oh, good, there's that whipped kitten look we all know and love."

"Were you born, Kitchel, or did you just spring full-grown, frothing at the mouth."

"The spunky hero of the stacks has just put in an appearance, bravo."

Chub took a deep breath, got control, then handed over the pages. "Maybe you might take a look at this," he said.

"This is a *carbon,*" Kitchel bellowed. "To the greatest critical mind since S. T. Coleridge you have the audacity to give a carbon? Would you give Tom Eliot a carbon? I think not. Not only is it insulting—the subtext is that I am not worthy of the original—carbons are smudgy and messy and blurry and they obfuscate the author's intention and—"

"—this is *important,*" Chub said.

"*I* am important," Kitchel said, and he shoved the pages back into Chub's hands. "And I do not read carbons."

Chub stormed out, shouting, "You are so fucking irritating I wouldn't let you read this now; I mean, there is no way on this earth you'll ever see this, Kitchel!" and he slammed the door with all he had and went back to his room, threw on a coat, started for the No-Name, took off his coat, grabbed the original and went back up to Kitchel's room. "Me," he said, throwing the door open.

Kitchel was lying on his bed now, reading a copy of *Serendipity,* which was a semiannual class paperback that contained wonderful stories and poems. Probably, if he had his choice, Chub would have wanted to be published in *Serendipity* more than anyplace, *The New Yorker* included.

"Fuller," Kitchel said cheerily, putting the book down. "How *are* you, good to see you, have you written anything lately?"

"As a matter of fact, I have," Chub said.

"Is that it in your hands?"

"Not to shock you, but it is," and as Kitchel held out his hands, Chub gave him "The Girl(s) of My Dreams."

Kitchel put it down on the bed beside him without a glance. "Now: What do you want me to do with it?"

"Aw shit, Kitchel, isn't that obvious?"

"For most mortals, it would be, but you, Fuller, being an acknowledged whacko, must be approached with considerable care. I am assuming you would like me to read it, nod once for yes, twice for no."

Chub gave him the finger.

"I'm being serious, Fuller. Because after I've read it we are into something of a quandary—the last time any criticism was directed your way, you came quite unglued. The question on the table, Fuller, is do you want my opinion or do you want my *opinion?*"

"I want everything," Chub said. "If you think any of it's okay, I want to know that; if you hate it, I want to know that, too; if you can tell me why it stinks, that would be terrific, I can take criticism."

"That has yet to be proven on this planet."

"Just tell me the truth."

"The truth you shall have, but it may not set you free."

Chub left then, and this time he did go to the No-Name for a couple of beers. Del was working and B.J. was sitting in her special seat at the end of the bar and they were all over each other when Del could get away. Chub joined them briefly and B.J. said thank God the stupid pizza fight was a thing of the past and Chub said thank God, too, but he remembered her tears from less than forty-eight hours before and he wondered. He was bushed, and after chugging his second beer he went back to his room and slept for twelve hours.

When he awoke the first thing he did was glance toward his door because probably that was the way Kitchel would return his story, along with whatever comments he might have, and Chub was glad the story wasn't there. At least he'd given Kitchel something to think about. Maybe by that night, when he got back from the library, it would be returned.

Only it wasn't.

And it wasn't there the following morning either. Chub was beginning to get nervous now. He felt sure what he'd written wasn't garbage, but there was a limit as to how much praise a guy like Kitchel might bestow.

When it wasn't returned the third morning, Chub realized it wasn't praise that was keeping Kitchel. He wrote long papers, Kitchel did, and sometimes they were vitriolic, and Chub realized he was going to have to brace himself for the coming onslaught.

The fourth morning when there was nothing he began to get ticked. Shit, it was only a story, how much bad stuff could you say about it, how many pages could you fill?

He found out that night when he got back from the

library and there, shoved under the door, was a manila envelope. Chub went to his desk, sat, got ready, opened it up, reached in for his story and Kitchel's lengthy comments. The front page said this:

RE: THE FULLER EFFORT

1) Some critics might consider the title to be smart-ass. I consider most critics to be smart-ass. You may keep the title.

2) Your knowledge of the Isle of Manhattan is less than encyclopedic.

3) On to the next.

Chub, nervous as hell, flipped to the next page for the rest—

—there wasn't any rest.

On the next page was the start of his story. Confused, Chub flipped to the end because maybe Kitchel had put his real remarks there—

—no real remarks.

Stunned, Chub went over the whole thing page by page.

Nothing. Just that goddamn moronic note. Steaming now, he grabbed the note and took off for Kitchel's room and knocked. "Stand and unfold yourself," he heard from inside.

Chub opened the door. Kitchel was sitting on his bed, rubbing dry shampoo in his incredible mass of curly hair. "I . . . I don't know what . . . don't know how to begin, really," Chub said quietly. He sat in the chair across from Kitchel. "Talk about food for thought."

Kitchel went on rubbing.

"I don't know enough words to thank you, Two-Brew. I mean, the way you compared my use of the symbol of the swimming pool with the water images in Conrad—shit, I didn't even realize in a conscious way that I was doing that."

Kitchel said nothing, concentrated on his hair.

"And the philosophical implications you pointed out in the way I chose the pizza flavor to be pepperoni instead of mushrooms and anchovies, my God, my head was spinning."

"Do I detect a note of disenchantment?"

"Shit, you fuckhead, you keep me waiting a fucking fortnight damn near and then what do I get? *This!*" and he waved the single sheet of paper with Kitchel's writing on it. " 'You may keep the title.' Of course *I* may keep the title—it's my story, I can call it anything I want. Arrogant prick. 'You may keep the title.' "

"I think you should consider seeing a psychiatrist, Fuller, to discuss your deep-seated problem with criticism."

Chub exploded—"I don't have any goddamn problem with criticism, fart, *you didn't give me any criticism!*"

Kitchel stopped rubbing his hair and looked at Chub. "Have you ever heard of George Abbott, Fuller?"

"No, is he another critic with a lot to say?"

"Hush your face and listen—George Abbott is the most successful director in the history of the American theatre. Have you ever heard of the American theatre, Fuller? It's an event that happens on a platform called a stage and real people walk back and forth and say things. It is not *Leave It to Beaver,* which I *am* sure you've heard of."

"Fuck you."

"Fuck you. George Abbott is known as the quintessential professional and I once met an actress who had been in a musical he'd directed—*Fiorello,* Fuller, it only won the Pulitzer Prize. And this girl was a great success, only she told me that during rehearsal she *knew* she was going to be fired. Because when the other performers did their scenes Abbott would work with them intensely and for long periods of time. But when this girl did her scenes, he didn't say anything. Just listen and when she was done he'd excuse her. Without comment. Which is why she was convinced she was going to be terminated. Later she found out that if he was pleased with someone's work, he didn't see any need to work with them so he excused them. If he wasn't pleased, he would keep the actors rehearsing for hours. Now do you see?"

"What I see is this little pissant piece of paper you wrote."

Kitchel sighed. "I, too, am the quintessential professional, Fuller. The crucial words I wrote are the last four."

Chub looked at the page. "You mean 'On to the next'?"

Now Kitchel exploded—"Yes, you churl, because that means I want to see your next story, if I hadn't wanted to see it I would have said something like 'Thank you for letting me see this.' But I didn't, did I?"

"You mean you want to see more of my writing?"

"Talk about pulling teeth," Kitchel said.

"You mean you liked it?"

"I was pleased, Fuller, pleased, pleased, pleased, Jesus Christ."

"Fuck you—"

"—fuck you."

"Well, shit, why didn't you *say* you liked it?"

"Oh, my God, you come on talking about wanting the truth when all you really want is praise—I shall give you praise—" He crawled across the room toward the chair, grabbed Chub's hands. "Oh, Fuller, I wept, rarely have I had such an epiphany, not since I first studied Homer have I come across such a master of the art of narrative, not since Milton or Keats has anyone understood the poetic nuances of language—"

Chub shoved him on his ass, headed for the door. "I'll be right back, I've got lots of other stuff to show you."

"I am not interested in yesterday's news."

"You'll like these, Kitchel—I've got one about an astronomer who discovers Heaven behind Mars—"

"—*Byuk*—warmed-over Heinlein."

"Well, I've got another about a librarian who hates this guy who always dog-ears the pages of the books he takes out and she loves Jane Austen and when he dog-ears *Pride and Prejudice* she kills him by hitting him over the head with a copy of Emily Post."

Kitchel clutched his stomach and rolled on the floor. "*Double Byuk*—warmed-over Dahl."

"*What the hell do you want?*"

"Just what I said I wanted—*the next*. Get to work. Create something."

"I can't just 'create' something on order, for Chris-sakes."

"You can *try*, you prepubescent fart," and before Chub could come up with an answer, Kitchel forced himself up into a sitting position and pointed a finger at him. "Hear me now, Fuller. Hear this and remember it! *Anyone* can be a writer. To be a *good* writer sometimes you have to put words on paper." Then he reached for his dry sham-poo and went back to working on his hair, while Chub contented himself with slamming the door as he left.

But well before he reached his room one floor down, Chub knew damn well he wasn't angry, not anymore, at Kitchel. Why should he be?—Chub had *pleased* him. Kitchel *liked* the story.

And besides that, you couldn't stay angry at Two-Brew. Yes, he was insufferable; bingo, he was supercil-ious, sarcastic, overweening, ego-ridden, contemptuous, snobbish, snooty, bloated beyond the bounds of reason. Shit, he was probably the only human who swaggered on crutches.

But he was funny (at least some of the time) and human (at least on occasion) and so fucking smart (al-ways, always).

In his room, Chub lay down and went back over the scene up in Kitchel's and he realized that more than anything, what they were like was two snot-nosed kids scrapping in the schoolyard. Chub's most memorable encounter of that kind was with his best friend, Johnny Roberts, when they were eight, and it happened after Assembly when some old yawn of a guy had given a speech to Athens Grammar School on the necessity of overlooking appearances as you made your way through life, and that some of the best people came in weird sizes so don't be fooled, and then he did this incredible thing—

—he took out his false teeth and put them on the rostrum.

None of the students was ready for the move and there was a very loud reaction, not one of joy, and this old guy put his teeth back then and said how probably they thought less of him but that was just being fooled by appearances, he explained, because back in World War II he had been in the same company as Clark Gable and he also had false teeth.

Chub knew that was bullshit, it had to be bullshit, and if it wasn't it would bomb the hell out of his mother since Gretchen was the world's number-one Gable fan. She talked about him a lot and she didn't go to movies, but whenever one of *his* pictures hit the local theatre, guess who was first in line?

After assembly, Chub and Johnny Roberts were heading for the playground and a hot challenge match of pom-pom-pull-away when Johnny said that he never knew that movie stars could have false teeth and Chub said they didn't, at least Gable didn't, and Johnny said it had to be true, you couldn't go around lying in Assembly like that and Chub said if you believe an asshole like that you're an asshole yourself and within another minute of talk, they were into action, hitting each other and rolling around on the gravel and pretty soon they were still hitting each other but now they were crying and before anyone broke it up they both had torn clothes and bloody noses and Chub had a shiner starting but Johnny's lip was gushing pretty good so Chub wasn't really sure who won—

—but as he ran home, trying to make the tears stop, he knew his mother would be pleased. He had defended Clark Gable with every ounce of strength and you couldn't do better than that.

In his room now, Chub got out of bed and put some typing paper in his machine. Because the story had a

kicker—Gretchen was furious. She shrilled at him over
his clothing and she was humiliated by his blackening eye
and what if his nose had been broken and she sent him to
his room for the rest of the day and even though he tried
explaining why it all had happened, she couldn't have
cared less. He had disappointed her with his hoodlumlike
behavior.

Chub needed names for his characters so he reached
for *Mixed Company,* and *Sailor off the Bremen* had been
about a fight and the names Shaw used were Ernest and
Stryker and the girl was named Sally, so Sally became
Gretchen, and he and Johnny the other two, and he
began to write, starting with Assembly, going through
the incidents, ending with the surprising displeasure of
the mother.

Eight pages long.

Chub, done by three, fell asleep with pleasure and
expectation. What was it Kitchel had said? To be a good
writer you have to put words on paper? Well, he had
done that, surprisingly done that, and he looked forward
to rereading his efforts the next morning.

It was gahr-bagh. Or close to it. Chub, before coffee,
read the story again.

Fug.

He dressed, went to the cafeteria, drank three cups of
coffee as hot as he could bear, desperate to get awake
fast. That semi-accomplished, he returned to his room,
glanced through the story.

```
          ''CLARK GABLE'S WERE REAL''

                    by

              Charles Fuller
```

He reached for a sheet of scratch paper, rolled it in,
began to fiddle.

```
    kitchel would eat this alive--
    true
    true
```

```
why though?

it's not as bad as I thought.
it's not even all that bad.
it's just . . .
what?
```

Chub stared at the paper for five minutes, trying to think of the right word.

```
fluff is what it is.
no weight at all.
no core, no center, no . . .
```

Chub got up from his desk, lay down, got up again, went down to the bathroom, pissed, washed up, brushed his teeth, nodded to a couple of other Obies who were using the facilities at the same time, and a couple of them wanted to BS but he excused himself, went back to his room, sat.

```
got it got it got it--
it's not a story, jerk--

IT'S JUST AN INCIDENT.

fug . . .

so fix it.
```

Chub stared at the paper again and as he did, he felt it again, that *impulse* that had been the foundation for "The Girl(s) of My Dreams."

```
yes yes yes--
yes yes, oh shit--

what you left out wasn't her displeasure--
it was that you were so good at arousing it.
```

Chub took out the scratch, put in the Eaton's and the carbon, and while he did it dozens of incidents trooped by, and he picked two, the dog and the book. The dog had been Gretchen's love. (Chub hated the fucker, a mean growling giant of a shepherd, and he sometimes *knew* it was going to rip his throat out while he slept.) And when it got run over Chub went to his father with his great idea and begged Mike and kept at it until finally Mike drove him out to "Orphans of the Storm," where they gave strays away, and he picked a shepherd pup and brought it home and Gretchen was in the kitchen making supper when Chub burst in the back door with the animal in his arms and Gretchen saw and the first thing she did was just laugh, throw back her head and let fly, and then she said, "Who's gonna walk him, huh? Who's gonna take him out in the snow and who's gonna clean up after he messes, huh? huh? me, well, I clean up enough messes with just you two heroes to look after," and after dinner Chub sat with the dog in his lap while his father drove him back to "Orphans of the Storm."

The book had been her birthday gift, the one that came just after Mike's suicide and Gretchen had been in bad shape before only now she was sliding abruptly down and Chub went by himself into Chicago and visited a bunch of bookstores before he found it—a leather-bound copy of *Gone with the Wind* and it took almost all the money he'd been saving but that didn't matter spit, and on her birthday morning he'd handed it to Gretchen all neatly wrapped and she opened it and stared and then wept with Chub watching, nervous but ready to crow because she was touched, only when she could speak it turned out she wasn't, because all she said was, "Jesus, no money coming in and this is what you piss yours away on?"

Chub, the impulse with him, worked through the day, and if it had been a painting he was doing it might have been a triptych, because he rolled the three incidents together, one popping into the next, in and out and back without much regard to chronology.

And just as the pessimistic movie theatre owner always saw business as half empty, never half full, that was how Gretchen saw her world, her life, her home, and the story ended with the protagonist son aware of two things: He knew he would never be able to please his mother; and he knew that he would never be able not to try.

''THE HALF-EMPTY HOUSE''

by

Charles Fuller

Nineteen pages.

Sumbitch.

Chub got it all carefully in order, put a paper clip in one corner, stretched, stood, grabbed it and went off to do battle with Kitchel.

This time he didn't take the carbon. . . .

CHAPTER 3

Eight Ninety-Five

"Would you enjoy," Two-Brew asked a month or so later, "a brief visit to New York?"

"More than almost anything," Chub said. It was true. Ever since he was probably twelve and had for the first time held a copy of the Sunday *New York Times* and had turned page after page of the entertainment section, experiencing infinity. There was no doubt from then on that someday he would, when he could afford it, move there and revel. Athens was where he lived, but a mistake had been made: New York was home.

They were walking back to their dorm. Chub had just taken Patty McLean home. They'd been dating for several weeks, and though it wasn't serious, Chub suspected that might change. Patty was also a sophomore, a psych major, not quite plain, not quite clever, but where it mattered she was luminous, being totally kind. More often than not, when he took her for coffee after his job, Two-Brew butted along, and she didn't seem to mind. "A long weekend, perhaps, in Manhattan. Does that strike your fancy?"

Chub smiled, shook his head. "No *dinero*."

"Certainly a problem, but not necessarily insoluble. Hear me now: I do not drive, but you do. I do not own a credit card but my father possesses one. He arranges with a Hertz in Elyria. You chauffeur me home. Once there, we can find room for you, my parents won't mind, and then I will supply you with a bus ticket home, which, knowing you, you will probably cash in and hitchhike. Your fee will be precisely one hundred and twenty-five dollars and—"

"—that's a strange amount," Chub said. "Why not a flat hundred?"

"You interrupted me, that is a no-no. Shut up till I'm done. There also may be a surprise in the city—"

"What is all this elaborate shit?" Chub wondered aloud. "They've got this new invention—it's called a *plane.* I'm not sure, but I think there's an airport in Cleveland and I'll bet if you check around, you'll find there's got to be one in New York somewhere."

Two-Brew stopped, whacked Chub across the ass with a crutch, then continued on. "Prepare yourself for disillusionment: I know you and the rest of the world considers me without flaw. Now you must know my secret. Acrophobia. I hate fucking airplanes." (That was but half true; Kitchel did hate airplanes, but it wasn't acrophobia. Chub did not know the whole until years later, when he and Two-Brew were flying back from Dallas the black and barren day when B.J. Peacock's wondrous little girl had been lowered in her obscenely small coffin into the unforgiving ground.

(He and Two-Brew took the plane back together, and it was jammed in the waiting area and just before boarding, one of the mechanical stewardesses made the standard speech, announcing that anyone with small children or anyone needing special assistance would be boarded first.

(They were traveling under the seat and Chub stood, waited for Two-Brew to do the same.

(Kitchel stayed in his chair.

(A few minutes later when the regular boarding began so did their troubles. There was a long entranceway from the gate to the plane and inside the aisles were full and it was bad for everybody—

(—except for Two-Brew it was worse.

(His crutches were hard to work in the aisle and the bag was hard to handle with the crutches and pretty soon there was a jam-up and they were causing it and Chub reached for Kitchel's bag but Kitchel ripped it free and kept trying to plod on and behind them now a stewardess was saying, "Excuse me, excuse me," her voice getting nearer, "Excuse me, what seems to be the trouble, excuse me," and when she was just a step behind them she said that again, "What seems to be the trouble?" and Two-Brew said, "There is no trouble," but his voice was louder than it should have been and now the stewardess said, "Sir, we said that anyone requiring special assistance would be boarded first," and then Two-Brew lost it: "I do not need special assistance! Not from you or the pilot—*I need no special assistance from anyone!*"

(Chub, with what remained of his brain that day, realized his weird and dearest friend could only deal with his infirmity when he set the ground rules. He could joke about the two dead appendages with intimates. But in the unknown world, in dealing with strangers, the legs were humiliations beyond his ability to bear. . . .)

They left ten days later, very early, in a rented Chevvy picked up from a Hertz in Elyria. The previous morning had been graduation and they both needed to hang around for that, Two-Brew because of some seniors he was friendly with, Chub because after the diplomas were passed out, B.J. and Del got married.

Chub met the Peacocks and the Hiltons and had a drink with them at the Oberlin Inn. B.J. said she'd never been as happy and the way she sounded, it had to be true. Chub kissed her good-bye, wished her all the best, Del, too, and they all promised to get together somewhere soon, but that was, and they all knew it, unlikely.

Chub had a little trouble, leaving Elyria, before he found the Ohio Turnpike but once he did, the rest would be a breeze, straight turnpike all the way, the Ohio into the Pennsylvania into the Jersey. He was glad the driving wouldn't worry him, because he was, even before he set foot in the Chevvy, exhausted.

The last ten days had been murder on him. He

couldn't sleep, couldn't write, made a bunch of mistakes in the library.

New York was too much with him.

He read and reread Shaw's *Welcome to the City,* the great story where the young actor, Enders, is having just a rotten time in Manhattan, he's new there, nothing much goes right, until, on a pissing-down night, he meets a girl who looks like Greta Garbo, who is "full-breasted, flat-bellied, steel-thighed, supple as a cat," only it turns out her teeth are bad and she's down on her luck, too, and as they go to bed together Enders feels that somehow, in its own way, the city was calling out to him, in its own voice, saying, "Welcome, Citizen."

Chub wondered who would call out to him? Or, more precisely, would anyone? And, more precisely still, why should they? He was a jerk, a putz, who had his heart set on whirling happily in the center of the universe, and what if he hated it? Or worse, what if he loved it too much? And could never afford to live there?

As they picked up their card on the Ohio Turnpike, Two-Brew said, "Excellent."

"That I finally found it, you mean?"

"No. Nine A.M. Five hundred fifty miles to cover. We should make it there by suppertime." He seemed as slobby as ever but in excellent spirits. He no longer wore lumberjack shirts, they were too hot; his spring costume consisted of spattered painter's pants topped with baggy Hawaiian tops worn loose, the most sedate of which gave the word "garish" a bad name. The only thing different about him was his crutches—they seemed relatively new and had no decals on them at all.

Chub wore jeans and a T-shirt and had his small bag tossed in the backseat. His hands were already moist as he gripped the wheel.

" 'Why so pale and wan, fond lover?' " Two-Brew asked a little later.

"Hung over," Chub said quickly. "A few too many at the wedding."

Two-Brew looked at him, nodded, settled back, closed his eyes awhile, dozing, till just outside Pittsburgh.

Chub checked his map. Four hundred twenty miles to go.

Two-Brew stretched, belched, looked out at the gloomy road. The day was overcast, no breaks in the clouds. "Low sky," he said. "Like Holland."

"That's a long way, I thought you were acrophobic."

"High school tour," Two-Brew answered quickly. "They flew, I boated."

" 'Boated,' " Chub mimicked. "*Très* fucking fancy."

"You are so prehistorically boorish. Fuller, in the unlikely event that you ever grow up, what in the world are you going to be?"

"The truth? I always hoped if my grades were good enough I could get a scholarship and go to grad school."

"And major in what?"

"I don't know; maybe boating."

"Oh, shit, you'll probably be an English major and spend your life pretending to spread the joys of Beowulf. Snooze." He reached into a large paper bag full of food he'd brought, reached around for an apple. "I know what I'm going to be."

"Let me guess: a fashion plate."

Two-Brew ignored him, bit hard into the apple, chomped for emphasis. "I—and there is simply no doubt about this—am going to be famous. . . ."

Harrisburg. Over halfway.

"Where is this legendary Journal of yours?" Two-Brew asked as Harrisburg fell away behind them.

"It's not legendary, it's just a journal."

"You brought it?"

Chub had told Kitchel about the book when Two-Brew returned "The Half-Empty House" with the note that said simply, "I managed to stay awake. On to the next." Which pissed Chub off, naturally, and they went round and round about if only there were a Mr. Insufferable contest, Two-Brew would be a cinch. As they were getting ready for the trip, he asked would·Chub mind him looking through it. Chub agreed as long as Two-Brew promised not to be insulting. "In my bag back there."

Two-Brew turned, unzipped the bag, brought the Journal into his lap. "I hope there are some good dirty-story ideas in here. You never write dirty stuff, it's a terrible lacking. Is it because you're not good at fucking? Are you good?"

Chub thought a moment. He'd been to bed with maybe half a dozen girls. No. Lie. He'd been to bed with exactly three girls. And they provided him with many of his happier memories. "That is not a question I choose to answer, fink, because it is not a question anyone knows the answer to."

"Wrong. I happen to be magnificent as a fucker, does that surprise you—don't lie, you've secretly wondered if my pee-pee is dead too."

"Did you just say 'pee-pee'?—I'm getting out of the car."

"That was Wildean wit—juxtaposing an Anglo-Saxon word with a child's expression. Humor, and you may write this down, is the unexpected juxtaposition of incongruities."

Chub snored.

"You were asking about my fucking," Two-Brew went on. "Well, the truth is this: I have been to bed with a dozen women and they have all—*all*—praised me."

(Probably, Chub realized years later, that was true. Not the number, necessarily, but the compliments. Two-Brew never dated, at least till he was in his middle twenties. He visited whores. Exclusively. The legs again.)

Now he opened the Journal, flicked around. "How's it divided up?"

"Mainly first lines and titles and story ideas."

Two-Brew stopped at a page. "Ah, yes: first lines." He ran his finger down a list, read out loud: " 'Youth is the illusion of infinite choice.' "

"Well?"

"Putrescent." He moved his finger down again. " 'I have, except for the murder, no real reason for telling the story of my life.' " He paused, thought a moment. "Vomitous."

"Is 'vomitous' better or worse than 'putrescent'?" Chub wanted to know.

"Dead heat."

"At least you're keeping your word and not being insulting," Chub said.

Two-Brew flipped on. "Perhaps your titles will be less stomach-turning." He stopped, read: " 'Roses, Roses.' "

"One of my favorites," Chub said.

Two-Brew nodded. "There is no question that it provides magnificent opportunities for sequels. The next you could call, 'Tulips, Tulips'—"

"—it's a quote—"

"—and then perhaps 'Hyacinths, Hyacinths' and certainly 'Camellias, Camellias' could follow hard upon—"

"—I said it was a quote, you asshole—"

"—I know it's a quote, 'I-have-forgot-much,-Cynara-gone-with-the-wind,-flung-roses,-roses-riotously-with-the-throng'—"

"—*just gimme the goddamn thing, all right?*" Chub said, and he grabbed his Journal, put it on the seat beside him away from Two-Brew. "Go fuck yourself, that was my father's favorite poem."

"I'm sorry," Two-Brew said after a pause. "I didn't know that."

Chub didn't answer, just gunned the Chevvy, because what he'd said was true, but his exploding wasn't because of that, you spent time with Kitchel, you learned to survive; what had set him off was a sign saying they weren't all that far from Philadelphia and Philly meant a hundred more to New York and what he wanted was to get there maybe at dusk, the magic hour, with the sun back-lighting the city and—

—and as they reached, in silence, Philadelphia, the drizzle began.

It stayed like that till into Jersey, when it really started pissing down. It was after five when they hit New Brunswick, and traffic began to snarl.

"Let me look at your story ideas," Two-Brew said then. "I promise to be as sweet as Snow White and as gentle as Bambi."

Chub hesitated, then passed over the Journal, because at least if Kitchel was concentrating on that there was a chance he wouldn't catch the nervousness Chub was barely keeping under control.

Two-Brew opened the Journal, asked, "What's 'The Bethlehem Scene'?"

"Oh, that, Christ, that," Chub began, the words pouring out fast, glad for the chance to keep his mind off his mind, "that was in third or fourth grade and I was the smartest kid in my class and I loved my teacher, Miss Roginsky, and the week before Christmas holiday the class had made this papier-mâché model of Bethlehem on a card table, we called it the Bethlehem scene, and we slaved and it was—I thought it was beautiful, and the first day back after vacation we had a test and I was done first and gave her my paper and she said since I had the time, would I please go to the rear of the room and break up the Bethlehem scene and I went to where the card table was and I figured I'd misunderstood what she wanted, because you couldn't break up something like that and what if I started and she got mad so I went back to her desk and asked again and she said to yes, break it up and when I got to the papier-mâché I was really confused because I couldn't figure out what she'd been saying but I knew it wasn't what I'd heard so I stared and stared at it and then I went back up front again and asked just what it was she wanted and she snapped, 'Oh, sit down,' and a girl was done with the test and she told the girl to go break up the Bethlehem scene and the girl got a wastebasket and broke it into little pieces and when I got home that night and told my folks my mother was angry at how stupid I was but my father, he thought I'd done just fine, and I understood later why he thought that—for the first time I knew he wanted me to be like him, he wanted me to fail."

"On to the next," Two-Brew said, louder now, because there was distant thunder. " 'The Innocent Eye.' "

"That must have been after I'd started jerking off—"

"—a dirty story, at last—"

"—wrong, I was just trying to place it in time, but my mother had taken a trip to Lauderdale because her father was sick and my dad was sober enough to drive to O'Hare to pick her up and I went along but her plane was late so we sat on the second floor to wait. We were facing an up escalator—you've got to see this now—it was like a movie—people were coming into view rising slowly and people are people, nothing particular, and we were waiting and waiting and then just this fabulous pile of beautiful brown hair was visible—and then a blink later these deep blue eyes—then a straight nose—she's rising into our sight, you get the picture?"

"Just go on."

"Okay, well her mouth was pouty, like Bardot's, and she was wearing a thin white T-shirt and her breasts jutted out and her T-shirt was tucked into her slacks—maybe she was eighteen, nineteen, and she had no waist practically at all, but her hips were round—I don't know if she was the sexiest girl in the world or not, maybe it was the way she rose up, but she had long legs and high-heeled boots and when she got to the top of the escalator she looked around and then smiled and went running into the arms of this guy, maybe he was thirty, it's hard to judge age when you're a kid, and he brought her into his arms and I couldn't not watch because she was this vision from nowhere and I wanted to touch her breasts so bad and I could feel my dick starting to harden and naturally that made me feel guilty as hell so I quick looked away from her and smiled at my father—but he wasn't watching me, he was watching that girl and I was so innocent then, and I'll never forget what I saw in his eyes."

"He wanted to leave your mother and run off with the piece?"

"No, Christ, no, I knew for years they weren't madly passionate about each other—see, we had this shelf at home of ribbons and medals—my father had been a hero in World War Two, but I never really believed it till that moment because when I looked at him that second I knew he wanted her so badly he could murder for her, I realized my father could kill."

"On to the next," Two-Brew said, but then he shut the Journal. "Has it ever crossed your mind you have a thing about your father?"

"I don't know, maybe, I guess, he was a great man." Chub shook his head. "He just wasn't great when I knew him. . . ."

It was after seven before they got through the Holland Tunnel and then Two-Brew said to take a left and Chub did, driving through the driving rain, past ugly buildings and skittering pedestrians and as a drunk came staggering in the middle of the street dead into the oncoming traffic Two-Brew spoke again: "Welcome to Magic Town."

Chub stared at him. "This is Manhattan?"

Two-Brew nodded. "Sometimes it's even prettier. This is Eighth Avenue—people from Hawaii come *here* to vacation."

Chub made a smile, but inside there was only disbelief—he remembered in *Welcome to the City* what a dump the place could be, and he'd seen *Midnight Cowboy* twice so he'd seen what a dump the place could be—he knew all that—

—he just never believed it. Now he had no choice. Sure it was thundering and the rain was a bitch but on the sunniest autumn day, you'd still only want to get the hell out.

"Cat got your tongue?"

"I just . . . I thought there'd be more . . . I don't know what."

"Ah, yes, with Fred and Ginger spinning on tabletops.

It can be very beautiful here—I remember one day my junior year in high school it was very beautiful all morning."

Chub continued to drive through the uptown traffic and when Two-Brew said, "Hang a right," he did, and that was the first of a series of instructions, "Go right one block, then left, then left again," and Chub, peering through the windshield wipers, felt more lost than he could ever remember but that feeling squared when Two-Brew said to stop, because once that happened a uniformed man appeared holding an umbrella for Two-Brew to get out and another man slipped into the driver's seat when Chub got out and the next thing he was in an elevator with another uniformed man who pushed a button and when the elevator reached its destination Two-Brew opened a door and Chub followed him into a room that was bigger than the whole downstairs of the house he grew up in, or at least it seemed that way, and Chub looked around a moment until he realized it wasn't a room, the rooms were beyond, this gigantic marble-floored rectangle was the foyer—

—and to the left of the foyer, a winding staircase.

Chub looked at it a moment, gestured up. "Is that another apartment?" he asked.

"Ever the sophisticate," Two-Brew replied, adding, "Those are the bedrooms, come along," and Chub did, and at the top there was a wide corridor you could have practiced track in and Two-Brew stopped and opened a door—"This is yours," he said, "I'm down the hall, I've got to freshen up, see you in the library," and he started off.

"Hey!"

Two-Brew turned.

"You live here?—you have to be rich to live here—how the hell can you be rich when you go around dressed like a Martian?"

"I told you there might be surprises," Two-Brew said. "And listen—if you beat me down there, my mother's no problem—she doesn't make sense a lot of the time but if you smile a lot you're set. My father is a businessman and he's got this kind of odd habit: He gets pissed if anyone disagrees with him. You smile at the one, you nod at the other, good luck."

Chub entered his room, studied the canopy bed, inspected the bathroom, stared a moment at the terrace outside. Beyond he could see, through the storm, lights and what must have been trees—Central Park, for Chrissakes—just *there*. He dropped his small bag on the floor, wondered what the hell he could do to "freshen up" beyond showering—decided not a hell of a lot, so he showered, toweled off, opened his bag, took out the one pair of trousers he'd brought along, the lone white shirt. He decided they wouldn't look so hot with his tennis shoes and thanked God he'd brought along his loafers.

Then he wandered downstairs. He peeked into the first room he came to—it contained a pool table and a dollhouse that was lit and probably twenty feet long. Clearly not the library.

The next room was, but there weren't a lot of books. He was about to sit down when from behind him a voice said, "Can I get you anything, sir?" and Chub was facing a thin woman in a white maid's uniform.

For a moment he was silent, wondering what he might ask for. He shook his head. "Thank you, though."

"Very good, sir."

"Can I help *you* with anything?" Chub said.

Now she was silent for a moment. "I don't know how to answer that," she replied. "No one's ever asked me before. But thank you. If you change your mind, just buzz." She pointed to a button by the fireplace.

"I'll be sure to do that," Chub said, and then he was alone again.

But not for long. Now a lovely woman fluttered into the room, forty-five or fifty, and heads must have turned when she was young. "You must be Mistuh Fullah," she said, her accent heavily southern. "We're so glad you could join us."

"Thank you very much," Chub said and as she held

out her hand, he shook it, but gently, because too much force seemed as if it might shatter her.

"Can Ah get you anything?"

With newly practiced skill, Chub replied, "No thank you," without so much as a pause. "The lady in the uniform was already in."

"That's why Minnie is such a treasure; she's so dutiful." She touched her hands together then. "Whey-ah have mah manners flown to? Ahm Bernice Kitchel, Stanley's mother."

"I knew that—he's told me all about you."

"And just precisely what did he say?"

"That you were very beautiful and from the South," Chub said, faster on his feet than usual.

She gestured to the sofa and they sat, and then she took Chub's hands. "And how is ouah Stanley?"

"He weathered the trip just fine."

Now she dropped her voice. "Ah meant at school. He doesn't write or call as often as he might. Has he many acquaintances?"

Chub nodded.

"Ah worry so about Stanley's shyness."

Chub blinked. "I don't really think you have to fret a lot about that, Mrs. Kitchel."

"He's conquorin' it, then?"

"He's working on it very hard, yes, ma'am."

"Oh, that is *ex*cellent news."

"He's just blossoming lately, Mrs. Kitchel," Chub said, and he was about to go on when a perfectly attired sartorial vision appeared in the doorway—black shoes that glistened, white trousers with a slash for a crease, a white shirt that could have been silk, a perfectly knotted red tie that was silk, a black blazer that must have been tailor-made.

"Good evening, all," the vision said.

"Two-Brew," Chub said, stunned. "You're gorgeous."

"When am I not?" Two-Brew replied, and he hugged his mother, who had risen, gone to him, opened her arms. "Good evening, Scarlett," Two-Brew said.

Mrs. Kitchel looked at Chub. "That's Stanley's way of teasin' me about mah manner of speech." Then she turned back to her son. "Weeah havin' yoah favorite meal. Mistuh Kitchel won't be home till nearly nine, he works too hard."

"When does he not?"

"Shall we enjoy a little aperitif in the interim?"

Two-Brew nodded, went to the fireplace, buzzed, only dutiful Minnie did not respond. This time it was a man, also in uniform, who carried a tray of filled, bubbling tall glasses. Chub recognized him as the one who'd driven off in the rented car.

The three touched glasses and Chub took a sip. Odd— it tasted delicious, like lemonade, but it looked like champagne. He was very thirsty and he finished half the glass before the others had begun to sip, and by the time he was through with it, he was astonished to discover he was buzzed. "You can have another but I'd advise against it," Two-Brew said. "It's a southern concoction, a diamond fizz—it's champagne but it's also loaded up with ice-cold gin and sugar to get it faster into the blood stream. Three can bring on amnesia."

"I'm cool," Chub said, and they talked a little longer until Mrs. Kitchel said, "There's the elevatuh, your fathuh must be home," and she fluttered into the foyer and out of sight while Chub waited, watching as Two-Brew drew himself up very straight, a soldier at attention, and then his parents were in the doorway, arms around each other and Chub felt, watching his friend, Two-Brew's fear.

He felt it in himself, too, which was strange, if you looked at it logically, because Mr. Kitchel couldn't have been more than five five. But broad-shouldered and jut-jawed and Chub wondered if the man had smiled since Eisenhower left office.

"Sir," Two-Brew said.

"Stanley," his father answered.

"This is my friend, Chub Fuller."

"Sir," Chub said.

Mr. Kitchel made a perfunctory nod, said he was hungry, and when could they eat?

"Why, now, of co'ose," his wife said, and they headed into the enormous dining room beyond. Mrs. Kitchel fell in step with Chub, took his arm. "Ah do hope you like salmon," she said. "Stanley adores it so."

"Love it, yes," Chub said quickly, though the reverse was true. Salmon was that hot chunky fish his mother always overcooked because she didn't serve it often, only when it was on sale.

The large table was candlelit and rectangular and there were silver bowls with flowers. Mr. Kitchel sat at one end, his wife at the other, Two-Brew and Chub in the center, across from each other. In front of each was a plate with something thin and pink covering it, and alongside, a smaller plate with a funny-looking fork and wedges of lemon. Chub looked at it a moment, decided he didn't know what to do with it, so he waited while the uniformed man appeared, filled one of the several empty glasses in front of each of them with white wine. Mr. Kitchel swirled the wine around, sniffed, sipped. Chub looked to Mrs. Kitchel for assistance. At last she took a lemon wedge, squeezed it gently over the cool pink whatever, took a fork and a funny-looking knife, cut a piece.

Chub did the same, put a piece of the whatever into his mouth and almost instantly wished his portion were ten times as big—not only was it delicious but he could fill up on it before the salmon came.

"William Poll does have the best salmon," Mrs. Kitchel said then.

Two-Brew, halfway through his portion, nodded. "I swear I can always tell his salmon from anybody's."

Shit, Chub thought—*this* is salmon? He swirled the wine in his glass as Mr. Kitchel had done, didn't quite spill, took a good swallow. Probably he should go easy, he knew, but the wine was wonderful, too, and he didn't have to worry about faking his way through the main course, whatever it might be.

When he saw it, he was more baffled even than by the

salmon. It was a large round something that could have been chops because there were bones sticking out on top only each of the bones was covered with these little white paper ruffles or maybe they weren't paper, maybe you ate them, too, and while the butler cut it up the maid removed the white wineglasses and brought in a bottle of red for Mr. Kitchel to inspect. He nodded, and she poured their glasses full and when Chub cut into his food he discovered it tasted like lamb, only better lamb than anything he'd ever had. Chub drank the red wine greedily, knowing he shouldn't, but it tasted so damn good with the meat, he couldn't help it. He knew he was on the road to getting squiffed, so he was glad there hadn't been much conversation directed his way.

"I assume you're pleased," Mr. Kitchel said then, staring at Chub.

"Oh, yessir," Chub dabbed at his mouth with his napkin. "This isn't exactly dorm food."

"I was not," Mr. Kitchel said, "talking about food."

"Yessir," Chub said.

"He doesn't know," Two-Brew said then. "I thought it might be best for you to tell him."

"Tell him what," Chub said—"I mean, tell me what?"

"*Serendipity*," Mr. Kitchel said. "*Serendipity* is publishing your story about the boy who learns to swim."

"That's right, I wrote that, yessir," Chub said, and he was halfway through cutting his next piece of lamb when he realized what he'd heard. "Pardon me, sir, how do you mean, 'publishing' it?"

"Stanley sent me a copy along with a request for my opinion and it was positive."

Chub reached for his wine, then thought, You don't need any wine, you've had enough wine, and then the words started coming—"Just one thing—I'd like to get something straight—you mean the book, when you say *Serendipity* that's what you're talking about—the book that publishes stories and poems, *that Serendipity?*— we're talking along the same lines."

"I don't know what lines you're talking along, Mr. Fuller."

"I just—I mean you're sure and everything—like it's all set and everything—"

Mr. Kitchel turned to his son. "Are you sure this is the writer of the story—he's acting rather stupidly."

"Father publishes *Serendipity*, Chub."

"But you said he was a businessman—"

"I *am* a businessman," Mr. Kitchel said, very loudly. "I have run Sutton Press for a quarter century, and not once have I considered myself anything but. I deal with writers and I detest them one and all, I have made many of them rich and not one has ever thanked me, they do nothing but revel in their neuroses and complain about their bank accounts. It takes a bottom-line businessman to keep them in line. Now, you will receive one hundred and twenty-five dollars for your story, not that I think it's worth that but that is the rate, and I consider this part of the conversation closed."

Chub nodded; he couldn't have talked anyway, not coherently because Sutton was one of the few publishing houses he'd ever heard of, along with Knopf and Random, and more than that, he was drunk now and more than that, more than anything was the dawning that something he had done, something he had put down, was going to be in print.

Jesus God, did that mean he was a writer?

The rest of the meal went quickly—dessert turned out to be chocolate cake and vanilla ice cream and Chub knew instantly what it was and how to eat it, and Mrs. Kitchel, over coffee, chatted on and on about her friend Mercedes who had finally found a co-op she liked and was moving to eight ninety-five in a month and Mr. Kitchel grunted perfunctorily at the news and something about that, Chub realized, was odd, but he couldn't quite zero in on what, and then after dinner the doorbell rang and Mrs. Kitchel said, "That must be Paige, she promised she'd try and stop by for a moment," and while she and her husband both went to the elevator Chub asked who Paige was and Two-Brew said she was his three-year-older sister and the reigning Jewish Princess of the eastern seaboard, and then Chub stood when this girl who looked like Natalie Wood entered the library where they were having liqueurs, and the parents left the siblings alone for a moment while Paige said, staring at her brother's girth, that obviously his new diet had done wonders for his looks and Two-Brew ignored that, introduced Chub, saying what a talented writer he was, and Paige said, "If you don't mind, I'd like another opinion," and Two-Brew said, almost childishly, "Oh, yeah, well, Father's going to publish a story he wrote," and then Paige shook Chub's hand and she was distant, and said little, but there was something in the pressure of her hand that made Chub know she was interested and then the senior Kitchels were back and there was some family banter, Chub listening only, Two-Brew doing mostly the same, and then Paige left and it was late, the Kitchels excused themselves, and when they were alone Two-Brew became his Oberlin self, belting away about how much he hated Paige and that eight years ago she'd looked like Tiny Tim but the nose was fixed and the ears were fixed and her tits were last year's addition, molded by some surgeon in Brazil and—

—and then Chub remembered. "At dinner," he cut in, "your mother said some friend of hers was moving and she gave a number but she didn't name a street."

Two-Brew laughed. "Mercedes is her oldest friend and a Park Avenue snob. She would never live anywhere else."

"But why are you laughing?"

"Because she's also Father's mistress and Mother knows it—where do you think he was till nine o'clock? He probably bought her the apartment. She was letting him know she knew. She does it every meal. It's a fun family."

They said good night a little later and Chub, exhausted, went to bed but not to sleep. The rain had stopped and he opened the terrace door. He could see nothing. A fog had wrapped the city. Central Park was there but it wasn't there.

He felt the impulse then, so he went to his Journal and began taking notes about a young man who came to New York for the first time, knowing it would be his home.

''EIGHT NINETY-FIVE''

by

Charles Fuller

And what Chub's hero would discover was what Chub now knew: that there would never be the voice of the city saying, "Welcome." Because he had started his run too far behind the starting line ever to catch up. And not even the sudden startling glory of being published could close the gap.

For this was a world where salmon was thin and cool and lamb chops had ruffles to cover their bones; where girls who looked like movie stars were made not by God but by stitching; where publishers hated writers and had affairs with intimates of their wives; where slobby friends became fashion plates and stilled their tongues because if they ever spoke their anger they would blow their families apart; where street names never needed mentioning, not once you knew the code.

Chub would never master the deciphering. It was too late for that. In a way, he loved the city, but not in any way he had imagined. And he would come here. Someday. And live here. Somehow. But always as an alien, an immigrant from the outback of Illinois, always, alas, a stranger in this very strange land. . . .

CHAPTER 4

Rock-the-Cradle

Serendipity being a biannual, Chub did not receive his copies until December, and the arrival came as a surprise. Partially because in some part of his lunatic mind, he expected maybe half a dozen guys dressed up like courtiers blowing those long horns that announced that the king was coming. More than that, though, was the fact that he had been hoping they would arrive in October, been sure they would be there before Thanksgiving.

By December, he had waited so long he'd stopped waiting. This day (the twelfth) he opened his mail slot to find no mail—he never got mail, not real mail, only announcements or junk stuff—but a note saying a package had arrived. He took the note around the corner to the package room, handed it to the old lady who seemed to live there, Chub could not remember the package room without her lurking somewhere inside. She returned shortly with a plain brown envelope and he opened it on his way out the door—

—the two copies slid into his hands.

His first thought was this: "Oh, good, my copies came." His second thought was a bit more exultant: "Holy shit!" Then the third and longest thought took hold and it wasn't really a thought at all but, rather, panic—what if there wasn't room or what if the printer was drunk and goofed and left his story out or what if

Mr. Kitchel had changed his mind only Two-Brew didn't
have the heart to tell him or—

—page 89.

It was there—sandwiched between a Cheever and a
Borges—not too far from an Oates—reasonably close to
a recently discovered Plath fragment—less than one hundred pages from a Nabokov essay—

A *FULLER!*

Chub sat down on a nearby sofa and flipped to the
back, where the author's biographies were listed. His was
the shortest:

Charles Fuller.
Illinois born, Mr. Fuller attends Oberlin College. This
is his first published story.

But who cared if it was the shortest—how could you
care when it was so obviously the best? Practically iambic
fucking pentameter. How did Bellow begin *The Adventures of Augie March?*—"I am an American, Chicago
born . . ."

That echoed here. "Illinois born," Chub thought. My
God, you could hear the drums pounding under a phrase
like that. He began tripping off:

Illinois born,
I'm Illinois born,
I can take your scorn,
Cause I'm Illinois born.

Illinois born,
Yes, Illinois born,
On a special morn,
I was Illinois born.

It was then that he thought of his mother.
Gretchen was living in Lauderdale with her folks, and

sure, there'd been some bad times, but wait'll she saw *this*. (For a moment Chub suddenly was moved—Mike was less than five years dead and he would have come apart at the seams if he'd been around to see a FULLER! in print.)

He got up from the sofa, shook the thought away. Gretchen would have to do and she'd do fine, thank you. He'd never come out and told her exactly of the publication. (He wrote her dutifully twice a week and though she wasn't much on letter writing, he knew from the notes his grandmother sent that his letters meant more than a little.) He'd hinted around some, said that maybe there might be a surprise in store, but that was as close as he came. He needed to be sure. (What if the printer got drunk and left out his story, what if Mr. Kitchel changed his mind, etc., etc.)

Vacation was a week away, but if he mailed her the extra copy, she'd have it by the time he got there. Then he decided against it. Presents were fine, sometimes terrific, but they were always better in person.

Chub had spent a lot of the last month typing papers and theses for other students and he'd earned enough to fly both ways, so on the seventeenth, right after classes broke for the holidays, he lucked into a ride to the Cleveland airport and flew south. The plane was a little late taking off and there was a long layover in Atlanta, but he got to the Lauderdale airport at not much after nine. Then a bus ride to the center of town and a cab ride from there to where his grandparents lived. It was ten when he rang their bell and after a pause he heard his grandmother's voice going, "That must be little Charley, little Charley's here." Then a long wait till the door opened, because the old woman could only get around with a walker, but finally they were face-to-face.

"Joe College, isn't that what they say?"

"Yes, Grandma." He kissed her on the cheek.

"Well, let's have a look at you."

Chub put down his bag, smiled, did a pirouette. He could see his grandfather, who was more decrepit than the old woman, sitting in a recliner, staring fixedly at the black and white television set in the living room beyond. Chub went over to him, knelt by the chair, gave another kiss. The TV picture wasn't holding; it kept rolling up every few seconds. The watcher didn't seem to mind. "How are you, Grandpa?"

"Oh, he's just fine," Chub's grandmother answered. Then she said, loudly, "It's little Charley come to visit."

"I know that," he snapped. He looked at Chub now. "I was caught up in the story." He reached out, mussed Chub's hair. "Joe College, isn't that what they call you?"

"Yessir."

"Damn picture."

Chub stood. "Maybe I can fix it." He went to the set, fiddled with some knobs, got the rolling to stop.

"You must get that from your father's side of the family," his grandmother said then. "None of us can so much as plug in a plug."

"I could fix things," his grandfather said, more angrily than before. "I was good with my hands."

"That must have been when you were in the cradle, because we've been married going on sixty years and on our wedding day you couldn't so much as plug in a plug."

"I fixed Dad's Hubmobile—it was stalled on the highway—outside of Buffalo—he couldn't do a thing with it but I got it going in nothing flat. Cruised straight into Buffalo without a knock." He glared at his wife.

She dropped her voice. "That is *not* the first time I've heard that particular whopper."

"Cruised straight into Buffalo, I'm telling you. Purred. Motor purred the whole way." Now a frown came over his face. "Now damn," he said, staring at the TV again. "I've lost the story."

"Sorry if I bothered you," Chub said.

"You didn't bother me—how could *you* bother me?— you made the picture good. It's her. All the time her." He shook his head. "Par for the course. Par for the course."

Chub made a little wave, went to his grandmother. "Where's Mom?"

His grandmother pointed. "Out by the pool. She likes to watch the boats going by." The little house was on a side canal, and during the day there was water traffic. Less at night. "I'll bet you want to go say hello to her."

"I do, yes." Chub knelt, zipped open his small case, took out the copy of *Serendipity*.

"I'll just leave you two alone, you know the way."

Chub nodded. Then he said it: "How is she?"

His grandmother paused. Then she said it: "Well, you know Gretchen and her moods."

"The Moods," Chub thought, watching as his grandmother piloted her walker across the room, sat in a chair alongside her husband, took his hand, put it in her lap, held it there.

He had always known his mother had a temper. And then again, sometimes she liked to talk and sometimes she didn't. But he never put a name to it till the summer after his high school graduation, two years before. From then on, whenever he thought of Gretchen, the phrase "The Moods" came right along.

He had been out late to a party and was surprised, when he got home, to find the light still on downstairs. Gretchen was sitting on the floor, thin legs crossed, watching an old movie on television and silently weeping.

Upset, Chub went to her, asked what was wrong.

She pointed to the movie.

He watched it a moment. It was one he'd never seen but Pat O'Brien was in it and he looked very young.

"Oil for the Lamps of China," Gretchen said.

"And it's sad, is that it? Everything's okay, except the movie's sad."

"It was the book."

"What was?"

"It was a big best-seller I think. *Oil for the Lamps of China.* I didn't read it when it came out. Later, though. While your father was fighting in the war, I did a lot of reading, I must have read it then. It was that book killed your father."

Chub couldn't think of much to say. Because the book hadn't killed his father, he had killed his father, he was the one responsible. A year and a few months before.

"Watch and you'll see," Gretchen said. "It's about a guy who works for this big company and he goes all over working for this big company, he works his ass off because he loves the company and he knows the company loves him, too, and will take care of him no matter what except in the end the company screws him."

It must have been four in the morning when the movie was done and Gretchen had cried most of that time, never out loud, but the tears still streamed.

"Do you know what your father did when you were a little boy?" Gretchen asked when she had a momentary control.

"Not really, I guess. He was a businessman. He wore a suit. He took the 8:08 to Chicago every day."

"He worked for Finkelstein's. They were a big office supply company headquartered in the Loop. He started working for them right out of high school. When we got married in 1940 he'd already been there a dozen years. Worked his way right up to a good position. Then he enlisted. He didn't have to except he said he did. And I read a lot when he was gone and when I read this book, I knew that Finkelstein's was going to do him in. He was their best man, everybody said so, Old Mr. Finkelstein who owned the place and his son who was the president, they were all the time saying Mike Fuller, he was the best they had. And after the war, when he had his health back, they took him in again with a big promotion and he was a vice-president the year you were born. But there were a bunch of them and I knew he'd never get where he deserved—the top. So I started."

"Started what?"

"I got after him to go out on his own. The only way he ever was going to be the best was if it was his company.

He knew everything there was to know about office supplies. He had all the contacts. I got after him and I wouldn't stop. I told him how the company always ruins you unless you're a member of the family. You're only safe if you're the boss and he'd never be the boss at Finkelstein's, there were too many family between him and where he deserved to be. I never let up. Every night I begged him to go out on his own before they ruined him. He said I was crazy, that they liked him. I said they only were *saying* that because they needed him. It took a couple of years, but I beat him down. They gave him a big party when he left."

"Was that when he wore a tuxedo? I know once I remember him dressed up like that."

"Only time he ever wore one. We rented it in Chicago. I was all dressed up too."

"I know you were," Chub lied. "I can see you both."

"He started his own company—small, of course, but you got to start small. He planned it all out very carefully. He started his own and it destroyed him."

"He couldn't get it going right, you mean?"

"No. *No.* He did great. He was a success with it—but he was out there on his own and he couldn't take it—you remember a time you came along when I picked him up in a bar?"

"Sort of, I guess."

"That was the day he bankrupted the company. He couldn't take being a success on his own. I didn't know that. If I'd known that, I would never have made him leave Finkelstein's. If he'd stayed there he would have been the top man. Old Mr. Finkelstein told me at the funeral. See, his son died and none of the other family were in a class with Mike—he would have had the company like he deserved. But I made him quit and—" Now the tears were strong, the strongest they'd been all evening. Silent but you could sense the power. "I killed your father, I killed him as if I'd shot him dead but at least that would have been quicker. If—if only I hadn't done so much reading during the war." She shook her head then, waved for Chub to leave her.

He hesitated.

Then she gestured again, and you could sense the power.

He left her in the living room and went to his room. Chub didn't have much of a night. Of course, there wasn't much of a night left to have. It was almost nine when he awoke and got up and went to her room only she wasn't there. He found her in the living room. It had been dark when he left her but now it was bright. That was the only change, though. She still sat cross-legged on the floor with the silent tears for company.

The doctor came as soon as Chub could get through on the phone and gave her some pills and put her to bed. His name was Dr. Robertson and he had been to the house often, when the drinking was getting out of control. He wasn't old, but there was always a slight tremor to his hands. He asked Chub what had led up to this and Chub shorthanded it, said a movie had reminded her of bad things, the worst of which was that she killed her husband. The doctor told Chub to stay around the house and call if anything happened and that he'd be back after office hours.

Nothing happened. Gretchen just slept. Dr. Robertson woke her, talked with her quietly before she drifted back to sleep. He told Chub he'd be back in the morning before office hours and to call him if anything happened.

Nothing happened. Gretchen just slept. When the doctor came and woke her she rolled over in bed so that her back was to him and said nothing. She said nothing that whole day.

The next day she talked and talked and made Chub a wonderful dinner of meat loaf and mashed potatoes and gravy. The next day she was silent again. And the day after that. And that evening, Dr. Robertson spoke with Chub in the living room.

"I'm not sure you're old enough to understand what's

going on. The truth is, Chub, I'm not sure I'm old enough to understand what's truly going on. But I like to think that even if I hadn't spent all those years in med school, I'd be smart enough to know that your mother is not a very happy lady."

"But no one's happy all the time."

"True. And she may be fine tomorrow. But I don't think she will be fine tomorrow. Chub, is there any money in the family?"

"I don't think so. I wouldn't be going off to college if I hadn't gotten the scholarship."

"Because what she needs is very, very qualified help, and alas, that costs a great deal of money. Is there anyone who can take care of her?"

"I don't have to go to college. You just tell me what to do and I'll take care."

"I think that would be—I *know* that would be—among the least beneficial solutions. Has she family?"

"Her folks are in Lauderdale."

"Can they take care of her?"

"They can hardly take care of themselves—they're awfully old, Dr. Robertson."

"*Will* they take care of her?"

"I don't know, I could find out."

"Do that."

"Yessir, thank you, I will."

Dr. Robertson did not move.

"You mean now?"

"I do."

Chub went to the phone and called Florida and explained to his grandmother that Gretchen was kind of blue and would they mind if she visited awhile?

"They'd love her to come down," Chub said after he put the phone down.

Gretchen, the next morning, didn't seem to mind. At least she didn't say she minded. And the next weeks she was fine. There was a lot to do. Packing and garage sales and trying to get rid of the house and late summer they said good-bye to Athens, Chub and Gretchen, and flew south, and Chub stayed till everything was running as smoothly as he could make things run, and by this time it was early September and he stored some boxes of things he thought he might like to keep from his growing up days in the tiny basement, and then he left for Oberlin, where, that very day, he fell up the stairs to Peters Hall as B.J. Peacock started coming down. . . .

Now, the copy of *Serendipity* in his hand, Chub moved out toward the swimming pool area where he had first crossed beneath the water. It was unlit but Gretchen was visible, sitting cross-legged on a chair, staring out at the narrow canal beyond.

"Hey, Gretchen," Chub said softly, kneeling beside her, kissing her cheek.

"I thought it was tomorrow you were coming."

"Probably you're right," Chub told her. "I just couldn't wait." He studied her as well as he could. She had never been fat, but now she was bony almost.

"Trip okay?"

"Fine. A few kids played basketball with the chicken but other than that, not much of interest."

She looked at him now. "On the plane? They played basketball?"

"Bad joke—it was rubbery was all I meant." He was aware his hands were perspiring, so before he soiled the *Serendipity* jacket, he handed it to her. "Take a gander at page eighty-nine, why don't you?"

"What's this?" She looked at *Serendipity* in the darkness.

"Book."

She bent the soft cover back and forth. "Doesn't feel like a book."

"It's not a real hardcover I guess, but it counts."

She kept bending it in her hands.

"Page eighty-nine," Chub said again.

"This a college thing?"

"No; it's published in New York. Twice a year. Stories and poems and essays. Short pieces."

She nodded. "Um-hmm." Then she was silent, studying the canal. "Here he comes," Gretchen said finally.

"Who?"

She nodded toward the canal. "Fella lives a few houses down. He commutes to his office by boat. Isn't that wonderful?"

Chub watched as a twenty-foot boat slowed on the canal, began a slow turn toward a dock across the water. "I'm on page eighty-nine," he said finally. "A story."

Gretchen kept studying the boat.

"I just wanted you to have it," Chub said softly.

When the boat was moored, she looked at *Serendipity* more closely. "Can't really see much out here."

"Where's the light switch?"

"I like it better dark," Gretchen said. "Anyway, I can't read without my glasses."

"Just tell me where they are, I'll get them."

She shook her head. "I'm not much in for reading."

"You don't have to read it," Chub said quickly. "I just wanted you to have it, was all."

"I'll *read* it, Charles," she said, for the first time her voice sharp. "I just don't want to read it *now*."

"Fine."

"Who else is in here?"

Chub named a bunch of the others.

"Well, I've never heard those names."

"Most people haven't—but Mr. Nabokov, he wrote a novel called *Lolita*—it was made into a movie."

Gretchen thought a moment. "Wasn't that the dirty one?"

"I guess a lot of people thought so."

"Are there any Jews in here?" Gretchen asked then.

"I'm not sure, Mother; I don't think many."

"Well, that's something; it was the Jews killed your father, you know."

They talked a little longer, then Gretchen put the book on the glass-topped table by her chair, said she was tired. They went inside and Chub kissed her on the cheek again before she went into her bedroom. There was only one other in the place, where his grandparents slept, so Chub made do with the living-room sofa. But not till very late because his grandfather watched television until he was able to sleep, and there was only the single set.

Chub got as comfortable as he could on the sofa. It was okay. He didn't expect to sleep much anyway.

And he didn't. He was up a little after eight and his grandmother was also up, puttering in the kitchen, making coffee. "I'm the only early bird," his grandmother said and then she asked a favor: Would Chub go with her to the market, she always liked to get the marketing done as soon as she could and Gretchen was always going on about how much Chub liked salmon the way she made it and that meant not just going to the supermarket but also to the fish store because the supermarket was great for produce and staples but she didn't like the look of the man who handled the fish department and Chub said he would consider it an honor, so after coffee they went out to his grandparents' car and Chub drove, first to the market for produce and staples and it took a long time, not just because of the slowness of the walker but because his grandmother checked every item for price, since she saved sale stamps and she told him once how she saved two dollars just on laundry soap alone. Chub pushed the cart and she trailed behind, checking for savings, and after the market they drove to the fish store and it was ten before they had the salmon paid for and were back at the house.

His grandfather was back in his chair, watching the TV. And Gretchen was out by the pool. Chub put the groceries quickly in the kitchen and went out to say good morning to his mother.

She was different now, smiling at his appearance, not sitting but walking around the area with a lot of energy, and she held the copy of *Serendipity* in her hands. "I'll tell you the truth," she said. "I didn't read it, but I did look at page eighty-nine and there it was: Charles Fuller. You're not upset because I just looked at your name."

" 'Course not."

"Oh, good." She took his hand and led him to a sofa and sat beside him, looking into his light-brown eyes. "Probably I wouldn't have understood it right anyway. Would you mind to tell me what it's about?"

"The story?"

"I looked at the title—that's a funny way to spell the word 'girls.' "

"With the parentheses? You're right, it is a funny way."

"So now you just tell me and I'll be sure and understand."

Chub shrugged. "It's just a little thing about a couple—"

"—how old?—"

"—early twenties—"

"—named?—"

"—well, the guy's name is Chris—"

"—Chris—"

"—and the girl is Louise—"

"—*Chris* and Louise, okay, I've got it in my head, you just tell and I'll just listen."

"Well, they're both actors in New York and they both are up for parts in a road company of a play and they're in love and they decide if they both get into the play they'll get married and they do both get the parts, only at the end Chris realizes that maybe, as he puts the ring on her finger, just maybe he's making a terrible mistake."

And then his mother was screaming—"And what about the fight?—what about the fight by the swimming pool—by *this* pool—" and she jabbed her finger at the nearby water.

Chub just blinked, but in his mind he wondered how could he be so stupid, thinking his mother was full of energy that morning because it wasn't, not energy, it was fury hidden by a smile and there was a storm coming fast.

Now Gretchen was up and pacing— "—you did not learn to swim in *this* pool—not in *this* pool you didn't—that was a lie but you've always been good at lying—but I never thought you would lie about your father and your

mother because we never never not once in all our years
had a fight—not one fight ever and now you put this lie
in this thing you say is a book and the whole world is
going to think it's true—"

"—Mother, listen—please—"

"—Chris would never have lied—"

Chub, confused, sat a moment, then got up and went
to her but she spun free and half ran around the pool,
where she stopped, and when he tried to move she
moved, too, always keeping half the pool between them,
and Chub for a moment thought he was in a time warp
and it was a kid's game of tag—

"—Chris was perfect—*Chris's eyes were blue!*"

Behind him now, Chub could hear his grandmother
crying out, *"There's no need, Gretchen—"* and here she
came, but so slowly, on her walker—

Chub stopped moving because he didn't know what to
do, where to go.

"Blue," Gretchen screamed again, "and he never once
cried, never was trouble, he slept through the night when
he was a week old, and you had the colic and were born
to make trouble and when he died we had you—God, I
wish I knew why," and then she threw the book into the
pool and ran into the house and into her room.

Chub managed to keep standing and when his grandmother finally made it to where he was she said, "There
was no need for her to tell you that," and Chub nodded,
but now that he'd had the news he wanted it all only
there wasn't much. His grandmother spoke for less than
a minute, saying that the firstborn in the Fuller family
had caught the crib death before he was a year, it wasn't
nobody's fault, and then she left Chub to see after her
daughter while Chub stared at the copy of *Serendipity* at
the bottom of the pool.

But his mother's room wasn't far away, and he could
hear the two women, the older one saying, "Now,
Gretchen, now, Gretchen," while the younger kept crying, "I want him out of here, I don't want to see him, get
him out before he starts telling lies about *you,*" and Chub

was all packed before his grandmother could leave his mother alone.

"She'll change her mind," his grandmother said.

Chub gave his case a final zip.

"She's just—well, I don't have to tell you about your mother's moods."

Chub nodded, went to his grandfather who sat in his chair, watching the TV, and shook hands good-bye.

"It's Christmas," his grandmother said. "Where will you go?"

"Oh, I have a lot of places. A friend in New York kept after me to spend time there."

"Well, just so you won't be alone for the holidays."

"Don't worry."

"Don't you worry, either—she's just going through a bad patch."

"We all do."

"That is the truth."

"Bye." He started for the door.

"Charles?" his grandmother called out. "You be sure to keep on writing her letters. They just cheer her so. . . ."

The trip back to Oberlin was remarkable—Chub hitched a ride from a guy who lived next door who was driving past where the bus left for the airport and when he dropped Chub off, the bus was about to go. He reached the Lauderdale airport without the least idea of how long he would have to wait but there was no wait—a plane was leaving almost immediately that would put him in Cleveland inside three hours.

But it wasn't the consistency of connection that made it a remarkable journey; it was Chub's realization that his mother's shouted secret wasn't truly a secret at all. He had always known—not that there had been an earlier sibling precisely—but he had always known *something*.

Because there had to be some reason for their treatment of his crucial years. He had tried, always, to be so good, to please in any way available. Maybe he wasn't the smartest kid in school but no one got better grades. Certainly he wasn't the best athlete but he had gone out for all the teams, had slaved, arrived early, stayed late. And he never gave them cause for worry, never wised off, never you name it.

And they never looked at him.

So there had to be some other, some finer place for their attention. Always, he had sensed some wraith around him, a tracking shadow, a doppelgänger they preferred. He had never known his sin until now and it was this: He had been born.

The Oberlin campus was deserted when he got back— barely thirty hours after he had left. He went to his room in the empty dorm, dropped his bag on the floor and immediately sat down at his typewriter. A story had literally dropped into his head during the flight, perhaps over Georgia, perhaps the Kentucky mountains, and it was about an eight-year-old kid.

Chub picked up *Mixed Company,* and "Little Henry Irving" was about a kid named Eddie, so that became Chub's hero. Eddie had been given a yo-yo for Christmas. Not just an ordinary toy but a *real* yo-yo, a Duncan that slept when you snapped it down.

At first, Eddie wasn't that adept at making it work, but in a week he was. And the week after that, he was hooked on the thing, took it everyplace, practiced for hours. Once he was able to do Walk-the-Dog he moved on to the next hardest trick, Around-the-World.

When that was conquered, he began to learn Rock-the-Cradle.

To really make Rock-the-Cradle look spectacular, you had to fling the yo-yo down and the instant it's asleep and spinning you carefully raise the string with both hands and form a triangular cradle and then rock the yo-yo back and forth through it and then release the string and bring the yo-yo rolling perfectly back up into your hand.

And perfection was what he was after. You had to be perfect if you wanted to be the greatest in the world. And you had to be the greatest in the world if you wanted to make your folks see you.

And making them see him was what he was after. He was an only child, but they both led busy lives, and it was great and all, but this would make it greater.

In a month he was ready.

After dinner they were busy but he promised it would only take a second so they went into the living room and Eddie said, "First, Walk-the-Dog." And he spun his yo-yo down, raced it halfway across the carpet before he brought it neatly up into his hand. He was building his act, and before the Rock-the-Cradle had to come Around-the-World and he announced it: "Around-the-World."

He took a deep breath, snapped the yo-yo straight out, began to bring it into a perfect circle over his head but the string was frayed and the yo-yo burst free and as Eddie stared, it streaked across the room and broke the biggest window in the living room.

Banished, crushed, he ran outside and tried so hard not to cry while inside, he could hear his father swear while his mother picked up the pieces of the broken glass, and as he listened they talked, talked of their curse of a son and how their lives would have been different, better, everything, if only their firstborn had not died unbreathing in his crib.

And Eddie, hearing the news of the unknown-till-then sibling, took a new string out of his pocket and put it on and began to do Rock-the-Cradle—

—he hadn't even gotten to *show* them—

—but then he realized it wouldn't have mattered. He did the trick in darkness, again, again, always perfectly. But it didn't matter. Because even if he had been the greatest yo-yo wizard in the history of the world, he could never have been champion. The champion had retired, unbeaten, untied and unscored on, the year before Eddie was born.

''ROCK-THE-CRADLE''

by

Charles Fuller

Chub typed the title page, took the original (the story wasn't long, barely ten pages) and was the first one at the Oberlin Post Office the next morning. He spent a ton mailing it off to Kitchel the fastest way possible, because these were the Christmas holidays and the mails were flooded and he didn't want to wait for Two-Brew's reaction.

It came on the morning of December twenty-first, bright and early. Chub was barely awake when there was Kitchel's voice booming over the phone. "You will not, I repeat not, believe this."

Chub waited. He could have asked, "Believe what?" or some other dumb remark just to keep things humming, but he could tell Two-Brew was in one of his rhetorical moods, and needed no help. Sometimes, he could go for half an hour or more building to climax.

"I don't know why these things happen to me. Someone stern Up There is testing me. Can *I*, the unique and delectable fellow that I am, make Job seem like a piker? Probably, if I don't overrate your intelligence, you will have surmised that something has entered my life of late and you would not be incorrect and what has entered my life is—are you sitting down? Sit down—where was I? Yes. Some fool, some mewling incoherent who has an interest in fiction, has sent me *something,* I'm not sure what, about—brace yourself—*a fucking yo-yo.* I, Kitchel, whose only peers are Eliot and Coleridge, have been sent this missive to decipher, which I and only I have now done."

"How was it?" Chub asked.

"On to the next."

"I kind of thought so—it wrote very easily."

"Jesus, Chub, did that happen? How the hell did you survive—assuming you have."

"All made up; just a notion that hit me on the plane."
Two-Brew's voice was quieter now. "And Florida?"

"Florida was fine."

"Also lengthy."

"Well, they don't really have a lot of extra space down
there. I was in the way."

"And how is Oberlin?"

"Fine."

"Bustling and festive I assume with no one there."

"You'd be surprised, there's a lot going on."

"Chubbo—when campus is booming and there's a lot
going on, there's still nothing going on." He paused a
moment. "I have just come up with my hourly inspiration. Get on a plane and come here—you're always
welcome at Walgreen. Two weeks I offer you."

"That's really nice, but I can't."

"What's wrong?"

"Nothing, I'm really fine."

"No, you're not."

"No, I'm not."

"Want to talk about it?"

"I don't know what it is," Chub said. Then he added
quickly, "See you in a couple of weeks," and hung up.

Chub didn't like it when he got in the dumps, and most
of the time when that began to happen he forced himself
into extra activity, which usually took care of things.
Now, alone in the empty dorm, he felt rotten—even
though Two-Brew liked the story, it wasn't enough to put
him over the top.

He half dressed, then reversed the process, got back
into bed, slept till early afternoon. When he awoke, he
started to shave, decided not to, threw on some clothes
and headed across the deserted campus toward the No-
Name. It was deserted, too, except for Dr. Wallinsky, the
town rummy, who was already talking to himself in a
corner. Chub ordered two hamburgers, rare, though it
was an exercise in futility and he knew it—whatever meat
the No-Name used for its patties was always pounded far

too thin to be anything but overdone. He downed the burgers with a beer.

He left the No-Name, checked what was playing at the Apollo. *The Poseidon Adventure* was the special pre-Christmas new release, and after that *The Getaway* was due. But the Apollo didn't open till six, so Chub went back to his room, lay down, got up, went back to the No-Name, ordered a pitcher of beer for himself and started slowly to drink.

Before the second pitcher, he went across the street to the drugstore and picked up *The Plain Dealer*. Harry Truman was still close to dying. Two young guys who were thought dead in a plane crash in the Andes had made it out to safety. *Life* magazine was throwing in the towel, whipped by television. . . .

Everything in *The Poseidon Adventure,* Chub realized in his six o'clock stupor, was upside down. His stomach was in no condition for the special effects, so he left halfway through. It was snowing outside now and he headed across Tappan Square and when he got to his room he fell in bed and the next thing he knew there was another morning to be faced.

There was a terrible ache inside him and at first he put it off to too much beer, but after coffee and breakfast the ache was still there. And he was still in the dumps. Usually writing something helped, but as he went through his Journal, he found nothing that gave him any appetite.

The ache was really bad as he lay there in his bed, tossing. He stayed that way for hours, seeing Gretchen down in Florida, hearing her voice rise, watching her throw him, figuratively, into the pool to drown.

He knew what was inside him now and he also knew the only way the ache was going to leave was if at last, alone with nothing but his memories, he put down on paper how he had killed his father.

Mike Fuller had been a peculiar drunk. After the one terrible night when Chub and Gretchen had gone to get him in the graffiti-filled men's room, he never again touched the stuff outside the house.

But inside, my God, the bottles. Little ones, tenths, some even smaller, the kind they give you on airplanes. Those were the best. They fit in closet corners and the toes of slippers and the backs of drawers and the basement of the house was heaven for bottles that size.

Sometimes, more than sometimes, Gretchen would go berserk and wake Chub in the middle of the night and scream, "Fifty cents—I'll give you fifty cents for every dirty bottle you can find," and she would drag Chub up and they would ransack the house and Mike would stand at the top of the stairs, using the banister for support, saying, "Don't, Chub, it's late, you go to bed," and Gretchen would scream, "*You* go to bed, that's all you're good for, lying down and sneaking booze under the blankets with you," and Chub, eight, nine, ten, would run around, trying to block them, hoping to find bottles, hoping not to, hoping—

—and then the good days would come. Before Chub was even up, Mike would be downstairs making breakfast for him, and then over the round coffee table he would reach out and take Gretchen's hand with his right, Chub's with his left, and beg them to forget the past because it was bad, sure, but it was gone, he was mixed up, sure, but not anymore, believe that, and he would hug them both and sometimes cry because he was so happy that his curse was finally beaten. "I'll be good, you'll see, these will be good days to make up for the bad."

And they would be. Sober, Mike would sit around the house reading the *Tribune* and cluck-clucking about how the world seemed to be getting crazier all the time. And these periods would go on for weeks, even months, always long enough to make you believe.

Then there would be the silence.

Chub could tell the minute he threw the door open when school was over and hollered out his greetings.

Silence.

He would stop, stop dead, because even though he

knew he still had to know for sure, and he would creep upstairs and peek into his father's room and the alcohol stink would be back and there Mike would be, toad eyes blinking slowly, helpless on the bed.

"Under the weather," Gretchen would say when people called and asked them anywhere. "Oh, we'd love to but Mike, he's under the weather, it must be that bug that's going around."

Chub grew up under that weather.

During the good days, Mike sometimes did little odd jobs for people. Mowing lawns in the neighborhood as a favor. Sometimes going out to the golf tee where a friend of his worked and he'd pick up golf balls for hours.

The day he died he was working for another friend, at the dime store in Athens, helping out. Chub would join him after school, helping out too. Mike had been sober for over a month, the first time he'd been that way for over a year, and an old woman came in and asked Chub for a tailor's thimble and Chub said, "Yes, ma'am," and went to his father and said, "What's a tailor's thimble?" and Mike smiled and said, "And you're going to be the college boy—a tailor's thimble, my young scholar, is like an ordinary thimble only it doesn't have a top, it's hollow, a little cylinder," and then he went to the old woman and said, "My pleasure to serve you," and he made a bow and went on, "Let me escort you to our sewing department," and she followed him to the little area off in a corner where there were spools of thread and tape measures and Chub watched as his father opened a drawer and said, "I think this is where we keep those babies," and after a moment he closed it and opened the next drawer down and rooted through that—

—and suddenly they were into it. Mike flung the third drawer open and the fourth and that was it, that was the extent of the drawers of the sewing department and then he scrambled through the ribbons and measures and spools of colored thread that hung from a board above the drawers and then he was back at the drawers again, only now he was pulling them all the way out, dumping them onto the floor, and Chub ran toward him and the old woman backed off and Tony, who owned the store, followed on Chub's heels but by the time they got there Mike was on his knees, spreading everything around on the floor with his big hands and Tony said, "Christ, Mike, easy," and Mike kept at it and Tony said, "Mike!" and that did it, Mike stopped, stared dully up and shook his head. "Aw, God, I'm sorry," he said, "but I just can't fight the battles anymore."

"Maybe Mike wants to go home, Chub," Tony said, and Chub nodded, saying he'd come back and clean up the mess but Tony said not to bother, he'd take care of it, so Chub led his father home.

When they reached the spare room where his father now lived in the back of the house, Mike said, "Better go do your homework."

"I finished it during last-period study hall. There wasn't much." Not true. There was a ton of reading and a paper to finish on how barbed wire changed the course of American history, and it had to be better than good because Chub was to be the first to go to college in his family. He was just finishing junior year in high school but college was to be part of his future—assuming he could get a full scholarship. Neither Mike nor Gretchen had dreamed of college, the same with both sets of grandparents. Chub was the hope.

"I don't want company."

"I do, though—I've just got a bunch of problems I need to talk about." Not true. Right now he had only the one problem and it was across the room from him. Chub sat in the chair near the bed and started making up things. "This history teacher of mine—he just hates me, I don't know why—but today, right in front of everyone, he made me stand up and answer a bunch of questions—but we hadn't gotten to the stuff he was asking about and I didn't get a single answer. . . ." And now his voice went dry on him because while he'd been going on about the history class his father had gone into his closet and come out with a dozen or more tiny bottles of liquor.

"Hey, Daddy, come on, now."

Mike said nothing, twisted open the first bottle, drained it dry.

Chub knew he should move—race across the room, grab the goddamn things but he couldn't, not quick enough: In all the years he had seen his father drunk a thousand times, but he had never actually seen him take a drink. The results were all he'd ever had to deal with and they were bad, but watching Mike now, seeing the way his lips glued themselves to the tiny bottle neck, wasn't so red hot either.

Mike looked at him. He sat heavily on the bed cradling all the bottles in his lap and he shook his head. "I couldn't even find a tailor's thimble," he said finally.

"Fuck the goddamn thing!" Chub said, and now he was up and out of the chair and grabbing for the bottles in his father's lap.

Mike backhanded him hard and Chub fell. Another first: His father had never hit him before either. Oh, sure, the usual spankings when you're a kid. But this was meant to hurt.

"I told you: Go do your homework."

Chub shook his head, got up, started toward the bed again, but his father made a fist and Chub was frightened, not by the pain of another blow, but at the fact that now his father's face was full of tears. He ripped another top off, drained another bottle, did the same with a third. "I'm not special," Mike said then.

"Yes you are."

Mike shook his head. He lay back on the bed, the bottles beside him. He closed his eyes next and Chub thought Mike was going to go to sleep.

Instead, he started talking about the dead pile.

"I was with the Eighty-second. A paratrooper. I served under Gavin—he was a great man, not much older than I was, but he was a general and I was a sergeant and we wouldn't have traded him in for Ike or anybody. I would have been a lot more scared except for him. See, when you jump behind enemy lines, there's a rule of thumb: A third of you are going to get blown away. The first time it isn't so bad because, sure, you've heard the rule of thumb but you figure that's just the Army, trying to do a number on you. Then, after you've done it once and you've seen it's true, the second jump is all that much harder. When we went in at Arnhem it was my fourth jump and I knew I was going to get blown away. But it was Gavin's fourth jump, too, maybe his fifth, I don't know, and that helped." He stopped, twisted off another bottle cap, chugged the whiskey down.

"Give me the rest."

"You can have the empties."

"Please."

"I never once talked to you about the war, Charley. I thought you'd be interested."

"I *am.*" Chub sat in the chair across from the prone man and tried to figure what he could do. Mike was stronger than he was, even now; bigger and stronger, so he couldn't overpower him. And the time was a few minutes after five, which meant he couldn't get hold of Gretchen—she was working in Chicago as a secretary for a big law firm. It paid well, and someone had to bring in money. But she left work at five and then walked to the station, so she would be gone now, not to be home till just before seven.

Mike seemed to be getting tired, though, and that was good. As he rambled, his words were already beginning to slow. Maybe he'd doze off. "I want to hear. But promise me you'll go easy."

"Where was I?" Mike asked.

"Your fourth jump."

"I knew—just wondered if you'd been listening. The fourth jump. September, '44. And it was the first time a major drop had ever been done in daylight. Always the others had been in darkness; you had a better shot when it was dark. Anyway, they packed us in and we took off and when we were over Holland we jumped and the group I was with, our job was to take this little bridge and hold it and I was so scared 'cause I knew I'd get killed in the sky before landing. They'd just pick us off, the Germans, we were helpless when we were in the sky. The odds—my odds, anyway, well, there weren't any. One third times three is a hundred percent and this was my fourth and when I was drifting down I could hear the Germans firing and I wondered where I was going to get hit and how much it was going to hurt and I prayed until I saw the ground rising up and I'd made it that far, and our group, once we were untangled and everything, we saw our objective, this little shit bridge and there were Germans on both ends of it but we charged—and the minute they saw us coming the fuckers ran away and we all, every goddamn one of us, just let out this crazy scream because we were safe and we'd never have to jump again. I remember that sound, Charley—Christ, it was like it happened this morning." Mike raised his head. "You never heard this, did you?"

"No, Daddy."

"I hate guys who go on all the time with their war stories. Where was I?"

"You know damn well where you were."

Mike almost smiled. "Couldn't fool you again, could I?"

Chub shook his head.

Mike lay back on the pillow. "We ran toward this little shit bridge while the Germans ran away and we knew our jumping days were done but nobody knew they'd mined the area and I didn't either till I saw a bunch of guys over to my left go flying through the air, and then it was my turn to go flying through the air and it didn't hurt like I thought, not near as bad. But when I landed you know what?—I couldn't open my eyes. I could feel the blood on my face and I could feel I still had fingers and toes but I couldn't make them move. I couldn't see and I couldn't move but I could hear. And I don't know how long after but the medics were working and there was a field hospital set up not far away and someone was lifting me and then carrying me and a lot of what they said didn't make any sense at all, the sound kept going in and out, but pretty soon there was a lot of noise and I knew I was at the field hospital—people were shouting and all kinds of orders were going on when some guy said, 'Put him down here.' You know where they put me down?"

"No."

"In the dead pile. They thought I was dead. I knew I wasn't but they knew I was. But I couldn't open my eyes to tell them. It was a slaughterhouse and we didn't have all that many supplies and what they were doing was the ones they could save they were working on, the ones they couldn't, the dead ones like me, they piled up until they could begin burial. They didn't have the least idea but they were going to bury me alive. They weren't dumb guys, Charley—I was dead. I was blown up and nothing moved, and I didn't know it then but some of my head was gone and I lay there getting weaker—it's hard to imagine a guy who's not strong enough to move anything getting weaker still but I could feel I was. I couldn't hear as well. I couldn't feel my fingers anymore. I didn't know anymore if my feet were still attached. But I did know if I didn't do *something* that I would be dead."

He drank another bottle.

Chub watched. Was that four or was it five? He couldn't remember, but his father's words were slower still.

"I moved the only thing I could—I put everything I had into it and I got my eyes open a little. I couldn't see much, because of the blood, but down at one end of the pile I made out something moving—it turned out later he was a doctor but I didn't know that then—it was just movement. He was hurrying along past the dead pile and I couldn't talk or wave but I had to get his attention. So I did the hardest thing I ever yet did, Charley—I moved my eyes toward him. 'Cause I thought if I could just catch his attention maybe it would help. But he was walking so fast, from my left to my right, and I made my eyes go to the left and as he went to the center I made my eyes go straight ahead—*and he looked at me*—I thought I was safe. Only he looked away. I wanted to die right then, I knew I was going to die right then, except I kept my eyes on him—he was past me now but I made my eyes go to the right and he glanced back and then he stopped and stared and then he moved back toward the center of the pile and I made my eyes go that way and the next thing he was hollering, *'Get this one here—get this one here—we may have a shot with this one here.'*"

Another bottle.

"That was when I left the dead pile. They kept me alive and later they moved me back to a real hospital, and they put a plate in my head and after that I went to England for a long time until I was ready for discharge, and that was a lot of pain, those months, but I didn't mind because of one thing: I knew then I was special. I was the only one lifted off the dead pile and that was because I was special. When I went back to work at Finkelstein's I knew I was special and when I started my company I knew I was special and when it went bad I knew it was only temporary, because I was special, and all these years I knew what I was going through was only a tunnel, and I was going to come out bright and shining on the other end because I was the one that left the dead pile, I was special."

Another bottle.

"But I'm not, Charley. I learned that today once and forever. I couldn't even find a tailor's thimble in a dime store. Nothing special about a man like that."

And now, as Chub watched, his father's body convulsed and the big man was crying. He turned his face into the pillow and Chub went to him. Mike was trying to say something and it took Chub awhile to figure it: "I wanted so bad to be special, Charley." Over and over.

Chub sat beside his father, massaged his neck, rubbed his back, took off the old man's shoes.

"I really need to be alone, Charley."

"Not with those bottles."

"Take 'em. But Jesus Christ, leave me alone."

Chub grabbed up the full bottles and left him alone. He went down to the kitchen, unscrewed the bottles, poured the contents into the sink, dumped the bottles into the garbage can, put the lid on. Then he took the lid off, reached around inside until he had the bottles again. He put them into a thick plastic garbage bag, put that bag inside another, went to the tool chest and found a hammer. He went outside in the back and knelt by a tree, placing the plastic on a protruding root. And as his father wept upstairs, Chub went through his ritual in the open air, because his anger was out of control and he pounded the hammer against the bag until his arm was hard to raise. There were no lumps left inside the plastic. He had, he hoped, reduced the containers to sand. Sweating—it was hot for May—he sat against the tree, getting his wind. Then he got up, dumped the remnants of the bottles into the large outside garbage can.

It was after five-thirty when he entered his room and probably five–thirty-five before it hit him: His father would never have given up his treasures so easily if he didn't have their equal and more squirreled away someplace. He stood in his room and thought. He had to go in and face his father down.

There is a psychological theory that can be summarized thus: If a vagrant sees an apple tree and his desire for food is sufficient, he will risk climbing the tree for the fruit. If his fear of falling has dominance, he will walk away. But if his fear and his desire are roughly equivalent, he will simply stand at the tree and stare.

Chub stayed in his room and stared at the wall. His desire to help his father had been etched on record over the past years. But his fear of what he might find now— either the man drinking again or crying helplessly into his pillow—was something he could not shake.

For a moment he simply stood frozen. Then he walked around in a pointless circle. Then he reached into his desk drawer and got out his old Duncan yo-yo and began to play with it. Finally he put the toy away and got to work on his paper.

Joseph Glidden had invented barbed wire in 1874 and

nothing in the West was ever the same again. Instead of being forced to let their cattle run free, ranchers now had a way of marking off their territory and keeping their livestock controlled. Giant empires began. Land wars intensified. Rich men were murdered and others hired murderers for protection. The entire western United States began an upheaval that—

—that—

Chub looked at his research, looked at what he had written, looked at his watch—

—half past six.

He stood. The fear that had held him an hour ago was present but weaker. His desire was enough now, so he got up and left his room and walked to the back of the house to look in on his father. From the hall he could not see much of the room, just the dark-blue rug. He crept inside, a step at a time, and even though it was bright outside, his first thought was of a dark-blue sky filled with glistening stars. The sky had fallen into the spare room and Chub marveled at how incredibly beautiful it was, all the stars, all the peaceful stars there for his pleasure alone, and how long the image held he wasn't sure, probably a few seconds only, before he realized the stars were pills and as he was in full view of the room he saw his father sprawled on the floor with the large empty medicine bottle by his body—

—Chub knelt—Mike was breathing—Mike was definitely still breathing—Chub stood—ran for the phone— called the hospital—the ambulance came—he rode inside with Mike to the emergency room—they took Mike on a stretcher inside—doctors were there—they put Mike onto a table—the doctors started to work—the door was closed—Chub waited outside—on a bench outside— waited—then a friendly nurse—she sat beside him—"Are you with Mr. Fuller?"—"I'm his son."—"Then could you help me with a few of these questions?"—she held a form—"Address?" Chub blinked—"Address?" again— "How is he?"—"Oh, he's dead."—Chub burst from her—into the room with the table—his father still there—Chub flung himself across his father's body—some doctors tried to intercede—Chub grabbed his father's arm, felt for pulse—*and it was there, the pulse was still beating*—he told them—*"It's beating."*—they wouldn't feel—he told them louder—he told them screaming—they wouldn't—wouldn't—they gave him something—something to calm—he called home—Gretchen answered—"Where are you?" she asked—Chub told her—she came—they left—the mourning—the funeral—her Moods building—the days going by—

—and in the days and months to come, Chub would often stop on a street and whirl, because down the way, just turning a corner, he saw his father walking. Sometimes he would even chase the figure until he saw it was only someone who had Mike's step, carried his big shoulders in the same way.

Finally Chub made himself try to believe that his father was truly beneath the tombstone. But it wasn't the Nembutal that put him there. It was his very own chickenshit fear. For surely, if he had been able to conquer it and not play with his yo-yo and work on his Glidden, the world would have had a different environment; yes, surely, he had put his father in the ground. . . .

Until he began trying to deal with this material, Chub had never had all that much trouble writing. The normal panics, the inability to start, all those and more were standard. But once he was under way, once he had a stretch of uninterrupted time, he didn't suffer a whole lot.

But this story (he finally decided, halfway through, to title it "The Tailor's Thimble") made up for all that. The memories he needed to dredge, the guilts that surfaced, racked him. And the material kept shifting—where was the really right place to begin? Where did you properly climax? He was dealing, he supposed, with the most incandescent event of his life and the heat kept him at bay.

He had two weeks—Kitchel would be back by then

and he had to have it ready—and as he began, he thought that would be more than enough time. But he couldn't make it come alive. The first week was a waste—sludge, crap, garbage—and halfway into the second week he was drinking more than he ever had. His head hurt in the mornings—no hangover is worse than a 3.2-beer hangover—and that didn't aid his cause. But it was, in his head, somehow that—a cause—and finally the story began to open. He stayed up the final forty-eight hours before vacation ended. And then he had it—the longest piece he'd ever tried. Fifty pages. And he knew, as he held it at last in his hands, that maybe it didn't have much quality when compared to the work of real writers, but he also knew that it was by far the finest thing he'd ever done.

What Two-Brew might think, though, was up for grabs.

In the preceding six months, Stanley Kitchel had become, in his own words, "irreversibly insufferable." And all because of one Emma Heather Lathery.

In June, after Chub deposited Kitchel in his home and had his first encounter with Manhattan, he returned to Oberlin for the summer, did a bunch of jobs around campus, wrote when he could. He had been back less than two months when a thick envelope arrived in the mail. It was a Xerox of a badly typed book entitled *The Bluest Eyes in Africa* together with a note from Two-Brew saying, in its entirety: "Your immediate reaction is demanded." Chub read it that night. The chapters were very short and the first one went like this:

The man was white, his body tan, his hair the color of sky at evening, his eyes tranquillian blue.

He stood six and a half feet high, and everything about him was massive where bulk was needed, slim where slenderness the aim.

The girl was white, her body pale, her hair the color

of wheat at harvest, her eyes like lush grass after a rain. She stood five and a half feet high and everything about her spoke of feminine perfection, curved and rounded and soft, belying the underlying strength of both soul and body.

She wore her nurse's uniform.

He wore . . .

He wore . . .

He started toward her slowly through the lush African veldt.

She closed her eyes. She was a nurse, experienced in the ways of men, but still she closed her eyes. "Go," she managed.

"If I leave, you will be dead, madam."

She opened her eyes, began to turn.

"If you move, you will be dead, madam. BELIEVE ME."

Such was his tone she could do nothing.

"There is a spitting cobra poised behind you in the tundra grass. If I move slowly, and you move not at all, perhaps we shall laugh about this later."

He spoke no more but behind her now, she could hear something.

He came closer, closer still, closer till within arms' grasp of her—

—Then his giant body sprang like a champion diver entering a blessed pool—

—When she turned, the cobra was dead in his giant hands.

From then on things really got bad. She was a nurse. She was engaged. He was a scientist. He had amnesia. They kept saving each other in an Africa remarkably less authentic than Burroughs's. At the end they were in love. But she still had her fiancé. His amnesia was cured by a fall, which was good, only among the things he remembered was a wife back home. On that note, the book ended.

Chub shot Two-Brew an air mail letter saying, in its entirety: "Would make a great sketch for Carol Burnett and Harvey Korman."

The rest was silence: no reply to his reply.

That September, Chub went to New York a second time and after a couple of good days, he and Two-Brew began the drive back to school. They were barely out of Manhattan and on the Jersey Turnpike when Two-Brew said, "Fuck you with your Carol Burnett and Harvey Korman."

"Just trying to be kind.".

Two-Brew turned in his seat, punched Chub on the arm. "That," he said, "was for not recognizing genius. I was speaking, obviously, of myself."

"Somehow I guessed."

"As you may or may not know, Fuller, publishing houses have slush piles where smartasses fresh from the Ivy League deal with unsolicited manuscripts. I have worked on the slush pile at Sutton for the last two summers. Last year I found nothing. But this year—on my second day—lo—*The Greenest Eyes of Africa* appeared. Totally dog-eared. God knows how many houses it had been to. And there was an accompanying scrawl from the author, Miss Emma Heather Lathery, informing the reader that this was the first of a twelve-book saga she had spent her years completing. I almost put it down after the first pages. Most would have. But that special wisdom that only I seem to possess made me endure. And by the end I thought, 'I think she actually believes this.' I phoned her and went to visit—she's this dotty old crippled lady who lives in Nutley, New Jersey. She's spent her entire existence in Nutley, New Jersey. I asked to read the next few books, and when I did, I asked my father to read just the first. Now, being a publisher, I knew full well my father never reads anything, but he has lackeys and when they gave him their reports, I requested a meeting."

"Requested a *meeting?*" Chub said. "With your own

father? Couldn't you have just talked to him during dinner?"

"*Fool.* Of course I couldn't. This had to be official. Anyway, he kept me waiting half an hour just to let me know what a prick he was and then his secretary ushered me into his sanctum sanctorum. Being an intellectual, he began our encounter on the highest of levels: 'Stanley,' he said. 'What is this shit?' 'Father,' I said. 'When my beloved sister Paige turned twenty-one, you gave her a BMW plus a trip to Brazil for new breasts. I have no plans on tampering with my bosom, and clearly a car will never be of much use to me. Did you plan to give me a present on my twenty-first?' He said that he did, though I suspect he'd forgotten it was coming up. 'Well, here is what I want—I want you to publish this and option the others. Paperback original. Right away. It can't cost you much more than what you spent on Paige, and I'd guess a good deal less.'"

"Did he say yes?" Chub asked.

"Not without a fight. He waved his reader's reports at me and said, 'She doesn't know squat about Africa.' I said that didn't matter, because she believed in the love story. And I pointed out that Harlequin was making a fortune on this kind of thing. Then I hit him with the clincher: 'I've got the advertising line for the jacket. *The geography may not be authentic—but the passions are real.*'"

"Aw, shit," Chub said.

"What's wrong?"

"I hate to say what I'm gonna say—but that's really good."

Two-Brew beamed. "So my father thought. As did the head of our paperback arm. The book is going full speed ahead and will come out in November. I'm going to be irreversibly insufferable from now on, I fear. The book will be a smash."

(It was or it wasn't, depending on your definition of "smash." Four hundred thousand copies sold. Her second book, published six months later, edged up to half a million. The third—*The Coldest Eyes in England*—was the breakthrough. Triple the second. Six years later, by the time the "Eyes" saga was done—all Emma Heather's books had that word in the title, as all the Travis McGee's had a color—sales were close to twenty million copies. In the United States alone. She also did extraordinarily in Canada, England, Australia and, for reasons no one could fathom, Hong Kong. One movie and one television series had also been made.

(Not to mention a fortune for Sutton Press.

(Plus Stanley Kitchel's reputation. He was the one who discovered Emma Heather Lathery. People in publishing never forgot that—twenty million copies tends to linger in the memory.)

It was late and starting to snow when Two-Brew returned from vacation. "Young Lochinvar has returned," he announced, barging into Chub's room without knocking. "Minnie insisted I bring you sustenance," he said, indicating a package in his hands. (Minnie, the Kitchels' maid, had taken a liking to Chub since his first visit when *he* asked *her* if he could do anything to help. "That boy will make his mark," she told anyone in the Kitchel household who would listen.) "Fudge brownies."

"Trade you," Chub said, taking the food, handing over "The Tailor's Thimble."

"More of your juvenile prattling? Excellent—I needed a cure for insomnia."

Very carefully Chub said, "Your immediate reaction is demanded."

It came in the middle of that night—Chub and Two-Brew had adjoining rooms and Chub was awakened by a pounding on his wall. Two-Brew always whacked at the wall with a crutch whenever he was ready to go to class or dinner or a flick.

Chub had a hard time coming to. It was four and outside the snow was turning into a blizzard. Chub got up, went to his door, opened it. His story was there with a covering page on which was written, slashed really, three large words—

WRONG!

WRONG!

WRONG!

Chub, stunned, stared at the page. It was the worst criticism he'd gotten and this was the best writing he'd ever done. Two-Brew had to be mistaken, only Two-Brew didn't make mistakes—not on his stuff anyway. Chub took the story, went back to his bed, lay flat and stared quietly out at the snow. Confidence was never his longest and strongest and he started looking at the pages, flicking through, not reading it at all. He shook his head and wondered.

A few minutes later Kitchel entered, wearing plaid pajamas. "I expected you to come roaring in for combat."

After a while Chub said, "Tomorrow we'll talk."

"No sir, we will not talk tomorrow. I'll get dressed, you do the same, let's go for a walk," and he pivoted on his crutches, left.

(Chub knew then that something was up. Weather was a bitch for Two-Brew. Snow more than rain. And there was ice on the ground before the snow began. Sometimes he fell. More than sometimes.

(The walk wasn't all that long—less than half an hour. But as the years rolled, it became a fly in amber for Chub. He forgot nothing.)

They met outside their rooms in five minutes and moved silently through the dorm halls. Chub opened the main door of the dorm, Two-Brew took the steps carefully, and then they started toward Tappan Square, through the cold and swirling night.

"I have to talk about myself a little bit," Two-Brew began, and there was none of the brashness about him. "All my freak years in Manhattan, I've been preparing myself. I didn't go to Harvard/Yale/Princeton/Brown because every other shit at Dalton went there. I needed to come someplace where no one knew me, and I did. I want to be the best editor and the best publisher and since I didn't have to spend a lot of time playing field hockey, I've read. There's a story Father told me about a remark that was made at Knopf—that's the best publisher, or it was when this remark was made. The year Camus won the Nobel and one editor said to another, 'Did you hear? Al got the nod.' They weren't hysterical because they have a ton of Nobel writers on their list. No big deal for them. Well, I want that for Sutton, but I want more. I want to publish shit that sells—but good shit. And I want to publish quality. I want it all and that nut woman whose book I sent you, she's one kind of writer. And you're going to be the other if I have to kill you."

Chub was silent.

They were almost at the Square now, and Chub took it slowly as they crossed toward the trees. "Now your story—"

"—I thought it was the best I'd ever done."

"It is the best writing, it's wonderful writing, but—" And now one crutch hit a patch of ice and Two-Brew tried to brace himself but no way, and he fell sprawling.

Chub dropped alongside him, started to lift.

"I'm quite capable myself now get the fuck away."

Chub watched in silence as Kitchel got his crutches, tried to leverage them so he could rise, but they slipped again. The second time he made it and then he was talking again exactly where he'd been. "—but it's wrong. All all all dead wrong."

Wonderful writing, Chub thought. That was the best he'd ever gotten. From anyone, let alone Kitchel. He began to relax. As long as someone thought he was talented, he could deal with anything.

"Two things are crucially incorrect—first, what you've done is write about how guilty you feel. What's that line?—'Every suicide kills two people'?—It's old news,

Charles. I knew twenty pages in where you were going, and you skilled your way along, but alas, not to much avail. Your father didn't die because of you and your goddamn barbed-wire paper. He was already a corpse, it was just a matter of when he decided to finally lie down—he would have killed himself anyway."

In the middle of the square now. Two-Brew started to slip again. Chub made no move to assist. Kitchel got his balance back unaided. "Second and the most important thing I've ever said to you—it shouldn't be a story, Chub, *it's a novel* and it shouldn't be about you but about your father."

Chub stopped.

Kitchel turned on him and his voice began to build. "It's fabulous material—and it's yours and you can write the shit out of it. A guy—no schooling—gets a job—does okay—then the Army and that incredible stuff when he's tossed in with the corpses. We should come on that as he does—we should *feel* the belief that he's special. *And he is.* And then the wife forces him out on his own. This is America and America's about success and what kills your father isn't that he failed, *it's that he succeeded*— and then the alcohol. Don't you see? It will make an incredible book."

Two-Brew went on, getting more and more excited, and Chub resisted as long as he could but eventually he began to see that Two-Brew was right. And once he came to admit that, he felt terrified.

"I can't write a novel—I'm twenty-one, for Chris-sakes."

"Vidal did at nineteen but let that pass. This book should be called *The Dead Pile* and I'm not saying write it now, stay with the short stuff now, but when we're done and out of here, that book could make you. *Believe me.* This material cries out to go where I'm suggesting. Do you agree?"

"I don't know."

"Are you frightened?"

"Yes."

"Excellent: Anyone can be a writer; to be a good writer, you have to feel panic. And never lose your sense of revenge." He paused. "We're understood then?"

"You may be."

"It's very simple—when we graduate, we will go to New York and you will live in a pit and scribble; I will luxuriate and shape."

Chub watched as Two-Brew balanced on one crutch, slashed at the storm with the other. "It's all going to be so goddamn wonderful—I'm going to be your Maxwell Perkins and you're going to be my star."

In the eighty weeks between the walk and graduation, Chub kept busy. Socially, he stayed with Patty McLean, who lived off campus and was as obsessed with psychology as he was with writing, so there was no pressure for Commitment; they liked each other, both as friends and bed partners; no problem there.

No problem with the writing either. He managed to turn out thirty-seven pieces of fiction (garnering from Two-Brew sixteen "Byuk"s and twenty-one "On to the next"s). Two of the stories were printed in the Oberlin lit magazine, of which Kitchel was the editor, Andrew Cheyney the advisor. Cheyney and Chub had a rapprochement, and it wasn't long before Cheyney was convinced that he was Chub's discoverer, because *Serendipity* published a second story, "Eight Ninety-Five," and Chub was also printed in *Prairie Schooner* and the *Evergreen, Kenyon* and *Hudson* reviews.

He also worked nights at the library and typed endless papers for other students for fifty cents a page. He was, no doubt, busy as hell.

But what he did, most of all, was fret about New York.

Because the dream—double dream, actually, of not just writing but writing *there*—didn't deal much with reality. Chub did some research of his own in the library, figuring what it would cost to live for two years in New

York. Two years being what he figured it would take to do *The Dead Pile*. And the answer was approximately fifteen thousand dollars.

Fifteen *thousand*.

He had earned, from his published work, three hundred and sixty-two big ones, and that was spent as soon as the checks arrived. Sure, he could go to the city like everybody else and get a job waiting tables and write when he wasn't—except he knew that was disaster. He needed time when he worked. A stretch all his own. Twelve-hour days, fifteen when the going got good. He was never much when he had to snatch two hours here, another three the day after.

The answer, the only answer, that seemed satisfactory was a full scholarship to a decent grad school in or near Manhattan. That way he could study toward a doctorate, which he'd thought about before he ever even came to Oberlin. He'd get someplace cheap to live in or around campus, he'd type papers or something to stay ahead of the game.

And he could write during vacations. Between Christmas, spring and summer that was four months plus. School for eight, the rest his own for writing. Writing *there*.

He was a bit dismayed to find only four places that gave Ph.D.'s in English in the area. Columbia, NYU, City, and St. John's. He applied to them all early in his senior year, got through his Grad Record Exams breezing.

On one remarkable April morning of his senior year, Chub heard from all four. And they all rejected him. Forget the full scholarship, they wouldn't even take him.

Staring at the letters, Chub could feel the center starting not to hold.

Because it wasn't possible—he'd been *published*. He'd included Xerox copies of his stories with his admission applications. It had to be a mistake—he locked himself in his dorm room trying to figure it out. It didn't take long. In all he'd been doing the last year and a half, there was one thing he hadn't been working at—school. His grade curve was fine the first two years—"A"s mostly—but junior year he'd managed only one "B-plus" and first semester this year he'd gotten a preponderance of "C"s.

When he was steady, he hurried to the employment office—it was late—he'd never conceived somebody wouldn't accept him. The best the employment office could come up with was a nibble as an instructor at someplace called Central Piedmont, a tiny college outside of Evansville, Indiana.

"Don't take it!" Two-Brew said. They were having coffee in a corner of the Campus Restaurant with graduation only three weeks away.

"Teaching is not so terrible."

"Especially at Central Piedmont—why, only last year the freshman class had an IQ average of close to ninety."

"I've checked it out a little—it's got a very nice reputation around Evansville."

"Do you *hear* what you're saying?"

Chub preferred not to answer.

"What's the salary?"

"Seven thousand."

"And what do you expect to live on?"

"Hundred a week."

"Which comes to a saving of two thousand a year. Only it won't 'cause you'll need wheels. And you need fifteen thousand. You may actually get to New York by the twenty-first century."

"Knock it off, all right?—I don't need this."

"You do—you fucking well do—don't you understand? If you take the job, *you won't write.*"

"Oh, bullshit—teachers get a lot of time off."

"Let me outline your future," Two-Brew said. "You will spend the first year stuffing *Mill on the Floss* down the throats of cretinish freshmen. That's if you're lucky— instructors always get the shit courses—you'll probably get four sections of English composition—though they may not get to that at Central Piedmont till sophomore year. Perhaps you'll teach remedial reading."

Chub started to stand.

Two-Brew put a crutch on one of Chub's shoulders, forced him down. "That was the good part I just told you. And you actually may write that first summer. But then you'll start to get lonely. Lonely is not so terrific, but lonely in Evansville squares that. And you'll need somebody. And you'll find her. And she'll be okay. Sweet. And she'll think you're wonderful. And I'll come to your wedding and you'll be smiling like a bastard but inside you'll be dead and I'm right and you know it."

Chub blew into his coffee.

"Go home, why don't you—sponge—write there."

Chub just looked at him.

"I'm sorry," Two-Brew said. "I forgot you don't have one."

Chub said nothing, sipped the last of his coffee.

"Come to the city, for Chrissakes. Give it a shot."

"I don't want to go there like everybody else and fall flat on my ass and leave in a year. When I have the money, I may not make it, but at least I'll have a leg up. And Central Piedmont will be fine."

"Spelled 'd-o-o-m,' " Two-Brew concluded.

Whether Kitchel was being overly melodramatic or not turned out to be beside the point. The week before graduation Central Piedmont called to say, with some embarrassment, that they had located another teacher who had a master's and they hoped Chub understood.

Chub was very polite. But how the center was shattering.

Graduation came, and while he was going through the paces, Chub knew he was blocking it all. Gretchen couldn't come up so he spent most of his time with the Kitchels. After the ceremony, he went to Patty McLean's and helped her parents load her stuff into their station wagon. It took awhile but he enjoyed the physical labor and then they embraced and she was gone.

Two-Brew was gone too. Just a note on Chub's door was all: "Sentiment does not become us; we shall meet at Philippi."

Chub packed. The dorms were closing for the summer so he had to get out and there was a small room over Gibson's bakery that rented by the week so he took it. Then he heard about a summer replacement job at the No-Name and the guy who owned the place always liked Chub because of the beer-drinking contest and when he said yes so did Chub.

Working the No-Name didn't pay much, but there wasn't much work to do. You sold 3.2 by the glass or pitcher, you sold Coke and ginger ale by the bottle. And since the place survived on college trade, it was mostly empty in summertime. Dr. Wallinsky was there every day, of course, drunk usually when he arrived.

Sometimes Wallinsky would reminisce hazily about his Oberlin days, forty years earlier. Before he went off to Yale and got his doctorate in languages. It seemed to Chub that all language had left him—his English was barely distinguishable. He liked to talk to Chub about the great beer-drinking contest and how thrilling it had been, and at least twice a week he would ask, "Where's that crip? Haven't seen the crip much lately," and Chub would explain patiently that Stanley Kitchel was starting his career now in New York in his father's publishing firm. Satisfied, Dr. Wallinsky would usually retreat to his favorite table in the corner and watch the bubbles in his beer flatten.

And it also seemed to Chub, watching him, that there was a story in there someplace—maybe thirty years down the line he would be watching the bubbles flatten—only he didn't feel much like writing it.

June was dry and steaming, and the No-Name was air-conditioned but not his room over the bakery. The smells that rose from below were wonderful but sleep was hard to come by.

Chub developed a taste for Wild Turkey. He'd walk out of the town limits to the nearest liquor store and buy a bottle or two. Every night he would sip alone, perspiring heavily, not getting plotzed or anything, but it helped him to doze off.

And it helped him to try and figure things. Because that was what was important—his next move and what and where.

He had always thought teaching would be good, but now that didn't appeal much. He was sick of school and he couldn't afford to go on. Probably there was some graduate faculty somewhere—there had to be—that would give him at least a partial scholarship but he would be wasting his time and their money.

He was twenty-two—born with the half century—and he had a degree in English and that wasn't worth a whole lot. Starting factory work, assuming there were job openings, averaged just under four bucks an hour and that didn't appeal to him much either.

But to hell with "appeal," he had to strike out somewhere, and he could handle the language and in the back of his head there was always the thought of working as a copywriter for an ad agency. New York was the obvious goal—if he could get a job there he'd at least have an honorable line of endeavor and he'd be where he so desperately wanted to be.

But what if the New York agencies said no?

He spent three days typing up an acceptable resume and then researched the half dozen leading agencies in Cleveland. If he was wanted there, he might accept, but then again he might not, might just sail with that confidence toward Magic Town.

The Cleveland agencies, all six, said no.

Chub sat in his room over the bakery, wondering if he'd somehow fallen like Alice, only this was no wonderland. Three months ago he was on the come, on a roll, moving like a bastard. He would not allow himself to believe the roll was finished, but he sure wouldn't have objected strongly to a little evidence to the contrary.

Then, thank God, came the brick factory.

"Is this the Elyria Brickworks?" Chub said into the phone in the hall outside his room.

" 'Tis."

"Well, my name is Charles Fuller and I'm calling from

Oberlin. I saw your ad in the Elyria paper this morning. It said you had openings with 'top pay.' "

"That was my ad, I run the place. I'm Mulloy."

"I've got to tell you, Mr. Mulloy, I don't have any previous experience."

"None required."

"Could you tell me what the 'top pay' is?"

"Yessir, seems only fair I do that. Starting out is ten bucks per hour, forty-hour week. Non-union. I won't let those fuckers near me."

Chub closed his eyes and started figuring. Ten times forty was four hundred times fifty-two—no, make it fifty, easier to multiply—was—was *twenty thousand dollars* the first year. He could be in New York by next summer.

"Overtime starts at fifteen. Saturdays. Eight hours. We usually need overtime."

How much was that? Thousands; it had to be. "When could I have an interview?"

"You're having it, Mr. Fuller. It's not the hardest work in the world to learn. You live in Oberlin?"

"I just graduated."

"Very hoity-toity—only joking—I won't hold it against you. Got a car?"

"Nossir."

"Well, you won't need one. Just take the Oberlin bus past the center of town here—Main—get off and walk two blocks south. Can you handle that, did you take geography?—only joking; I do that a lot."

"Yessir, I can handle it."

"I'll be here at eight-thirty. Good-bye, Fuller."

Chub was outside the Elyria Brickworks at seven–forty-five. Until he actually saw the place he worried that the whole thing was some cosmic put-on applied for his benefit. After the past months, he didn't feel his paranoia was unjustified.

At eight-thirty Mr. Mulloy arrived. Leprechaun type. He reminded Chub of Mr. O'Malley from the Barnaby comic strip he'd loved when he was young. They talked a little—Mr. Mulloy had a niece who he said was smart as a whip and was thinking of Oberlin and what was Chub's opinion of the place? Chub gave it high marks, they had coffee out of plastic containers and then when it was almost nine, Mr. Mulloy gestured for Chub to follow.

They entered a small shed where half a dozen middle-aged men were grouped, talking. "This here's Fuller and he went to college and I want him treated with respect."

"Hi," Chub said.

They kind of grumbled and went back to their conversation.

Chub put on his newly purchased work gloves while Mr. Mulloy pointed around. There was a chute in the center of the shed and a number of chairs set alongside. He ushered Chub toward the front chair. "Here's the drill—bricks are made behind that wall there"—Chub nodded—"and then they come down this chute here and what you do, Fuller, is you sit in the chair and you see those boxes alongside?" Chub nodded again. "Well, when the bricks get to you, you lift 'em, two at a time, and you put 'em in the box. When the box is full, give a holler, I got a kid with a wagon who'll come take the box away, give you a new empty. Got it?"

"I just reach over into the chute, take two bricks, stack them in the box?"

"College boys, God love 'em—just joking."

Then there was a whistle and Chub sat in the lead chair, turned, smiled at the middle-aged guys behind him. They weren't the friendliest but probably he wouldn't have been either if he'd been a veteran and a new kid came along.

At nine it got noisy and the bricks began coming down the chute. At first, Chub had trouble—asshole—getting the hang of it right; the bricks weren't as smooth as he thought and he thanked God he'd remembered to buy the gloves yesterday. But it was, he soon realized, a rhythm. You reached over with your hands to the right, grabbed the bricks, brought them across your body, put them carefully into the box. He was pleased at how easily they stacked and inside of five minutes, he called out, "New box, please," and as if on cue, a kid arrived with a wagon, gave Chub an empty.

It wasn't for a few minutes more till the old guys began needing new boxes and Chub knew he'd made a mistake working too fast. He was going to be practically living with them for the next year, and the last thing they needed was a show-off in their midst.

So he began, carefully, to slow his rhythm down. The second box was filled at the same time as several of the others and that was good.

"New box," Chub shouted at nine–twenty-five, his mind set now on the problem of overtime. Should he do it every week? It would be a lot more money but six days a week didn't allow for much writing time. The work required no mental strain and he could easily figure out what to write while he worked, maybe take a few notes at lunch break, and do his own work on weekends.

It was hot now in the shed and Chub stood quickly after he'd finished another box and took off his shirt, tossed it close by. There was a lot of dust, too, and he quickly figured not to inhale when he was reaching for the bricks, because that was where the dust was heaviest. You *ex*haled while picking them up, breathed in while you did your stacking.

By ten he was bored but that was fine—one hour meant ten bucks and he wondered if Mr. Mulloy paid by the day or the week or what—he should have asked but he was too nervous to. Probably by the week. Probably by the four-hundred-dollar week. Would it be in cash or check? Chub didn't know quite what "non-union" meant and cash would have been better but what the hell, four hundred was four hundred and fifty times four hundred was New York and two free years and sonofabitch if that wasn't worth all the boredom you could eat and then some—

—"Son of a bitch," Chub said out loud, angry at his goddamn fingers for starting to cramp on him, but he quickly took care of that, stretched them back to normal without missing a brick and—

"—what the hell *shit*," Chub said as someone put a knife into his shoulder blades. He gasped with the sudden pain, but then it dulled, there was no knife, it was his shoulders locked into a sudden cramp and as he stood he heard a sound—

—behind now, was laughter.

Fuck them, Chub thought, and he sat back down and reached out for two more bricks and he had them up off the chute but then as he tried to reach across for the box he dropped them. His shoulders were worse but probably not as bad as his forearms. He knelt, managed through his pain to get the bricks into the box, sat, tried reaching for two more, got them up, dropped them back down in the chute.

And now from behind him came a chant: "Easy money at the brick factory, easy money at the brick factory," and Chub, in anguish and humiliation, turned and looked at his co-workers and they had their shirts off, too, and he saw that so what if they were older than he was—My God, they all had arms like Popeye.

"What's so goddamn funny?" Chub shouted.

"I'm gonna win—" the guy behind him said—"we got a pool on how long you'd last and I picked ten-forty-five." Chub looked at his watch. Half past ten. "Screw," he said, and he sat back down and reached out for the bricks.

At just before eleven Chub, throbbing, was back in Mr. Mulloy's office.

Mr. Mulloy looked up from his desk. "Was it the shoulders that got you? It's usually the shoulders."

Chub was able to make a nod. His neck, at least, still almost worked.

"Cramping should be gone by tomorrow, Fuller. Take a nice hot bath, they say that helps. And don't feel bad—the last two kids quit before ten."

Chub, the cramping worse, asked could he have the money he'd earned.

"Can't pay you, sorry about that—never pay unless there's a full day's work, you understand."

Chub stood there, trying to massage his forearms, but his fingers were cramping too badly for anything to be effective. *This is funny,* he told himself. *This is wonderful material.*

Only he didn't feel much like writing it.

Mr. Mulloy walked him to the brickworks entrance. "So long, Fuller—if you ever get your arms and shoulders in shape, give a holler—I've always got openings."

Chub took the bus back home.

No, not home, just back to the room over Gibson's where he spent the afternoon in the tub, rubbing in Ben-Gay, waiting for his muscles to stop cramping. The bath didn't do much but the Wild Turkey helped, and he and Dr. Wallinsky were both drunk when they entered the No-Name that evening.

"It's the crip!" Dr. Wallinsky cried the first night in August. The weeks since the brick factory had been bad for Chub; really the worst for Chub, but now he turned and there in the entrance was Two-Brew, dressed in a blue seersucker suit and blue button-down shirt and red tie. "How are things in Glocca Morra?" Two-Brew said, moving on his crutches toward the bar.

There was no one in the bar except the three of them. "Swamped," Chub said.

Kitchel smiled, took a seat, and they shook hands.

"You look good," Chub said. "Not exactly sylphlike, but immaculate."

"We both look good."

"Jesus Christ, what are you doing here?"

Two-Brew sighed. "My prick father insisted I spend the day in glorious Cleveland. We've got a hot-shot doctor at Western Reserve who's doing a diet book for us. Only he's late. We're in deep on our advance so Father said I should see him and explain how thrilled we are that the book is coming along so well. But the subtext was: *Where is the goddamn thing?* Father believes in scaring writers, especially when he's paid them money. And I figured, as long as I was in Cleveland—may I never see it again please God—I'd say hello."

The clock behind the bar indicated seven-thirty. "I get off at eleven," Chub said. "Can you spend the night?"

"Can't you get off? I've got to catch the last plane back and it leaves before eleven."

"Shit," Chub said.

Two-Brew leaned forward on the bar. "What I wanted to see you about was this: I've come up with a crazy idea and I want to try it out on you. It could be important."

"I'll try to pay attention between all my chores."

"Okay—it's crossed my mind that maybe, just maybe—"

"—God, that was a great night, the contest night," Dr. Wallinsky said, sitting down next to Two-Brew. "I wish we could do it again."

"May all your hopes be granted," Two-Brew said, turning away from the doctor toward Chub. "What crossed my mind was this—"

"Nothing's touched it since," Dr. Wallinsky said, smiling at them both. "I see it all plain as yesterday."

"I'm sorry, Dr. Wallinsky, but we're trying to talk," Chub said gently.

"I like to talk," Dr. Wallinsky said. Then he said, "Oh, you mean *talk*." He asked for another glass of beer and took it to his table in the corner.

"You know all those stories you've fumbled out over the last couple of years? All of them about people with different names because of your obsession with Irwin Shaw?"

"I'm aware of what you're talking about," Chub said.

"Well, on the plane ride in today—maybe I was thinking of our time here, I don't know—but I realized they don't *have* to be about different people. The kid who breaks the window with the yo-yo is the same guy really who marries the actress when he shouldn't. I mean shit, they're all you."

"I guess maybe."

"Well, what if we took say ten of those stories—and did some minor rearranging when necessary—and made it all the same people. It's ripping off Salinger and the

Glass family, I know, but if you did what I'm suggesting, you'd have the future of a guy growing up, starting when he's six or so and ending when he's screwing up his life by marrying someone who's going to slaughter him. I even found you your title. Try this: *Under the Weather.*"

Chub thought a moment. "Good title."

"Put that in your pot and let it stew awhile."

"Why?"

"Because, nerd, publishers hate books of short stories. But if they were connected, there might be more interest. I could bring it up at the next sales meeting."

"That would be fantastic," Chub said.

"Not really. I can go on all night about how it's not really short stories only they're dumb but they're not that dumb. They'd turn me down. And I, being as is common knowledge, flawless, don't like being rejected."

Chub poured himself a beer.

"But—" Two-Brew said then.

Chub drank it down.

"—they *might* be interested in publishing the book if they knew there was a novel coming they were hot for. That way, if I could snooker them, twenty-five hundred would be a reasonable advance on the short stories and maybe fifteen thousand advance on the novel. What I want you to do before I try anything is really ponder do you want the stories changed a little so as to make them more connected."

"The answer is yes. There. I've pondered."

"You fool," Two-Brew said.

Chub looked at him.

"You actually believed me."

Chub didn't say anything.

"You're dumber now than when we met and there wasn't a lot of room for deprovement." And now he banged a crutch on the bar and the sound exploded. "*I did it, you buffoon!* The sales meeting was today—and there isn't any diet doctor in Cleveland—the fifth 'Eyes' book just hit two million, they couldn't turn me down. And even if it hadn't they couldn't turn me down—I was so brilliant, Chubbo—I told the part where your father was pitched in with the corpses and they didn't fucking *breathe.*" Two-Brew began to cackle now—"Look at you—your mouth is open—Bo-Bo the Dog-Faced Boy would appear more intelligent. Don't you understand?"

"Say it slowly."

"*Under the Weather* will be published in a year. *The Dead Pile* will follow when finished." He handed Chub an envelope. "Two checks inside totalling seventeen thousand five. You don't even have to pay an agent's fee, you worthless shit. So get ready, Tonto—Silver's hitched outside."

Chub shrieked and leapt over the bar, grabbed one of Kitchel's crutches and began waltzing with it around the empty room.

"What's up?" came from the old drunk in the corner.

"I'm going to New York to write a book!"

"I wrote a book once," Dr. Wallinsky said. . . .

PART II

The Dead Pile

CHAPTER 1

Singer

Chub knew he was going to rent the apartment before he ever saw it.

It was certainly not the location—Ninety-eighth Street, between West End and Riverside—that won him over. Across the way was a Single Room Only hotel, and derelicts lined the sidewalk. Also, it seemed to Chub that an inordinate number of transvestites were in the vicinity. (This, it turned out, was a permanent part of the area's ambiance. The block was known as Transvestite Heaven.)

And the tenement was probably not built in this century—security seemed nil, the front door opened to anyone who had a shoulder to shove it.

The super—a heavyset woman named Gonzales—sighed when Chub inquired about the "Apt. Avail." sign in front. "I hope you got strong legs," she said to him, which made more and more sense to Chub as they began the climb. The empty was on the top-floor rear, ninety-seven steps up from the street. It made the newlyweds' place in *Barefoot in the Park* seem like a ground-floor flat.

As they paused on the third floor for Mrs. Gonzales to catch her breath she said, "It's almost got a view of the river." Chub assumed, correctly, that it didn't have a view at all. Mrs. Gonzales nodded. "If the three buildings over get knocked down, you'll have a clear shot. But even now, when the wind's coming in from Jersey, you get the breeze."

Between the fourth and fifth floors, Mrs. Gonzales, perspiring heavily—it was late August and the wind was not coming in from Jersey—said, "Singer lived here once."

"Which singer?" Chub asked, trying to keep the conversation going.

"The Yid. The Hebrew guy."

Chub stopped. "You mean *Isaac* Singer? Isaac Bashevis Singer? The writer?"

"I think. I don't know for sure. I only been super five years but someone said that once, a long time ago, he did. Maybe. He lives around here now. Shouldn't be hard to find out if you want to know."

I don't ever want to know, Chub thought. But he knew then that no matter what lay above him, it was going to be home.

Fortunately, what lay above him wasn't so bad: two decent-sized rooms overlooking a number of cement courtyards down below. Two large windows in each room. A wall kitchen with little shelf space but who cared, he hated cooking. And a bathroom with both a tub and a shower head and a toilet that almost flushed completely.

Chub signed a three-year lease at $285/month, and set out almost immediately for the Salvation Army. Within a week the place was habitable—desk, bed, tables, rugs took no time at all. What took him the most time was his wall.

He had always wanted a cork wall. Where he could tack notes and anything else that might help jog his memory. He went to a paint store, bought over a hundred squares of brown cork, several large bottles of glue, set to work. He wasn't all that good with his hands ("Easy money at the brick factory") so it took more time than he thought, but finally he had it done. The entire wall, floor to ceiling, was covered with brown cork. Chub bought a bottle of Wild Turkey, soaked off the label and, when it was dry, tacked it on the wall above his desk. He went to the Strand Bookstore and found an old copy of *Oil for the Lamps of China* and tacked the jacket beside the liquor label. In an Eighth Avenue pawnshop he found a World War Two Purple Heart and he placed that so that the jacket was tacked between the liquor and the prize. Then he got his notes in order, because he knew he had to have the novel really under way before the reviews came out for his stories. (He would manage over a hundred pages, protection enough.)

But before he did any of that, the very first thing he tacked up was a small typed note that was eye level as he sat at his desk.

"Welcome to America," the note read.

From *The New Yorker:*

BRIEFLY NOTED

Fiction

Under the Weather, by Charles Fuller (Sutton; $5.95). A grouping of ten inter-connected stories centered on the growing up of Peter "Pudge" Irwin. Young Mr. Fuller has studied his Salinger and Shaw, to most excellent effect. The book jacket informs that he is at work on a novel; one cannot but await it with interest.

From the *New York Times Book Review* (reviewed by Joyce Carol Oates, the fourth of four collections of short stories):

... It would be logical to expect Mr. Fuller, being the youngest by far of the authors under discussion, to be the most experimental. This is not the case. Any of these stories could have been written in the past forty years.

But such is his control of his material that it is impossible to hold that against him. In a relent-

lessly and unsparingly ugly story, "The Men's
Room at Meroni's," the ten-year-old hero waits
in a graffiti-scarred hellhole to help his drunken
father home. What makes the scene so moving is
the author's sure knowledge of shared pain.

The final story (somewhat too cleverly titled
"The Girl(s) of My Dreams") brings the book
full circle and successfully; the hero is doomed
to repeat the mistakes of his parents.

One might long for a growing audacity in Mr.
Fuller's future work. But that he has a future is
beyond question. He already has this considerable achievement behind him—at the age of
twenty-three. Probably that ought to be enough.

From the *Oberlin Alumni Magazine:* Reviewed by
Andrew Cheyney:

UPDIKE, FULLER AND ROTH?

A presumptuous title? Without question.
Charles Fuller ('72) is nearly two decades younger than the others. And I must admit to a
certain bias—he was a student of mine during
his years here, when these stories were written,
and I like to think I did not damage his growth.

But the growth was inexorable. At similar
ages, Updike and Roth had similar accomplish-
ments behind them. And today, of course, they
are among the best we have.

Will Fuller, two decades hence, be among the
best we have? I have neither the space here nor
the inclination to detail the stories—all Oberlin-
ians should hie to their bookstores and support a
fellow alumnus. But it is my hope and firm belief
that in time the question mark in my title will be
erased. I like to think said title will prove to be
precognitive, not presumptuous, after all.

Chub read his reviews, both good and bad—and there were some bad—with great care. The negative notices he went over several times, often taking notes, trying to find a consensus on where he'd gone wrong. For the raves, his reaction was always the same: "My God, I got away with it."

Considering it was a book of short stories by a total unknown, *Under the Weather* did well. The first printing of thirty-five hundred copies came close to selling out. (Eventually, less than three hundred were returned.)

The people at Sutton were sufficiently encouraged to put out a paperback edition, and to celebrate that occasion, Kitchel invited Chub to have lunch. (The paperback was the shocker. Nothing to compete with Emma Heather Lathery, of course, but it went through five printings, total sales over a hundred thousand. Chub received an offer to lecture for a semester at Iowa, which he politely refused because of his novel. And fifty or so fan letters, all of which he politely answered. The letters were all from college students and there was a reason for that. Because, for one brief month or so, collegians all across the country put down *Siddhartha* or *Bury My Heart at Wounded Knee* and gave *Under the Weather* a try.)

Chub met Two-Brew in his office at Sutton, and by now he was almost used to Kitchel's work costume. Blue button-down shirt, grey flannel suit, striped ties from Brooks. Probably the whole works came from there. And Kitchel's curling hair was normal length. One thing was new though: He seemed thinner.

"Where's that pornographic novel you're working on?—I want your goddamn book."

"It's coming along," Chub said. (It was. He had, that morning, finished page 255, his father had been planed to England for rehabilitation. What particularly excited Chub was what he had found in his recent research—he was totally at ease with the library facilities all over the city by now and it was probably the best in the world. What he had found was a series of marvelous articles in some old medical journals dealing with the salvaging of the wounded during the war. Not just the delicate operations, but the mental and physical treatments that followed. He hadn't quite digested it all yet, but he would soon, and he felt as confident as he ever did that he could write what his father went through and make it work.)

" 'Coming along,' Fuller, is the writer's equivalent of the man who owes you money saying, 'The check is in the mail.' "

"I'm around two hundred fifty. He's entering rehabilitation."

Two-Brew groaned. "What are you, a third of the way through? I don't want the fucking *Forsythe Saga*. There go our hospital sales—you can't push groin-busters to the invalided. They need something they can lift. How dull is it?"

"Oh, it's very dull, I promise."

"Well, that's something at least—"

"—May I come in, Stan?" a female voice asked, and Chub turned to the doorway and was aware, instantly, that Somebody was there.

Lydia Katz was wearing a grey tweed skirt and a white button-down shirt. A red scarf at her neck set off her dark skin and hair. She was tall, five seven, and perhaps inside her was a fat girl trying to get out. But as Chub watched her, the fat girl was losing. She was enormously sensual, but the intelligence was there too. She seemed almost on the verge of tears and when she spoke, a slight impediment was evident. "Fuller" was never quite "Fuwwer," though there was no denying that "l"'s gave her trouble.

Two-Brew started mimicking immediately. " 'May I come in, Stan? May I come in, Stan?' Lydia, if you had the least knowledge of spatial relations you would already have deduced that you *are* in. What you can do is state your business and then go out."

"I don't even hear it anymore, Stan," she said, then crossed to Chub, who stood. "We haven't met but I'm

Lydia Katz and I really wanted to meet you. I'm a real fan and I had to tell you that."

Chub thanked her.

She turned then after her smile, went to the door, stopped. "Oh, yes—if you ever need a *real* editor, I'm just down the hall." A quick glance toward Kitchel. "That was a joke, Stan."

"Lydia Katz, for Chrissakes," Kitchel said when she was gone, his face red with anger. "Have you ever heard a phonier name?"

"How 'bout Paige Kitchel?" Chub said, mentioning Two-Brew's sister, whom he had dated after his first reviews came out—not for long, though; she had the habit of always crying after intercourse, which put a permanent damper on things.

"We're entering her in the National Preppy Contest next spring—I suspect she sleeps in button-down nighties."

Chub looked at Two-Brew's button-down shirt, said nothing.

"Miss Hot Shit—the only reason she's a junior editor is she's the godchild of one of our vice-presidents."

Chub wondered aloud when Kitchel had turned his back on the glories of nepotism.

"I am employed here, shit-for-brains, because of my acumen, sensitivity, and sagaciousness. The fact that Daddums owns the joint is an inconsequential issue. Let's eat."

Ordinarily, they lunched at little French places like Le Moal, where Two-Brew had the pâté, anything with a sauce, and either one or more desserts. Now, he explained, he'd found a new eating experience that surpassed the Frogs.

On the street, he took off again on Lydia Katz, on her rudeness and incompetence, her speech—"The office Barbara Wah-Wah"—and how Yale's allowing her to graduate two years ago was proof of the fall of the Ivy League.

They dined—Chub couldn't believe it—in a vegetarian restaurant. Chub had tuna salad while Two-Brew ordered cottage cheese and carrot strips.

As Chub watched his dearest friend down the white curded stuff, he decided that very clearly *something* was most definitely in the air.

The situation began to clarify that Saturday when he was studying surgical techniques for head wounds and the phone rang, the caller being Lydia Katz, they had met at Sutton, and could they meet please sometime soon, like, if possible, now.

She was standing outside a coffee shop on Ninety-fifth and Broadway half an hour later. It was a cool September day, and she was wearing jeans, tennis shoes, and a baggy Princeton sweat shirt.

"I thought you went to Yale," Chub said as they sat in a corner and ordered. It was close to eleven in the morning, and the place was empty.

"Christ, he can't even keep that straight," Lydia said. Her eyes were red and moist.

"Don't be upset," Chub said quietly.

"I'm not upset—it's these goddamn contact lenses—I switched from my horn-rims a month ago and I'm in agony and he didn't even notice."

Their coffee came. Chub waited for it to cool.

"I don't suppose I have to identify who 'he' is?"

Chub shook his head.

"I'm 'interested' in Stanley Kitchel," Lydia said then. "I was not infatuated at first sight. I almost cried the first time he insulted me and I'm not a weeper. I did not fantasize about him thereafter, except occasionally about revenge. I avoided him at the office wherever possible. My answers, when spoken to, were curt and as cutting as I could make them. But the last couple of months, I don't know—he's just so fucking weird and I can't stop thinking about him."

"If you think he's bizarre now, you should have seen him in school."

"Okay, here's why I'm bugging you—you know him

better than anybody—I think he's interested in me too. I mean, lately, he's just been so *horrid,* that's got to mean something, don't you think?"

"With a human being, yes."

Lydia sighed. "You mean he isn't interested?"

"I didn't say that—I have seen him with my own eyes eat cottage cheese. He isn't slimming down for the next sales meeting."

"Well Jesus Christ, thank God I'm not crazy," Lydia Katz said. She lifted her coffee cup. "What do we do now, Coach?"

Chub shook his head. "It won't be easy."

"Did he date at Oberlin?"

"I am reliably informed he was sexually active. But he did not socialize to excess."

Lydia nodded. "The goddamn legs." Then she said, "Do you mind?" and she turned her head to the wall, took off her contacts, reached into her purse for her horn-rims.

"You're pretty either way," Chub told her.

"I don't know about that, but I've never had trouble getting boys before. What the hell can I do, drop my handkerchief?"

"Two-Brew wouldn't understand that. He'd just think you were clumsy."

"Look—I don't want his money; my father owns more stupid McDonald's franchises than anyone else in New England and he wasn't poor going in. And I'm totally devoid of Florence Nightingale instincts—the one time I was engaged it was to a basketball player."

Chub looked at her. He had never thought much about Kitchel getting serious with a girl. This one across from him now seemed like a steal. Assuming her skin was thick enough and that no one could predict. "I'd like to help you get started," he said. "I just don't know how."

"What about honesty—I could just ask him out, don't you think?"

"Death."

"Fug," from Lydia Katz.

They sat silently for a few minutes before Chub said it: "Lydia?"

"What?"

"Ask us *both* out. . . ."

"How could you have accepted?" Two-Brew railed at Chub as they walked through the drizzle on East Eighty-third Street toward the new large, white, boxlike building up ahead. It was Wednesday, several weeks later, and talk of a second printing of the paperback was growing stronger.

"Don't ask that again, huh?" Chub replied. "It's the middle of the week, you'll be home early."

"I do not do not do not do not understand!"

"I made a mistake, I'm sorry—when she asked me I thought from what she said you'd already accepted, so I accepted too."

They entered the building, asked the doorman for Katz, were buzzed on in. At the elevator Chub took off his raincoat. He was wearing slacks and a white shirt, open at the throat, and a blazer. When Two-Brew took off his raincoat Chub saw he was wearing the kind of jogging suit—this one was purple—he'd costumed himself with at school.

"Don't look at me that way," Two-Brew said. "She said 'casual'—to me this is casual."

Chub just shook his head.

They got into the elevator. "The meal will be splendiferous," Kitchel said. "Our main course will be Eggs McMuffin; my secretary did some checking. The divine Lydia's father manages a McDonald's."

Chub watched the numbers above the elevator door.

"I'll tell you something you won't believe, Chubbo—when she first came to the office, she wore horn-rim glasses; she was much less unattractive then."

Lydia was waiting in her doorway on the seventeenth floor. She wore dark silk slacks, a white silk shirt, and she ushered them inside. She lived in a large studio apartment. By the kitchen a small table was set up with three place settings, an unlit candle serving as center-piece. There wasn't much view, but the room was not, Chub observed, filled with relics from the Salvation Army. "Really nice," he said.

Two-Brew nodded. "You majored in home economics at Yale?"

"Harvard, Stan."

There was a large couch by the main window, a table in front. There was a bowl of dip surrounded by fresh-cut vegetables. Lydia gestured toward the area. "Why don't we all sit there to begin. Dinner is theoretically in the oven." Chub and Two-Brew started toward the couch while Lydia darted into the kitchen, returned a moment later with a bottle and glasses. "I thought, in honor of the second printing, we might start with champagne."

"Terrific," Chub said.

"I didn't know Manischewitz made champagne," Two-Brew said.

Chub shot him a look but Two-Brew was already resting his crutches by the back of the couch, dropping heavily down.

Lydia got the foil off the champagne but the cork gave her trouble. Chub reached over, took the bottle, began pushing hard with his thumbs. During this, Two-Brew examined the dip. "What is this, calf's-foot jelly made from your own calf?"

"Stan, if you're going to quote Kaufman and Hart, at least quote Kaufman and Hart. The line is 'Made from your own *foot,* I have no doubt.' "

"They taught you that at Harvard, I'm impressed."

"Yale," Lydia said.

Chub finally got the bottle open, poured carefully. They lifted their glasses to *Under the Weather* and drank. "I can't wait for your novel," Lydia said.

"You won't be able to finish it, my pet; it's going to be long and your lips will get tired."

Lydia smiled, looked at Chub. "The terrible thing is, he actually thinks that's funny. Here's another new one, Stan: It's a book, *The Yellow River* by I. P. Daily."

Chub laughed and started talking quickly. "God, I loved those when I was a kid. *The Hole in the Mattress* by Mister Completely. *The Open Kimono* by Seymour Hair. *The Russian's Revenge* ... who wrote that, do either of you guys remember?"

There wasn't a lot of interest in pursuing the subject so Chub shut up and drank his champagne. They would have to battle it out themselves. He wondered if Lydia was equal to the task. A few minutes later he wondered if anyone was equal to the task.

Lydia said she'd just seen *Amarcord* and *Scenes From a Marriage* and they were both wonderful. Chub said he totally agreed with her. Two-Brew said he loathed and detested any movies where he had to read.

Lydia tried theatre. *Equus* was in previews and she heard it was wonderful. Chub said he'd heard the same thing. Two-Brew said he heard it was faggy.

"You'll have to excuse him," Chub tried then. "He's had a terrible shock earlier tonight—his pet python died."

Two-Brew looked at him contemptuously and bit down loudly on a carrot stick.

Eventually, Lydia glanced at her watch and stood. "I've got to go look in the oven, cross your fingers; I haven't done much entertaining before."

"She still hasn't," Two-Brew said when she was gone.

"What was that?" Lydia called from the kitchen.

"He said entertaining was hard," Chub said quickly. "I said the guests make the party." He looked at Kitchel then. "You've been fabulous so far."

Two-Brew crunched another carrot.

Lydia put a glass salad bowl on the table, made another trip for a bottle of red wine. Chub got up to help. He stood by the kitchen as Lydia emerged carrying a casserole. "This *began* as beef bourguignon," she said, putting it on the table.

"I'm not fussy," Two-Brew said, reaching for his crutches. "Just as long as everything's dead inside, I shan't complain." Chub stood behind Lydia's chair and pulled it out and she nodded thank you and Kitchel crossed the room toward the table and the candlelight, Chub thought, made Lydia look particularly stunning and even Kitchel had to notice that, so maybe things were on an upward curve now, except they weren't, because as he approached the table one of Two-Brew's crutches slipped and he screamed out loud and began to fall, grabbing for a chair to support him but the chair gave way and he frantically reached for the tablecloth and then he was on the floor along with everything else, the salad, the casserole upturned, the emptying bottle of red wine.

It took twenty minutes to get it cleaned up, and Two-Brew apologized and Lydia said not to and eventually they ordered in pizza, ate it in silence, and by ten Chub and Kitchel were back in the elevator, heading down.

"Prick," Chub said.

Two-Brew said nothing.

"Prick," Chub said again in the foyer.

"I apologized plenty, now shut up."

The rain had stopped but it had gotten colder. They started walking away from her building. The street was empty.

"What a miserable prick you are."

"And what a glorious vocabulary you have—you might consider taking up writing."

"You did it on purpose."

"Did what?"

"This," Chub cried, and he kicked at Two-Brew's nearest crutch, watched as Kitchel spun, fell hard to the wet pavement. Chub grabbed the other crutch and moved a few feet away. "Admit it."

Two-Brew, stunned, lay where he'd fallen.

"Admit it, prick."

Two-Brew blinked.

"You were so chickenshit scared you had to ruin it all. With *these*." He lifted the crutches into the air. "Boy, these fucking things make you king of the world, don't they."

Two-Brew reached for his crutches.

"Not till you admit it."

Two-Brew crawled toward a car, began pulling himself up.

Chub poked his hands with the crutches and Two-Brew fell again. "Chickenshit and dumb—she's not interested in you, she's interested in me."

"Is she?"

"Never shit a shitter. You know goddamn well what she's interested in—it's your money."

"She has money," Two-Brew said.

"Then there's only one answer isn't there?—She's got a thing for freaks. You buy that?"

Two-Brew reached for the crutches again.

"Admit it."

"Please."

"Admit it."

Two-Brew sat huddled on the sidewalk for a long time. Then he said, ". . . I thought the chair would hold me. . . . I never meant to pull everything . . . everything over like that. . . ."

Chub dropped the crutches alongside Kitchel, started walking away.

"Wait."

Chub kept on walking.

"Chuuuuub!"

The tone was so whipped Chub pivoted.

"What'll I do?"

"You might go back and apologize."

"I couldn't do that." He forced his crutches into position, got to his feet. "You see that, don't you?"

"I just see you, and I don't like it."

"What if she won't talk to me?"

"I hope she won't. No. I hope she does and takes your fucking head off."

He turned again and walked away until he was out of sight around the corner. Then he looked back. Two-Brew was standing in front of Lydia's building. Chub waited. Finally, when Two-Brew went in, Chub went home. . . .

The following months were almost more than Chub's stomach could stand—Two-Brew was in love before November and he took to calling Chub at all hours and singing, "Ahhhh, sweet mystery of life at last I've found you," before hanging up. When the three of them had dinners together, he was forever kissing her hand and attempting Rudolph Valentino flickers with his eyes. When they waited in line to see *Lenny,* he tried pawing her; when they sat through *The Wiz* all he wanted to do was nibble at her shoulder. Lydia fought him off with skill and ardor, but not too much of the latter and he knew when Two-Brew invited him, early in January for drinks at his place and dinner at The Four Seasons after that before the evening was done, gold bands would be in evidence.

He felt terrific about it and he felt even better about the novel. (Page 380 now and counting. The rehabilitation section in England, complete with a plate being put into his father's skull and the agonizing physical suffering before his body would properly obey him, was, Chub thought, probably a section in need of cutting, but maybe the best thing so far. Because none of the nurses gave the veteran much chance at coming all the way back, but the man knew the one great secret: He was special.)

The only thing Chub didn't feel so terrific about was there was little heat in his apartment. He wrote in sweaters and, on very bitter days, his overcoat. He was still cold when he got off the crosstown bus and walked to Kitchel's. Two-Brew had a two-bedroom place a block from his office. It was a zoo, naturally, but a comfortable one.

"My dear dear friend," Two-Brew began, as Chub walked in. "My own Horatio." He moved to embrace Chub but Chub gave him the slip, tossed his coat over Kitchel's arms and instead embraced Lydia, who stood smiling and watching them both from across the room.

Two-Brew went to the kitchen, returned with a bottle. "A little champagne to start the festivities?"

"Only if it's Manischewitz," Lydia said.

Chub smiled. There was no doubt they would hammer and tong each other blissfully for years.

Two-Brew poured. "A toast: to our best man, Charles Fuller."

Chub was honored and said so.

They touched glasses and as Lydia began to drink Kitchel said: "Hold—look at the way her arm moves, Chubbo. Note the grace. Behold her form: the perfect breadth of shoulder, the bosom jut, the waist a wasp would envy."

"Oh, can it," Lydia said.

"I liked him better mean," Chub said.

"I think I'm beginning to agree with you," she said.

"Can it the both of you—? I promise to be demeaning by dinnertime."

It was still before eight and they weren't due at the restaurant till half past nine, so Two-Brew opened another bottle of champagne when the first one was empty. Chub begged off. The stuff tasted funny. Or at least he thought it did. He sat down suddenly and Lydia asked was he okay and he said yes, fine, because if there ever was an evening he didn't want to bitch up, this was it. He was just so goddamn cold, though. Lydia suggested a nap and Chub said thanks no, he didn't do that. But she insisted, promising to wake him in a half hour and a half hour later she did. He put some water on his face and went out to the living room where they were watching the tube.

"Fix the set," Chub said.

They both looked at him.

"The set," Chub said, pointing. "It's a double image." Christ, he was freezing.

They still looked at him. "There isn't any double image. The set is working perfectly."

Chub sat down then, or tried to, but he never would have made it to the couch if Lydia hadn't supported him there, and he didn't have a doctor but the Kitchel family did, and by the time Two-Brew had him on the line Lydia had taken his temperature, which was a hundred and three, and when Kitchel relayed that message to Dr. Stein along with the business of the double vision, the doctor suggested they meet at the emergency ward of the hospital he worked through and they didn't go to The Four Seasons that night, they went to Manhattan General instead, where Chub was to stay for a week.

Or maybe it wasn't a week, his time sense was wobbly. The one thing he was sure of was this: The doctors wouldn't leave him alone. They came by constantly, many of them young hotshots, and they all had the same routine, some early bullshit about how was his fever, the aches and the chills, and then, oh, yes, they began to ask about his eyes.

Because nobody knew what was wrong with him.

Dr. Stein was elderly and austere and when Chub thanked him for all the attention he pooh-poohed it, explaining that ordinarily you could buzz for hours and no one would come around, but when something unusual happened, all the interns and younger men got excited. After a few days his fever was down but the double vision was worse—he could see perfectly out of either eye singly, the two just wouldn't work together, and the night the two hotshots came in for the spinal tap Chub was confused, because Stein hadn't mentioned it and his fever was normal and were they sure they had the right guy and they both said yes, the spinal tap was for Fuller, and Chub said he didn't want it, he really didn't, and that couldn't they wait for Stein to come later and they said no, and please to lie on his side and Chub, frightened, did that, and they began trying to hook the needle into the base of his spine and he didn't want to scream and he told himself, *'This is going to be material, you'll write about this someday, it's great material, it is, it is,'* but then the pain was too much and he was screaming, he couldn't help it, he couldn't, the pain was that bad and the young guys were having a bitch of a time finding the entry spot with the long needle but they persisted, the pain increasing and Chub wanted to pass out but he couldn't, couldn't do a thing but lie there embarrassed at the sounds he was making until he heard Stein in the room, and now Stein was the one screaming, vilifying the hot-shots for doing an unauthorized procedure, and they said they thought he might want it and Stein said over and over, "I'm putting this on your records, both of you, I won't forget this."

Chub didn't forget it either. The next day, an ancient neurologist came across a similar case in a text. Chub had had pneumonia, but a rare strain that for some reason attacked the nerves of an eye. He would be fine, but it would take a year for the nerve to heal itself, and he would have to wear an eye patch until then.

The day after that, eye-patched and feverless, Chub went home. He was terribly weak and Kitchel said to come rest up with him, Lydia seconding, but Chub said no, thank you but no, he wanted to go back to his place.

Lydia helped him up the stairs—the ninety-seven were too much for Two-Brew. So he waited below while Chub and Lydia made the ascent. Chub had to stop at each floor but they made it finally and he fell in bed. Lydia left, came back with bags of food. By the time she'd put them all away, Chub was drifting.

It was several days before he felt strong enough to try a walk. He bundled up against the cold, slowly descended the stairs. The eye patch felt funny, his depth perception wasn't right, and twice he had to grip the banister in surprise. He decided what he would do was walk the block and a half to Broadway for the *Times* and he rested a moment in the foyer of the securityless building. Chub never minded that—anyone who wanted to get him was going to have to be a practiced mountaineer and the odds against that were unlikely. He opened the door, moved onto the sidewalk, his body bent forward against the January cold—

—and coming toward him—the first human he saw—was an old guy wearing an eye patch. As they passed, their good eyes moved toward each other, slowly, in wounded recognition.

Fantastic, Chub thought. He had to put that in his

Journal. They were like two old lizards considering each other on a summertime log.

He made it to the newsstand, got his paper, made it back to his place. But the stairs depleted what resources he had left and by the time he flopped back in bed he'd forgotten what the hell he thought was so fantastic in the first place.

When he saw Stein the good doctor examined him, told him all was coming along, asked what Chub was doing with himself. Chub answered, basically watching game shows in the morning, sleeping in the afternoons, watching the evening crap at night. Stein allowed that such activity was certainly good for his mind but it wasn't doing much for his body, and if Chub wanted to get his strength back quickly, mild exercise would be beneficial; walking would be fine, but not till the weather warmed, so he suggested swimming, cautioning Chub (a) not to overdo it and (b) to be sure to dry off thoroughly before returning home. Chub located a health club not far from his place that was open from two till ten and that accepted monthly memberships, so the next day he was there promptly at two, paid for the ensuing weeks.

The pool was big, the staff small. A fat lady working the desk, a college kid playing at lifeguard, an old guy named Tom who kept the dressing rooms clean. Chub changed, went down to the empty pool. He hadn't been near one since the visit to Gretchen—was *Serendipity* still moldering at the bottom? No. Ridiculous. Probably Gretchen had taken it out once he'd gone, taken it out with great care and toweled the pages dry, making sure it was a book again. No. More than likely she'd gone around and bought a dry copy. It was in a lot of stores, she wouldn't have any trouble finding it. Probably it was in her room, by her bedside table, maybe, or across the room where she could see the cover before she slept.

Chub slipped into the shallow end. The water was very warm and felt healing. He'd been a good swimmer ever since he had first learned; now he pushed off, doing a slow, well-formed crawl. And was astonished to find he could barely cover the twenty yards to the other end. He rested in the deep water, holding to the edge, till he got his breath back. Then he pushed off, only got halfway.

The next day he was the only one in the pool again when he arrived and he hesitated a long time before giving it a shot. This time he made the first length without terrible fatigue and didn't pause, almost making it back to where he'd started before his strength gave out.

The third day the fat lady was in her spot at the desk and the kid lifeguard was reading *Playboy* but Tom was late. Chub undressed, went down to the water. There was someone already in the pool, a women doing a breast-stroke, her black hair piled high. She wore dark sunglass-es, which is what first made Chub study her. She was probably mid-sixties, and her head didn't bob much as she swam. Chub thought, as he watched, that he knew her from someplace, Athens maybe, maybe Oberlin. Then he realized he didn't know her, she just looked familiar.

She looked like Hedy Lamarr grown old.

Chub got in the water, swam up and back, the entire forty yards without stopping. Pleased, he decided to make it all the way to a hundred before he left for the day. But he was breathing heavily, so he got out of the pool and rested in the chair, his eyes half closed.

When the woman who looked like Hedy Lamarr was done, Chub watched her leave. She was thin and tan, but her skin was wrinkled with age. He waited a little longer, tried another forty, almost made it. Then he rested again, did a final twenty without as much effort as he feared. He grabbed his towel, went to the men's locker room and before he was inside, Tom was on him: "Didja see her?— the one day the fucking subway's late and I miss her— Hedy Lamarr was here, *shit*." Chub went to his locker, took off his wet suit, started for the shower. Tom, almost in a frenzy, followed along. "*Ecstasy*. I saw that three times. She swam on her back and she didn't have a top on. Greatest little tits in all the world *and I missed her*."

Chub looked at the old guy. Tom must have been close to seventy. He was in good shape for his age but the way he was going on now couldn't have been good for a young man's heart.

"Easy," Chub told him. "Maybe she'll come back tomorrow."

He showered and when he was done Tom was standing outside the stall. "Goddamn right she'll come back tomorrow—hell, who goes to a place only once? This is a good place, you like it, don't you?"

"Excellent," Chub said, moving past him to where the hair dryer hung on a hook.

"I keep it clean, don't I? Goddamn right. You know what I'm gonna do?"

Chub turned on the hair dryer, shook his head.

Tom's voice rose to compensate for the noise of the machine. "I'm gonna swat her right on the ass—friendly like, nothing crude. Them movie stars, they like a gentleman, everyone's all the time after them. And then, once we've struck up a good conversation, I'm—" He shook his head now. "I can see her tits in that water. The best. Do you think I should tell her that?"

Over the dryer Chub said, "Well, probably you'll have to see how the conversation's going."

"Right. I'll get her talking good and once that's over, I'll take her out to dinner, someplace not too fancy—them movie stars, they get sick of always going someplace fancy," and when Chub's hair was dry Tom followed him to his locker, talking about Hedy Lamarr and while Chub dressed, Tom talked on, but Chub was hurrying now, anxious to get home, because the impulse was on him and as soon as he got back to Ninety-eighth Street he rolled some paper into his machine and began to fiddle.

--great story idea--

--the last little while spent talking about where this attendant should take Hedy Lamarr for dinner.

```
suggested Yorkville, she's German, he went ba-
nanas.

what if she comes back tomorrow and it turns out she
isn't Hedy Lamarr--

  no, no,

what if she is--
and he asks her out and

and she won't give him the time of day--

  no, no

maybe she says yes and
  and what?

HE STILL THINKS SHE'S TWENTY.
```

Chub stopped, stared at the scratch paper awhile.

```
so? so what if he still thinks she's twenty?
well?
well . . .
```

He got up, went into the bedroom, lay down, turned on
the television. The soaps were on. Chub flicked from
station to station. Boring, boring, boring. The next thing
he knew it was an hour later. He must have napped.
Whipped from the swimming. He got up, went to his
desk again, read what he'd written.

```
odd.
looks like sludge.
boring, boring.
```

He ripped the paper out of the machine, pitched it into
his wastebasket—two points—lay down again. It wasn't
a great story idea. Besides, Updike did it better in "The
Persistence of Desire." And besides besides, what the hell

was he doing messing with a short story when he had a novel working?

The problem was energy. Energy and concentration. He wasn't strong enough yet. But if he couldn't sit down and whip off pages, at least he could research, and Chub did. He found a lot of articles on the whys of people starting boozing and two books were helpful and he got a doctor on the phone who specialized in the problem and they talked for fifteen minutes.

But best of all was the COA.

There were maybe a dozen sitting around the table when Chub slipped in and sat quietly down; all were children of alcoholics and the sense of shared pasts, shared griefs, was unmistakable. They were of varying ages, some of them drank coffee out of containers, most of them smoked.

Chub was the only one with an eye patch but he'd gotten not to mind it anymore. As he glanced out at the early February sun, he realized the eye patch gave him a glamour he'd never possessed before. He had panache now, like Burt Lancaster in *The Crimson Pirate,* one of his all-time favorite flicks. He took out a pen and paper; he had no intention of talking, just wanted to take notes. At three precisely the leader said, "My name is Ross and I'm the son of an alcoholic." He was a fine-looking mustachioed man, twinkling-eyed, and he gestured toward the person to his left, and they went around the table:

"Frank."

"Ruth."

"Judy."

"Ilene."

"Ed."

"Pete."

"Chub."

"Bill."

"Dave."

"Stevie."

A girl raised her hand then and the leader nodded toward her.

"My name is Ilene and this is my first meeting, so probably I shouldn't talk—" She was going very rapidly.

"All the time you want," the leader said.

"—well, my mother was an alcoholic and it was— what I wondered I guess was this: Nobody knew that she drank, it was all kept inside the family and is that unusual or not?"

Half the people at the table burst out laughing.

"I think you can tell from the response," the leader said, "what the answer is. It's like there's an elephant sitting in the corner of the living room but nobody will acknowledge that it's there."

"Elephant in the living room," Chub scribbled down. Christ, what a phrase. Maybe it was good enough for a chapter title. Damn right it was.

The next two hours zipped. The only problem was he hadn't brought enough paper along, there was that much wonderful stuff.

Even better, though, was when the meeting broke at five. It had taken place in a church basement and the leader had to put the chairs back against the wall. Chub helped him. "The eye patch is new," the leader said.

Chub didn't get it.

"Aren't you the author of *Under the Weather?* I took the hardcover out of the library. Your picture was on the back."

Chub nodded. (Two-Brew had insisted on taking the photo and Chub thought he was barely recognizable but Two-Brew, claiming he could be Karsh of Ottawa if he so desired, blasted him by saying the only people more ego-drenched than actors and politicians were feebleminded authors.)

"You're a wonderful writer," the leader said then. "I read it through twice."

They parted outside and when Chub was alone he looked at his notes, then executed a dazzling thrust and parry—Burt Lancaster threw down his sword and begged for mercy.

The leader this time was an older woman, very thin; her name was Ruth and both her parents were alcoholics. She gestured around the table.

Chub sat in the church basement, staring at the cold February sun; no note paper this time. His stomach was tight, tight with anger at himself for coming, for wasting two precious hours.

"Ilene."

"Bill."

"Donna."

"Mike."

"Debby."

Pause. Finally the leader said, with a smile, "If you wouldn't mind."

"Sorry," Chub said. "Wasn't thinking. No. I mean I was thinking, I just wasn't thinking about here. Chub."

"Jenny."

"Brett."

"Susanna."

"Clarence."

Then a woman raised a hand and spoke about the bad week she was having, she'd just broken up with her boyfriend and she got all choked up until the leader said the important thing was that she'd be fine, she was here, one day at a time was what you had to remember and then another woman raised her hand and she'd had a bad week, too, she'd lost her job and was it her fault or not, she wasn't sure and could she hold out.

Chub, listening a little, realized that this Children of Alcoholics meeting was different—most of those present were alcoholics themselves. Recovering alcoholics. Trying to stay that way.

Chub glanced at his watch. Half past two. Ninety minutes to go. Could he last it? He didn't have to stay, he knew it was an asshole move before he got there. But it would be rude, just taking off now. He could trip off for ninety minutes. He had no intention of speaking, so he could wander wherever his mind wanted.

At five of four he was stunned to see his right hand rise.

"Yes?" the leader said.

"I haven't had a bad week or anything, so I guess I shouldn't be going on like this—I'm not going on actually, am I?—I mean, I've just started."

"We have time," the leader said. "We can run a few minutes over."

"I guess I just had this question is all. Actually, it's not a question." He paused. "Then again, maybe it is."

"Please," the leader said. "Don't feel pressured."

"I don't."

"You don't have to."

Chub nodded.

Everyone was watching him.

"Okay, I'm writing this novel about my father—he didn't hit the bottle bad till after the war and I'm having a little trouble easing into that part—no big deal, but I wish it was going a little quicker is all and I wondered if anyone else ever had kind of the same trouble and how they got through it."

"How long have you been having trouble?" the leader asked.

Chub shrugged. "Maybe since the pneumonia."

"I'm sorry, the what?"

"I had this weird pneumonia two years ago and since around then it's been slow going."

"You haven't written in two years?" the leader asked.

Chub smiled. "No, nothing like that; I mean I've started a couple other novels and they're cooking and just last week I went over a story of mine—it's a nutty idea about how this astronomer discovers Heaven behind Pluto—Pluto or Mars, one or the other, it doesn't matter—the kicker is another astronomer discovers it isn't Heaven out there, it's Hell. It was always too cute before but now I've got it right."

"Is this your first writing?" the leader asked.

"Oh, hell no, I had a book of stories published four years back, it was called—" *Stop,* he told himself. If you tell them the title they'll know who you are. They might. One of them might. One hundred thousand copies.

"The reason I asked," the leader said, "was that I wondered what suggestions your editor has given you."

Chub laughed. "We've got this special relationship and I want my book to be a surprise to him—I just want to drop the whole goddamn thing on his desk some morning out of the blue and watch his face."

"You haven't told him then."

"Right."

"Why don't you talk it out with him? I don't think keeping secrets does anyone much good."

Chub couldn't believe it. "Secrets? Who the hell said anything about secrets? It's a surprise, I told you, *can't you fucking tell the difference between a secret and a surprise?*" They were all staring at him now, and Chub said, "I'm sorry, I really am," and then he stood and took off out the door, grabbing the first subway for Queens, where he picked up his taxi. He'd been driving a cab most nights for the past twenty months now, ever since his money had run out; Gretchen had died about that time and he told Two-Brew and Lydia that he'd fallen into a terrific inheritance because they knew how big his advance had been and had to be wondering what he was living on now. Driving a cab wasn't bad, it kept the days free for work and as he pulled out of his garage he got a ride from three blue-haired ladies who wanted to go into Manhattan to see Streisand in *A Star Is Born.*

They tried to be friendly but he wasn't in the mood—traffic was murder coming over the bridge and more than that, how could he have shot off his mouth back in the church? Well, really he hadn't, and if anyone recognized him, he'd just say it was gathering material, material for his book.

He dropped the ladies behind Bloomingdale's and they stiffed him on the tip but you had to expect that when you picked up women with blue hair. Traffic was a bitch all over—it was Friday night—and he almost got into a fight with some jerk from Jersey who tried pulling a right from the left lane. At seven-fifteen he picked up some out-of-towners who were heading for *Annie,* a bigger hit now than even *Chorus Line,* and at Fifty-second he told them they'd get there faster if he didn't have to turn in but could just let them off on Eighth, but they didn't trust him, they thought he was pulling something, so they said no, no we want the theatre and Chub cursing to himself turned into Fifty-second.

Gridlock.

After five minutes they said maybe it would be quicker so they got out, leaving him trapped for twenty minutes on Fifty-second Street, which didn't do a lot for his mood.

Maybe because of his mood he picked up the three black guys. Badly dressed, drunk, and they wanted Harlem, a side street off Lenox and a lot of drivers carried baseball bats when they worked nights and Chub wished, as he drove uptown, that he had something to protect himself except it turned out he didn't need anything—they paid when they got to the building they wanted and they tipped him plenty and he had almost forgiven himself for his behavior at the meeting when he stopped at eleven in front of the Waldorf, where a bunch of couples were waiting in line for cabs. The first couple got in—a young guy, swinger type, with a girl he knew he was going to score with, you could tell that before the door was even closed and Chub was about to pull off when he heard his name called—

—and Paige Kitchel, standing with some guy, was knocking at his closed front window.

"Hey, Paige, great," Chub said, rolling down the window, throwing on a smile. "Just be a sec," he told the swinger in the back. "Old friend."

Paige Kitchel of course was no friend. Her name wasn't Paige Kitchel anymore—she'd gotten married awhile back, then gotten divorced. But "old" was valid.

The last job she'd had done on her face had been too tight; she was thirty, looked forty, and all resemblance to Natalie Wood was gone.

"Very fancy car," she said.

"Oh, this," Chub laughed. "Just gathering material. My father drove a cab awhile after the war, so I wanted to be able to feel it before I wrote about it."

"Um-hmm," Paige said.

Chub raced on. " 'Course, that was in Chicago and this is New York but what the hell, I figured the job's the same no matter where."

"Um-hmm," Paige said again.

"Can we get a move on?" the swinger in the back said.

"Yes, *sir,*" Chub said. He looked at Paige. "Gotta scoot."

She laughed a little.

Chub started to reach for her then, reach for her and say, "Please don't tell Two-Brew," but there was no point. She hadn't believed a thing he'd told her and even if he begged, there was no way she wasn't going to call her brother with the glorious news.

The only question was when.

It was early afternoon the next day when he heard the answer. Slow sounds on the stairs. Crutch sounds. He went to the door, opened it slightly. He could hear the exertion as Kitchel mounted the ninety-seven stairs. Probably his crutches were digging hard into the soft area under his arms. It seemed that every half floor there was a pause. Chub started to call out, decided against it, decided to leave his door ajar and he did, heading for his desk, slipping a piece of scratch paper into the roller, pausing, taking it out, pitching it toward the wastebasket.

Perfect.

"The buzzer didn't work," Two-Brew said, pale and exhausted, leaning in the doorway.

"Never does."

"But the door was unlocked."

"Always is. Want some coffee?"

"I didn't come for coffee. Paige called me last night."

"Was that a fantastic coincidence? My third time driving a cab and I run into someone I know."

" 'Guess what your genius is doing?' she said. Many times over."

Chub shrugged. "Gathering material is all, like I told her."

"What is my genius doing?"

"See, my father drove a cab and I figured—"

"*Can it!* My secretary's spent the morning on the phone with the Taxi and Limousine Commission. You've been 'gathering material' for over a year and a half."

"I gotta eat, right?"

"And the money from your mother?"

"Didn't last."

"Was there any?"

"Not as much as I thought."

Two-Brew came inside, closed the door. "Are you lying?"

"If it makes you happy to think so."

"It doesn't make me happy. Chub, what the hell have you been doing?"

"What the hell do you think—writing my ass off."

"Last month at dinner you told us you were eight hundred pages plus and your father was in the ground. The funeral scene was the best thing you've ever done. Could I see it?"

Chub shook his head. "Not till it's reworked and smooth."

Two-Brew held out his hand. "I won't read it. I promise. Just let me hold it."

Finally, Chub said, "I'm not quite there. That was kind of a fib. What I should have said was it's going to be the best thing I've ever done."

"Let me see the book."

"No. I've never let you see anything till it was done and I'm not going to change things now, not the great way we've been going."

Two-Brew sat heavily by the desk. "Enough with the games. I'm not leaving until you show me what you've done and we both know that so give me the goddamn thing."

"Not in the mood you're in."

Two-Brew shook his head. "I don't know what mood I'm in. I just know you're going to show it to me."

Chub got up suddenly, went to the bathroom to put some water on his face. "It's in the top drawer, you arrogant son of a bitch." When he came back, Two-Brew was holding *The Dead Pile*.

"Three hundred eighty-two pages is very impressive," Kitchel said. "It seems to me that's where you were on the night of my engagement. What the fuck's been going on?"

"I've been writing—writing, just like I said—I put it aside is all—I've got two other novels and they're cooking like crazy."

"What are they?"

"They're not done or anything, but they're terrific. One's about this guy who writes obituaries—I read about a guy who does obits for the *Times* and he goes around and visits people who are old and sick, just getting the record straight, and he goes to Chicago to interview this financier and strange things begin happening because— and here's the kicker—see, the financier's family has just poisoned him before he changed his will and they can't risk being discovered."

"And the other?"

"It's even better, Two-Brew—I swear—see, it's about this actor who can't cut it in New York and he finally decides to leave, there's this shitty deli owner who's always been a prick to him, so just as a gesture—like a symbolic farewell to the city—he breaks the glass front of the store and steals some stuff, nothing valuable, he's not in it for gain, it's like I said a symbol and he gets home to his crummy cold-water flat and—and here's the kicker— *he loves it.* So he begins doing other robberies, only what makes it great is he uses all his actor's skill, voice changes, makeup, and he begins getting written about in the papers—*he's a star.*"

"Where are they?"

Chub's voice got louder. "Right here, bastard, right here," and he shoved two folders over. "I've got thirty pages on the one and almost forty on the other."

"May I read them?"

"I don't care what you do," Chub said, and he went into the bedroom and lay down and tried to watch the tube while Two-Brew read in the next room, only his stomach was bad, worse than at the COA meeting, so he closed his eyes and wondered which of them Kitchel would like the most, because they were good, not perfect maybe, but he'd slave at them until he got them right.

From the next room, Two-Brew said, "I'm done."

Chub looked at his watch. Not an hour had gone by. "I don't like you speed-reading my stuff."

"I didn't. They're very skillful."

"Goddamn right."

"Skillful and slick and shitty and there's not an ounce of you anywhere in them."

"That's not true."

"I didn't like saying it."

"Oh, sure you did—you like pissing on people, it makes you feel so goddamn smart—"

And then Two-Brew was standing: "Christ, Chub, it's me, what's happened?"

And Chub never knew what, the look on Kitchel's face, the sadness in his tone, but suddenly he knew he had to let it out, let it all pour out, and he said, "I—" don't know, he almost finished. "I—" just know that it's bad, he almost said. "I—" need to talk, I really do, I need so goddamn much, *and you can help me,* so he reached out his hands to Kitchel, stretched them as far as they'd go.

Two-Brew began shouting at him then—backing away and shouting: "Listen to you—'I—I—I'—that's all you give a shit about is 'I.' Look at you—whining about yourself. *What about me?* I brought you here! It was your goddamn dream and I made it happen! I got you published! I did all that and you betray me!"

"—I didn't—I swear—"

"—lies—for two years, lies—"

"—I didn't betray you, I only wanted it to be a surprise, I swear—"

"—you succeeded—betrayal always comes as a surprise—"

"—don't say any more—please—"

"—you have my word on that—" He worked his way to the door, threw it open, whirled. "I trusted you and in my world, there is no sin worse than betraying a friend and I promise it will be a long time before we ever speak again."

And it was. And it was.

Chub was done with his first bottle of Wild Turkey by suppertime and that got him through the night and the next bottle got him through the next night and probably it was the day after that when he was drinking his breakfast that the phone rang and it was Andrew Cheyney calling from Oberlin, asking a favor, because he was late on his book of Kafka papers and would Chub possibly consider taking over his writing class this semester, just this one semester, the money wasn't all that much and he didn't want to interrupt Chub's novel but Chub had done so well writing at Oberlin before that perhaps he could thrive again and Chub realized, even drunk in the morning, that a life preserver was being pitched his way, because it had gone well at Oberlin and it couldn't go worse than here so he managed to interrupt and say, "Yes," and "Yes," and "Yes, I'll come right away," and he did, locking up his apartment, packing what clothes he had, heading back, back to where it had all begun so beautifully, with perfect B. J. Peacock coming down the stairs. . . .

CHAPTER 2

Shaw

Before the end of his first afternoon back, Chub was pleasantly stunned to find himself sharing his bed again with Patty McLean.

Professor Cheyney had picked him up at the Cleveland Airport, driven him to the college. First Cheyney took him to a large room on the top floor of Westervelt Hall and asked if this would do for an office. It was bright, with a desk and typewriter in one corner, a large round table in the center where the writing class would be held. Cheyney was solicitous; was this satisfactory? Chub said more than.

Next Cheyney took him to a lovely suite of rooms he'd engaged tentatively for the semester. It was the ground floor of a large house on the north side of town, on a quiet street, just two houses away from the home that Cheyney shared with Durning, the librarian. Were the rooms all right? Chub said palatial. Cheyney, still the small dynamo he'd been when Chub first asked admittance into his class, left him then, adding that he and Durning would have Chub to dinner soon. Durning still remembered Chub's years in the library and referred to him fondly as the first freshman who knew of the existence of Sheehy.

Alone, Chub unpacked, went out to the front porch and stood in the February wind and contemplated renting a bicycle. Everyone at Oberlin used them, and Chub had, too, until Kitchel entered his life, but that was then.

And while he was on the porch, a familiar-looking figure pedaled by, saw him, shouted, "Chub," wheeled her way to the steps and then ran up into his arms. Chub held her, embarrassed almost because they had been intimate for over a year and so much of her was gone from his memory. He told her what he was doing there and she explained that she was almost finished with her dissertation in psych at Ohio State and that she worked as a shrink here in town for the many college students that needed gentling. He showed her his rooms and she looked at her watch and then her coat was off and he never made the first move with a woman, couldn't imagine that he ever would, what if he'd misread things, who needed that?

When they were in bed he decided he hadn't misread things. The first time he kissed her breasts she almost giggled and he remembered that that was one of Patty's ways, her breasts were ticklish, so he concentrated on the rest of her and it was a splendid homecoming.

Chub caressed her tenderly, running his hands through her curly brown hair, touching his fingertips to her skin, and when she laughed he said, "Sorry," because he figured he was coming too close to her breasts again.

"It wasn't you, I was remembering something, my speed-writing book. I taught myself speed-writing the summer after our freshman year and I was home in Columbus and my father's boss needed a temporary secretary for a week while his regular girl went on holiday. I campaigned for the job—I could type and answer the phone and with speed-writing under my belt I figured I'd be perfect. Dad set it up for me.

"His boss was this terrifying authority figure—I was scared to death of old Mr. Kron, but when I went to work the first day I hid all that and did great and after lunch he asked me in for dictation and I got up all bright and shiny with my yellow Ticonderoga and pad and I sat across the desk and he said was I ready and I nodded and he started, you know, name, address, all that stuff, and he wasn't half a paragraph past the salutation when I realized—*I couldn't do it.* I'd never taken a letter before, I'd only practiced from the book and I thought should I interrupt him but I didn't have the guts, so I figured after he was done with the letter I'd go out and try and reconstruct it from memory. Only he didn't stop with one. He dictated *nineteen* letters, it took an hour and then some and I just sat there nodding and doodling and trying to figure out the best way to kill myself. Finally he said that that would be all so I thanked him and went outside and kept right on walking. Never went back. I cried for more than a week after, thinking my father was sure to be fired, but he wasn't and I lived." She kissed Chub on the mouth, then lay back. "Second biggest error of my life." There was a pause before she said, "Even you have to be interested in what the biggest was."

"I am, I definitely am," Chub said, wondering what the "even you" part meant. He liked the anecdote; it was sweet material.

"Never telling you straight out how I felt," Patty said then.

"Felt about what?"

"Same old Chub—*you,* jerk. I just adored you so."

Chub looked at her. "We were comfortable was all."

"That's what you thought. If you thought. I don't think I ever made a dent on your memory all our time together. You weren't even sure who I was on the bicycle outside."

"Wrong and wrong. I knew who you were the second I saw you and I remember every date we had, damn near."

"Don't look now, but a lightning bolt is headed in your direction." He started to sit.

She held him, brought him back down. "And the reason it was the greatest error was not because I thought you'd swoon and propose—but because I cared for you so and you were in such trouble and I knew it and I never faced you with it. It would have been good if someone had. You seem so open and look so kind and you're the bestest good boy in all the world—that, I suspect is your ambition, anyway—and you never talk to anybody about anything."

"Sure I do."

"Not in this life."

This time Chub did sit on the side of the bed. "Look— I know you're this genius shrink and everything and I'm proud of you, but save it for your patients, all right?"

Patty sat on the other side of the bed. "Okay. But at least I said it now." She began to dress. "How bad are things?"

"Why do you even ask a question like that?"

"Because it's so obvious—why the hell else would you be back here?"

"Because I've always wanted to teach, you know that, and the timing was perfect."

"Here comes another lightning bolt."

"I'm sorry if it pains you to be wrong with your analysis, but things are going great with me."

"I'm glad I'm wrong." She hooked her bra, smiled at him. "Dan and I would love to have you for dinner while you're here. Dan . . . pause for effect . . . is my husband. For three years. He's a professor in the science department."

Chub's eyes flicked toward the rumpled sheets.

"Things are going great for us too," Patty said.

"I can't make you writers," Chub began, looking around at the undergraduates, young people sitting around the large table in his office. "I don't think anyone can make you writers. All I can do is make you write."

Heads nodded. They were watching him with such intensity and it was difficult for him, because he knew he was their ambition.

"When I was in high school I heard an old expression: 'Want to be a writer?—write a million words.' Since we only have these few weeks together you will be pleased to learn, I suspect, that you will not reach that goal this semester."

Light laughter now, along with the intensity.

"I've cleared all this with Professor Cheyney and here's the drill: You will write one page a day. Seven pages a week. And I'll meet with you privately for an hour and discuss what you've done. Class time will be spent in discussing the work of major storytellers. Any questions so far?"

A thin girl raised her hand. "I heard that when Professor Cheyney taught this he read our work out loud."

"I've heard that too," Chub said. "But this semester we will discuss the masters in public and your own work in private. I hope that's satisfactory."

It was.

"One last important note of business: There will be no grades—this is purely a pass/fail course. All you have to do is meet the writing requirement and you survive. I want the pressure off you, I want you to feel free to doodle or experiment or tell me the secrets of your heart. There is no way that I can see—since this is a course you all elected to take—that any of you cannot pass. I hope that's satisfactory too."

It definitely was.

"Okay—I'd just like to ask who your favorites are so we can discuss them here—I hope none of you are passionate about Melville's shorter efforts and I also—"

"*Late!*" boomed from the doorway.

Chub looked around toward the giant figure moving into the room. Six three, six four, probably two hundred solid pounds at least. "You're all late since I am always early." He sat across from Chub. "Now that I'm here, we may commence."

"Cool it, Hungerford," one of the boys said.

Chub, watching as Hungerford gave the guy the finger, knew he was in the presence of someone trying very hard to be a road company Kitchel. "I'm Peter Hungerford," the giant said, looking at Chub. "Who the hell are you?"

Chub almost smiled, picked up his train of thought. "Who would you like to discuss in class?" he said. "Who do you admire?"

Hungerford's hand shot up. "There's one book that's changed my life. I don't just think it's the best book of the decade, I think it's the greatest work of the century. And the name of the masterpiece is *Under the Weather*."

Chub sighed. "Hungerford—you missed the beginning but this is a course you can't fail so there's no need for brown-nosing."

"Ah, well, then, let me make one slight amendment to what I've said. I thought *Under the Weather* sucked, and not only that, I didn't read it."

Chub broke out laughing; at least life wouldn't be dull.

The letter from Kitchel contained no salutation:

Please read this through.

My behavior was unconscionable and I do not ask forgiveness. I just want to try and explain.

Chub, do you remember when I first sought you out in the library freshman year? Because you knew the bartender at the No-Name? That was true—you did know him—but it was at the same time false—I'm sure the event would have transpired anyway.

I didn't want your contacts, I wanted *you*. I'd watched you those first weeks and the way people responded. People like you, you see; probably you don't even know that or want to know that but it was and is gospel.

I grew up as this embarrassment—do you know why my first name is what it is? Because my father admired a great fighter named Stanley Ketchel. He already had a daughter and now he wanted a *son*, with all the manliness implied.

Well, after my glorious bout with polio, that was out and I was left to live through his disappointment.

Once I realized, once grammar school started and I realized I was a thing to be avoided, I decided to attack, to make all the little shits avoid me. And I was immaculately successful.

Then, in the Cheyney class when I realized that you were not just someone I coveted but someone with your gift, you became a gift to me. If you hadn't come to me with your stories, I would have found reason to come to you.

The fact that you survived your childhood and still had strength—I needed to be near that fire. I'm twenty-seven years old and you're the first friend I've ever had, not counting Lydia and that was in no small part your doing.

So why did I behave as I did in your apartment? Because, you see, I *need* you. I need to have you to rely on. And when you began to come apart before me—when *you* reached out to *me* with your needs, it was more pressure than I could bear.

You weren't *supposed* to need anybody. I was the only one allowed that.

I've been writing this letter for ten days, over and over, and the only reason I'm sending it now is because I realize I'll never get it right. Christ, you didn't betray anybody, I did it all.

When I think of the anguish you must have gone through these last two years—humiliation so deep you couldn't even speak of it, not even to me—

—I simply could not face it. I did not have the strength to be your rock. That wasn't our deal—you were supposed to be mine. Except, of course, you never knew we had a deal.

After I left your apartment, I told Lydia what I'd done and like the great good wife she is, she listened with perfect attention. Then she said that, knowing you as she does, she was sure you would eventually forgive me. Then she added she wasn't so sure that *she* would.

She has. One down and one to go.

Don't answer this. But when you get back to the city if
you give me a buzz, I promise my secretary won't put
you on hold.

One final note: In case it has escaped your woefully
underdeveloped mind, this was sort of kind of meant
to be an apology.

K.

Chub didn't answer the letter, but the week after it
came, he was having coffee in the Campus and a beautiful
young high school girl was sitting alone, reading some
literature about the college. Obviously, a prospective
freshman. A professor of history with a very fat wife
stopped briefly by the girl and asked if her last name was
Henderson. She nodded. The professor said four words:
"I knew your mother." And then the girl was alone
again.

As Chub eavesdropped, he felt such weight in those
words and he knew, or imagined he knew, that the
professor had not just known the girl's mother but had
loved her too. And as he watched the professor's wife
waddle toward the exit door, he paid and went to his
office and wrote a little sketch, called it "I Knew Your
Mother."

The next day, between meetings with students, he
remembered Patty's dictation anecdote so he wrote that,
too, six pages, mainly dealing with the mind of the
terrified girl as she catalogued possible ways to end her
life, beginning small and building to a public execution
with the man she had taken dictation from being in
charge of the guillotine.

If it was anything, it was hopefully sweet, no more, but
he wrote and rewrote it several times, the same with the
professor and his lost love, and sent them off to Kitchel.
They weren't much, but at least they were his, and Two-
Brew would know that things were the way they had
been between them.

Kitchel's answer came in a few days, a solid page single-spaced, and it began with this: "I'm not sure if these are the best things you've ever done, but I'm not sure they're not. There's a maturity here—you've always understood sadness but I don't think this deeply (speaking of the prof and the young girl). And the dictation piece is just a wonder—I roared when I read it and I don't do that a lot, trust me, and . . ."

And Chub, stunned, read the words, the well-intended lies, but halfway through the page he crumpled it and threw it away. All the while thinking only this: Jesus God, I've slipped back that far.

That very night he decided to seek out Dr. Wallinsky. Except he wasn't at the No-Name and the bartender didn't have much clue as to whom Chub was talking about. But Chub kept asking until somebody told him Wallinsky had moved away and somebody else said no, he hadn't moved, he'd died.

Chub went to the wall phone in the back and picked up the directory beneath it and there was the name, Felix Wallinsky, on Prospect, and Chub thought about calling, decided the walk would do him good, and when he reached the right number he rang the bell and an old woman opened the door. Chub asked if Dr. Wallinsky was in.

"What'cha want him for?"

Chub explained that they'd known each other in his student days.

"Third floor on the right," she said. "Just follow your nose."

Chub understood what she meant as soon as he reached the third-floor landing and turned right. There was an odor, growing stronger as he approached and knocked softly. "It's Charles Fuller," Chub said.

There seemed to be a sound from inside so Chub turned the knob; the door was unlocked. He stepped in. Whether the smell was one of liquor or decay or a mixture of both Chub was never sure. But clearly, the old man on the bed, stomach swollen like a woman soon to birth, was dying. The wall light was on, the bulb weak, but Chub could see the yellow skin.

The room—with one exception—was in chaos. But the exception was so strong Chub went to it. A glass case, with a dozen or so books inside, all preserved in clear plastic covers. *Language as an Act of Faith* by Felix Wallinsky. Published by Yale University Press. There was one copy of the American edition, one of the English, and the rest were translations into other languages. Chub carefully opened the case, took out the original, looked at the young author in the photo. He put the book back, brought a chair to the bed, sat down.

"I just was walking by, sir, and I thought I might pay my respects. I worked at the No-Name one summer."

Dr. Wallinsky moved his eyes toward Chub, breathed.

"Charles Fuller? People called me 'Chub'?"

The eyes were very dim.

"There was a beer-drinking contest when I was a freshman. I was kind of helping. You were there."

Now a flicker: ". . . the best night . . ."

"It sure was, yessir. I'm back here teaching this semester and I wondered how things were going with you."

". . . two . . ."

Chub nodded. "That is right, Kitchel quit after two."

Dr. Wallinsky closed his eyes for a time then, concentrating very hard on breathing.

Chub sat with him.

After a while, Dr. Wallinsky said, ". . . two . . ." again.

Chub waited for a long time.

Just breathing from the bed now.

Chub turned out the wall light, found his way back to the chair and started to talk, first about Dr. Wallinsky's book and then about Roth, the *Call It Sleep* guy, and Harper Lee with her evocative *To Kill a Mockingbird*, and there was nothing wrong with being a one-book wonder, it was really kind of a distinguished tribe, after all, how many people could say even once they'd given pleasure and Chub had done that, he had the letters from college kids safe back in his apartment in a box some-

where. And in a way he was lucky that the pneumonia
had sideswiped him, had taken his energy and impulse
away, because if it hadn't, everybody would have known
what he knew, that he was just a kid on a lucky streak, a
fluke and a fraud, and that Two-Brew was the talent, the
real talent, Two-Brew was the one who'd seen how to
make a book out of the stories and so, Chub ended up,
the fact was that what he really ought to do was count his
blessings.

". . . best night . . ." Dr. Wallinsky said.

Chub agreed, turned the light back on, said good-bye
and walked back to his place. He felt, no question, really
good about the evening. It was nice to see Wallinsky
again but more than that, he had made Patty McLean
out to be wrong in what she had said about him: When
he *really* needed to talk to someone, he could do it easily.
It wasn't a problem at all.

If he had a problem it was just getting through the rest
of the semester. He had hoped his return would help him
breathe again, renew stirrings. But he was just an outsid-
er, not really accepted by the students or the faculty—too
old for one, too young for the other.

Patty dropped by his house the second week of his stay
and it was clear what was on her mind, but she was
married and "bestest good boys"—her phrase for him—
didn't do that kind of thing, only they did, twice a week,
skillfully, but there wasn't much mirth in the room.

Chub became obsessed with his students. Or he tried
very hard, but they were an odd group, sombre, well
grounded in the basics, but none possessed flights of
fancy. Any number of stories by the boys in his class
began with sentences like "After it was over, he rolled up
on one elbow and looked at her." The girls tended to
write *New Yorker*–type stuff—the kind of story where a
couple would have a walk in Venice and then sip a *citron
pressé* and not talk and then an insect would crawl across
the table and the girl would "understand."

Hungerford wrote about nothing at all. He was obviously a goof-off, in college undoubtedly because of parental pressure. His pages always had incredibly wide margins and they were obviously slapdash fragments, one about butterflies and weren't they pretty—that was his best effort. Chub's hourly meetings with Hungerford rarely took twenty minutes. The giant didn't say much, kept calling Chub "pal" and looking at his watch.

At last, in typical Oberlin weather—steady rain—May marched in. School was over before the final week and Chub was packed a week before school was over. He'd made it. Or almost. Because Hungerford had the flu with two weeks to go and handed in nothing and the next week he had "these vicious allergies" and couldn't begin to think and Chub, with the last days coming up fast, dropped a note in his mailbox saying that twenty-one pages were needed by that Friday or Hungerford would have a lot to answer for.

On the stated morning, Chub arrived in his office for his last day and shoved in the box outside was a twenty-five-page wide-margined beautifully typed piece of work entitled "Saturday's Child."

Gratefully, Chub sat down and began to read. The hero of the story, Chris, was a football hero at Oberlin who had run for eighty yards and a touchdown his sophomore year, assuring Oberlin of its first conference championship in history. Chris's girl friend, Lou, slept with him for the first time that night. She was rich but he was the golden boy until an injury to his knee in practice junior year ended his athletic career but he was still the golden boy. They married after graduation and Chris went to work for Lou's father's business, but things didn't go well.

Halfway through the story, Chub began to feel sick.

Chris and Lou's marriage held, but as his life began to slip away, hers built. She became a decorator and a successful one and then there were other men after her but she remained faithful. Then, fifteen years after graduation, Chris, a two-bit salesman now, happened to be back at Oberlin and he wandered alone on a spring day to the empty football field and before he knew it, his memories had him, and he stood on the twenty-yard line as an imaginary football came into his arms and then he repeated his magical run, eighty yards alone on the grass, scoring for the championship. It was only after he had done the act that he noticed a couple of undergraduates in the stands, staring at him. "Once I played here," Chris managed to say, and then, sweating, finished forever, he walked away.

Alone in his office, Chub wanted to walk away. His plane would leave the next day but his instinct was to change that, just get the hell to Cleveland Airport and stand by for the next plane to New York.

He sat back at his desk and studied the story again. It was by far the best writing Hungerford had ever tried; there were stylish phrases reminiscent of Irwin Shaw. But then, that shouldn't have been surprising. Because what Chub was reading had been written by Irwin Shaw: "The Eighty-Yard Run."

Hungerford had handed in a piece of plagiarism.

If you subscribed to Murphy's Law, as Chub had come to, if you truly believed that everything that could go wrong would, it didn't make much for an optimistic outlook on life, but at least it braced you against disaster.

Chub was not braced for this.

He pushed the story away, rested his head in his hands, trying, trying desperately, to think. The whole reason he had handled the grades of the course the way he had was so that he would never have to fail anybody. But if you're a soldier, the worst sin is cowardice, and if you believe in the printed word, plagiarism takes precedence.

Chub sat without moving, trying to figure what would be best, what action, but then in his mind he saw a mirror and he was remembering a terrible murderer in Chicago who used to scrawl "Stop me before I kill more" on the mirrors of his victims.

Chub realized then that it wasn't just plagiarism, it was worse than plagiarism, it was a cry for help. Hungerford wanted to get caught. He must have wanted to get caught. If you were going to copy something, well, Chub was reasonably well read—so steal something slight from Camus, or pick anything from any issue of *Playboy* and he never would have known.

But don't crib Irwin Shaw. He loved Shaw, the class all knew that, he'd told them, he'd spent two weeks discussing "The Girls in Their Summer Dresses."

Hungerford was obviously a very disturbed young man. Just how fucked up, Chub had no way of knowing, but he knew that he had to find out.

He left his office and went to the library, where old Durning was, as ever, at his main post. Durning smiled as Chub approached, saying, "You've decided to come back and save me, I accept."

Chub kind of smiled, shook his head. "I need a big favor."

Durning said nothing.

"Mr. Durning, you know everyone on campus; there's not a person in the administration you can't get to, am I right?"

"I'd like to think so."

"Well—I've got a student—Peter Hungerford—and I want to look at everything the school has about him. Whatever folders, background, school record, the works."

"They don't much like to let those go around loose."

"I wouldn't ask you if I didn't have to. Please."

Durning looked at his watch. "Be in my office at four o'clock. You'll have to read whatever I can get my hands on there. And I'll need to return them before the offices close."

Chub thanked him. It was barely noon and he wished he hadn't packed so he could pack then. He wandered across Tappan Square and there was joy in abundance— the weather, oddly, was bright and dry and classes were done. Kids threw Frisbees. Groups picnicked. Couples necked at the base of the giant elms.

He went to the Campus, ordered a BLT on white toast, fiddled with it, left it untouched. *Exorcist II: The Heretic* was playing at the Apollo and Chub had heard it was so bad, people were barfing out loud at the screen and a little laughter would have been welcome but the Apollo didn't open till six. The No-Name was shut too.

Chub went to his rooms and lay down; he closed his eyes and dreamed of sleep, but inside of five minutes he was making a pot of coffee. He drank three cups the next hour, and by the time he was done he had decided several things. He already knew that Hungerford was just in school for the ride. Sure, he was a senior but probably, if his work for Chub was any indication, he'd be way short of the hours for graduation. Certainly he must have caused trouble before. If Hungerford was a semester or so short, it would mean that Chub could get him to drop the course, take something else in the fall. That way he wouldn't have to fail him and he could talk to the kid, explain that the best thing would be to get help. Hell, he was young, he'd be straightened away in no time. Maybe he could even get him to go see Patty—she was a good shrink, he knew that much.

The folders lay on Durning's desk. "I used up many favors," he told Chub as he let him into his private room.

Chub thanked him.

"You have an hour," Durning said, and he closed his office door, leaving Chub alone. Chub opened the top folder, began to read, feeling almost immediately the center sliding away.

Hungerford's father (Oberlin, '50) had gone on to Harvard Medical School, taken advanced study in surgery, was on the staff of New York Hospital, a man of not yet fifty, was already much honored in his field. Hungerford's mother (also Oberlin, '50—they married graduation day) had also attended Harvard, earned a doctorate and was a psychiatrist and noted writer working in Manhattan. They had obviously been outstanding students.

But their son and only child, Peter, put them both in the shade. He wasn't just Phi Beta he was *junior* Phi Beta, and in his first three and a half semesters he had managed, as his worst grade, the grand total of one "A-minus."

And he was accepted at Harvard Med School in the fall.

And he needed the writing hours to graduate.

It was shortly after five when Chub knocked on the door to Hungerford's room. "It's me," he said. "Fuller."

"Hey, pal, door's open."

Chub walked in. Hungerford, massive and perspiring, was playing an Atari game.

Chub said they had to talk.

Hungerford said great, but he had to finish the game first.

Chub said it was important.

Hungerford kept battling the video game. He wore a T-shirt and jeans and the power of his body was never more evident. He had taken to affecting a crew cut and his dark hair and Germanic features made him seem almost frightening. The only thing about him that wasn't frightening was his fingers; they were long, thin, almost feminine. Surgeon's hands.

When he couldn't take the wait any longer, Chub went to the wall, pulled the plug out, and the machine died.

"Ordinarily, that's an act of war, but since it's you, pal, all is forgiven." He smiled, studying Chub. "You don't look happy. Sit down, tell Petey all your troubles."

Chub closed the door to the room, began talking almost in a whisper.

Hungerford interrupted—"Hey, is this top-secret stuff, great."

Chub began to speak. "If I fail you, you won't graduate; if I let it be known why I failed you, I can't imagine Harvard Med's going to greet you with such open arms. So do us both a favor and cut the wise-ass shit, all right?"

"Hey, are you serious or something?"

"I said cut it!"

"You've got to drop the shoe, Professor—I don't know what the subject is under discussion."

"The subject is plagiarism and we both know it."

Hungerford stared at Chub in total disbelief.

"It's up to you now—explain yourself."

Hungerford shook his head. "What is this vendetta thing you've got?"

"Vendetta?"

"Oh, come on, pal, you've had it in for me from the first day when I was late. I worked my ass off for you and every other kid got a full hour of your time but you always had me out the door in twenty minutes. I don't know why I rub you wrong—I shouldn't have made that remark about your book, maybe. But Jesus Christ, I never thought you'd try and ruin me out of malice."

"It isn't malice, believe me, and I don't want to ruin anybody. You plagiarized 'The Eighty-Yard Run' and I want to know why."

"What the fuck is 'The Eighty-Yard Run'?"

"Peter, don't do this."

"You're the one that's doing something."

"I'm not. I'm just as confused as you are. I don't want to fail you. I've come up with a compromise—I'm supposed to leave tomorrow but I'll cancel that. I'll stick around here until you've written me twenty-one pages. That's the requirement left. I don't care how wide your margins are and I don't care if all you do is type 'All work and no play makes Jack a dull boy.' That's as fair as I can be. I'll pass you and nothing will go on your record. Isn't that fair?"

Hungerford sat in his chair, the look of disbelief still on.

"Plus one more thing—you've got to promise me to see somebody."

"Explain, please?"

"Someone to help you. Someone that's qualified."

Hungerford smiled then. "Oh, that's easy—I can always see my mother over dinner—she gets a hundred an hour, does she qualify as being qualified?" And then the smile was gone and Hungerford was out of his chair, slamming Chub against the closet door, and his hands were twisting Chub's shirt and he was hollering now— "There's nothing wrong with me, pal, if there's a whacko in this room I'm looking at him—I'm not writing shit for you—I broke my ass for you and I don't know what you're after, but I wouldn't advise you to try getting away with it! *You do and are you gonna suffer.*"

He dropped his hands, jerked the door open, and Chub, suffering, left. It was worse than he had thought— Hungerford was crazy.

At shortly before seven, Chub rang the bell to Andrew Cheyney's house. He carried a copy of *Mixed Company* along with "Saturday's Child." Durning opened the door, saw who it was and said, "Oh, no, another favor." Chub explained that he needed to talk to Professor Cheyney. "Andrew's a bit under the weather," Durning said but then he looked at Chub's face and said, "I know, I know, it's important." He led Chub into the living room, which was large and very contemporary. Chub had expected antiques.

"Andrew," Durning called then and a few minutes later, Cheyney, looking pale, entered. He was wearing slippers and dark socks with garters and a paisley print robe, and Chub started right in, explaining that he was new, he'd never taught before and maybe Cheyney had dealt with plagiarism before but would know what to do with the story turned in by Hungerford—

"*Peter* Hungerford?"

"Yessir."

"Doesn't ring true. I taught both his parents, I know them. They've been very kind to the college. I've kept tabs on Peter during his years here—he's been a student leader all the while."

Chub handed over what he'd brought. "Here's 'The Eighty-Yard Run' and here's Hungerford's work."

"What is 'The Eighty-Yard Run'?"

"It's by Irwin Shaw—"

Cheyney shook his head. "Fuller and Shaw, locked together for immortality."

"It's very famous," Chub said.

"Fuller, I'm a bit waspish this evening, what with a hundred-degree fever and all, but may I say that if it were *very* famous perhaps I might have heard of it."

He took the written material. "Let me go read."

"Thank you, and I'm terribly sorry to be barging in but there's one thing I want you to bear in mind while you're reading—he wanted to be caught. I taught Irwin Shaw in class."

"This story?"

"No, another one, but that's not the point—he knows, just like you do, I'm a fan, and this is more than just plagiarism—it's a cry for help from a very sick human being."

"Oh, dear God, just what I needed tonight, an invasion from a Freudian. Allowing Sigmund Freud to be translated into English is the greatest mistake America has made since we allowed women the right to vote." He gestured toward a chair. "Sit. I shall read quickly."

Chub didn't sit, he paced, and Cheyney didn't read all that fast, but when he returned he looked paler than before.

Chub watched.

Cheyney sat down heavily. "I admit I'm biased—I like the family, I know the boy. And only a fool would fail to see the similarities."

"Then we're agreed: It's plagiarism."

"I don't think so at all."

"What else could it be?"

"Oh, dear God, Fuller, there must be fifty stories about football heroes whose lives go bad. I think perhaps we're dealing with coincidence—there is no reason for as brilliant a young man with as wondrous a future as Peter Hungerford to do a thing like this."

"I told you, he's sick!"

"If you wish to stay in a civilized house you must behave in a civilized manner."

"I'm sorry."

"And since his mother is one of the leading experts in the field of mental illness, I suspect she might have seen chinks developing, if chinks there were." He dropped the writing on the sofa beside him. "There is only one thing we must do, and that is speak to Peter himself." And with that, he reached for the phone.

Hungerford, wearing sneakers and chinos and a clean white shirt, arrived after nine. He shook hands readily with both men. "What is this, a meeting of the Nobel Prize committee?"

"I wish there were more wit displayed on campus, but now is not the time," Cheyney said. He indicated the sofa. "Sit down, Peter."

Hungerford sat down quickly.

Chub watched him. He looked so self-possessed, so goddamn calm.

"Professor Fuller has some qualms concerning 'Saturday's Child.' Although I am in theory in charge of him, he is, in this case, in charge of you. I have read both your story and 'The Eighty-Yard Run.' "

Hungerford raised his right hand: "I swear on anything you want I've never read that story."

Cheyney gestured for Chub to speak. "Peter—Peter, listen—the names of the main characters are the same—the last line, 'Once I played here' is the same—the thrust of the narrative is the same—and there are eighty-yard football runs in both pieces. Tell me how you explain that."

Hungerford said nothing.

"Peter—" Cheyney said. "This could be—is—a matter of some seriousness. You understand that?"

Hungerford nodded.

"Then I feel it incumbent upon you to explain."

Hungerford said nothing.

"Peter?" Cheyney said, more urgency now.

Hungerford buried his giant head in his beautiful hands. "I never should have done it," he said.

"Tell us what you did, Peter."

Chub watched. When Hungerford raised his head again there were tears in his eyes. "I saw a TV show once—years ago—I think Paul Newman was in it, and his wife too. I didn't get the name but I remembered it was an adaptation of something by Irwin Shaw and—" He looked at Chub now. "—and Professor Fuller, I knew he loved Shaw and he's been so fabulous to me this semester, he's kind of one of us, being young and all—" He looked at Cheyney now. "You would have been fabulous, too, sir, I don't mean any criticism, but I've just loved the course and the great long talks Professor Fuller and I have had, these intimate kinds of one-to-ones, and I thought . . ." A long pause now. "I wanted to let him know how much I appreciated what he's done for me, I wanted him to have a going away present."

"Present?" Cheyney asked.

Hungerford dried his eyes. "See, in the TV show, the main character's name I remembered because my best friend's name was Chris, and the girl's name I remembered because I was in love with a girl named Louise then, and the last line I remembered, well, because it's such a great line, how could anyone forget that?" Now there were tears again. "The crazy thing is I thought it was a *ninety*-yard run in the TV show but I know little about football and a run that long, well, I didn't believe it, so I changed it to eighty to make more sense."

Chub stared, thinking, omigod, *he's* the one making sense. He shut his eyes now, opened them again, stared at Hungerford. He looked so sad, wringing his exquisite hands, his voice rising and falling perfectly. In his mind, Chub kept seeing the mirror with the lipstick message getting brighter.

"I decided what I'd do was write Professor Fuller an Irwin Shaw story. I thought he'd love it. I couldn't just come out and tell him what he's meant to me, so I thought the story would send the message I wanted so badly to say. It was supposed to be this gift and now it's a nightmare."

"Then you didn't plagiarize at all," Cheyney said.

"I'm so confused I don't know anything anymore," Hungerford said. "The names, sure, the last line, sure, maybe some of the plot's the same, you tell me. If you think I plagiarized, I'll accept your word, Professor Cheyney. But I wish you'd tell me why in the world I'd do it."

"I don't think you did anything wrong, Peter, but I can tell you now I didn't think it when I phoned you. Go in the next room a moment and wait, would you mind?"

Hungerford dried his eyes a final time. "Whatever you say, Professor Cheyney."

When they were alone, Cheyney said, "Well?"

Chub sat silently, staring out at the night.

Then Cheyney was on him: "Why do you want to make trouble, Fuller?—what is it in you that thrives on trouble?—I remember our first day in class you began making trouble and obviously you've never stopped."

I hate trouble, Chub thought, and then Patty's phrase "the bestest good boy, the bestest good boy" was echoing.

"I'm totally satisfied, Fuller. But you're the professor in charge. If you want to take this up a step, we'll visit the dean of men tomorrow. Side by side. And I will let you make your speech and then I will say when you are quite finished that I think you are wrong—dead, dead wrong. But that, of course, is your decision. How much trouble are you interested in stirring?"

Isolated and alone and yes, beaten, Chub thought of the plane taking off in the morning from Cleveland. "No more trouble," he muttered.

"Peter," Cheyney called out then. "You are summoned."

Hungerford filled the doorway.

"I am pleased to inform you that this incident is history. Men of good will can settle anything, I wish our leaders understood that." And then he turned toward the sideboard. "Nothing puts a period on a disagreement like a glass of port, I insist you both be my guests." He filled three glasses, made a toast. "To the end of an era of hard feelings."

Hungerford and Chub touched glasses. "Hey, we're pals," Hungerford said, and he smiled at Chub and Chub realized, just before he drank, that never before had he seen a face that so desperately wanted to kill him. . . .

CHAPTER 3

Seuss

If it had not been for the rainbow of B. J. Peacock's reappearance in his life with her flashing green eyes, her pale red hair, Chub's ensuing days would have been without color at all.

The afternoon he got back from Oberlin he figured he'd put in a call to Kitchel except he didn't. No deep reason. He just needed the time to readjust to the noises of the city after the quiet of the college town. He unpacked, decided, while the incident was still fresh, to put some Hungerford notes in his Journal, except he didn't do that either.

It was a week before Kitchel called him. "Hey," Chub said excitedly, eyes closed, lying on his bed, "what have you got, detectives on me?—you have caught me in the act of unpacking."

"Want to call me when you're done?"

"No, Jeeves is here, taking care of the brute work—ironing my shirts and stuff. I'm just overseeing that he does it properly. They don't make butlers like they used to."

"Well, then, hear this: There is going to be a magnificent dinner party *chez* Kitchel come Saturday and you—it's against my wishes but the divine Lydia insists—are invited."

"Formal?"

"I shall be resplendent in my purple jogging suit, you may dress accordingly."

Chub accepted and arrived, as always punctually, at seven-forty-five. It turned out that *he* was the magnificent dinner party. Just the three of them was all. A catching-up time.

Two-Brew was trimmer than ever. Lydia, horn-rimmed and smiling, was as dark as before only even more *zaftig*. They were going to move eventually, but they lived still in Kitchel's old apartment, near the office. The place was still large, but a zoo no more. Lydia had decorated it. Danish modern, but not so much you couldn't find a place to sit that was comfortable. There was the standard Manischewitz oldie to begin things, then a magnum of Taittinger, icy chilled. The appetizer was smoked salmon from Poll's, the main course a rack of lamb from Lobel Brothers. A lot of zinging back and forth, Two-Brew dominating with one overbearing pronouncement following another.

It should have been terrific but it wasn't. By the time the lamb had disappeared, along with two bottles of Gruaud-Larose '70, Chub, finally given the floor, was working his way toward the end of his Oberlin semester, and he told the Hungerford story with great care, because he was buzzed a little and he wanted to make all the story points clear and before he was finished, Two-Brew said, "Incredible material," followed quickly, too quickly, by Lydia's "Absolutely fantastic," and Chub dabbed at his lips with his napkin, trying to forget the eye flick that shouldn't have passed between them.

Over coffee and brandy, the zinging got worse, Lydia leading the way, arguing, nitpicking. Chub, silent now, did his best to concentrate on his brandy. There was no outright warfare, but when Lydia left early to go to bed, saying, "You two talk," it was clear she didn't care if they talked or not, just so she didn't have to be around to listen.

Chub finished his brandy.

Two-Brew refilled his snifter.

Chub swirled the liquid.

"Lydia's not herself," Kitchel said finally

"Ah, well," Chub replied, hoping that would do.

"It isn't her work," Two-Brew went on. She was proving to be a splendid editor, hardworking and not uncommercial, considering she was cursed with an Ivy League background.

Chub said her success certainly didn't surprise him.

Eventually, the trouble turned out to be children. Or rather, the lack thereof. They hadn't really made a scientific attack in their first year of marriage, they didn't need the burden. But these last months their needs had shifted, and they did several months of planned intercourse, the middle of the month, that kind of thing. And they didn't dwell on their failures, Lydia was too kind for that, because they both knew that the sin was his: He had to learn to live with the fact that his third leg had proved faulty. It swelled, it grew hard—no problem there, thank God. But it was difficult for him to accept the fact that his seed was insufficiently strong. Then, recently, he had screwed his courage and gone for medical testing. He was not the culprit. This past week irrevocable word had come from the doctors that Lydia, with wide-curving hips and a shape seemingly made for birthing, was barren.

Doctors had made mistakes before, Chub said.

"Of course," Two-Brew agreed. "But for the nonce, you'll have to forgive her. As I said, she is most definitely not herself these days."

Just how far Lydia had swung from her natural orbit came clear to Chub in July. She called him at home and he could tell the strain before she'd finished, unnecessarily, introducing herself.

"I've heard of you," Chub said.

"Yes, well, here's the thing—we've never been much into paperback novelizations of movies but there's a market, it's there, and it would be foolish of us to keep ignoring it, and we've got the screenplay for a Charles Bronson movie—he's really a fine actor, don't you think?—underrated. And very popular in Europe too. And we've contracted for a novelization and I wondered if you'd do it, I'll messenger it over and it's thirty-five hundred dollars, and we need it in six weeks and I thought of you, you'd do it so well."

"That's very sweet," Chub said, wondering what Two-Brew would say if he ever found out she'd made this call, how much anger would spill?

"We like the story quite a lot—so you'd just have to flesh out scenes, add description, we don't want a total reconstruction or anything like that, may I send it over?"

Chub read the screenplay that night, the first he'd ever seen, and of course he was ignorant as to the ultimate success of the film. But writing quality was not something that interested the scenarist—gore was clearly foremost in his mind. It was a bloodbath picture, a bang-bang flick, with violence, it seemed, in at least every other scene.

He glanced over it a second time without spotting much improvement, then put it down beside him on his bed. He had fifteen hundred dollars in the bank, he'd saved that much from his Oberlin semester, so the money wasn't absolutely essential.

But Lydia was going through a bad patch, and he'd never done anything remotely like it; technically, it might have some interest.

He did the first seven pages that night. He awoke the next day early and by noon had gotten up to page eighteen. Before he went to bed, he was closing in on thirty.

And he felt sick.

As a kid, he'd always been a reader and there was a time when nothing was more important than would the engine get the toys over the mountain, would Pooh rescue Piglet with the honey jar. Then, as the battles from surrounding bedrooms began to escalate, his own room became increasingly important; it was there he first met Poe and O'Neill and so many other Americans, before taking a breath, going across the oceans where Chekhov was waiting for him, and Turgenev and The Don riding with Sancho. He knew that he could never match the masters. But he also knew that what he could at least try to do was bring something into being that had never been put down quite that way before. More than any other single wish, he honored that.

And there was no honor in the thirty pages that lay scattered around his typewriter. No human could contemplate the gore and be the better for it. Even the crap he'd written growing up at least was his crap.

On his desk now was nothing but orphan shit.

Chub got up, thought of Wild Turkey, forgot about it—he'd been nearly off the stuff the past months and it wasn't going to make him feel better now.

It was steaming in his bedroom. The building wasn't wired for air conditioning though Mrs. Gonzales, the super, kept promising in both Spanish and English that "all that stuff" was "in the works."

Chub walked down the stairs and sat down on the steps of the building. Ninety-eighth Street was pulsing even though it was two in the morning, it usually was on hot nights, and the drunks in the single-room-occupancy buildings were hurling insults at the transvestites who managed, even in the worst weather, to parade in finery. Someone threw a bottle and it shattered, and for a moment Chub thought there might be combat, but then the street began to quiet and he looked toward Riverside and saw a black policeman begin walking toward the commotion. (It was Rory L. Baylor and he was to become more than a good acquaintance in the future, but Chub had no way of knowing that then.) The cop didn't seem overly impressive physically, not much taller than Chub's five nine plus, but he moved with graceful purpose and without fear, nodding and naming various drunks as he passed them, doing the same to the men in drag. Then he took a seat a few buildings down from Chub and sat, clearly in no hurry, and he stayed there till the potential combustion abated. (Chub asked Mrs. Gonzales about him the next day—clearly the man had some power and he wondered what it was. The answer from the fat lady came accompanied by hand slashes: karate. The cop had killed with his hands. He had been a champion, had won the world a few years back in Tokyo, Japan.)

Chub sat for an hour, then climbed the stairs, lay on his bed, thinking of Lydia, and how would she feel if he called her up and told her about this great book he'd just come across on the joys of adoption?

Sure, she was entering a bad patch, but she wasn't the only one walking through some joyless days. Yes, the money cloaked the offer in propriety. But what she was really doing was trying to spread her pain around and you didn't do that. No, you did not. He had never, not once knowingly in his life, demeaned another soul.

It was close to five before his eyes began to close. He had several large fans in his bedroom and eventually the heat released him and he slept. He was up before nine, made a pot of coffee, drank enough for his head to clear, because he had to handle the phone call to Lydia with skill.

"Hey, don't hate me," he began, when her secretary put him through, "but this Bronson thing—I can't find the handle."

"How so?"

"Well, I've tried and I've tried but I can't get started and I know you're in a time bind and it's really great of you thinking of me and all, but I suppose it would be best if you thought of someone else."

"You mean you're passing?"

Chub sat at his desk, the thirty pages in one hand. "I'll never get it done in time. I've taken notes but I haven't written word one. I think it must be seeing a screenplay for the first time that's got me whipped."

"I thought you'd be perfect."

Chub laughed. "Well, of course, I am, personally speaking, without flaw, everybody knows that, but I don't think I'm perfect for this job. I really appreciate the offer, though, Lydia."

There was a pause. "I'll send for the screenplay this afternoon." Another pause. "Chub, there's a call waiting, gotta dash, 'bye."

Chub hung up. He could tell she was pissed but he didn't think she could read anything in his voice, so that was one for his team.

He went to his sink, cleaned his coffee pot, was half-way through shaving when the phone rang and Kitchel's voice way saying, "What the hell is this with you pissing on the Bronson novelization?"

Oh, Christ, Chub thought; *you knew.*

"Well?"

You couldn't have, you couldn't have.

"Chub?"

"Dropped my watch, sorry. What were you saying?"

"I was saying that when I thought up the idea I felt pretty goddamn good about the whole thing."

It wasn't your idea; it couldn't have been. You were going to be my Maxwell Perkins, don't you remember? In the blizzard you said that. And I was going to be your star.

"I couldn't think of anything better to get you untracked."

"It's the time element, maybe—if I had a month, I could knock out thirty pages, I'm almost sure I could, but—"

"It didn't have to be a masterpiece. Graham Greene didn't turn me down first."

"I'm flattered you even thought of me."

"How could you say no? You could have forced yourself, you know. Writers have been known to do that. Thirty-five hundred is thirty-five hundred." Agitation. "We'll talk." Click.

"I'm not a fucking charity case," Chub shouted when the phone was dead. He slammed the receiver down then, ripped the thirty pages apart, decided to burn them, decided that was overly dramatic, decided he wanted to be overly dramatic, took his biggest pan, dropped the paper in, lit a kitchen match, stared till there were only ashes. Then the Wild Turkey for company, he lay down in bed, brought the fans close, nursed the bottle along. So what if Kitchel thought he was a figure on the dole? Fuck

Kitchel. Fuck Kitchel and fuck Cheyney and fuck his father and anybody else who wandered along. Sure, thirty-five hundred was thirty-five hundred but there were things you did and things you didn't do and no one was going to have to pass a hat for his funeral. *He had talents.*

What, though?

Chub closed his eyes and listened to the fans, waiting for lightning. He always thought he was good at people, but maybe he wasn't. He always hoped he'd be good at writing, but maybe he wasn't. And he never thought he'd be good at taxis, and he certainly wasn't. Or brick factories either.

But—

—and now he capped the bottle, got up, looked out at the blue summer sky—

—but no one was better at libraries.

EXPERT EXPERIENCED RESEARCHER

Speed matched only by accuracy. No subject too arcane. Low rates. Call 212-555-4001; seven days 9–5.

Three Sundays later, Chub stared at his ad in the back of the *Book Review* section. There were half a dozen competing researcher ads, but his was unquestionably the best. He had not been in the Sunday *Times* since Joyce Carol Oates had called *Under the Weather* a "considerable achievement" (some things you just remember) but the way his ad jumped out at you was something you just couldn't feel bad about.

And the day—you couldn't bitch about that either. Cool and dry, that first hint of fall. He dressed, went out and celebrated by buying a couple of buttered bagels, along with a container of coffee, from a deli around the corner and spent the next hours watching a tight baseball game in Riverside Park between really good competing teams of Puerto Ricans. Then he took a long walk by the Hudson, stopping at the Seventy-ninth Street boat basin, where a couple of big yachts were anchored. On one of the yachts a party was blasting along, and there was a lot of laughter but, watching the tanned faces, Chub doubted the sounds.

He lay down on the grass awhile, getting a start of a tan, and when the afternoon was moving along, headed back up into the Nineties, where his luck held: The Thalia was playing a Bergman double feature, *Winter Light* and *The Seventh Seal,* masterpieces both, and he was amazed when he left that they were better even than he remembered.

Getting dark now. He hadn't eaten since the bagels and he treated himself to a pig-out at the local Hunan spot that had recently opened. It was after seven when he got back to his place and after eight when the phone rang.

Chub answered and a male voice said, "Is this the 'expert experienced researcher' that ran an ad in today's *Times?*"

"Yessir, it is."

"Well, I have but one question."

Chub grabbed a pad and paper, got ready. "Shoot."

"How in the name of bleeding Jesus am I supposed to reach you between nine and five when there is no one there to answer the fucking phone between nine and five?"

Chub tried not to laugh at himself but sometimes he really was the asshole of the world: Obviously he had intended to be absent—who gave a damn about Puerto Rican baseball?—because what if the phone didn't ring? Or what if it did? Or both. "Busy on a job," he said.

"I have waited for you, young man, because you were the only one who had the audacity to use the word 'arcane'—most writers haven't the least idea what it means."

See? It really was the best ad.

"I am Elliott double 'l' double 't' Carter," the voice said. Then: "Yes, *the* Elliott Carter to forestall your question."

Chub didn't know who in hell the guy was, though maybe he should have. (Carter turned out to be a Donald

Westlake type—only without Westlake's talent—a factory in himself, who turned out close to a dozen books a year, mainly mysteries, under several pseudonyms.) "A pleasure, Mr. Carter."

"And what is your name?"

Chub told him.

"Well, Fuller, it comes to this: I am very hard on my researchers—I fired my most recent one this very weekend."

"I've never been fired yet, Mr. Carter."

"You are not the first to claim that. Here is my situation: At my present rate of speed, I expect to deposit my heroine into some quicksand by the end of this week and I find, to my dismay, that my *Brittanica* is of no use at all. Obviously, I do not intend to let her expire there."

Chub wrote the word "quicksand" at the top of his pad, asked a few pertinent questions: Did it matter where the quicksand was, seacoast or inland? Did the time of year matter? Was the heroine conscious or otherwise? When he was done he said so.

"I'll have to read whatever you can come up with," Elliott Carter said. "So I'll need it by Wednesday."

"You'll have it tomorrow," Chub promised.

It was so easy. There were over twelve hundred libraries in the greater New York area but a thousand of those weren't much use at all. Chub didn't need to ferret around in those two hundred though; it was all at the main branch of the public on Forty-second and Fifth. Chub arrived before the place was open, was one of the first into the card catalog room on the third floor. There weren't whole books on the subject but my God, the periodicals. In the next hours he looked at probably thirty or more articles, scanned them to see if they fitted Elliott Carter's needs, ended up selecting a dozen: from *Scientific American* (June '53) and *Science Digest* (June '75) and *Reader's Digest* (December '64) and *American Family Physician* (volume 19, number 2), on and on. Then he went to the Xerox room and waited in line for copies to be made. He bought a large manila envelope, shoved the hundred or so pages inside and set off for the subway.

Elliott Carter lived in a brownstone off Macdougal. He was probably close to sixty and could have passed for Nero Wolfe. Standing in the foyer of his home, he quickly examined the material Chub brought him. Then he beckoned for Chub to follow him into his study. "Now to finances," he said, taking out a checkbook. Chub handed him a scrawled paper on which he'd listed his expenses, travel, Xeroxing, etc. "You don't list your hourly rate."

Chub hadn't known remotely what to ask for. "Sometimes I'm really stupid, leaving off a thing like that."

"I paid my last researcher ten dollars an hour."

"That's what I always get."

Carter looked at him. "I'm a liar—I paid him twelve per hour."

"I'm a liar too," Chub answered. "You're my first job."

Carter smiled, wrote a check, and Chub found himself on the sidewalk five minutes later, thirty-six dollars richer, not counting expenses. *Thirty-six bucks.* He taxied home.

An unwise gesture, since that thirty-six was the sum total he earned in the next two weeks. But then Carter called again—"Could you kill a man by forcing him to swallow an entire tube of toothpaste?" That one took awhile. (Yes. But it would take a pretty dumb cop to let the cause of death go unnoticed.)

Carter wrote a lot and he also talked a lot, fortunately to other writers, and by Christmas, Chub was out so much he bought himself a present: an answering machine so he wouldn't miss any more calls.

When the libraries didn't supply the proper information, Chub's clients had him set up interviews with experts—a historian at Columbia who specialized on the slave trade in Zanzibar in the last century; a wonderful Italian in Queens who explained the intricacies of the workings of a motorcycle dealership. Sometimes Chub did the interviews for his clients, sometimes not. Sometimes the research was tedious (debutante balls in prewar London) more often not (crime—a lot of his work dealt with murder; that was how he first came to know and like the black cop, Rory L. Baylor).

But all of it kept him off the streets, and within a year he had dozens of clients, and his price was up to twenty per, and he was earning four hundred dollars on a good week. And, of course, he was associating with real writers, sometimes every day.

Soaked, Chub tossed his raincoat over the shower rod, kicked off his shoes, tossed them near the bathroom radiator to let them dry. He toweled his hair, cursed as another blast of thunder hit the city. It had been raining for three days, more on than off. He went to his desk, saw there were messages on the machine, clicked it on. The first was from an old lady in Maine, a friend of Carter's, who hated Stephen King because she had been working that side of the street before King was born only she'd never hit it big. She needed information on lake monsters, not just Nessie in Scotland, but also the one in Chesapeake Bay and anything else. Chub made a note, waited for the next message.

A female voice said, "If this is Charles Fuller, and I mean *the* Charles Fuller, that noted author and literary figure, and if whoever's listening is his secretary, *please* be sure that he is told that— Now don't you beep at me, don't you dare hang up. . . ."

Excited, Chub listened to the next message: "Chub, this is B.J. I just hate machines. If you're free for dinner, I can unthaw anything," and then she gave a number.

Chub dialed the number quickly and a little girl's voice answered with "Whoever can this be?"

"B.J., *hi*," Chub said.

"*B*.J.," the kid said. "I'm not B.J."

"Sorry," Chub said. "You must be the maid. Would you tell your mistress that—"

"I'm the daughter. I'm Jesse. You must get things straight."

"Sorry," Chub said. "It's just you have a very deep voice. Anyway, this is Mr. Fuller returning your mother's call."

"She's in the potty."

"Fine; when she gets home, tell her—"

"She is home. The potty's *here*." Now a pause. "Just you hang on."

After a while, B.J. was on the phone. "I'm so sorry—I was hanging stuff up in a closet and I didn't hear the phone."

In the distance, Chub could hear giggling.

Then B.J.'s voice: "Did you tell?"

More giggling.

"There are no secrets," B.J. said back to Chub, and then, before they started to deal with the years, Chub asked was the dinner invitation still operational because he happened to have a break in his busy schedule and she said it was so they agreed to meet at her place at half past seven.

That gave him several hours, enough to get some work he'd done ready for mailing off and to transcribe an interview he was behind on. What he did instead was this: fuss about his wardrobe. Should he wear a tie or not. Should he wear his suit? Maybe the summer blazer? Still undecided, he went into the bathroom and shaved a second time. He'd never done that before—his light-brown beard didn't require it and it didn't require it now but he hacked away, drawing blood at the crappy spot just under the nostrils. Now he got into the tub, soaked a long time, finally stood and showered with much soaping.

Done, he studied himself in the mirror over the sink. Except for the little puffiness under the eyes, he looked okay. The same. The same 160 pounds, the same light-brown hair cut short, the same cursed round cheeks.

He lay down next, closed his eyes to rest, realized it didn't matter a whole lot how he looked, it was B.J.'s appearance, that was the thing. What had it been, seven years since she graduated? She was probably closing in on thirty, no sin, but goddamnitall, it was adolescent on his part, still he hoped she hadn't faded. Redheads did that and B.J.'s hair, long and tumbling, was a very pale and very special red. At least special to some people. Some stupid people.

The address was on Central Park West in the Seventies and Chub hoped for a cab. As soon as he hit Ninety-eighth Street an empty came by. Chub hailed it. The driver ignored him, roared past. Assuring himself that was not an omen, Chub ran for the bus. B.J.'s building was old but fancy, and he told the man at the door that his name was Fuller, to see the Hiltons, and after a phone check, he was directed to the automatic elevator with the instructions that it was the apartment on the right, fifteenth floor.

He rode up accompanied mainly by a gnawing stomach. There were two apartments on the fifteenth floor and Chub took his time before ringing, taking off his raincoat, shaking it awhile. His grey slacks had lost their crease in the rain, so he licked his fingers, went over the area by his ankles, doing what he could at restoration. Finally he rang, waited, and when the door opened he knew B.J. had entered into a pact with the Devil.

Her hair was still long, still tumbled across her shoulders. But her green eyes seemed somehow brighter, her face the same face, perhaps younger, her starlet's body as he remembered. She wore a white gathered skirt, a pale-blue blouse open at the throat. "You dear man," she said. "Braving the elements for Swanson's chicken." She kissed his cheek, ushered him in. Chub followed. His wet loafers squeaked. "Those," B.J. said, pointing down. "Off with them at once. Comfort is the order of the night. And how dare you wear a necktie in my presence?" She went to the hall closet, hung up his coat, snapped her fingers at his blazer and she hung that up, too, draping his tie across it.

The apartment was large, the living room enormous and dark, filled with overstuffed furniture. "Excuse this place," B.J said. "It's a two-year sublet and you can't always be as choosy as you'd like."

"You're here, then?"

"Ensconced this very week."

"There is no way that can be considered bad news."

"I'll give you the grand tour but let's have a drink to accompany us." She walked ahead of him through some double doors into a library with a bar set up by the window. There was a terrace beyond. Chub watched the way her body moved, wondering if Del ever got annoyed with the world, knowing he had that to return to.

She was putting ice in his glass when the phone rang. B.J. answered, said "Hiiiii," then put her hand over the mouthpiece. "It's Daddy, I'm sorry, he takes forever," and she gestured for him to continue with his own bartending.

Chub didn't feel the need, so he paused momentarily by the terrace doors and Central Park beyond in the storm, and beyond that, on Fifth, was the Kitchel place and he thought of his first trip, the *Serendipity* trip, and quickly turned away. He didn't like eavesdropping so he pointed back toward the living room and she nodded and smiled and when he was alone by the foyer Chub heard a child's voice raised in incantation. "Rain, rain, go away, come again some other day," over and over.

He tracked the sound, paused noiselessly in the doorway to the nearest bedroom and saw, for the first time, Jesse kneeling by the window, looking out.

She was probably five and he felt from their phone call that there was no world in which she was going to be a dummy. Her father's brains, at the very least. Also, her father's features. Square head, prominent chin, hair that was thin and straggly. He must have shifted his weight because she turned sharply and Chub put a smile on fast, fast enough, he hoped, to hide his sad surprise: The entire upper right quarter of her face was on fire, the forehead, the eye, half the nose, the top part of her cheek. Chub had seen bad birthmarks before but never one like this.

"I'm Chub."

She looked at him a moment. "The potty man."

"In person."

"Well, *I* am Jesse," she said, and then she held up a large doll that was kneeling beside her by the window. "And this is Big Baby." She held out Big Baby's right arm.

"Pleasure," Chub said, crossing toward them, shaking both their hands. As he grew nearer, the birthmark seemed to burn a deeper red.

She turned back to the window, adjusting Big Baby into a position parallel to her own. "Did it rain when you were five?" she asked then.

"Indeed." He sat on her bed a few feet behind her.

"I just hate it," Jesse said, and she half turned toward him briefly.

He smiled, looked away from the birthmark, the sad red eye. "I loved it," Chub heard himself saying. "Best time of my life."

"Why?"

"Why," Chub said. "An excellent question. Because of my adventures," he said then.

"You mean like putting on galoshes and splashing the puddles away?"

"That's not an adventure, that's a game."

"What's an adventure?"

"Danger. Travel. Excitement."

"When you were five?" She shook her head.

"Forget it," Chub said. "You wouldn't want to hear about it anyway, you're a girl." He got up off the bed. "Girls don't understand about adventure. They don't believe."

She was looking at him carefully now. "Tell me one."

"Okay, here's the deal: I'll *start* my first real adventure, but the second you don't believe me, that's it."

She nodded.

Chub thought a moment more, then started talking quickly. "I come from a big family—lots of brothers and sisters, only they were older and I was the baby and they never liked to play with me much, and we lived in Chicago and then, when I was five, we moved to this small town called Athens miles away. All the rest were excited—my father had gotten this great new job and we took a big house, it was terrific—except, see, I was frightened. I didn't know anybody in Athens and I was really blue. And to make things worse, the first week we moved in, all it did was pour. All my big brothers and sisters, they didn't mind, they got to go out but I was stuck in the house and I'll tell you the truth, I was one miserable kid. Alone, new place, no friends, all that."

Jesse nodded.

"Well, what I did was I'd sit by my window in my room and sometimes I'd just be quiet but a lot of the time I'd do just what you were doing, sing 'Rain, Rain, Go Away' over and over and that's what I was up to when suddenly I heard this voice saying, *'Stop—that—song.'* And then, right outside my window, I saw the Rain Man—of course, I didn't know his name then, but that's who it turned out to be. 'I hate that song, it gives inclemency a bad name.' I didn't know it either then, but he only appeared when it was raining."

"Why?"

"I asked him that later, of course, and he looked at me like I was from Mars or someplace weird, and he said, 'Why would anyone bother to come out at any other time?' Anyway, when he told me to stop singing, naturally I stopped and I opened the window so I could hear him better and he asked me what was the matter and I said I didn't know anybody and I was bored and he said, 'Excellent, come along with me, I'm in the midst of a great adventure,' and I said I couldn't, I'd get soaked to the skin and then he was talking loud again: 'No, no, you don't get wet if you do it my way,' and I asked what his way was and he said, 'You run between the drops, obviously.' "

"No one can do that."

"Forget it," Chub said, standing. "It was only one of the high points of my life but you would have probably thought the part where I captured the Umbrella Fiend was dull anyway, your mother's going to be off the phone soon, I'll see you." He looked toward the door.

"That was Big Baby," Jesse said then. "She doesn't understand about things. She told me to say that." Jesse took the doll, put it in her lap, held it there.

Chub hesitated.

"It must be hard, though," Jesse said. "Running that way."

"Don't you think that's what I thought? I told him. He said for me to stick my hand outside. I did. Guess what?—my hand got wet. Then he said, 'The only reason your hand got wet was because you didn't concentrate. Look at me—do I look wet?' "

"Did he?"

"He didn't look so much wet as he looked strange; he was shaped kind of like a tube, I guess; you know, the way a raindrop is shaped when it's falling, and he had a nice round head and then he began to wiggle his hand like this." Chub made his hand spin and circle and his fingers danced. " 'Do that,' the Rain Man said. I did and guess what?—my hand was still wet. 'You're not concentrating,' he said and this time I really concentrated and when I pulled my hand in it was dry and—"

"Completely dry?" Jesse said and before Chub could stand again she said, "Yes, Big Baby, completely dry, didn't you listen, he was *concentrating.*"

And now Chub began to wave his hands again, watching Jesse watch them, and he lowered his voice and said, *"Almost* completely dry and suddenly he was excited, the Rain Man was really *up* and he said, 'You have the gift, I can tell, you can be one of the chosen to race between the drops and have adventures undreamed of by the ordinary,' and I was getting a little scared now that he was going to ask me to come with him and I said, 'I'd love it, I would, but I'm only five, maybe when I'm six we can go off together,' and he said, 'No! No! It has to be now, six-year-olds don't believe anymore, they stop and they can't concentrate and four-year-olds are babies, I can't risk

what they might do if the going really got tough—and
believe me, the going gets tough when your job is to
capture the Umbrella Fiend, which is where I'm going
now, this is your chance, now, you're not a baby but you
still believe and you have the gift but have you the
courage to use it? *Have you the courage?*' "

"Free at last," B.J. said, staggering into the room,
feigning exhaustion.

"Unfair," Jesse cried.

B.J. put her fingers between her lips and made a very
creditable whistle. She pointed toward the bed. "Scoot."

"But I'm not *ti*red."

"*Jess*ica."

"Big Baby is the one who's tired."

B.J. looked at Chub. "Blood is soon to be spilled. I
suggest you remove yourself."

" 'Night," Chub said.

B.J. picked up Big Baby in one hand, tugged at Jesse
with the other.

Chub waved, left the room.

Behind him he could hear Jesse shouting: "Did you
have the courage, I simply must know."

Chub called back: "It wouldn't have been an adventure
if I'd stayed in my room alone."

Five minutes later, B.J. was back in the library, and
this time she didn't have to feign exhaustion. "Chub—
who in the name of Christ is the Umbrella Fiend?"

Chub shook his head. "I'm not sure yet—I didn't
know the Rain Man existed till a few minutes ago."

"My own Dr. Seuss. Will you tell her to please go to
sleep, say you'll tell her the next time."

Chub went back into the child's dark room. "The next
time, I promise." He bent down and kissed her.

"I knew you had the courage," Jesse whispered. "Big
Baby said you didn't. She's just wrong wrong wrong all
the time."

"Sleep now," Chub said. She closed her eyes. He
wasn't sure if she was tired or faking it but he watched
her for a while.

Dinner was not totally frozen. The lettuce salad that preceded the Swanson's chicken was clearly fresh, and the strawberry Jell-O—Jesse's favorite—was recently made. There were just the two of them, Del being at work, and the conversation stayed mainly with college.

It wasn't till close to ten, when they were back in the library, finishing instant coffee, that it began to change. "I thought by now you'd have asked how I succeeded in locating you."

Chub didn't get it.

"I thumbed through my college directory—you know, the one they issue every five years. And there you were."

"I'm also in the phone book."

"You're *listed?* I never dreamed. I figured there would be ninety Fullers and none of them would be you." B.J. shook her head. "But you're so well known. I mean, everybody *I* know read your book—of course, seeing as I was the heroine, that probably accounted for some of it— I was the girls of your dreams, that's so."

"My inspiration," Chub said, embarrassed but touched.

"I thought everybody famous was unlisted. In Washington, *page* boys are unlisted. Don't you get pestered?"

Chub shrugged. "You learn to deal with things."

"Is that why you've got that monstrous machine that goes 'beep beep beep' before a person can finish talking?"

"I guess it helps." He didn't want to lie, he hated it, but as she pressed him it became apparent that she wanted so to believe in his success. Yes, *Under the Weather* had been wonderfully reviewed and one hundred thousand copies of the paperback had sold. (She clasped her hands: "A best-seller, I just *knew* it!") And the novel, well, it was going great, it just wasn't going fast. (A sympathetic smile: "That's why you *creative* artists have such a bum road. I'm an *interpretive* artist, so it's easier; I wouldn't be anywhere without Tennessee Williams.") The first four hundred pages, they were typed and retyped and ready for publication—only they weren't even half the book. The next five hundred, well, they were done, but so rough you wanted to throw up, you couldn't show them to anybody, and getting them right, getting them up to the standard of what was ready, well, it wasn't coming—no, it was coming, but it was taking so goddamn long. (A nod: "Well, that's the way some people are—this Styron?—his new book *Sophie* something?—twelve years it took him, think of that.") So doing research was turning into kind of a salvation—because that way, he could pick his own hours, do his rewriting when he was fresh, and the old juices were flowing.

And you?

Well, the first year at Yale she'd played Blanche in *Streetcar* and *that* was an experience, because she didn't think she was ready but it turned out she was, they'd all been knocked sideways, and of course she'd done Juliet, which was fun. (Chub remembered her Lady Macbeth and wondered if she remembered that as being fun too.) And Del had studied and Del had studied, that was all he did, until second year, when he began talking about a baby and she didn't want one, not yet, but then he'd forced himself on her one night, literally used his strength to bring her down and when she was pregnant she didn't know what to do, so she talked with her Daddy and he said women could always act but they couldn't always bring life into the world and that was what she'd already decided—she was from Texas, she was a good Baptist and when Jesse came, that was a real high point. Except it meant she couldn't do her acting so she dropped out and Del studied and Del studied and then when he made *Law Review* that only meant he had to study harder and when he graduated he was given the chance to clerk in Washington, for a Supreme Court judge, no less, so off they traipsed to Washington and next Del got a job with one of the most influential law firms and he worked and he worked and she became his ornament. She gave parties—"catered; believe me, he didn't want me cooking"—and went to parties and everyone thought they were the most delightful young couple until she went last summer to visit her Daddy and they were doing a little production of *Streetcar* in a little Dallas theatre and he practically forced her to audition and, well, it wasn't surprising she got the part, after all, she'd *played* the part, and the run was only for a week and the reviews—just little ones—were all for her and the night the show closed she cried her heart out and her Daddy said, "I raised you to be happy, are you happy?" and all she was was this ornament and when she told him that, that and how empty it all was, he said, "Child, leave him," and she said she couldn't do a thing like that and she went back to Del but it was the same only worse because the days were getting emptier so she packed up and went back home and yes, when she said before that Del was at work that was true, but he was at work in Washington and their divorce would be final soon and her Daddy sent her packing to the big city, with two years of money and then some, two years to pick up what her life had been before Del had used his strength to bring her down.

"So I guess you could say you're looking at a fallen woman."

Chub looked at her as he had throughout the night, but probably he didn't see her. She had dazzled him when he was a freshman; nothing had changed.

"After that endless recitation I am positively parched," B.J. said. "I think a Scotch and soda might revive me."

Chub knew it would be polite for him to fix it, but the bar was set up across the library and he was hard, and the bulge in his trousers kept him seated on the sofa.

B.J. rose from the chair across from him. "You?"

"The same."

She made the drinks, came back to the sofa, gave him his drink, sat on the far end of the sofa. They sipped and talked about the city and B.J. asked would he take mercy on a newcomer and show her around.

No problem.

Then they were quiet, listening to the rain until B.J. asked would he like a refill. He didn't but he said fine and while she was making them, Chub glanced at his watch. It was after midnight. She gave him the second drink and then they were together on the sofa again.

She stared at him for a long time before she said it: "You're boring him, B.J."

"Not even a little."

She tilted her head back, stared at the ceiling. "He is looking for the exit door." Her voice was more southern now than it had been. "You get up to make the man a drink and he looks at his watch."

"I thought you might be tired. Moving takes a lot of work."

"B.J. remembers when he used to like to enjoy your company. But he's forgotten that."

"Not a minute."

"That first time we met? In the Square at school when you tripped in front of me?"

"That was the second time. The first time was on the stairs of Peters Hall."

B.J. smiled. "Well, at least he hasn't forgotten everything." She was looking at him now. "Blanche always put her faith in the kindness of strangers. Is he a stranger now?"

"No."

"Put your drink down—if a departure is in order, at least have the decency to leave the glassware."

They both put their drinks down.

She reached out then, took his hand, placed it on her breast, held it there. "How much did he want to do that, I wonder, all those years ago? What would he have given then?"

"Everything."

She dropped her hand away. Chub pulled his back.

"It won't bite."

He touched her blouse again, gently, rubbing a circle. Under he could begin to feel her nipple pressing against the fabric of her pale-blue blouse.

"Is he still hard, I wonder?"

"See for yourself."

She touched his trousers lightly, pulled her hand away.

"It won't bite," Chub said.

"Promise?"

Chub moved toward her on the couch and they kissed. His hand went inside her blouse, inside her bra; her nipple was already firm. "Come, baby," she said then, taking his hand. "Jesse isn't the soundest of sleepers." They moved into her bedroom. She locked the door, turned out the light. The only illumination came softly from the bathroom beyond. Chub took her into his arms again; her lips parted and he kissed her, moving his tongue inside her mouth, pressing his body up against her.

She moved a step away. "Consider that the appetizer. B.J. has her rituals—she only beds when she is immaculate and her partner the same. You shower first."

Chub undressed in the semidarkness. She stood as before, watching him. When he was naked she moved to him, ran her hands across his chest. When his nipples were firm, she kissed them, then gave a quick bite. "Just another appetizer, now be off with you."

He went into the bathroom. There was a shower with a glass door and when he got the water right, he stepped in, began to lather up. B.J. watched him. "Close your eyes," she said. "Keep them that way until otherwise instructed."

Chub closed his eyes, and then her hands were on his penis and he stared at her, the glass door open, a bar of soap in her hands. "You were not otherwise instructed."

"C'mon—"

"—*you were not otherwise instructed,* now, unless you want to forget about any main course at all, I suggest you do as you are told."

Chub closed his eyes; she soaped his testicles, then both her hands were on his penis again. "This was called a 'dohicky' where I came from. You'd be amazed at how many men are slovenly when it comes to keeping their dohickies clean." Now her fingers traced their way across the upper side, paused and circled around the tip, then began to massage the underside and Chub, hard, pulled away.

"He doesn't like it."

"He likes it a lot," Chub assured her. "He just doesn't want to lose it in the shower."

She nodded then. Her clothes were soaked but she didn't seem to notice. "Off to bed with you," she said.

Chub grabbed a towel, began to get dry.

She just stood there. "A lady undresses alone."

Chub wondered what the hell that was about, but he finished drying off, went back to the bedroom. It was still dark but the bed had been made ready. He lay on the sheets, listening to her singing as she showered. "It's a Barnum and Bailey world, just as phony as it can be, but it wouldn't be make believe if you believed in me." Blanche sang that. In *Streetcar*.

When she appeared, she was wearing a half-slip, the elastic top barely covering her breasts, the bottom of the slip reaching her thighs. "I stole this from my Dallas performance; this was my costume when I inflamed Stanley Kowalski. Of course, I was wearing undergarments then." She began to dance slowly, gracefully circling the bed. Then she flicked off the bathroom light and there was darkness. "Would he care to dance with me, I wonder?" Chub got up, followed her voice, took her in his arms and awkwardly moved back and forth, until Chub took the elastic top of the slip and pulled it down and her breasts sprang free and they were large, his hands covered them, larger than he thought and firmer than he'd hoped and he kissed her nipples, tried pulling the rest of the slip off but she resisted that, which was fine with him, he wasn't interested in tonguing her navel, all he wanted, all in the world he wanted, was her body beneath him on the bed and he reached out for it, found it, brought her down and they kissed as he touched her breasts and she liked that, and then he reached down and put his finger into her pubic hair and she didn't like it, reached for his hand, and that was fine with him, too, he just wanted to make sure she was moist and ready because he was, his cock had never felt as hard and he straddled her, spread her legs, and ramrodded home. She made a sound, a quick gasping sound, as Chub put his hands beside her body, thrust deep, pulled halfway back, thrust again, again, and as he kept on it was wonderful, yes, great, all that, except he couldn't get deep enough inside her so he reached up, took her shoulders, turned her as he lay facing her and the movement made him lose her but that was quickly handled, he grabbed his cock and found her vagina and plunged again, and she was making her sounds but he still couldn't get deep enough, couldn't bury his cock up to her throat, so he pulled out again, lay flat on his back, took her, brought her up on top and she wasn't sure she wanted that but he knew what he wanted. He wanted her above him, and when her knees were spread he put himself back inside and began to jerk up with his hips and at last he was there, totally penetrating with his hands reaching up, fingering her breasts, which were swelling. Now all he wanted was to last. Last forever or at least until she came, and sometimes he could do that, could bring a girl to orgasm before he'd come, but usually to make that happen he had to take his mind away, concentrate on the multiplication tables, forget his own throbbing, desperate needs. He loved that, he loved to feel the female body out of control while he still had his. But that was out of the question now. B. J. Peacock was riding him now. And soon his cock was on its own, and as he started to shoot he grabbed her shoulders as hard as he could and pressed her down as he moved his hips into her and then he was into orgasm, so he released her shoulders, brought her so that her breasts hung above his mouth and he sucked the nearest nipple until he was still. Then he rolled over on top of her and said, "Squeeze me," and she said, "What do you mean?" and he said, loud, "Your thighs, squeeze my cock, goddamnit," and she did, getting the hang of it soon enough to satisfy him, keeping at it until his final drops were gone.

She started talking to him then, quietly, tenderly, praising him, and Chub was stunned—because she thought it was over—

—he kissed her mouth and then down to her nipples and then he was kneeling on the floor, bringing her toward him, spreading her legs and at first she didn't resist but then she said, "No, no, don't do that," but by then his tongue was inside, and her clitoris was between his lips. She tried again to roll away but he held her and he buried his head in her pubic hair and used his tongue and he could tell it wouldn't take long, even though he wanted it to. And as he took her clitoris with his lips and moved his head side to side he could hear her and she wasn't saying no anymore. She was starting to come now, and Chub reached far up, felt her nipples begin to engorge, and then he left them and touched his hands as lightly as he could to the skin above her navel, because he could feel beneath the surface the delicate movement inside. He never knew what it was but he loved it, loved being able to feel it happen, it was like a river was moving just beneath her skin. Her body was out of control now, her hips rising involuntarily, and he kept his mouth pressed down, kissing her clitoris, until she cried out and exhaled and lay still.

He moved back onto the bed, and before he could reach for her she was reaching for him and holding his face with both hands, and then she was talking, the words coming in bursts, about how Del would never do that, no one had ever done that, Del had been her only man till now and he said it was dirty and Chub kissed her mouth to quiet her. He didn't want to hear about Del or anybody else, Del didn't matter, no other man mattered, nothing mattered except that he, Charles Fuller, had startled and pleasured the girl of his dreams, made flesh out of fantasy.

He got dressed a half hour later. She put on a robe and

saw him to the door. She stood in the doorway till the elevator parted them. It was still pouring when he reached the street but Chub didn't look for a cab or a bus, he wanted to walk home.

Between the drops all the way.

The next night Chub had to bus to Princeton to tape an interview with a professor who was perhaps the leading expert on the actual day-to-day workings of the Kremlin. (One of Chub's clients in Oregon was writing a love story between an American journalist [female] and a Russian diplomat [all male]. The client had sent Chub pages of questions, Chub asked them, recorded the answers, paid the prof fifty bucks an hour, mailed the tape from New Jersey before catching a late bus back to Port Authority.) When he got back there was a message on his machine that said, "I am attempting a sirloin tomorrow, in case you feel brave."

Jesse met him at the door, dragged him off to her room because her grandfather was on the phone. Chub was to learn that B.J. talked to her father every evening. Sometimes for fifteen minutes, sometimes longer. Chub never eavesdropped, but it was a habit set in stone, and had been ever since Carlos Peacock's wife died.

Chub sat on the bed and explained to Big Baby and the child about the Umbrella Fiend, who was as ruthless as they come. He was also a master of disguise, so it was impossible for anyone except the Rain Man to be sure who and where he was. The Umbrella Fiend was responsible, in his own Machiavellian way, for every broken umbrella in the universe. Every trash can that contained a maimed and useless umbrella was his doing. He and his vast army of henchmen always appeared on street corners when a drizzle was about to begin and sold their wares for a great deal of money, knowing that within minutes the umbrella would turn inside out and break with the least puff of wind, thereby amassing a fortune second only to the entire International Brotherhood of Teamsters, plus also making the common citizen despise precipitation. The Rain Man, who understood the beauty found in mists, was sworn to stop him.

When B.J. appeared, Chub realized he needed a kicker fast, so he told Jesse that on his first adventure, just when he was about to grab the villain, the weather cleared suddenly and just as suddenly, the Rain Man disappeared, leaving Chub alone and frightened and a long way from home.

Jesse shouted "Unfair" again but Chub promised more another time and the sirloin wasn't half bad. The accompanying baked potatoes could have used an extra half hour or so but Chub swore to B.J. that he preferred them nice and hard and crunchy.

They made love again in total darkness and again the night after that. (The weather turned damp quickly, the Rain Man reappeared, and they caught the Umbrella Fiend and handed him over to the local authorities, who let him slip away as he changed into a different disguise between the police car and being booked, and at dinner that night, when all his large family was sitting around the table and telling of their days, Chub, smallest and last, explained that he had helped bring in the Umbrella Fiend and when he was done, his wonderful mother just shook her head and said, "That child—what won't he think of next?" That became the tag line of all the Rain Man stories. "That child—what won't he think of next?" Jesse picked it up and soon it became a part of her vast, for five, vocabulary.)

"Listen," B.J. said as they lay in the dark room that third night. "Are you going to disappear on me or what? I mean, are you seeing women?"

"Many. It's almost like a harem."

"I'm *serious.*"

She was; it was clear from the nervous tone to her emphasis.

"I'm right here," Chub said. "There aren't a whole lot of places I'd rather be."

"Then you better know it all, the good and the not so good." She flicked on the bed light—she wore her half-

slip as she had before. This was the first time there had
been brightness in the bedroom.

Chub watched.

B.J. stood, removed the slip, looked at him.

Chub looked back. Her skin was splotched across her
neck; her hair was in disarray. That was about all that
was different.

"Well?"

"Well what?"

"You see it."

Chub shook his head.

"This," she said, and she pointed to just below her
navel. A scar ran down into her pubic hair. "Jesse was
cesarean. Fucking doctor should have gone sideways but
he didn't."

Chub didn't get it. It wasn't that much of a scar. But
she was working her way into something.

"The stomach muscles were cut, don't you understand.
I could never lose this." She gripped the flesh above her
pubic hair. "I'll never be flat again."

"Turn off the light," Chub said. "And come here."

She did. Chub held her for a moment, then bent down,
ran his tongue along the scar. "This is farewell," he said,
and he was about to go on when he could tell tears were
approaching, so he held her again until she had control.
Weird. That was the only word for it. Here was this glory
confessing in embarrassment that her stomach would
never be as flat as when she was a teen-ager; this head-
snapping creature who made love only in total darkness
lest her "disfigurement" be seen. Weird, indeed.

But then, for some people, an "A-minus" was the same
as an "F."

Dinner with the Kitchels ten days later graded out to a
"C." No flaws with the meal—they ate at El Parador, the
wonderful restaurant on East Thirty-fourth Street, which
was one of Two-Brew's favorites, and when it turned out
that B.J. preferred Mexican to any other food, the destination became obvious.

Chub and B.J. were together constantly during those ten days. He was worried that she wanted time off, but if she did, it didn't show, since she was the one who always set up the next night's assignation. "It's not me who wants to see you, Lord knows, it's Jesse."

For his part, Chub wanted to see them both.

The only problem was B.J.'s insistence on reading Chub's book. He put her off and put her off—it wasn't ready. But when she began to assume he thought she was probably too stupid to understand it, he gave in, at least partially, letting her have the section that dealt with the war and the wounding. She was the first to see it and he asked her not to talk about it, and she said she wouldn't, except to him. Which she did. Going over it with him, because she was rocked by its power, rocked and moved and how did he do it, how could he just pick words out of the atmosphere and make people, strangers, *care?*

Two-Brew and Lydia were already at the bar when they arrived. The restaurant didn't take reservations so they had a forty-minute wait until a booth was ready. They drank a couple of margaritas apiece and Lydia emptied a bowl of chips without much help, asked for a second when that was done. They were all a little buzzed when they finally sat down, and that wasn't all bad, because the Kitchels had been scratchy from the beginning, when B.J. held Two-Brew in her arms for a very long time.

Lydia watched from behind her horn-rims. Chub thought she looked fine, a little tired maybe, maybe a little heavier. At the booth they had another round of margaritas and B.J. tried explaining about the great beer-drinking contest at the No-Name. Two-Brew sat quietly, and Chub did his best to help but clearly it was the kind of experience you had to be there for.

Menus came and Lydia said, "You all go first, I need time," so the other three ordered. Lydia still wasn't sure. Then she said, "Oh, what the hell, let me start with the guacamole and then the black-bean soup and the special fried chicken." The waiter nodded, took the menus back, when Lydia said, "And some nachos. With the peppers on them."

Two-Brew looked at her. "That sounds fine for an appetizer, honey, what'll you have for a main course?"

Lydia looked back at him. "What's that all about?"

"Why didn't you just order the whole right side of the menu?"

Lydia said, with great precision, "The nachos are for all of us. For the table, all right?"

Two-Brew shrugged.

Lydia finished half her margarita without talking.

B.J. raised her glass then for a toast. Chub thought it was going to be for old times' sake but instead B.J. said, "To my freedom: I am now officially divorced." She reached across, took Two-Brew's hand. "I'm officially on the prowl. If you know any young bachelors, keep me in mind."

"You can't do any worse than Young Lochinvar here, that's a certainty."

"True." And now she put her arms around Chub, kissed his ear. "Onwards and upwards."

They all had guacamole and the plate of nachos was put in front of Lydia, who insisted they all share. Then, when her second appetizer, the black-bean soup, came, Chub and Two-Brew excused themselves and headed for the men's room.

"Jesus," Two-Brew said when they were alone. "You must be in hog heaven."

"The evenings pass pleasantly, I'll admit that."

"Did you see the way people watched her at the bar. She's sure something, all things considered."

Stung, Chub asked what the hell that meant: all things considered.

"Well, Christ, Chubbo, what is she, thirty with a kid?"

"What are you saying, she's in the final stages of deterioration?"

"Skip it."

When they got back to the table Lydia said, "B.J. loves Chub's book."

"Just the part I've read—he's very secretive but you know how artists are." She smiled at Two-Brew. "You love it, too, don't you?"

Chub broke in: "He never reads anything of mine until it's complete. He gets a fresh reading that way. It's how we've always worked."

Two-Brew nodded but Chub could tell from the way he picked at his enchiladas that he was pissed. He grew more sour as Lydia ate her fried chicken. The others had long finished while Lydia concentrated on getting every last bite from the bones. Finally, they had a quick coffee while Chub took care of the check. Then they took separate cabs home. On the way, Chub realized what "all things considered" meant. Two-Brew was flat-out jealous but that was understandable. Here he'd arrived with the most sought-after creature either of them had known, while at the same time, Lydia had chosen to balloon.

The trip to Texas, in late September, was brief and terrifying. Chub had no intention of going and more than that, felt he had no business being there—the reason for the trip was personal on B.J.'s part. Her mother had died on the last day of September and she'd made a private vow to always be with her father then, to accompany him on the drive to Plano, where the family originated and where all the Peacocks finally came to rest.

When she first asked Chub to come along—it would just be a quick shoot, she explained, leave Friday afternoon, back the following Monday—he begged off. She came at him again but he told her he did not like feeling the part of the intruder. That night, during her talk with Carlos, she suddenly shoved the phone at Chub and he found himself in stuttering conversation, listening as the voice said he would surely like to reacquaint himself with the famous fella he'd met at his daughter's wedding. Chub thanked him profusely but explained that business matters made problems for him, clearing his schedule and all.

He gave the phone back to B.J. and encountered Jesse eavesdropping from the living room. She looked, the kid did, odd. Almost frightened, Chub thought. "I get to go to Texas," she said.

Chub said he'd heard.

"I love it there," Jesse said. "My granddaddy, he just loves me so."

Chub waited. There was more. He could see her face working.

"If only Big Baby wasn't so scared."

"I didn't know Big Baby didn't like to fly."

"Oh, she loves to fly, she just doesn't like getting there." Then she snapped her fingers, like a bad actress indicating. "Maybe you could come along." She brought Big Baby up to her ear, whispered awhile. "Big Baby would like it, too, she really really would." There was something in her tone.

Chub scooped them both up into his arms. "Anything for Big Baby," he said.

The flight to Dallas was uneventful; Chub discovered that he could play drums on his dessert pudding, using the round bottomed spoons for sticks, and Jesse got a kick out of that and if B.J. hadn't made a remark, *"People are watching,"* they might have gone at it a lot longer.

Carlos Peacock himself met them at the airport, and Chub found B.J.'s father surprisingly old and frail although J. Press would have found his attire impeccable. He stood at the exit gate and B.J. almost flew into his arms. She was five six and probably once he had been taller than that, but now their mouths were level when they kissed. Chub shook hands very firmly and looked the old man straight in the eye. (His own father had taught him that when he was young and he kept the habit alive, though he never was sure why—Stalin was supposed to have had a firm handshake and Dillinger was noted for always looking people in the eye.)

Then the old man bussed his grandchild and they started to walk, but in that brief touch, Chub saw it all—Carlos had carefully chosen the unscarred cheek and the look in his eye as he turned the birthmark away was so unchecked that Chub was suddenly back in Florida and Gretchen was screaming about his dead older brother: "*His eyes were blue. Blue!* And he never once cried, never was trouble, he slept through the night when he was a week old."

Chub took Jesse with one hand, lugged Big Baby with the other, following the Peacocks and wondering about people and how could they behave the way they did? From a hundred yards you could tell that Jesse was special. What the fuck difference did it make that an unjust God had chosen to fire her face?

Then he realized he was as bad as the rest; if B.J. had been a hundred pounds heavier back at Oberlin, there was no way he'd be in Texas now.

The Peacock mansion was located in Highland Park, the old-money part of Dallas. The walls were filled, not with paintings, but more with large color photographs of the family. B.J.'s mother was prominent (green-eyed, red-haired), and two handsome brothers, both of them living now in California, both in the aerospace business. (The old man spoke of them without emotion—they were both almost forty, they could take care of themselves.) Dozens of pictures of B.J. (She had been one of those few who never went through an awkward age.) And a single photo of Jesse, in profile, in the good profile.

Dinner was brought in by servants. "Good old Texas beef" but well done. Afterward, Jesse was sent off to bed and the three sat around, talking, until Chub excused himself—it was obvious they wanted to engage in personal conversation, memories of the dead mother predominated, so he left, went up to tuck the kid in. (The Umbrella Fiend had concocted a monstrous plot to try to capture the Rain Man once and for all, but with luck and guile, they both escaped, and that night at dinner, when Chub told the events of the day, his mother said—

("That child," Jesse interrupted. "What won't he think of next?")

Chub stayed with her till she was asleep, joined his host downstairs. The old man was tired now, too, but he carefully showed Chub the guest room and said, "I'm just down the hall, give a holler if you need anything, I can hear pretty good from there."

"He's old-fashioned," B.J. said as they finished their nightcap downstairs. "But he likes you."

"Mutual," Chub lied.

The next day was taken up with going around and meeting friends—which seemed odd to Chub, since a party had been laid on for that evening and all the friends came to the Peacocks. But he got through it—"No, he didn't know James Michener; no, he didn't know Harold Robbins either." Jesse stayed out of the way upstairs except for once when B.J. brought her down and led her quickly through the large rooms.

Chub watched the other people watch the child. Half the ladies shook their heads in sadness when Jesse passed by. From what he'd heard, California was the place that put the most premium on physical beauty; from what he saw, Dallas could give cards and spades to Los Angeles anytime.

Sunday morning after church they started the drive to the cemetery. Jesse had never been before, but B.J. insisted; she was old enough now. Carlos agreed but insisted the doll not come along. This was not a time for frivolity. Chub steadied the kid, went with her while she tucked Big Baby safely in her bed. Then she just stood there: What oh what if someone decided to steal it. Chub got a piece of paper and wrote a note and read it to Jesse: "This is *not* Big Baby." He put the note beside the doll's head, took Jesse's hand, led her to the Cadillac and they both got in back.

B.J. asked her father if he wanted her to drive but he said no, he knew the way best and they began. He drove very slowly, not only in Highland Park but when they were outside of Dallas, aiming for Plano. Chub had no idea how far the place was, but as the flat land passed by, he decided it was a great spot not to come for your summer vacation.

After what seemed like hours and well might have been, the car came to a halt by a river. Chub looked around for the cemetery, saw nothing.

"Remember?" Carlos asked.

"How could I not?" B.J. answered.

Carlos turned now and pointed down toward the murky water. "Almost lost your mother there," he said to Jesse. "If I'd been five minutes later, you wouldn't be here now."

"You almost drowned?" Chub asked.

"Drowned?" the old man said. "Heck no—that ain't water, it only looks like water. You know what that is, Jesse?"

Jesse shook her head.

"Quicksand," Carlos said. "Good old Texas quicksand. You know what that does?"

Jesse shook her head.

Carlos looked at his granddaughter. "It sucks you to death."

Jesse stared at the water. "No it doesn't, you're teasing."

"Hope to tell you I'm not—see, we were visiting here when B.J. was, oh, maybe ten, and we went for a horseback ride and she got ahead of me and the next thing I knew she was screaming. See, she thought it was like a river or stream and then the quicksand had her and thank the Good Lord I had the strength to grab a branch and drag her safe but her horse, it just got sucked to death." He put a hand on B.J.'s shoulder. "Almost lost my girl."

Jesse was terrified now.

"That's all pure plain one hundred percent unadulterated bullshit," Chub heard himself say.

Now the old man glared back at him. "I'm not a liar, son."

" 'Course you're not," Chub said. "But I know a little

bit about quicksand and it doesn't suck anybody anywhere."

"It happened, Chub. Daddy saved me."

"I know that, and I hope you know I'm grateful that
he did. All I'm trying to get across is that he didn't have
to." He looked at the kid now. "Y'see, Jesse, I did some
research once on this and quicksand isn't something to
fear—it's just a sand without enough foundation to hold
you, so what you do is lie down on the top and just roll
over and over until you're on safe, solid ground."

"I saw her horse go down with these two eyes, son."

"I'm sure you did, Mr. Peacock. And I'm also sure
that the animal probably thrashed and kicked and pan-
icked. And it sank beneath the weight of its own body."

Jesse was watching the two men now, her eyes flicking
from one to the other, the terror still there.

"For a writer, he sure don't know a lot," Carlos
Peacock said to B.J.

"Ah, now there you're right, sir." And then Chub
opened the car door, stepped outside. "Why don't we
prove how stupid I am. How about if I walk into the
quicksand till it's, say, up past my knees and then what if
I lie down on the top and roll back to shore. I promise
you I will be gooey"—almost a smile from Jesse on that
word—"and I promise you my shoes will slosh, but I also
promise you there is nothing to be afraid of because I will
be here, *all* safe and sound. Does anyone believe me?"

Mr. Peacock said nothing, just gripped the steering
wheel. B.J. said, "Get back in the car."

"Does anyone believe me?" Chub said again, standing
his ground.

A quick nod from the backseat.

Chub got back in the car.

The rest of the drive was quiet. The cemetery, when
they reached it, was small and might have been pretty
had it been on a hillside. But they were in short supply in
Plano, Texas. B.J. and her father led the way to the
grave. Carlos had brought a bouquet of flowers and he
rested it beside the impressive stone, by far the largest in

the place. Chub held Jesse's hand, watching from a discreet distance. B.J. knelt when he was done, said a
prayer, then beckoned for her child. Reluctantly, she
released Chub, joined her mother. She was frightened
again—who wouldn't be; it was ridiculous bringing her
along. The first grave Chub remembered belonged to his
aunt and he was around Jesse's age when he was taken
there and it scared him then. When Jesse was done she
hurried back to him and B.J. knelt again and when she
was done the old man took a very long time, talking to
the flowers and the stone, sometimes directing his speech
toward the ground.

Finally they all trooped back to the Cadillac and Chub
felt enormous relief. No more scares today.

He could not have been more wrong. They had been
driving no more than a half hour back toward Dallas
when Carlos cried out, "Willya just lookee there," and he
was genuinely excited as he pulled off the road, staring
and pointing into the distance. Chub squinted, unable to
make anything out at first, but then he saw the dark
spiral moving fast across the horizon. "It's goin' away
from us, but just lookit the size," Carlos said. "I'll bet
you don't get twisters in New York."

Jesse was already inching toward him when Chub said,
"Are we ever lucky—see?—that's how Dorothy got to
Oz." Jesse stayed close to him and when the car started
at last Chub assumed they were at last soon to be safe at
home except the old man, excited, turned off, tracking
where the twister had been, and in twenty minutes they
reached the destination, a nameless crossing in the road.

And the shacks on one side were as they always had
been. But across the road, no more than forty feet, all was
destruction. Trees uprooted, trailers on their sides, children out of control, and Chub, watching the old man
watch with building excitement at God at his most capri-
cious, realized that Fitzgerald had been wrong: It wasn't
just the rich who were different from the rest of us.
Texans were too.

Jesse, in his lap now, said, her face against his neck,

"This is how Dorothy got to Oz," whispering it over and over until they at last drove on, and Chub, holding her more and more tightly, knew one thing: This kid in his arms now, this child with the fire on her face, was going to be safe. At least while he was around. He would protect her. From you name it on up and down. Even if it cost him dearly; pain, suffering, death.

The weeks following their return to Manhattan were filled with change. Jesse got a late acceptance at Little Dalton and B.J. lucked into a wonderful Colombian woman named Alicia who not only was good with children but could also *cook.* They arranged for Alicia to work from noon to eight at night, which for B.J. was only heaven. She also found a great acting teacher, "Better than Lee or Stella but low-key," named Theo. He was Greek and his last name was unpronounceable but he had classes two afternoons a week and taught privately as well, so B.J. signed up for two extra sessions on her own. Not to mention singing lessons with an even-tempered Italian lady who was very old but had an impeccable reputation.

Chub, for his part, found Rory L. Baylor.

One of his clients who lived in Schenectady (half of Chub's people now were from out of town) had signed for a series of superhero spy novels with a paperback house and he needed some difficult information on karate. He explained to Chub, via letter, that he was ripping off the famous torture scene in the first Bond, *Casino Royale,* and what he needed to know with accuracy was how badly could his villain wound his hero via karate and still enable his hero to quickly be able to function. There wasn't much in the libraries; not much of use anyway, it all tended to be how-to material. Chub was actually kind of pleased. He had wanted to meet the black cop since the night before he began researching, when Baylor's very presence had quieted a potential explosion on West Ninety-eighth Street.

Chub lucked out, finding Baylor during a shift change at the Twenty-first Precinct house just around the corner on West 100th, and he spent five minutes explaining who he was and what he did and what his needs were and, of course, compensation.

Baylor said not a word during this time, just stared Chub up and down. "Fifty bucks an hour to talk about karate?" Baylor said. "You shitting me?"

Chub, hoping the guy wasn't going to blow his stack and decapitate him with some chop he'd learned in the Orient, rushed to assure the man that he was in no way shitting him.

"Cash?"

"Or check, whatever you want."

"Cash."

"Fine."

Baylor looked at his watch. "Tomorrow night do?"

"Yessir."

"You've got an honest face, Fuller."

"Thank you."

"Don't thank me—I hate people with honest faces."

They met the next night at Chub's place a little after eight. Chub offered him a beer and Baylor accepted and Chub was no more than five minutes into the talk before he realized the guy was fantastic. Lighter-skinned than Chub had thought, but more powerfully muscled in a T-shirt and chinos than in uniform, he spoke with remarkable precision. A little on the street side, but he could handle the language with wit and with color. He carried a typed sheet of paper, which he referred to constantly, on which were listed the proper spellings of various bones in the body.

He didn't mind if Chub taped and he understood Chub's client's problems perfectly. "If we start with the knee," Baylor began, "there are obviously four main points of attack. Do we slash at the inside, the outside, the back or the cap itself?" Then he ticked off the answers—the damage a karate blow would cause in each place, the bones that might be shattered, pausing to consult his paper so that the name of each bone itself was clearly put down. When he was done with the knee, he was equally thorough on various other body parts: the elbow, the shoulder, the ribs, on and on. If you did this to that, recovery time would be approximately thus and so. (Baylor was to become a godsend for Chub—a remarkable number of clients were into mysteries and ignorant of police procedure. Chub used Baylor constantly. Sometimes getting answers by phone; sometimes doing the interviewing himself; on other occasions, if the author lived in town, sending Baylor down himself.)

It was almost ten when the cop was finished and Chub, happy he had gone to the bank that day, handed over five crisp twenties. They shared another beer, BS-ing awhile, and finally Chub felt that Baylor wouldn't be offended it he asked a question of his own: Had Baylor actually been forced to kill people? With his own hands? And what did it feel like?

Baylor took a long swig. "You mean karate-style?"

Chub did.

"And this money here is mine, no matter what."

"It was a great interview, one of the best ever."

"Well, then, Fuller, I like you, in spite of that honest face you're cursed with, so I'll tell the truth: I don't know shit about karate."

Chub, stunned, sputtered that the entirety of Ninety-eighth Street knew of his championships.

"That was a fucking rumor—started by me—I'm scared shitless of all that chop-socky stuff—I'm one-quarter Jewish, man, and we *hate* violence."

Chub broke out laughing.

Baylor held up his typed page—"Now, my wife—*she* knows karate—little minute of a girl, she decided to learn to protect herself. She typed all this bone crap down for me. We need the money. I'm starting law school this fall and it's gonna take six years but when I get my diploma, I am leaving the force posthaste. A man could get *killed* out there." He stood up, put on his Windbreaker. "This is our secret, Fuller, and it's gonna stay that way because first, no one in the area would believe you. And second, if they start to, I'll just send my little minute of a lady up here to pay you a visit and she *loves* violence."

Chub thought, when they shook hands good night, that they both knew it would not be for the last time.

He was busy the next evening too. He had to cancel dinner with B.J. because when he was working up in the Bronx at the Museum of the American Indian Library (an honest biography of Geronimo was his client's project) he beeped in at lunch to get his messages and found that Elliott Carter (*the* Elliott Carter) said to call.

Chub did, immediately, and found that Carter needed some material dealing with how would you make tarantulas bigger, how would you enlarge a cobra? (A mad-scientist epic was clearly in the works.) Carter asked if Chub was busy and of course, even though the answer was yes, he said no. Carter had been the reason for so much of his business that even though he never told the old man, he always put everything else aside, regardless of the hassles it might cause.

So he subwayed to Forty-second and Fifth, and they didn't have much (who could possibly have much), so he took the Lex local number six, got off at 103rd, legged it quickly through the dangerous streets until he reached the New York Academy of Medicine stronghold, probably as good a medical library as any anywhere.

They had material on cobra venom and serum and a lot of unpleasant-looking pictures of tarantulas (Chub was as squeamish as the next guy) with accompanying text, but it wasn't until he tried "Growth" that he found much that Carter might find useful. But the material was scattered and also overpoweringly scientific in jargon, and Chub had to ask the librarians more questions than they wanted to hear. He Xeroxed what he could but he realized as he did so that he had a long night ahead—he would have to type up much of the material, collate it into coherent groups, put down as many definitions as he knew.

It was three in the morning before he slept, then he got up early, handed it to Carter before ten. He was due at B.J.'s that night at six, which gave him time to do a little more Geronimo stuff, take a nap and write a stern letter from the credit manager of Bloomingdale's complaining for the *very last* (underlined) time that Big Baby had overdrawn her account.

After Jesse hugged him he handed her the note. "Doorman gave this to me. You better read it."

Jesse, proud of her reading—she was a whiz from watching *Sesame Street*—squinted at the typing, handed it back to Chub. "You read and I'll tell if you're doing it right."

They went into her room, sat on the bed along with Big Baby, who was propped comfortably, her head resting on the pillows.

"Big Baby *what?*" Jesse said, when Chub was done.

Chub explained awhile: Bloomingdale's was a store that sold things, accounts were ways of paying without paying, overdrawing did not have anything to do with using real cash.

"But she never goes shopping alone," Jesse said.

"That's not what this indicates, kiddo. I'll bet she's been hitting the high spots while you've been in school." Chub shook his head. "This could be trouble." He reached out his hand. "Give me the other Bloomingdale's letters."

Jesse just looked at him.

Chub showed her the typed page: "See this part where it's underlined? See where it says *'very last'* time? Well, that means there must have been earlier letters. Let me have 'em, I'll try and get to the bottom of it."

"This is the very first one."

Chub studied her. "You're not just trying to protect certain people?"

"I promise."

Chub heaved a huge sigh of relief. "Well, if you promise, that means it's so, and if it's so, everything comes clear—it's those stupid computers at Bloomingdale's—they goofed. They're famous for that. Mind if I keep this?"

She didn't.

He folded the letter, stuck it in his pocket. "I'm gonna call that credit manager tomorrow and really let him have it. If he doesn't send a written apology, he is going to be one sorry cookie." (The credit manager was distraught, and from then on, not a week went by without some gift and accompanying note. One week a training bra, the next a copy of *Remembrance of Things Past* in the original. He was clearly a man of unpredictable tastes.)

"He is going to be one sorry cookie," Jesse told her mother the night the first letter arrived. They all three ate together now, early, because Alicia needed to be done with the dishes and gone by eight. Chub delighted in the early meals, because not only was Jesse with them, the food was fresh, warm and always bore a clear resemblance to what it was originally intended to be.

B.J. listened to the story of the computer mistake, and she nodded at the right times, always paid attention. But Chub sensed very definitely something. Later, after Jesse was asleep and they were alone on the couch he started going on about some of the Looney Tunes jobs he had, how he was up till three typing material for a writer who, a century and a half after Mary Shelley, was still spending his days inventing monsters and—

"I don't want to hear about it," B.J. said.

"Sorry. I don't blame you." He reached for her hand, and she let him hold it, but only for a moment before pulling it back.

"I don't want any sex tonight. I'm tired—no, I'm not tired, I've got a headache. You believe that? Well, don't."

Chub waited.

"I'm pregnant. You believe that? Well, don't."

"What's the matter?"

"You don't get to ask that, that's my question, 'What's the matter?' Only *I* know the answer."

"Well, I wish you'd share it."

She looked out at the October night. "Oh, come on," she said finally.

"Obviously I've done something."

"You sure have. You have changed, and I know when it happened—at that Mexican place—and I know why—because I told you my divorce came through, which makes me, what's that terrible word?—oh, yes, 'available.' You've been scared ever since."

"Oh, bullshit."

She looked at him with her green eyes then, and for a moment, Chub thought there might be tears. Then she was up, moving sharply away toward the bar. She started to make herself a drink, but her fingers couldn't get the ice out of the bucket. Her back to him she said, "I thought maybe we were into something. I wanted that."

"Same."

"Then why are you all of a sudden going on about your work—Del did that—I left him before I died of boredom—I've got a life, too, I don't hear you asking many questions. And why did you pick a fight with Daddy?—the place I almost died and you had to make a scene."

"I was just trying to calm Jesse."

"Jesse is stronger than either of us—when was the last time you tried to calm me?"

Chub started up toward her.

"You listen! You sit right there, because maybe you have other women, but I don't have other men and maybe you think that's because I can't, but believe me, I get hit on. In class the other actors, on the street, the goddamn strangers. Just because I'm damaged goods in your eyes doesn't mean I'm ready for the ashcan." And now she started slowly toward him. "Do you hear me? I need a man. But care has to cut both ways."

Chub reached out for her.

She took his hands, stood over him. "All I've tried to do for months now is make you happy but I want that too. I want to be an equal partner, I want a man beside me."

"I'm not going anyplace," Chub said.

Chub was married in what B.J. referred to as his "first grown-up suit." A navy-blue pinstripe she'd helped him select at Paul Stuart. Actually, she did the selecting entirely on her own, and when he went into the dressing room to try it on, she asked the salesman if he minded if she "took a peek," and when the salesman said, "Not at all, madam," B.J. went into the dressing room and pulled the cloth curtain shut and chatted with both the salesman just outside and Chub. "Is this the best fabric you have?" she asked and the salesman assured her it was of the very finest quality and "Do you think it will prove durable?" she asked and the salesman said he had no doubt that it would and she asked Chub to "turn this way" and "now that way" and all the time she chattered on her hands had unzipped the fly and were massaging his cock, watching it grow and finally B.J. said, "It may be too big but then it may be just right, I'll take it just the way it is," and then she zipped his pants, patted the bulge, left him alone to await the return of normalcy.

The ceremony was very brief and intentionally small. It took place the week before Thanksgiving in B.J.'s living room. Carlos flew up from Dallas. (This was after much scuffling—he wanted to give a "shindig" but B.J. said he had given her one of those, with half the town in attendance, and the marriage had been miserable. This time she was doing things the other way around. Carlos finally agreed when she said they would honeymoon over the Christmas holidays back home. Ordinarily, when given such news, Chub might have balked, but not much was bothering him these days.) Two-Brew was his best man, tit for tat. (Later, Chub and B.J. roared over the conversations between Kitchel and Carlos—they had eyed each other with extraordinary wariness from the beginning, each being convinced the other had descended without warning from some distant planet.) Lydia watched quietly and so did Alicia the Colombian maid, standing in the farthest corner of the room. Most attentive of all was the kid, who whispered occasionally to Big Baby. The minister was an oddball nondenominational type Chub had hustled up in the Village. He seemed a trifle buzzed when he arrived, blew the ceremony several times, most noticeably when he forgot the business with the ring. Fortunately, the chief participants remembered and after everything was legal, Carlos took the bunch to "21" for an absolutely ordinary meal.

Chub had arranged for a suite at the Navarro on Central Park South, and he insisted on a large terrace in the front. (He had seen the view once in a movie—the park, from up high, looked like a giant Christmas toy from Schwarz's, the tiny cars obeying the traffic patterns, the lights changing color, the skaters at the Wollman Rink like dolls.)

After they'd showered and before they made love, B.J. put quilts around them both and they went out into the pleasant evening. At the railing, they gathered together in a single quilt, their naked bodies giving warmth. They touched each other gently and B.J. repeated that now, at last, at thirty, she had had her happiest day. Chub kissed her breasts, his eyes shut tight, knowing at last he was on the come again, because of all the people in all the world, he alone held not B. J. Peacock or B. J. Hilton but B. J. Fuller in his arms.

It was early in January when Del Hilton made such a brief but telling reappearance in Chub's life.

When Chub beeped in for his messages at mid-afternoon, there was Del's voice, asking could they meet, say, at the Palm Court of the Plaza at five. He'd be there anyway, regardless, and listen, there's no reason for anyone else to know.

Chub recognized him immediately. Del was totally bald now, but he still wore the old-fashioned rimless glasses, still possessed the same quiet strength. They shook hands, ordered coffee and pastry, waited for the string trio to move on so they could talk. Over the familiar Viennese music, Del said, "I'm glad you could come, I won't take much of your time."

"Think of me as yours," Chub said.

Del smiled, but behind it, Chub could see the emotion. Then Del did a strange thing: He reached across and took Chub's hand and held it briefly while he said, "I'm just so goddamn grateful, I had to tell you face-to-face."

"For?"

"Jesse. I just came from a visit. I've never seen her in better shape. She really loves you, Chub, and God bless you for that."

"I figured I was doing okay—Big Baby asks to sit in my lap sometimes now."

"I gave her that doll the week she was born—new father, what did I know, I went out and bought her this 'thing' that was bigger than she was at the time. Almost filled the crib." He shook his head. "That was the hardest thing for me, Chub, when I left B.J. Leaving Jesse too."

You left B.J.? Chub thought.

Del caught it. "She told you she left me? That's fine. Probably now she thinks she did. It isn't so but it's okay. Why do you think I have such miserable visiting privileges? When I moved in with Michelle I knew it wasn't going to be a 'creative' divorce."

"Michelle?"

Del gestured toward a woman sitting by herself at another table. "I'd like you to meet her when we're done. Terrific lawyer but a better human being."

Chub glanced at the lone woman and thought how it must have racked B.J. when Del left, and not just the rejection. Michelle was older than Del—she looked close to forty—and she was very, very plain.

"I would have taken off two years sooner than I did except for Jesse. I didn't know if she could take it."

"I'm told she's very strong."

"She is again now, now that you're around."

"You two were so golden back in school. It's none of my business, but what happened, Del?"

Del Hilton took off his rimless glasses, got a handkerchief from his back pocket, took his time in cleaning. "I don't know—I suppose I realized I couldn't make her happy—and I'm not talking bed—and the harder I tried, the more I failed. It's hard to survive on failure." He put his glasses back on. "But obviously that's not your problem—I can see that in Jesse's face."

Chub smiled. "So far, so terrific," he said.

Which was, of course, sort of true, and sort of something else he didn't understand.

The week after Thanksgiving they were having breakfast coffee at the round table in the kitchen. It was after eight, Chub was dressed, while B.J. padded around the room in her nightgown. She said, over a second cup, that it seemed to her a little schedule-rearranging might prove beneficial to all. Chub asked how so and she said, well, since Jesse was picked up by the Little Dalton bus at eight, and Alicia didn't come till twelve, and all her lessons and classes were in the P.M., it seemed to her that four hours alone with the man she loved was something she could deal with and happily. Chub explained that she was right but if you researched in libraries and you got there when they opened, you had the places pretty much to yourself and could get a lot done quickly, whereas if you got there at noon, you were entering a zoo. And it meant that by the time he got up to West Ninety-eighth Street, which he'd kept as an office, he might have to work later.

She listened and nodded and smiled. Then she took off her nightgown and said, "B.J. understands. A nice new naked wife is okay, but a quiet card catalog is hard to find."

They compromised. Chub stayed until she began to dress for the day, around eleven or so. They compromised on his night work too. Unless a particular expert was essential and only available in the evenings, Chub found somebody else just as capable, which worked out well, because they could go to so much more theatre, on Broadway and off. They liked *The Elephant Man* and *Whose Life Is It Anyway?* and B.J. was insane over

Sweeney Todd because it would be a great part for her when she was as old as Angela Lansbury. But she hated *They're Playing Our Song* because Lucie Arnaz was younger than she was and not half as good and probably only got the part because Lucille Ball was her mother.

Chub survived the two weeks in Texas well enough, except for Christmas Day. He had known for a month what he was going to give B.J. but it took some doing—a leather-bound album filled with pictures from her Oberlin career. Chub called Durning at the library and explained what he wanted and cost was really no object and Durning came through for him, and then some, finding pictures not just of the leads she played—*The Philadelphia Story, Kiss Me Kate, Macbeth*—but also others from her freshman year, when she was just a figure in the chorus of *Oklahoma!*, a secondary part in *The Trojan Women*. He bought the album at Mark Cross, the highest-quality leather they had, and in a color of green that almost matched her eyes.

She loved it, she just loved it, and said so many times "B.J. is just so touched" and Chub was pleased, of course, until that afternoon when he began to remember Gretchen staring at her leather-bound copy of *Gone with the Wind*.

They had their first fight, squabble really, in January, a few weeks after his meeting with Del in the Palm Court. When they were done with coffee she said, taking his hand, that the most wonderful idea had come to her. Chub asked what it was and she said that it wasn't enough to tell him, she had to *show* him, and with that she led him to the library and gestured around. This, B.J. said, this would make the most wonderful office for you and you wouldn't have to trek to Ninety-eighth Street anymore.

Chub was surprised at the strength of his negative reaction. Because, in truth, he was ashamed of what had once been his home. He was embarrassed by the shabbiness, had never allowed B.J. to visit—it would have humiliated him to let her see the way he lived.

What was so wonderful about Ninety-eighth Street?

Nothing. But writers have offices to go to.

Of course they need offices; but they don't have to *go* to them.

"I need it."

"I would most certainly be interested in finding out why."

"I just do."

"A masterly explanation."

What could he say? That Isaac Singer maybe lived there once? Ridiculous. That it was *his?* A mistake—they were married now, everything was *theirs,* and she was being gracious enough to share. That having it made him feel like a grown-up? True, but he couldn't explain what that meant to himself, not logically, so how could he expect her to understand. "It's cheap and I've got a terrific lease."

"Will you at least consider sometime in the future working here?"

"Of course."

"We'll talk about it some other time, then." Pause. "This lease? When's it up?"

"June."

"We'll talk about it in June, why don't we?"

End of discussion.

They had their first fight—not squabble—early in March, the day Jesse turned six. A few weeks before, Chub asked her, when he was putting her to bed, if there was anything special a special six-year-old might want for her birthday and Jesse said, "Oh, yes, a 'lectric wagon with pedals." Chub registered it: an electric wagon with pedals, and the next afternoon he went to Schwarz's to buy one.

No one at Schwarz's knew what he was talking about.

Odd, Chub thought, as he walked up to Rappaport's at Seventy-ninth and Third.

Rappaport's was equally ignorant.

That night, after they were done defeating the Umbrella Fiend, Chub asked the kid what she wanted for her birthday, because Jesse had a remarkable ability for changing her mind. "I told you, didn't I? A 'lectric wagon with pedals."

Chub kissed her good night, buried his head in her neck till she was kicking with laughter, left her in the arms of Big Baby.

"I am having difficulty finding a goddamn electric wagon with pedals," he told B.J. after they'd bathed.

"A what?"

"You tell me, but it's what she wants from me for her birthday."

"Oh, don't pay attention, she just got gobs of stuff for Christmas and I've already bought her a ton more."

"I said I'd get it for her."

"Well, forget about it." She was sitting naked at her dressing table, putting lipstick on her nipples. "A girl in acting class told me that this turned her boyfriend on." She stood, flicked the bathroom light out, the bedroom light too. "Tell me if it turns you on."

It did.

But he couldn't forget the electric wagon with pedals.

He made his money researching, for God's sake; that was his job, finding things. And he knew, somehow, he was going to find this.

He called the national headquarters of Toys "R" Us. They were courteous and they gave him all the time he needed.

No electric wagon with pedals.

He got in touch with the people who manufactured Flexible Flyers, on the odd chance they made items other than sleds, such as maybe electric wagons with pedals.

He tried the Lionel Train people too.

No and no.

Ten days before her birthday, Chub tossed in the towel. He had work that needed doing, work that paid, and he'd tried.

Two days before her birthday he was consumed with the notion that he hadn't tried *hard*.

And so at last the Great Researcher did what any fool

would have done: consulted the Yellow Pages. There were three columns of retail toy stores and he started alphabetically. Naturally, Zeffman's of Canal Street was Valhalla.

"I'm sorry to bother you, sir, but by any chance, do you have an electric wagon with pedals?"

"A vat?"

Clearly Mr. Zeffman—that was who it turned out was on the other end—was not born in Darien.

"An electric wagon with pedals, sir."

"No."

"I didn't think so."

"A vagon vit pedals I got, but it ain't a plug-in."

Chub shifted the phone to the other hand, massaged his neck, which was killing him from three columns' worth of negatives. Maybe a plain wagon with pedals would at least prove he'd made the effort, whatever the hell it was. "If I came down, would you show it to me?"

"It's in a big box, you gotta put it together yourself. The truth? It's a crap item by me. Everything they make is a crap item by me."

"Everything who makes?"

"The goddamn company, the Lecto Company, who vants to assemble nowadays ven you can just shove a goddamn cartridge in a machine and blow up the world?"

"I'll be right down," Chub said, and half an hour later he was.

Mr. Zeffman went into his basement, returned with an enormous box. "This is the Lecto vagon vit pedals but by me you're a dummy for buying it."

Chub looked at the box. There were no pictures of the contents. "Can you describe what I'm getting? So I'll know what it's supposed to look like when I'm assembling it?"

"Vell, as I remember, it looks like a vagon. It's got a long handle. You put a kid in it and you pull the handle and it's a vagon. *But*—and I'm varning you, it's a dead item, I don't take no returns—the half in front of where the kid sits lifts out—and below is pedals. The kid *holds* the handle vile he's sitting, he vorks the pedals with his little pudgy legs, he's on a bicycle. Fifty-nine fifty without tax, and I shouldn't take your money?"

"Why?" Chub asked as he paid.

"You handy?"

Chub shrugged. "Like the next guy."

"The other two next guys who bought this lox, it took 'em four hours to put it together."

It took Chub eight. He closeted himself in the maid's room and sweated away. Eight hours, not counting breaks, or the vicious cut he managed to inflict on his thumb, or the blood blisters that appeared on the fingers of both hands. B.J., naturally, gave him no sympathy but probably he wouldn't have given her much, either, if she'd spent most of two evenings cursing in the maid's room.

But when the magic day arrived, and after all the other gifts had been opened, Chub said, "Oh, there was this thing today that arrived, maybe from the credit guy at Bloomingdale's," and when he wheeled it out, red and shining, Jesse screamed, "A 'lectric wagon with pedals," and hopped in saying, "Pull me, pull me, Daddy," and when Chub did she said, "Lookit, Mommy, lookit us go," and Chub wheeled her through the living room to the library and opened the terrace doors and it was cool and grey with a March wind building but neither seemed to care. They struggled briefly with the front part of the seat but when they got it lifted out Chub gave her the handle and she peddled and laughed, zooming around the terrace, circling endlessly, and when B.J. joined them she shouted, "See, Mommy, you thought it was a wagon but *it's got pedals.*"

"And we're into the one hundred and ninety-second lap at Indianapolis," Chub said, "and we may just have a major upset on our hands, ladies and gentlemen, because no electric wagon with pedals has ever won here in the past but with eight laps to go, *Jesse Fuller has the lead.*"

Jesse made another circle. "Seven," she cried.

"Six," Chub said into his microphone after the next terrace tour was done. "And the noise here is fantastic, ladies and gentlemen, a six-year-old girl with six laps to go may be about to make racing history."

"B.J. loves your birthdays so," Chub heard then, and he turned, stunned, not knowing what was coming but knowing more than likely that there was soon to be an end to the joy on the terrace. There were always changes when she began referring to herself that way, in the third person. (Their first night? "You're boring him, B.J." when she caught him looking at his watch.) Chub wasn't certain what brought it on, but it all was in the region of some terrible insecurity.

"B.J. remembers those other days so well."

"So do I, Mommy."

"Those other days B.J.'s presents used to fill you with such joy."

"They do, Mommy. I love your presents."

"Of course, B.J. knows you do, she can see all those other presents where you left them, left them all by themselves in the living room."

"And the crowd is giving Jesse Fuller a standing ovation," Chub said. "A hundred thousand people—"

The kid began to slow.

"Finish the race," B.J. said. "All those other presents don't matter when there's a race to be won."

The kid looked at Chub, then at her mother. Then she scrambled to her feet and said, "Oh, this old thing," and ran.

Chub began to clap.

She turned to him. "Does B.J. detect a certain sarcasm?"

"Cut the third-person shit."

"Oh, his command of the language is overwhelming."

"That was a shit thing and you know it."

"You want to know what I know, mister?" and they moved toward each other in the center of the terrace.

"Tell me."

"I know what you're up to and it's not going to work."

"Let's hear it."

"You are my husband and I am your wife and that is fine with me, at least on most occasions. But that child is *my* daughter, I have the scars to prove it, and none of your games with credit managers or stupid stories or goddamn gifts can change that!"

She whirled and was gone.

Chub made his way to the terrace railing and stared blindly at the park. Because the insecurities he knew about, and the possessiveness came as no surprise, and yes, her jealousy came with the territory. But now the extent of it rocked him—she was jealous of his relationship with his child, Jesus God, even of that.

And he realized as he stood there the depth of his bind. B.J. dazzled him, blinded him, she always had, always would. But he could never lessen his affection for the child. He adored her. *Adored* her. It was beyond relinquishing, outside his control.

And there was no way in this world that he could ever please them both.

He tried. That night, he explained—not apologized, *explained*—while B.J. listened silently, that sometimes he acted obsessively and this had been one of those times. He probably shouldn't have gotten involved with the wagon in the first place but the fact that he couldn't find the damn thing ate away at him, since his job was finding things. And putting it together, all those hours, not only drove him almost round the bend but at the same time gave him an almost cuckoo sense of pride, since he stank with his hands. Which was why he had brought it out last, after the other gifts. If he was going to give it to her, it should have just been there at the beginning.

And if he was fond of the kid, that was because the kid had been brought along beautifully, and someone in the room with him now was responsible for that.

B.J. liked that.

The next night at dinner Chub gave Jesse a letter and said she better read it. She looked at the letter awhile, handed it back, suggested Chub do it out loud. It turned out to be a note from the credit manager at Bloomingdale's, explaining that he had been transferred to a new shop they were opening in a mall outside of Tokyo, Japan. It was a big break for him, but he doubted that he would be able to keep up his correspondence, and gifts from Tokyo took ages to cross the water so good luck to Big Baby and the next time she was outside Tokyo, please drop in and say hello.

B.J. liked that too.

What Jesse liked was that Chub began altering his schedule. There were a couple of afternoons a week when Jesse was home from school while her mother was at class, and Chub turned out to be there on those afternoons, working. But he didn't mind interruptions. Sometimes they would tell stories then. Other times, if the weather was nice, he would get the wagon out of the back closet and sit in it and let her pull him around the terrace. She was six now, he explained, which was when you had to start to work for a living, at least that's when he did, so quit griping and pull, and he told her what it was like, being the youngest person to work in the local brick factory.

It was three weeks before B.J. felt like sex again, and when she did, it was because of a Katharine Hepburn picture. *Summertime.* They watched it on the tube one night and B.J. moved into his arms, talking not about the movie but about where it was located, Venice, and how she had been there twice with her folks and it was the most romantic spot in existence. Or at least the most romantic place she had ever been, because although she had always dreamed of going to an island in Hawaii, Maui, which a girl friend of hers in high school had said really was the best place yet invented, she had somehow failed to get there.

The weather warmed, and Chub began taking afternoon walks with Jesse, and the first day the carousel in Central Park was open, they were there. Chub gave her a quarter and told her to have a go but she hesitated, studying the horses as they went around and around, wondering were they all the same or were any of them better to ride than the others and Chub suddenly said, pointing to an all-black beast, "That one's the fastest."

She squinted at him. The fastest? How could that be when they all go around the same?

And then he was into the story of a girl named Jenny who was very poor, so poor that all she had was one quarter, and she used to come to the carousel every day and pretend to ride—she never could really do it because then her quarter would be all gone—but she studied and studied all the animals and one day figured out that the black horse was really a whiz and just holding back so the others wouldn't feel like plodders. Jenny knew that, and her knowledge almost made her the lifelong slave of the richest boy in all the world.

"Who?"

"You mean his name?" Chub said. "His real name or what people called him?"

"You know."

"He lives right over there," Chub said, pointing to an enormous apartment building on Fifth Avenue.

"The richest boy in all the world lives right there in a 'partment just across from me?"

"There's a little difference, kiddo—the Flibberty-Smythe's live in the whole building. Really just the top thirty floors. The rest is for their staff. By the way, the richest kid's name was Chauncey Van Rensselaer Flibberty-Smythe. I wouldn't want you associating with him, though. A rotten egg all the way through." Chub looked down at her beside him on the bench as the carousel music changed tunes.

"Well, there simply must be more to it than that," Jesse said.

Chub took off, explaining how that Chauncey Van Rensselaer Flibberty-Smythe was in a horrible mood, because usually when he came to the carousel his social secretary called the Mayor and cleared everybody away so he could have it all to himself but this time she had goofed and Chauncey, being eight, was furious to find other children riding, and he told his three butlers to throw them out but the parents objected and Chauncey, fuming, stood studying the horses a moment, and Jenny, not knowing his bad habits, tried to cheer him up by telling him what a good time he would have on the black horse since it was the one with *real* speed, and he said she was dumb, they were the same and she said she was right and he said wrong and she held firm and then Chauncey made her a bet—she could take the black horse and he'd take the white one alongside and if they finished dead even, then he was right and if he was right she would have to be his slave forever but if *she* was right, if the black horse won, then he'd give her a lifelong supply of quarters and Jenny was afraid, but he taunted her and made mean fun so finally she had to agree and they got on their horses and the carousel started and both horses were neck and neck, dead even, and Chauncey laughed and laughed because she was so dumb and Jenny didn't answer him, just bent forward and whispered "Giddyap, horsee" to the black, and the ride went around and around, the horses the same, exactly the same, and then the ride was half over and then three quarters over and then it was almost done, you could tell because the carousel began to slow and Chauncey was screaming, "At last, at last, a slave all my own," and Jenny kept on with her "Giddyap, horsee, please, please, you must giddyap."

Chub stood suddenly, waved toward B.J., who had just called out "Hello" and was walking toward them. Chub went to her, kissed her.

"Alicia said you might be here. Class broke early."

"Great. Sit, sit, we're just watching the animals and getting a little sun."

Jesse nudged him and whispered, "Did she win?"

"What was that, darling?" B.J. asked.

"Nothing," Chub said. "Just goofing around."

"Oh, then I'm interrupting, I didn't mean to do that." She stood, started walking away.

"We were finished," Chub called, grabbing Jesse by the hand, giving her a look, hurrying alongside his wife. He took her hand, too, and between his ladies he strolled awhile.

After dinner that night Carlos made his normal call and the instant B.J. was seated talking in the library, Jesse scooted out of her room, gestured for Chub and when he was seated on the bed she said, "I've told Big Baby everything up to what you said so go on."

"Right." Chub glanced at the door, started talking. "See, there was this rich kid named Chauncey Van Rensselaer Flibberty-Smythe and he lived in a whole building—"

"—the race, the race, Big Baby knows all this."

"The race." He paused, but only briefly, and when he spoke again his voice was very low. "The carousel was slowing, the horses were even, Chauncey was screaming because he had won, and Jenny closed her eyes. The carousel was barely moving. The horses were just the way they'd always been. Even. Absolutely even." Now his voice sounded strange. "And then. *Then.*" The words came very slowly, a breath between each one.

"And then the . . .

    and then the great

          black

             horse

               began

                 to

                  mooooooove.

"It reared up on its hind legs and Chauncey began to blubber like a baby he was so scared and Jenny hung tight, and the black horse circled the carousel, faster and faster, and then it gave a cry of freedom because it wasn't an ordinary horse, it was a magic horse and years ago an evil sorcerer trapped it in the carousel and no one knew, and it could only get free if someone believed that it was the fastest, and then it gave a great jump, right out of the carousel, and it ran a few steps across the grass and then it leaped, leaped right off the ground, because magic horses, they can fly when they want and that's what this horse did, this great black magic horse, and on its back rode the richest little girl in all the land."

Chub stood, started tucking her in.

"Did they have adventures?" Jesse asked finally.

"Oh, plenty."

Then she was quiet again for a while. "I wonder," she said when Chub had her all tucked in.

"Hmm?"

"I wonder did they ever meet the Rain Man?"

"We'll find out, kid, won't we?" He grabbed her then, probably too hard, and pressed his lips against her birthmark, against her beautiful special fire.

B.J. was finishing up when he joined her in the library. "Chub sends his best," she said, and then a moment later, " 'Bye."

"How is he?" Chub asked.

B.J. smiled. "Daddy? Daddy's clever. But he's not as clever as some people, is he, now?"

Chub made no reply, just opened the terrace doors and went out to look at the park, trying his best to figure, in the darkness, just where the carousel might be.

May turned quiet. No fights, no heated words, but more than enough silence to go around. B.J. went up for a couple of open calls, barely got through the door. Because of her acting teacher, it was his fault, Theo was just a faggot who should have stayed in Greece and she quit him. Jesse got sick a lot, nagging colds, and she didn't seem to mind missing school.

Chub, watching them as the days dragged on, realized in his own spectacular way that in trying to win them both he was, in fact, doing the reverse. There had to be a shift, sudden and good, and so he went to his bank, took out all his savings, did some heavy spending, and the next night, at dinner, he clanged his fork against his water glass for attention.

"I have news of some interest," he began. "Your mother," he said to Jesse, "is about to have her half-year anniversary, so she has cause for celebration." He turned to B.J. "And your daughter has just finished finally and forever kindergarten and first-graders-to-be also have cause for celebration." He took an envelope out of his pocket. "And I, not wanting to be in the way, have decided to take off on my own." He tapped the envelope. "Inside here is my plane ticket for the island of Maui in Hawaii. I leave on Monday."

Jesse stared at him. "You're going away?"

Chub flipped her the envelope. "Look inside if you doubt me."

Jesse fumbled with the envelope, spilled the contents onto the table top. "But there's three things in here."

"Impossible," Chub said, examining carefully. Then he shook his head. "Dumb travel agent. You're right. Three tickets." He gave a deep sigh. "I guess we're *all* off for Maui, what do you think about that?"

It made for a lot of flying. Five hours to L.A., then a wait. Five more to Oahu, then another wait. A short hop to Maui, a long cab ride to where Chub had booked. No one had trouble sleeping when they got there.

The resort strung out along the beach, a series of low cabins shaded by palm trees. They had connecting rooms on the second floor, Chub and B.J. took one, Jesse and Big Baby shared the other, but Chub took great pains showing her that all she had to do was open her door and there they would be, in case Big Baby had any worries.

They were punchy the next morning, but awake in time for a late breakfast and to catch up with the counselor who took care of children during the day. Jesse wore an enormous blue sun hat because she had to keep the birthmark protected, and B.J. made her *promise* to keep it on, which Jesse did.

When they got back to the cabin B.J. locked the front door and the door to Jesse's room and made love to Chub with the terrace doors open so they could hear the ocean. When they had come she held him and said "Thank you" and she gestured to the rooms, to the water beyond. "For this."

They swam in the waves after lunch. B.J. had bought

several new one-piece suits for the occasion, because she insisted she was five pounds over at the very least, the winter always did that to her. The suits were white, and they set off her bright-green eyes, her tumbling red hair. She looked, as always, stunning. Chub looked like Chub—he still weighed the same 160 as always, so he had bought nothing new, made do with what he had.

Jesse returned from camp in the late afternoon, fuming. All they did was splash in dopey wading pools and play with dopey clay and she *hated* it because there was only one thing she wanted to do and she hadn't done it yet, and that was play in the sand. She was a city kid, born and bred, D.C., Dallas, New York, and she had never seen an ocean beach like this before.

So the second day she got some cardboard beer cups and they let her alone in the sand, just in front of the cabin, so they could keep an eye on her. Chub went out with her at first, showed her how wet sand was better for building, but not to go into the water above her toes to fill the cups. And that was how she spent the day. Kneeling on the white beach, in her blue suit and giant blue hat, until B.J. went out and put a beach robe on her because the sun was strong.

The old folks rested on the terrace in lounge chairs, ordering lunch in when they were hungry. They talked quietly and dozed and read, B.J. ploughing through *War and Remembrance,* Chub the collected Cheever.

When it was five, B.J. suggested ordering cocktails and Chub yelled out did Jesse want her usual gin and tonic or what?

"I'm busy, can't anybody tell?" Jesse called back.

B.J. phoned for two very tall rums and sodas and a Shirley Temple, and when the drinks arrived, she told Jesse to leave some beach for tomorrow.

"No, no, no, no, no, I'm not *finished.*"

Chub went out to get her.

What she had built amazed him. It was a castle, five feet long at least, and beside it was another building, smaller, but there was a road connecting the two. Chub sat beside her cross-legged and watched her labor. "It's beautiful," he said.

"Well, it *will* be," she told him. "See, this is the Rain Man's home"—she indicated the castle—"and this other place is where the magic horse sleeps. Except the stupid side keeps falling down."

"Jessica," B.J. called.

"Give her a sec," Chub shouted back.

That brought B.J. out to join them. "You've really done wonderful work. I'm proud of you. But there's a Shirley Temple inside with your name on it."

Jesse shook her head. "No. Not not not not yet."

Chub stood. "Let's us get sloshed."

"Jessica, I told you to come along."

"But this is the Rain Man's house," Jesse said. "And the magic horse's house isn't finished."

B.J. grabbed her daughter's hand.

Jesse struggled free.

"Jessica, you are ticking me off and do I ever mean that. It doesn't matter if you finish it or not—the tides are going to take it away, now come along."

"Tides?"

B.J. pointed to the ocean. "The water comes in at night and washes everything away. Then in the morning it goes out and you can play some more."

"Take my castle away? It can't do that."

"Well, baby, it will, now get up."

"Maybe it won't," Chub said. "These Hawaiian tides are very unpredictable."

B.J. whirled on him. *"Just don't start, all right?"* With that, she was on her way back across the sand.

"C'mon, it sounds like Mommy means business."

"But I worked *hard*."

"I know. Get up now."

Jesse stared and stared at her creation. For a moment Chub thought she was going to burst into tears, but she was a tough one. She reached for his hand and held it. "I think the Rain Man is friends with the tides."

"Can't be sure; they're both water and all, but—"

"—*I'm sure,*" Jesse interrupted. "My castle will be there in the morning."

Chub shouldn't have done it. He knew it during drinks, he knew it during dinner. He knew it when they went to bed. But there was no way he could help himself, so he stayed awake and before dawn was more than a wish, he slipped out of the cabin, crept out the door and down to the beach, did the best he could reconstructing the castle and the house. He worked frantically, and probably the job wasn't perfect, but then, neither was he. When he was done he tiptoed back into the cabin and fell asleep.

"It's there!" Jesse cried the next morning, waking them both as she shook their bed.

Chub, exhausted, took a long time to wake and when he did, B.J. was already sitting up, rubbing her eyes.

"You must hurry come see," Jesse said.

"Come see what?" B.J. said.

Jesse started bouncing up and down. "Just you wait. Now I'm *serious,* put on your suits, put on your suits," and B.J. got up slowly, Chub, too, and when they were in their suits they followed her out to the beach where she shouted, "See? See? I told you they were friends," and Chub smiled, watching her, because she was just so goddamn bursting.

B.J. smiled too. "B.J. is just so happy," she began, and then she was on him, screaming, "You cute little miserable son of a bitch—" and Chub said for her to shut up because sure they had fought before, gone at it pretty good, but never like this, never in front of the kid.

"You and your fucking games!" she said and then began to kick at the sand castle wildly, and she lost her balance, fell, got up, kicked again and again until she was winded. Then she grabbed Jesse and shook her—"*He* did it, don't you get that, he did it, and he did it to get me, don't you get that, *don't you see?*" and now Jesse was crying, in fear, and Chub broke B.J.'s grip, telling her for Chrissakes to get control but she was past that, way past it. "Why do you do it? Why do you have to ruin everything, everything you touch you ruin, you know that? *Prick!*" and B.J. was crying now, and she slapped at Chub, slapped hard, and he didn't bother stopping her, just let her go on until she dropped her arms and ran sobbing toward the cabin.

Chub sank down on the sand. He bent forward, rested his head on his knees, shut his eyes. He wasn't aware for a while that Jesse was sitting beside him, mimicking his position.

Chub kissed her hair. "Go inside, baby."

"I like the sand."

"Please."

"It's so nice and quiet out here."

Chub looked around. He didn't know what time it was but it was still very early—the beach was empty. He watched the water. There was a blissful morning wind and little patches of white on some of the waves. They rolled in evenly and without conscience, maybe a beckoning foot high.

"Mommy has some temper, but it always goes away."

Chub stared at her. Jesus, six years old and *she* was tending *him*. He blinked.

"Are you going to cry too?"

Chub shook his head. He never cried. Not true. He had. In the sweet long ago. Probably when he felt his father's pulse on the hospital table, probably that was the last time. "No, baby, I'm not going to cry."

The wind was picking up but the sun was strong enough. A perfect day. A perfect day. "Scoot, baby, I mean it, now. Go on inside."

"With Mommy like *that*?" A shake of the head.

"You are some creature," Chub said.

"*Creature?* I'm a girl."

"Yes, the best girl." She was. And it was right that he should care so deeply; after all, wasn't he the bestest good boy? "I'm going for a walk," Chub said then.

"Me too."

They started along the sand, slowly, Chub on the water side, but after a little he veered away, moving into the calming blue, until he was almost up to his waist. Then he turned, walked through the waves.

"I wouldn't do that," Jesse called.

"Do what?"

"Go in the water like that."

"Why?"

"Why? *Why?* Because of the sharks, that's why."

Chub smiled. She was six and *Jaws* was four years old but it was still one of the main conversation cornerstones at Little Dalton.

"Don't worry," Chub said.

She skipped along the water's edge, peering straight ahead of his path. "I'm keeping an eye out," she shouted.

"Jesse, you can relax—the truth is that on this particular island, the sharks can't come within three miles of the shore because they can't break their deal with the dolphins."

"What is a dolphins?"

"Didn't I tell you when I was on Maui before—why do you think I decided on here if I didn't know about it?—and I ran into the dolphin?"

"Louder." They were probably forty feet away from each other now and the waves breaking on the beach made it hard for her.

"Anyway, this dolphin—"

"—is this going to be a story?" she shouted.

Chub shrugged. The sun massaged his shoulders and the water was warm. "Just something that happened is all."

She took a step into the water. "If it's a story I must hear it from the start."

Chub laughed, moved in, took her by the hand, very gently and gradually led her out, waiting each step until she wasn't afraid. When the water was almost to his waist he put her firmly on the shore side, and each time a wave came, it broke on his body and he lifted her high so that she laughed, and then put her down again.

"Well, this dolphin—"

"—what was his name?"

"Jesse, it's been years since this happened."

"Well, you must"—now she giggled again as another wave broke and Chub lifted her over it. "It makes everything better if you know the names," Jesse said.

"Umm, lemmesee, now, he saved my life, you'd think I'd remember—got it! Milton. His name was Milton—dolphins are very religious and they all have names from the Bible."

Another shriek, another wave.

Up ahead was a long breakwater and Chub decided to reach it before turning back. Maybe he'd even let her sit on it awhile and watch as he dove in and swam around.

"This Milton saved you?"

"He did indeed. Now, you may not believe this"—he paused to lift her past another wave—"but I learned to swim underwater. I've always been great at it, so naturally when Oberlin entered a team in the World Plunging Championship to be held here in Maui, I came along. Plunging means being able to go the farthest underwater."

She nodded.

The breakwater was closer now. "Well, I didn't know about this three-mile rule with the sharks and I swam way out to practice plunging where none of the Japs could spy on my secrets, and first thing I run into—"

"—a shark."

"Right. See, I was just past the three-mile limit and this shark—I want to tell you I was scared and the next thing I knew—it all went so fast, this shark was flying out of the water up in the air and it landed and made this huge splash and then turned tail. See, that's why sharks are afraid of dolphins—dolphins swim faster and they have this huge nose and they go *zap* right in the shark's belly and knock them flying and when I was safe Milton—he didn't talk so much as squeal, but they're smart, some people think they're smarter than we are—anyway, Milton indicated I was out too far and I said I'm sorry, I didn't know, and I was tired and I told him, so he said—squeaked, I mean—'Hop on, I'll give you a free ride.' "

"Did he?"

"It was like flying."

"Tell me, tell me every little thing."

Chub wanted nothing more than that, to tell her every little thing about his ride, and he was about to when suddenly he was spinning down into the water, his face was in the sand and his mouth was open and he fought the water, made it up, realized instantly what had happened, the waves had caromed off the breakwater and blindsided him and he had been so busy talking he hadn't taken proper notice—

—and then he realized that Jesse was gone.

He stared around, shouting, *"Jesse, Jesse, Jesse,"* but she was not to be seen, nothing was to be seen but the waves and the water and standing there, spinning around, shouting his lungs out, Chub knew she was dead. (She wasn't. She'd just been stunned longer than he had been, and the water was harder for her to fight. Perhaps it took ten seconds before she would reappear, gasping and frightened, eyes so wide, yelling, "Daddy, Daddy, I was scared.")

But in those ten seconds Chub's mind flew because he was a murderer now. He had killed the thing he loved, not with a sword or a kiss but with a cursed story. And that would take awhile to forget, ten eternities if God was on his side, only that would never be, God hated bestest good boys when they did bad things, really bad things, and then Chub thought of B.J., B.J. running down the beach toward him while he cried, "I killed her, I killed the baby," which meant she had been right all along, he had wanted to steal Jesse, only this was the ultimate theft, and before their marriage ended would be the lowering of a tiny coffin into the Texas ground, only she would deny him being there, she would be right, he had done the deed, wasn't that enough for any man, and then Chub's thoughts took a turn for the worse, because he knew he would never have the courage to do unto himself what he had done unto others, he would have to live with the knowledge that what B.J. had just screamed at him was true, he was a prick, a prick who ruined everything, everything he came near, always had, always would and surely there was a name for him except it had not been invented yet, no one had needed to make up such a word—

"—Daddy, Daddy, I was scared."

Chub lunged toward her, spitting sand from her mouth no more than fifteen feet away from him and another wave knocked her down but he managed to keep his feet this time, and before the third wave struck his fingers held her fingertips, but only briefly; it was that third wave that blasted her away.

PART III

The Predator and the Prey

CHAPTER 1

The Bone

Chub met The Bone the night Two-Brew was anointed.

Mr. Kitchel had not wanted to give up being head of Sutton Press, had no intention of doing so. He was but sixty-one in 1982 and yes, there was company policy involving mandatory retirement at sixty-five but since it was *his* publishing house, he didn't foresee any trouble sidestepping that problem. He was, in his own eyes, good for years to come.

The problem was that, in the eyes of others, he had not been good in the years just past. When *The Thorn Birds* came up for paperback auction, Two-Brew had begged, in company meetings, that they grab it, no matter what the cost. Mr. Kitchel scorned him. When James Clavell left Atheneum, Two-Brew pitched desperately that Sutton sign him, he was about to break out on a gigantic international scale. More scorn. The same argument took place when Stephen King left Doubleday. The same scorn.

No one at Sutton could accurately compute how many millions of dollars those decisions had lost but everyone knew that the son had become far shrewder than the father. And sooner or later there would of necessity come the changing of the guard. But it would be later—common gossip in publishing had it that what kept Mr. Kitchel in power and would keep him there at all costs was his deep supply of scorn: He loathed his son now. The more of a threat Two-Brew became, the more the father drew pleasure from disagreement, overruling, frustrating, winning, no matter what the bottom line might read.

Then came the offer.

Just as Atheneum had been formed a quarter century earlier by three top publishers leaving their firms and setting out on their own, so in '82 three more top men decided to begin their own firm.

There was a lunch and the offer was made by the three: They wanted Two-Brew not just to come along, they wanted him to head things. Two-Brew said he would think about it and get back to them. That afternoon, he wrote his resignation and met with his father. Mr. Kitchel read it, read it again, looked at his son and said, "You couldn't run shit." (This was the most cordial remark of the meeting. Chub heard it all from Two-Brew, via phone. That had become their most common method of communication of late, except for an occasional lunch at a local Hunan when Lydia hadn't "felt up" to joining them.)

The ensuing battle was surprisingly brief—less than a week was all. Mr. Kitchel discussed the betrayal with his latest mistress (another friend of his wife's) and with Mrs. Kitchel herself. And he was stunned to find they both felt the same: He had worked so hard, too hard really, all his life, and now was the time to begin enjoying his days.

Mr. Kitchel swore at them both and, now triply betrayed, spent a mostly restless night thinking of how he might most viciously rewrite his will. The next day he received two calls from Sutton's best-selling writers wondering, idly, if the rumors about the new firm were true. Mr. Kitchel explained that there were always rumors and pay no attention. But the meaning beneath both calls was clear: They were thinking of leaving.

That afternoon he wandered into his son's office and asked how long he had to make a decision. Two-Brew said he would give him till Friday. His father stared at him then and said, "After all I've given to you." Two-

Brew stared right back and said, "After all I've taken
from you." (Alone, he immediately called Chub because
the battle was, he knew, won. It was simply a matter of
surrender terms. "It's fucking Sophocles, Chubbo—only
I ain't marrying Mommy.")

On Friday, Mr. Kitchel summoned his son and said
that he'd just had his annual physical. (True. And the bill
of health was clean.) "The quack said that I should begin
taking it slower. I said that I couldn't slow down, it was
full-out or stop. He said couldn't anybody else fill my
shoes? I don't think you can but you're my blood, I'll
give you a shot. You can be CEO, I'll be chairman."

"You can be charwoman for all I care," Two-Brew
replied. "Who has the power?"

The answer to that question became clear when the
announcements were sent out, inviting very special
friends of the firm to a party in a private room at The
Four Seasons honoring Stanley Kitchel and his new position. Each invitation was signed by Mr. Kitchel himself,
with the word "proudly" preceding his name.

Chub dreaded going, but Two-Brew really wanted him
there, so there wasn't any choice. There wasn't much
reason for his dread, either, because, after he'd been in
the room a few minutes, he realized that very few people
there knew him. It had been a decade since Two-Brew
had rescued him from working at the No-Name.

Besides, if you had been a fly on the wall, you would
have clocked a lot of funny stuff going on.

Example one: At the center of the room five people
were greeting guests. Mr. Kitchel, his wife, his wife's
friend Helene, his son and a young girl who was trim and
Peck and Peckish, the assistant head of publicity. The
eyeplay was glorious. Mr. Kitchel ignored his son and
Helene (his mistress). Two-Brew ignored his father and
the girl assistant (*his* mistress).

But a really perceptive fly would have soon given up
this scene for what was going on at the glorious buffet
table, which was long, and had identical platters of deli-
cacies set up on both sides.

On one side stood a fortyish grey-bearded skinny guy who might have tipped the scales at a hundred and thirty pounds. His companion, a bloated brunette, *must* have tipped the scales at *two* hundred and thirty pounds. And across from them was a genuinely startling-looking girl: probably six one in heels, extraordinarily thin, with eyes like Paul Newman, chalk-white makeup, which contrasted with jet black hair. And what was going on was this: While the bloated brunette kept a continual motion going, stuffing shrimp into her mouth, the thin girl across was stuffing shrimp at an equal speed, first into her napkin, then into her purse.

It would have been, seen from above, a terrific race. Who could make more shrimp disappear faster?

The skinny grey-bearded guy noticed what the thin girl was doing.

"Bite your tongue," the thin girl said sharply.

The grey-bearded guy looked away.

Soon after, a small commotion began—the assistant publicist moved alongside the shrimp stealer, started asking questions.

"Don't bug me, okay?" the thin girl said, gesturing across the table toward the skinny bearded guy who was watching again. "I'm with him, he said it was all right."

The publicist looked questioningly at the grey-bearded man, who eventually nodded. The publicist moved away. A smart fly would have moved on then, too, because the race was done as the thin girl, her purse sufficiently full, moved off to the bar.

A moment later, Two-Brew approached the buffet table and grabbed the hands of the bloated brunette and said, "Jesus Christ, Lydia, leave some for the guests." He turned to the grey-bearded man then. "Chub, come on, can't you stop her?"

Chub stroked his grey beard and said he was sorry.

Lydia said, "Stan, I don't want to shock you but I *am* a guest, I'm sure as shit not a wife."

Chub excused himself quietly, moved alone to a corner of the room, stared at a painting, then at his watch. Nine.

He had been there half an hour. Half an hour more and he could leave. He could last half an hour more.

"I got cats," came from behind him.

Chub stared up at the tall girl with the pale-blue eyes.

"I don't make a thing of stealing, but if you got cats, you don't pass up free shrimp." She got out a pack of English Ovals, gave Chub some matches. "Light me."

Chub did.

"I'm The Bone, who're you?"

Chub said his name.

"How come you're here?"

Chub said how come.

"Friends with the new head of the firm, huh?" She spoke quickly, with a heavy Brooklyn accent. In the dark she would have sounded like Streisand. "You can do me some good—not now, this isn't a hustle—but I'm into writing this great book and when it's perfect, you could slip it to him." She inhaled fiercely, drawing the smoke powerfully into her lungs, making an almost imperceptible "sss—sss" as she dragged. "That's how come I crashed this job—I only crash when there's literati, you never know who you might meet, are you a literati?"

Chub gave his job title.

"A researcher, no shit, I could use a researcher for this fantastic thing I'm writing, how much you charge?"

Chub gave his rates.

"Twenty-*five?* For twenty-five an hour I can get someone to write it for me, go to hell with your twenty-five." She got out another cigarette.

He lit it for her, gave her back her matches, excused himself, went to the bar for a double Wild Turkey. At the bar the assistant publicist apologized for the fuss she'd made about the stolen shrimp.

Chub said not to worry. And she wasn't, at least not about the shrimp; it was his relationship with Two-Brew that caused her apology. She was frightened of that relationship because she didn't understand it, but she knew a bad word from Chub wouldn't do her cause much good. She had been seeing Kitchel for three months now and she didn't plan on staying the assistant head of publicity forever.

Two-Brew's mother cornered him then, saying, in her southern accent, that wasn't tonight simply wonderful and Chub said yes, absolutely wonderful, perfect and wonderful, and she was in the middle of saying that Stanley was going to be a great success, when she spotted her best friend, Helene, in a corner of the room, talking with her husband, so she turned abruptly, moving toward them, her best smile on, leaving Chub, who went off by himself and sat at a small table, sipping his drink and looking at his watch. Nine-seventeen. Thirteen minutes to go. Anyone could survive thirteen minutes.

"I get stuff backwards," he heard behind him then as The Bone stood over him. "Mind if I park it a sec? I just wanna explain."

Chub gestured toward an empty chair.

"See, it's a big problem, and I can't lick it always, the backwards thing. Like before. What I should have done *first* was to thank you for saying you were with me. *Then* I should have said you could go to hell with your twenty-five. See? Backwards. Light me."

Chub did, and then she stood and moved away.

At nine-thirty he shook Two-Brew's hand. They looked at each other for a longer moment than probably either of them anticipated. Two-Brew resembled Itzhak Perlman now, only more trim. And his clothes were made by Huntsman. For a blink Chub was back, standing on a library ladder, when this apparition in a black and red lumberjack shirt and a bulging stomach came noisily through the Oberlin stacks, going, "Where is this Fuller fellow lurking? Where is young Fuller?"

"Joy," Chub said then, and left the party.

"Some might think this a coincidence," The Bone said, falling into step with him as he descended the staircase toward the cold December night.

Chub kept on moving down.

So did she. "Here's the thing—okay, I left my place tonight with ten biggies, five for the taxi uptown, five for the return. I knew this party was a freebee, and I wanted to see *Gandhi*, you know the new flick? I was gonna sneak in there, too—the Ziegfeld's easy—and I was half-way inside, what with all the crush and all, when this usher flagged me and got very hard-nosed about my method of entrance. So I was in a bind. I could have paid the five for the flick or bagged it and saved it for the taxi home, which would have been sensible. Except it was crucial that I see the goddamn flick—the reviews said that there was some great bloody stuff, battles, really good gore, y'know what I mean?"

For a moment Chub was tempted to interrupt and ask the difference between "good gore" and "bad gore" except probably she had an answer that he didn't want to hear so the moment passed.

"Anyway, I paid for the four-o'clock show, which means, if you can add—I mean subtract—you get the idea. Someone's got to take me home and I thought why not give you a shot?"

Chub almost reached into his wallet to give her five, but he didn't. He looked at her. She was pretty enough, startling enough more accurately, to have any number of escorts. Why had she picked him? This was a strange one, no question. This one had secrets. His curiosity was strong enough for a nod, and a few minutes later, they were sitting in a cab, heading downtown.

Her apartment was like nothing else in Chub's experience. It took up the first floor of what had once been a factory in SoHo, on Prince Street, not far from Dean and DeLuca. Part of the special quality came from the fact that it was, except for a small toilet, all one room, a room perhaps eighty feet long or longer, at least fifty feet wide, with a ceiling at least three times higher than Chub was tall. There was a large, well-stocked kitchen spread along one wall, a dining area nearby. There was a king-sized bed, a vanity close to it that looked like something Joan Crawford would have used. There was a seating area across the way, with an oversized television set, a Betamax, a stack of movies. (Hitchcock mostly, or titles that indicated violence.)

The Bone gave him a tour, accompanied by three cats that kept getting in the way. And there was such a pride, a fierce pride really, in her tone. "Bought this with my first bread. Everybody said I was crazy but I plunked down the dough. Eight thou. Then twenty more fixing it up. Last month I was offered two *hundred*. I told them to stuff it. The only way I leave my home is in a box."

It was a remarkable place. Chub told her so.

"Don't say that, don't say that, you haven't gotten the whole deal, sit down." She indicated a long couch.

Chub sat. The room was faintly lit; he looked around, wondering what was coming. She moved to a far wall. "Close 'em."

Chub shut his eyes. There was a series of clicking sounds.

"Have a look."

Chub stared around the room now, stunned, because on all the walls were giant photographs, six feet tall, some eight. Photos of magazine covers, *Vogue* and *Mademoiselle* and *Bazaar* and dozens more, all with the face of a younger Bone gazing out, each face styled differently. "Narcissus had nothing on me."

They were lovely and so was she; Chub said that.

The Bone smiled. " 'Bonita-Kraus-she's-got-the-prettiest-eyes.' " She crossed toward the kitchen. "What're you drinking?"

Whatever she was.

"How old are you, Fuller? Forty?"

Chub gave his age.

"Thirty-*two*? You're only a few years older than me. It's that goddamn grey beard, you should get the hell rid of it." She was pouring liquor when she said that, but she stopped. "There I go, backwards again. See, what I should have said *first* was that you certainly had a distinctive beard. *Then* I should have said that some men, handsome men especially, didn't need the added maturity a beard sometimes lent them."

She returned with two Scotches, bent down, kissed Chub suddenly, her tongue darting into his mouth. A moment later she stood, handed him his drink, sat on a chair facing him. "I hope you're better in the sack than you were just then."

Chub had known sex was coming before she said that, and the notion didn't thrill him. He had not touched a woman since the Pacific pounded outside the open terrace doors. Would he be able to perform? It had not been a problem in the past, but probably it would now.

The Bone gestured toward the giant photos on the walls. "Name your fantasy."

Chub didn't get it.

"You want the me on *Cosmo?* The face of *Seventeen?* It's a trick I do—whoever you want, I make myself up to look just like I did. I'm great at makeup." She shrugged. " 'Course, I ought to be after my years in the business. Evidence of a misspent youth." She snapped her fingers then, lit another English Oval, inhaled deeply, the "sss— sss" sound dominating the room. "Got it," she said. "I bet behind that beard you're one of those closet romantics—*Modern Brides.* I even have the clothes." She pointed to a stunning photograph of the magazine cover, the blue of her eyes never more dazzling, set off by the white wedding dress, the white lace shawl. "I'll drive you into a frenzy." She reached forward then to the coffee table and opened a box, held it out to Chub. "You into grass?"

Very.

"Okay, you take a joint and get ready for bed and I'll take a joint and get ready for you, it takes awhile."

Chub didn't understand, but in a few minutes, as he lay naked and smoking in bed, he began to see. The Bone sat at her oversized vanity, a copy of the original magazine cover propped by her mirror. She took off all her chalk white makeup with cold cream, studied her face, then the photograph, then her face again, turning her head from side to side. When she finally began to work on her eyes Chub was reminded of a painter; no, more a forger really, recreating something that once had been.

"I wasn't allowed makeup when I was growing up," The Bone said. "My grandparents were some kind of crazy orthodox and they lived with us and convinced my folks it came from the Devil."

Where was this?

"Brooklyn—you notice how I sound like Streisand?— we both went to Erasmus and ever since I was little she was my ideal. On account of at the start people thought she was weird-looking but she made them see the truth. Well, I was weird-looking too."

Doubtful.

She looked at Chub a moment, went on with her work as she talked. "Listen, Fuller, when I was thirteen I was five eleven and a half, with the same magnificent lack of chest I have now, and the same habit of getting things backwards—my mother wouldn't let me cut my hair so it hung damn near to my fanny and no boy would come near me. The Wallflower of the Western World. In my room when I'd stop crying long enough I could hear them downstairs on the phone, trying to get someone to take me out. 'You must meet my granddaughter, Bonita-Kraus-she's-got-the-prettiest-eyes.' See, that was all they could find to brag about. I got so that I thought maybe my real name was 'Bonita-Kraus-she's-got-the-prettiest-eyes.' What got me through high school was that I knew I was going to be a nurse and work in a hospital and marry a doctor who was taller than Wilt Chamberlain. So summer of junior year I worked at the local hospital and guess what: I *hated* nursing. I didn't realize mostly what you do was futz around all the time with old people. What a crusher. I read up on becoming a nun but that was dumb: I'm a rotten Jew, how could I be a good Catholic? So after I graduated I went to secretarial school in Brooklyn, knowing I was going to live the rest of my life upstairs and a spinster with everybody getting sadder and sadder because no man would come near me. And then guess what? Danieli happened to me."

Who?

"Danieli. *Danieli,* for Chrissakes. The King. Bigger than Scavullo."

Who?

She had been working on recreating the style of her eyebrows. Now she put her utensils down and stared at Chub. "I thought you were a researcher. Scavullo only happens to take all the *Cosmo* covers. I never miss reading *Cosmo,* it's got the greatest articles in the world— how the hell can you call yourself a researcher and not read *Cosmo?*"

Stoned, Chub smiled, promised to alter the errors of his ways.

She shook her head, lit another English Oval, went back to studying her face. When she spoke again, it was quicker than even her usual cadence. Her secretarial school was on Fulton Street and so was Gage & Tollner, which was where Danieli liked to eat, and when he exited she was walking by and he followed her a few steps, caught up, asked if she had ever considered modeling and she asked if he ever considered getting a foot in the goheenees, which made him laugh, so he gave her a card, left her, and when she read the card she cursed her big mouth for a week, after which time, without telling her parents, she called him and was invited to his studio in Manhattan. Without telling her parents she went and that day he set about creating her. He liked to do that, Danieli did; every five years or so he got the urge to play Svengali and now the urge was on him. He had her hair cut short. ("My mother died—she's still alive and causing grief in Flatbush, but she told me when she finally kicks that's the date she's going to have on her tombstone, the day the wop destroyed my hair.") He redid everything, shot for weeks till he had a book he liked, then he took her to Ford Model, Inc., new face new name—*Bo*nita he called her, and from that he got The Bone.

Three months later she was on the cover of *Seventeen.*
It was a crazy period. She was living at home still, still

in their minds "Bonita-Kraus-she's-got-the-prettiest-eyes" and commuting mornings to Manhattan, where she became, within a year, according to *Women's Wear Daily*, "one of the five most beautiful faces in America."

When she was twenty, she earned six figures for the first time and finally moved to SoHo. When she was twenty-two, she earned half a million dollars for the first time. "A lot of girls might have had trouble dealing with that," The Bone said, working on her mouth now. "But me, I've always had this incredible amount of common sense. So when I was twenty-three, I married my pusher."

Chub had to laugh.

She smiled at him, told him to turn away then and stay like that until she said different.

Chub lay on his side, facing the far wall. Two cats jumped on the bed. He shooed them off. He could hear her walking, then a door opening, then the rustle of clothes. Then her walk was coming close. Then it stopped.

"Is it live or is it Memorex?" The Bone said, and she stood there, holding the magazine cover, wearing the white bridal clothes.

Chub watched her. She looked barely twenty, like the smiling bride on the magazine.

"What are you, some goddamn statue, I gotta do everything myself, is that it?" and just as she spoke fast, so she moved, dropping on top of him, her tongue moving deeply into his mouth, her hands going straight down between his legs, and she wouldn't pause, wouldn't rest, and when he was hard she pulled him over on top of her and brought her wedding dress high enough so she could lock her long legs around him and then she said, "Oh, Christ, I need you, in me, in me, now for Chrissakes come in me," and Chub moved for position, thrust forward—

—but she was dry.

"Quit messing around, goddamnit," and she tightened her legs, moving up and down, saying, "Now, now, you bastard," and Chub tried to force his way in but The Bone was still dry and he couldn't penetrate, couldn't even begin to, so he took his fingers and began to touch her but she slapped his hands away, saying, "I don't want that—I don't want your goddamn *hands,* I want *you,* now *do something,*" and Chub tried, tried to make it happen but he couldn't, his erection was already beginning to leave him, and he made a final effort, but he was softening too quickly, and in a moment he rolled off her, limp.

"What do you do?" The Bone said then.

Huh?

"I asked a question, that's all. I mean, you don't talk and you don't fuck, what do you do?"

"I don't stay here," Chub said, and he dressed quickly, left quickly, the only sound in the giant room the "sss—sss" from the figure in the bridal gown, chain-smoking her English Ovals.

"This is Brooklyn's favorite sex bomb," Chub heard the next morning after he answered the phone. "And I'm calling from the corner—I can see your building so you can't escape me. Gimme a minute, huh, just a quick face to face so I can explain."

No explanations necessary.

"*Puh*-leeze."

There was too much desperation in her tone for a rejection.

Five minutes later she stood panting in his doorway, "You share this place with Edmund Hillary, right?" Now she took a few deep breaths, walked to the center of the room, looked around. "You *live* in this armpit?"

"Yes, I do and yes, it is an armpit, but you might have asked first, discreetly, if this was my home and if I took pleasure in it and then, when I said that I didn't, *then* you might have called it an armpit, but of course you do things backwards."

"I'm working on it, I really am." She looked at the cork wall, thumbtacked now floor to ceiling with newspaper articles, scribbled notations, a few scattered pictures. "I don't like the vibes in here, it's creepy here, can we go someplace in the neighborhood?"

Chub selected the coffee shop where years before he had agreed to play Cupid so Lydia and Two-Brew could thrive and bloom happily forever.

"I knew I wasn't ready last night," The Bone said, when their coffee came. "I ruined it on purpose on account of I didn't think you were interested and I didn't much want to deal with that, you weren't interested, were you?"

"Doesn't matter."

"Don't bullshit me."

"I guess not much."

"I just goddamn knew it." She shook her head. "And me such a great girl."

"Oh? Where is that written?"

"Listen, I'm funny, I'm smart, I'm talented as hell, I'm loaded with modesty—that last was a joke, kind of to prove I'm funny—"

"—I got it," Chub said. "Are we done with explanations now?"

"Almost but not quite—remember last night when I said I married my pusher and you laughed? Well, it does sound funny except it wasn't when you lived through it. He left me for dead two years later. I was almost. I don't think a drug's been invented I wasn't expert at. I collapsed in the street one day and then I was in some hospital ward and as far as I was concerned, it was all over—until Danieli saved me. He paid for everything, got me dried out, gave me odd jobs working for him in his studio when I was strong enough. I loved him—he was an old queen but I loved him more than any man I ever met. He educated me, told me I was too smart to waste my time modeling, so I quit. When I need bread now I do two-bit catalog work to see me through. Danieli was the one who said I could use words, he was the one who told me about The Cherry Sisters—"

"—who?"

"Jesus, *The Cherry Sisters,* that's gonna be my first book, no one's ever done a book on them before—they're the greatest act that ever played on stage. They were so bad, they had to work behind a screen—true—because people threw eggs and stuff at them, that's how great they were."

Chub said nothing, just stirred his coffee, because she was speaking faster; whatever it was they were there to talk about they were going to talk about it now.

"Danieli packed it in a month ago and, I don't know, I guess you could say I'm in the market for a substitute."

"I'm flattered," Chub said.

"No you're not, you think I'm whacko but I'm not, it's just, well, I can feel myself starting to slide down the tubes again and I'm not looking for romance, I'm not looking for sex, I'm crappy at it, I just know we could help each other."

"I don't need help," Chub said.

"Don't bullshit me, the minute I saw you at the party last night I knew it—you got nothing too. You got the saddest eyes on the block, buster, that's why I went after you. I know about sad eyes."

Chub looked at the unusual girl across the table. The Bone, desperate and insecure, so wary of the world, so anxious to strike the first blow because if she chose to wait and counterattack, the power of the initial thrust might shatter her.

And her invitation *was* flattering; Lord knew, she'd never bore him. But he had to turn her down, for so many reasons she wouldn't understand. He was dangerous. That was the main one. "You're very sweet—"

"—no I'm not, I am not sweet—"

"Have it your way. What you don't know about me is I'm engaged." He saw at once she didn't believe the lie, so he quickly set out to embellish it. "She's a lawyer, she was out of town in Philly working on a case, we're getting married just after Christmas, that's why I didn't want to sleep with you last night—at first I thought I did, a final bachelor fling, but then when I saw you in the bridal

clothes, you were so beautiful I knew I couldn't risk it."
He paused then, because she believed him now and needed time to deal with the rejection.

She fumbled into her purse for a fresh pack of English
Ovals, got it open, struck a match. "You really thought I
was beautiful?"

"You were."

"It wasn't me then made you hold back?"

"Not you at all."

"Well, that's something, I guess." She scrambled up
out of the booth. "You take care now." She threw on her
coat.

"Don't worry, I will, I'm fine," Chub said, sitting
there, stirring the cold coffee until she was gone.

And he was fine. Not all the time, obviously, but then
who is? There were days when he didn't much want to go
toe to toe with Arnold Schwarzenegger, but that was to
be expected.

And there was no denying the early days after his
return from Hawaii and the scenes at the funeral in Texas
were not glorious. His memory would not leave overdrive
and when he tried working he got no farther than the
door.

The solution began with his beard. Stubble really, at
the time. He hadn't shaved since his return and after a
week he figured since he didn't count the Collier Brothers among his heroes, it was shape-up time. He ran some
hot water in the sink, got out his razor, looked at himself.
The stubble was grey, which surprised him, because his
hair was as always, light brown except for a few grey
flecks in his sideburns.

Chub stared at himself in the mirror, and his mind
wouldn't leave him alone, and then he realized the truth:
He didn't have to shave the thing. He could just let it the
hell grow because that was one less act per day.

Which was, of course, his solution: to iris everything
down. Everything, every person too. Socially, he saw
Kitchel only occasionally and later, Rory Baylor, the
cop, and his wondrous wife, the karate queen, Maya.

The day he didn't shave he did do something: empty his cork wall. He first unpinned the Wild Turkey label and the cover of *Oil for the Lamps of China* and the Purple Heart medal he'd bought from the Eighth Avenue pawnshop. Then he set to work on everything else, snippets of dialog, newspaper articles that someday might be material, titles, first lines, the works. When it was empty he went to the liquor store and got some unused boxes and took them back up the ninety-seven stairs and filled them. He took *The Dead Pile* and placed it on the bottom of the first box. Then he covered it with remnants from the wall. And when both boxes were full, he stuck them in the back corner of his bedroom closet.

He hated the naked look of the wall now, but soon that was not a problem—he quickly had it filled again, with research stuff, typed phone numbers of people he had interviewed, pages of Xeroxed lists that saved him time.

Time was precious now, because the work load began ballooning. Chub went to Elliott Carter, asked if he could use his name on a flyer he was preparing, and when Carter and his dozens of other clients agreed, he got a list from the Writers Guild and mailed out hundreds and hundreds of envelopes, all containing his name and address and rates and quotes from contented customers. He advertised again in the Sunday *Times*, running the copy every other month, and it worked. Soon he was working seven days a week to keep up, more often than not over a hundred hours.

Food he grabbed on the fly, at least at first, but then he discovered that he wasn't hungry often, which was good, another act discarded. Everything was good that irised down.

Sleep was a problem, because even though it was always after midnight when he left his desk, his brain was still working, and in order to iris that down he got into grass. It was easy to pick up—the transvestites on the street all had joints they were willing to part with for a buck or so. Plus, the final aid, Australian red wine. Elliott Carter had first put him on to what was coming

out of the Hunter Valley area and Chub had trouble
locating it until, by luck, a store on Broadway in the
Eighties began stocking it, so he bought several cases at a
time, lay in bed inhaling the joint, sipping the red. It
rarely took him more than one joint and one bottle to
sleep.

So what he said in parting to The Bone was true, he
was fine; which wasn't to say that his life held no surprises, few more unsettling than the evening of the twenty-second of December, a week or so after she'd left him
in the coffee shop, when Chub came home and flicked on
his machine for messages and listened as he undressed,
getting ready for a bath and a message began, "Hey,
pal—Hey, guess what?—*guess fucking what, pal?*—I'm
coming and you know what that means, don't you, don't
you, you fucking baby-killer, you're gonna *die!*" and as
Chub raced across the room to shut out the sound of the
madman his mind was already racing, racing back two
years and two weeks, to the day when Lennon had been
killed in the Dakota and he had gone down late and
alone, drawn by the sadness of it all, all the songs that
would never be sung, not now, and Chub stood for an
hour in the strange, almost balmy dark, watching all the
children weeping and holding their candles, and it was
probably two in the morning when he went home and his
mind, occupied, did not see the mugger waiting in the
foyer and the first blow sent him back across the small
space and he thought, that wasn't a fist, and it wasn't, it
was a garbage can lid and the second strike dropped him
and Chub knew what to do, just let it happen, let him
grab the wallet and go and it wasn't until the fifth blow
when there had been no attempt to take his money that
he realized it was no mugger that was on him, it was a
murderer doing his job. Something, that thought maybe,
that he was about to die, gave him strength to kick out
and the ensuing cry meant he had been lucky enough to
land, and he grabbed the doorknob, yanked the door
open, slipped on the steps, rolled down hard, lay there
stunned in the open as the garbage can lid struck again

and the street was crazy that night, there were drunks
and transvestites all over, but the Lennon thing had them
all, there was music blasting from boom boxes, Beatles
songs, and no one was paying attention, it was just
another ruckus going on, the kind of act you expected in
the middle of the night on West Ninety-eighth, and Chub
tried to call out, but his mouth was cut, his mouth was
full of blood and Chub wondered, dazed and helpless, if
this was Lennon's madman on him now, intent on killing
and killing until Doomsday and he crawled a little, got to
his feet stumbling but another blow crashed and he went
down again, with no strength left, no more moves, and in
the darkness, with the Beatles rising up the outside tenement walls, Chub lay still and thought of something he
had read once, something about a guy who was going
crazy and whenever he was on a plane and there was
someone famous also on board the guy got out because he
knew if the plane crashed the famous guy would get the
obituary and no one would know that he had also per-
ished in the fire, and fading, Chub held to the thought
that even though he wouldn't have gotten an obituary
anyway, at least he had a good excuse, because no one
would get an obituary, not the night John Lennon died.

And then there was a gun. And the gun was black.
And the gun was in a hand. And the hand was black.
And the gun rose in the night, paused at the apex for just
a moment, until it came flashing down into the side of the
neck of the madman with the garbage can lid. The
madman stopped. Turned. Then Rory Baylor struck
again, crashing his piece into the side of the madman's
head. And the madman sank to his knees. Baylor kept
the gun pointed toward the killer, knelt by Chub, calling
out, "Somebody get a fucking ambulance!" and Chub,
forcing himself to sit, emptied his mouth of blood before
he said "No" and then Baylor said, "Can you make it to
the station?" and Chub said "No" again. "No police,"
and as Baylor stared at him Chub stared at the stunned
madman. "I know him," Chub managed to say. "He was
a student of mine." And he wiped the blood away again

as he studied the crazed face of the plagiarist, Peter Hungerford.

A crowd was gathering now as Baylor slapped cuffs on Hungerford, yanked him to his feet, but during this Chub managed, over the noise, to plead with Baylor not to do anything official, not yet, not till he knew more than he did then and reluctantly, Baylor agreed, and so fifteen minutes later there were five people sitting in the living room of an expensive town house in the East Sixties. Hungerford got his size from his father, the surgeon, his facial characteristics from his mother, the psychiatrist. The Hungerfords were grateful, they both said so, for the return of their son.

Baylor told them to think of it as a loan, and a temporary one.

They sat, Chub on a couch with the parents, Baylor off to one side with the son. Chub explained what had happened that evening, what had happened at Oberlin. Then he waited for them to explain.

Mrs. Hungerford began by saying that, just as with shoemakers' children, it was not difficult for trained specialists like herself to ignore psychotic episodes when they took place within the immediate family, which was when Dr. Hungerford cut in and said, "Can the psychotic-episodes jargon," and Mrs. Hungerford said she was sorry, and he said don't be sorry, just be brief.

Briefly, two months before, in his third year at Harvard Med, Peter Hungerford had snapped. He was hospitalized, tested, probed. The overwhelming results, paranoid schizophrenia—"I'm sorry, goddamnit," Mrs. Hungerford said when she used the phrase, and before her husband could interrupt, "but that's what it is."

Peter, of course, rejected the medical findings. He was one hundred percent okay. That was one of his delusions. Another was this: If he could just remove a writing professor who had started all the rumors about him, the world would know he was a hundred percent okay.

The Hungerfords had placed their son in a beautiful sanatarium outside Boston. A lovely place, ringed with hills, quiet, bucolic, with a first-rate staff. Everything about it was first-rate, apparently, except security. Earlier that day Peter had overcome a guard, taken his money, and disappeared. No one knew where he was. Until now.

Chub sat back in the quiet room and closed his eyes.

The Hungerfords said they were terribly sorry.

Chub didn't move.

And it would never happen again, they could promise that.

"I'm just a poor illiterate," Rory Baylor said then, "and I know all you suckers are smarter than hell, but somebody please explain to me how you're gonna keep that promise you just made?"

The Hungerfords looked at each other briefly. "Wellspring," Mrs. Hungerford said.

"I don't know that anybody's answered my question."

"It's several hours north of here," Dr. Hungerford said. "We thought of putting him there first—"

"—but Peter liked Boston, so we thought he'd be happier up there," Mrs. Hungerford said. "Wellspring has the best security anywhere in the East."

"We'll transfer Peter there. Now do you see? We'll start making arrangements right away, you have our word."

"What I have," Rory Baylor said, "is an attempted murderer and *my* immediate arrangements are to put him smack in jail. You have my word."

"No," Chub said, his eyes still closed. Slowly he opened them, looked at Baylor. "There's been enough trouble. Everybody's had enough trouble. I won't press charges."

Baylor paused a long time before he said, "Son of a bitch if I don't have the cuffs on the wrong guy. Chub, this big fellow here doesn't have your best interests at heart, has that gotten through?"

Chub shut his eyes again. "I just don't want to think about things, Rory. Go along with me, all right?"

"You can leave Peter with us," Dr. Hungerford said. "He's fine when he's with us."

And then Baylor exploded. "You're *all* crazy—in the first place, Mr. Fuller here has saved your asses, but I didn't hear any thank-yous. And in the second place, if this Wellspring has such great security I'll bet they got men on duty day and night, and I'll bet they got vehicles and even maybe a used straitjacket lying around somewhere. So you call them and get them down here and then you can all get in and be fine with him on the drive back up."

It was dawn before the ambulance arrived. Chub and Baylor left the Hungerfords in the living room with their son while Baylor kept an eye on them from the next room. As soon as they were alone Chub started to say that it wasn't every night someone saved him and—

—"And shut up," Baylor said. "I could have been a hero, you dumb bastard. I could have had me an attempted murderer if it wasn't for you. I'm gonna send my little minute of a wife down to finish what this nutcake started."

The Hungerfords drove off in the ambulance with their son. And just before they left they thanked Chub for being so understanding, for not pressing charges, for everything. And Mrs. Hungerford repeated her earlier promise. What he had endured was history; it would never happen again.

She was right but not entirely. The security at Wellspring might well have been the best—there were no more physical assaults on Chub's person. But once Hungerford broke off the grounds; he was recaptured at the railroad station, waiting for the New York train, no more than ten minutes later. But in those ten minutes he was loose.

And sometimes he got to a phone. And then there would be the phone calls promising death, the voice always starting low, then building in volume and vituperation and this call, on the twenty-second of December 1982, as Chub raced across the room to slam off his machine, was the third time that year, the first to call him "baby-killer."

Chub sat still at his desk. He looked at his watch: six-fifteen.

He put his elbows on his desk and his head in his hands. He looked at his watch again: seven-oh-five. Finally at eight he picked up the phone. The Hungerfords had the town house and they had a place on the beach in Easthampton. He tried the town house first. A servant's voice answered.

Chub gave his name.

The Hungerfords were having a party.

Chub started to give his name again, slammed down the phone, threw on his clothes, ran down the stairs, ran to Broadway, ran into the street, stopped a cab, sat rigid till he was in front of their town house, jammed his thumb against the buzzer, kept it there until a uniformed woman opened the door. "I know they're having a party, tell them Mr. Fuller is here!"

The Hungerfords were dressed formally. They moved together toward the foyer where he stood. From inside came voices, soft music, lovely, baroque, Vivaldi.

"He called again," Chub said.

They looked at one another. "He's there—we talked to him less than half an hour ago."

"I don't care—I'm telling you he called again. And he's getting worse."

"We know," Mrs. Hungerford said.

"None of this is easy," Dr. Hungerford said.

"We're past easy, don't you understand that?—" His voice was loud, louder than he meant, and Mrs. Hungerford turned, glanced back at the party.

"We can't talk now," the doctor said.

"You can listen, though—" His voice was his own again. "Every other time this has happened I've contacted you and we've all been civilized. We've visited and chatted on about the sadness of the world but I'm done with that now."

"You have nothing to threaten us with," Dr. Hungerford said. "And we're giving a party. Now good night." He reached out, started to close the door.

"I'll get him before he gets me," Chub promised, and then he was out in the cold.

By the next day he had irised down the phone call and his ridiculous threat to the Hungerfords. It was important to forget all that because the following night was Christmas Eve, which had become one of his favorites, because some TV station, he never quite remembered which, spent their entire evening showing the glorious fireplace at Gracie Mansion with the flames so warm and constant, the andirons glistening, and there were no commercials, just carols, hours of carols, some instrumental, some sung by choruses. Getting stoned and watching and listening had become for Chub the most peaceful night of the year.

The afternoon of the twenty-fourth he did a little quick Christmas shopping. He and Kitchel had never been gift exchangers, but since the Baylors had come into his life, they needed remembering. Rory was easy—Chub bought a Dick Tracy comic and wrapped it. Maya took more time—she was special. Very dark, very pretty, *very* smart. She taught art at one of the fancy private schools up in Riverdale, so the subject matter was no problem. He finally decided on a new coffee-table book about Venice, wrapped it carefully, jotted a note that said, "When you get bored with what's-his-name, I'm available."

They lived five blocks up from him, on West 103rd, and he buzzed the super, said these were for the Baylors and to deliver them, please. He had no doubts they would be delivered—the super was so pleased to have a cop in the house he treated the Baylors as if they were something close to royalty.

And if they weren't quite that, they were terribly important to Chub. So many of his clients were writing violent novels and Rory was his main source for that kind of research. And through that, he met Maya and they hit it off from the start. He'd spent dozens of evenings in their place, dinners or just BS-ing away the hours. And she was insatiable when it came to Chinese food, any kind of Chinese food, and the three of them had visited most of the countless places that dotted the Upper West Side.

Around six on Christmas Eve, Chub bought some grass from one of his friendly neighborhood pushers, went upstairs. He did a little work, got caught up in it, didn't finish till close to nine, when the program began. He quickly lit a joint, smoked it, opened a bottle of Hunter Valley red, bathed and got into his pajamas and then lay on his bed, flicking around with his remote until he found the fireplace with the warm flames. He had a twenty-five-inch color boob tube now, remote control and all, even though he didn't watch much television. But the thing arrived one day with two angry Macy's delivery men accompanying it—they hadn't much enjoyed the climb. Chub thought it must have been a mistake but his name and address were right, so he let them set it up and get it working. As he tipped them Elliott Carter called, explaining that a gift might soon arrive. Chub said he suspected it just had and thanks, but why? He had done a great deal of rush work for Carter at less than his usual rate, but that had been months ago. Carter said he'd just gotten a main selection from the Literary Guild and was sharing the wealth.

Chub sat up in bed, swigged the Australian wine, made a few quick jiggles on the control panel, got the picture just perfect. He swallowed again, turned the sound up louder, then lay back, closing his eyes, listening.

> *The first Noel the angels did say*
> *Was to certain poor shepherds in fields*
> *   as they lay . . .*

Chub smiled, listening to the harmony of the chorus. He loved that song but when he was a kid, he didn't know what the words meant, especially "certain"—he thought maybe it meant the shepherds were being punished as they lay in their fields. He brought the bottle to his lips, managed an expert swallow. It tasted delicious, but the first joint wasn't all that strong, so he hopped out of bed, took a couple of tokes on the second. He looked at his watch. Shit. It was almost ten already and the program went off at twelve.

He lay back down, closed his eyes, kind of conducted his free non-bottle-holding hand along with the music.

> *Deck the hall with boughs of holly,*
> *Fa la la la la, la la la la.*
> *'Tis the season to be jolly,*
> *Fa la la la la, la la la la.*
> *Don we now our gay apparel . . .*

Chub began to sing now, quietly.

> *Fa la la*
> *la la la*
> *la la*
> *la*

He stopped almost as soon as he started. His skin felt cold. He didn't like to drink under the covers. Once he had been so blotto he'd spilled a half-full bottle and ruined a damn-near-new pair of sheets. He got up, went to the bathroom, grabbed his robe, slung it on, went back and lay on top of the bed.

His skin still felt cold.

No. Wrong. Colder.

He tucked the bottle between his legs, blew on his hands, rubbed them together. For a moment he remembered the pneumonia but this wasn't like that, this was different, he wasn't shivering or anything, it was more like his skin was beginning to tighten as it lowered in temperature.

Chub pulled his robe around him, got in under the covers, pulled the sheets up to his neck, kept one arm down against his side, just keeping the bottle hand clear.

We three kings of Orient are;
Bearing gifts, we traverse afar . . .

What a crappy song. Stupid rhyme. Not stupid but forced, incompetent. He closed his eyes, drank, drank a little more, waiting for the goodies to begin again.

On the first day of Christmas,
My true love gave to me:
A partridge in a pear tree. . . .

Chub lay very still, eyes closed, listening to one of his favorites, when he saw himself alone before dawn on the Maui beach, rebuilding the sand castle where the Rain Man lived along with the fastest horse on the carousel, and that was no place he wanted to be, he had been there, so he opened his eyes—

—or tried to, but the skin of his lids disobeyed him, they were cold, frozen cold, no, it wasn't that, it was as if his body had been clouded by a mist, a mist so tight it had him in its power and he tried to shake his head, shake the beach away, but his head was in the power of the mist, too, and he was in Florida and Gretchen was going, "Blue. *Blue,*" and then Chub watched as his book made the splash in the water of the pool where he'd first learned to swim—

. . . two turtle doves,
And a partridge in a pear tree. . . .

—Cheyney was reading his stuff now, the description of the men's room, and the class was looking around, one to the other, trying to find out who wrote it, and now back to Athens and his father was looking for the tailor's thimble, pulling out all the drawers, and now still in Athens in the back bedroom and his father had all the bottles, the little bottles, and was downing them so fast, his lips squeezing around the tiny tops—

. . . three French hens,
Two turtle doves,
And a par—

—Chub forced his lips apart, it was hard because they resisted, the mist had them, too, but he would not give in, because now he knew what was happening, all the irising-down mechanism, it was starting to give way, and he knew the only way to keep it was to get his body working the way he wanted it to, not the way the mist wanted it to, and he got his lips apart but he didn't stop there, he kept making them go farther and farther away from each other and his mouth was so wide it hurt and when that was done he did the same with his eyes, got them wide and staring, so at last he could see the TV set and the warming fire—

—mistake—Big Baby was sitting in the flames—

. . . calling birds,
Three . . .

—Big Baby raised her arms to him, sitting there on the blazing logs, and Chub quickly shut his eyes, where B.J. was crying and slapping him and slapping him while he stood there not even able to cry, not even now, and Chub opened his eyes, and there she was, Jesse, eyes so wide, saying, "Daddy, Daddy, I was scared," and then the third wave hit her and nothing could be worse than that but Chub was wrong because now in the flames there was the funeral and B.J. was out of her mind with fury, crying, "Don't let that bastard in here," and Chub was fighting toward the tiny casket and now, in the flames, as the tiny casket was lowered in the ground Jesse popped her head up and said, "Is this a story, too, Daddy?— Does the Rain Man rescue me now?"

And Chub, needing rescue, cried out alone and dropped the bottle and fell to the floor because he knew he had to TALK TO somebody only Kitchel was on vacation with Lydia somewhere warm and he got his

hands on the phone and forced the mist back long
enough for his fingers to dial and when Rory Baylor
answered, Chub said, "Just . . . just CHECKING," and
Rory laughed and said what about and Chub said, "Wondered if . . . ANYTHING WAS DELIVERED, MER-
RY CHRISTMAS," and Rory said that yes, they had
arrived, and Merry Christmas to him, too, and would he
mind to hold one second, Maya wanted to talk to him,
too, and Chub said, "Always HAPPY TO TALK TO
OLD MAYA," and then Rory was gone for what seemed
like a while and that was bad, because during the talk,
while he was in contact, the mist seemed less powerful
and finally Maya was there, laughing and saying, "Whatever it is, it weighs a ton," and Chub said, "HOPE you
like it," and Maya said I'm sure I will and would he
mind, even though it was Christmas Eve and all, if she
asked him a question because she had a problem with one
of her students she couldn't help but maybe he might be
able to and Chub said, "SHOOT," and she begin to
explain about this senior student of hers who had a senior
project and the subject was the early life of Van Gogh
and the school library didn't have all that much and
Maya wasn't sure where to direct the student to go and
Chub said, "THE MAIN library, Forty-second and
Fifth, THE ART DIVISION, room 313," and Maya said
would he mind to hold while she got a pencil and paper
to write that down and when she was back Chub said it
all again and then he said, "WAIT one sec, is this kid a
high school student, they DON'T ALLOW HIGH
SCHOOL STUDENTS," and Maya said, well, wasn't
that unfair, how could that possibly be, and Chub said,
"LET ME DO IT FOR THE KID, I'm down there ALL
THE TIME," and Maya said no, it was a learning experience for the kid and Chub said was the student a boy or a
girl and Maya said why and Chub said, "BECAUSE if
they LOOK OLD enough, sometimes they can GET
AWAY with it," and Maya went into a long, detailed
explanation of how the student looked; he was a boy, not
tall, but big-shouldered and he had a heavy beard and she

hated to send him down there and have him turned away, was there anyplace else in the city and Chub said, "MID–MANHATTAN," and Maya said damn, her pencil point had broken and please to hold and she was gone awhile before she came back, all apologies, asking where this Central Manhattan library was and Chub said, "NO, not Central, MID–MANHATTAN, *MID*," and Maya apologized a long time about how her mind was like a sieve and then she wondered what if this place didn't have what her student needed and he said, "DON-NELL," and Maya asked how to spell that and Chub spelled it carefully and then she said that she wasn't quite sure if she'd gotten it all down straight, could he please go over it one more time and Chub was in the middle of explaining it when Baylor burst into his room and grabbed the phone from his hand.

"I'm here, baby," he said. "Don't worry. Thank you, you done good." Then he turned to Chub. "What the fuck are you into?"

Chub mumbled something about the mist.

Baylor slapped him.

Chub blinked.

"Talk so I can understand."

Chub tried.

Baylor started making coffee. "Walk," he told Chub. "Just walk till I tell you not to. Ain't no fuckin' mist— you bought some bad shit from some asshole on the street and Christ only knows what was in it. Listen to me, Fuller, *can you hear me, Fuller?*"

"YES."

"I ever catch you buying shit on the street again I'll kick you *very* hard. Next time you want a supply of grass, *you come to me*—we confiscate a lot of stuff and I keep only the finest. You want grass in the future, where do you get it?"

"THE POLICE STATION."

"No, you fool, not there, I keep it at home. Where do I keep it?"

"Your place."

"Riiiight. Keep walking."

Chub walked until the coffee was done and then Baylor poured him a steaming cup, black. Chub blew on it until he could get it down. When he was done, Baylor poured again. Then Baylor had him walk some more. At one in the morning, he looked at Chub. "How you feel?"

"Fine."

"Hundred percent?"

"Pretty GODDAMN close."

Baylor slapped him again. "Lying fuck." He stood up. "Get your clothes on—you can't be alone tonight— you're spending Christmas Eve with the Baylors. You'll be fine by morning."

But he wasn't. The minute he awoke he could feel the mist around him and before he opened his eyes his father was watching him write his paper on barbed wire, wondering why Chub hadn't come in to save him. And then his father was gone and someone he had never seen was watching him.

A perfect blue-eyed boy.

"See how blue?" the boy said. "You'll never catch up to me, no matter what," and Chub knew he was looking at his dead older brother, Chris.

Maya came in then. "Thought I heard you stirring."

Chub stared at her. She was probably all of five feet tall and maybe once weighed over a hundred pounds. He had never done anything like this before but now he reached out and put his arms around her body. Because the minute she was there, he could feel the mist weaken.

He spent the day with them. Rory knew from a look that the trip wasn't over, the shit was still kicking the hell out of his brains. He spent the night with them, too, both of them sitting on living room chairs, talking till he fell asleep on their couch. Chub told them they didn't have to, but he was glad they did. He could feel the mist waiting in a corner of the room, waiting.

The day after that, he was up at the Medical Library as

soon as it opened. Because he didn't think it was drugs that had shattered his efforts to iris life down. He just didn't know what it was.

In less than an hour he found out. It wouldn't have taken him that long if he'd been more skilled at unscrambling medical jargon. What he had wasn't all that uncommon. He had entered into a state of panic. Not depression—depression was abnormal mourning; panic was abnormal fear. Medication might help, but not always. Being busy was usually good. What was bad, always bad, was too much time to think; solitude was an enemy.

Well, now.

Interesting news, certainly, a new element to add to his daily equation, but nothing to get unhinged about. Probably Baylor was at least in part right—something in the grass had triggered things. But that was no longer a worry, since Baylor, his friend and friendly neighborhood cop, was now his new source. Doctors, in Chub's pantheon, rated just above snake-oil salesmen—no, they rated right along with them because that's really all they were, and the last time he had been in their care, they had given him that terrific spinal tap, so fuck them. Solitude had been good company for so long now, he doubted it would turn on him completely. He would just have to get busier, that was all.

He closed his eyes after he closed the medical texts and was yawning when the perfect blue-eyed boy decided to keep him company and before his skin could begin to tighten, Chub leapt up, returned the books, and headed downtown to do some work that was overdue dealing with, would you believe, any actual evidence on how hung Rasputin was. (A client from Riverdale, who was working on a sexual history of the world.)

On the subway downtown he decided to get off near the Lincoln Center Library because it always cheered him, the young intense kids all convinced it was only a matter of time before they became Olivier or Stravinsky or Balanchine, and he decided, as long as he was there, he thought, what the hell, he might just clock the catalog and see if there was any mention at all about The Cherry Sisters.

There was, and the sisters were fantastic.

Chub laughed out loud as he read some about them.

Their act was nothing unusual: The ladies came out in discreet costumes and did recitations and banged a bass drum and sang songs, some of their own composition.

They were originally from Iowa and after their Manhattan debut in 1896, the *Times* wrote, "Never before did New Yorkers see anything in the least like The Cherry Sisters from Cedar Rapids, Iowa. It is sincerely to be hoped that nothing like them will ever be seen again."

It was the kindest review.

But clearly they were a force of nature: Within weeks they were earning a thousand dollars a week, banging their drum and singing their songs, always behind the crucial protection of a net strung between them and the audience. They were not nicknamed The Vegetable Girls without cause. Soon it was reported that produce dealers were having trouble supplying their regular customers because so many vendors were waiting outside the theatre where the ladies worked, their carts piled high with onions and carrots, tomatoes and cabbage. Everyone in the audience came armed, and while they fired away, the girls just went on and on with their routines.

They were very proper, and their hope was to someday earn a high place in Iowa society, so when Anna Held asked them to dinner, or Melba or Lillian Russell, they declined, remaining quietly in their hotel suite, anxious not to be tarnished by associating with such folks.

Then came the lawsuit.

Leaving New York at the height of their popularity, they took their act and their net on the road. Finally they returned to Iowa, where a review was *so* bad that Addie, the youngest, sued. (The review had referred to her as "a capering monstrosity.")

The trial was climaxed when the sisters, to prove their case to the judge, did their act in court. The judge, after

watching their talents on display, ruled *against* them—
the review, though certainly not flattering, was just as
certainly accurate.

Undaunted, they took their case to the Iowa Supreme
Court. In what was to become a landmark decision on
the side of a free press, the supreme court upheld the
lower court's decision (Cherry v. Des Moines Leader,
114 Iowa 298, 86 N.W. 323).

By two that afternoon, Chub had located the case in
some legal texts, Xeroxed the pages, put them in an
envelope because, what the hell, maybe The Bone didn't
have this data. He was about to mail the information
when he thought what the hell again, SoHo wasn't that
long a ride on the subway, so he went down and started
to stuff the envelope into her mailbox. On the outside he
scribbled, "Just happened to come across this; thought it
might be of interest." Then he went off to see what
reliable information existed on the dimensions of Rasputin's organ.

"Just *happened* to come across this," The Bone said
that night. "Talk about feeble." (Earlier—when Chub
had beeped in for his messages there was one from her
and when he returned it, she invited him down for
dinner, "Unless your lawyer fiancée is back in town." He
said he was free and she met him at the door, looking
spectacular—wearing the makeup from her first *Vogue*
cover, her Paul Newman eyes never as large. She was
also, as she made them drinks, obviously in a very good
mood.)

"I was doing some work on Jolson," Chub said. "His
early life and stuff."

She whirled on him from the kitchen area. "And
you're a fucking liar."

"I'm a fucking liar," Chub said softly.

"And there never was any goddamn lady lawyer."

"Not even one."

"I knew I was irresistible," The Bone said, and now
she set the table. With three settings. "Well, Fuller,

you're too late." She pointed to the third plate. "After you spurned me, I crashed a party for Judith Krantz and I met a doctor—he's only six feet tall but except for that, perfect."

"Tell you what—let's fix him up with my barrister friend, they'll make a helluva team."

"We could—except that would leave me stuck with you." She picked up the third place, put it back in the kitchen. "So much for my surgeon." Then she came over, sat beside Chub, pursued by her three cats, who clawed the furniture while they drank. " 'Your eyes is fool of de hasking,' " The Bone said then.

Chub was curious.

"That was the last guy who was as feeble as you, Fuller. He was some wop royalty, a prince, and it was my first trip over on a shoot and he liked to bed down with models and sometimes he married them. Lot of bread, *lot* of bread. Anyway, he took me to dinner and there was a fuss because he was this rich playboy type and I knew he was going to make a pitch and whammo, before my goddamn Campari and soda, he leaned close to me and smiled and took my hand and said, 'Your eyes is fool of de hasking.' It's a cornball line to start—'Your eyes are full of asking'—meaning, I guess, wonder, curiosity about the world, intelligence, I don't know, but the real meaning was 'Let's hit the sack after the pasta, baby,' except his accent was so terrible I couldn't help it—I barfed out loud, right in his face. That put a damper on the evening, may I add." She looked at Chub, shook her head. "Except for my big mouth, I coulda had a prince. And now look who I'm stuck with."

"I just brought you some research material is all."

"Oh, right. Fine. Why don't you leave then? Now."

Chub started to say something, stopped.

"Boy, you are one closed-in son of a bitch. Say it—you don't want to go."

"I'd like to stay."

"That's progress. Why? Because what I said in the coffee shop was right: You got nothing."

"If you think so."

She reached out then, touched his cheek. "Don't tell me I don't know about sad eyes." Then she stood quickly, went to the kitchen to work on dinner.

It was an evening neither of them was quick to forget.

Before they began to eat, The Bone announced that she was an even greater chef than she was a writer. Chub had no way of knowing, since he'd never read a word of hers, if she had skill in that direction, but she was a brilliant cook. They began with a fish mousse—"home-fucking-made, none of that Dean and DeLuca shit"—accompanied by a half-bottle of Chablis. Then came pepper steak, rare—"I had to practically screw a guy at The Coach House for their recipe"—accompanied by a vinaigrette salad and a bottle of '66 Gloria, Danieli's favorite. For dessert: chocolate soufflé with homemade chocolate sauce poured bubbling into the center. It was as good a meal as Chub could remember and he said so while, over her protestations, he helped with the dishes.

Then came conversation on the couch, accompanied by a '63 Dow (another Danieli favorite). "I know this is going to be great," The Bone said as she got comfortable. "On account of what I do best is talk and what you do best is shut up." What they did the next three hours mostly was to yell at each other. Over a subject Chub had never even heard of before the evening began: the relevance, no more than that, the total and sole supremacy, of Trash.

"Of *what?*"

"Trash. Trash. Jesus, don't you know anything?"

Trash, it turned out, was the final philosophical contribution of Danieli, and The Bone was his disciple. As Chub tried to slog his way through the maze, the best he could come up with was this: In 1945, the two explosions altered forever the value system that had been, for centuries, in operation. Trash was transcendent and its main tenets were (1) transience and (2) the reconfirmation of the certainty of violent death. Therefore, the only magazine of true quality was *People,* because you were meant to throw it away. The greatest artist was Christo, because his works were meant to self-destruct. The greatest athlete was André.

"Who the fuck is André?"

The Bone kicked off her shoes. "You live in a time warp? Jesus, Fuller. André the Giant is the greatest wrestler in the world and professional wrestling is the greatest sport."

"I'm waiting for the punch line."

"I know why you're so dumb—it's all those writers you worked for have polluted your head. All fiction is shit, because those assholes who write fiction try and tell us life can be beautiful when the truth is life is cinders."

"*Death* is cinders," Chub shouted.

"*Same* thing, *putz*," The Bone said, pouring them both some more port. "Except, of course, for Kafka."

"Kafka is okay?"

"No—more than okay—Kafka is the Nostradamus of Trash. Don't you know why? Because when he died he directed all the shit he wrote to be destroyed before it was published. He knew it was garbage and the era of Trash was coming—I study him—so did Danieli—see, Kafka died in '24 and no one can figure out how he knew."

Chub stared at her. She *believed* it. She sat there, stunning and slim, surrounded by the goddamn cats clawing away, gathering steam. Hitchcock was the greatest director, especially in *Psycho* (if only the shower scene had been done in slow motion) and that other one, *Saboteur, The Secret Agent,* one of those with an "S" title, where the little kid has the bomb on the bus and everybody waits for the kid to get rescued only ka-boom, the bomb gets everybody, the kid, too, genius.

Genius, Chub managed, because everybody dies unfairly?

Now you're getting it, The Bone assured him, and then launched into splatter films, the only worthwhile stuff, where you saw limbs come off and really good gore. Actually, she was writing one now, it was going to be the greatest splatter film and it was called *Skeletons* and maybe if he'd stop acting like such a *schmuck,* she'd let him read it.

Three hours they went at it and Chub, to his dismay, found he enjoyed it all. She was so fierce in her beliefs, so willing to defend as well as attack. Whatever else she was, she was different. And never dull.

At a little after one she excused herself for a moment, went to the bathroom, leaving Chub alone with the three goddamn cats—they were nameless, or sometimes she'd referred to them as "one," "two" and "three" but it seemed to him she did it in a manner best described as totally arbitrary. Chub had a way with cats—they were smart buggers and they knew he didn't like them, so whenever he was near one, they naturally climbed all over him, and these had claws, so he was careful when he told them "Getaway."

To his surprise, they did. They went to the door The Bone was behind and they began to claw there. Chub stretched out, thoroughly relaxed and more than a little smashed, wondering what nut notion she was going to come up with next, when he heard her voice, very loud, saying, " 'Night."

Chub wasn't quite sure he'd understood—obviously, he had not understood, she had given no previous indication that their battling was coming to an end so he got up and walked to the bathroom and asked, "Come again?"

"Good night!"

Chub stood there. It was suddenly weird, the cats clawing and starting to meow, her voice far too loud. "What's up?"

"*Nothing.*"

Clearly, something was. Her voice was odd now, not just loud, and the cats were beginning to cry out.

"Something the matter?"

"No, nothing, nothing, goddamnit, just get the hell out of here!"

"Something I said bug you?"

Now, from behind the bathroom door, a cry of pain.

Chub pulled the door open and saw her sitting in a corner of the bathroom on the floor, the right side of her face pressed hard against the wall. Chub knelt alongside, took her hands, but she pulled away, pressing the right side of her face harder into the wall now and this time Chub used his strength, turned her toward him.

She resembled no Bone he had ever seen. The right side of her face was totally contorted, the blood vessels in her temple protruding, her nose was running, her right eye was bloodshot, her right eyelid starting to droop. (Chub had never heard of, much less seen, a cluster headache before, but the next day he did some quick work in the medical library and read up on them. A cluster headache was vascular in origin, meaning they stemmed, like the migraine, from a widening of the blood vessels. But whereas the migraines gave warning, the cluster gave none. It hit in as little as three minutes, lasted sometimes a half hour, sometimes twice that. And because they came and went so quickly, there was little medication of use—by the time you took something and it got into the bloodstream, the attack might well be over.

(But while the attack was on, there was no questioning the severity. More than one victim described the pain as if a hot iron was being pressed slowly, slowly, in the affected eye, forcing its way, boring its way into the soft tissue of the brain, remaining there. Pain being impossible to quantify, there was no point in comparing the suffering of a cluster to that of a migraine. But probably the cluster was worse. People banged their heads against walls with a cluster attack. Or threatened suicide. Or attempted it. Or succeeded.

(All this and more Chub didn't know until the next day. Most particularly why the name. He found out that night—the attacks came in waves, clusters, sometimes half a dozen before the anguish ended.)

The Bone had four that night, and Chub got her through them all. When she wanted to talk, he talked with her; when she wanted to press her hands through her eye, he applied the pressure himself, making sure there was no damage. When she wanted to crash her head against an iron radiator, he stopped her, lifted her up, carried her to her bed, trying to ignore her cursing and kicking, held her down so that there could be no permanent damage to that once famous face. Between the attacks he sat with her, held ice to the afflicted area because sometimes that helped. She wept and begged him to get away but he remained, and when at last, well after dawn, the last cluster attack had been beaten, he sat on the bed, stroked her dark hair. She was wet with perspiration, and her face was splotched and she was almost exhausted enough to sleep. All the attacks had gone for the right side, and the area under her nose was raw from the running, the right eyelid drooping completely now, covering the perfect blue beneath. Chub held her until he could feel sleep begin to take her.

". . . I never . . . wanted you to see me . . . not like this. . . ." The Bone managed.

Chub carefully touched his lips to the sad drooping lid. "Your eyes is fool of de hasking," he said. It almost brought a smile before she slept.

Such was their beginning. Love was not in the air. Nor passion. Sex was absent too. But that was not of much moment to them—what they needed was a mutual support system, and that was what they supplied.

Within a week she had gotten him to shave off his beard, and when he presented his new face to her she said that sure it was an improvement, now he looked his age again, only he also looked like he'd spent his last years underground, so she bought a cheap sunlamp and saw to it that he used it every day. Next she set out to get him back to fighting weight, so she cooked meals calculated to make him gain, which he did. She ate right along with him—weight had never been her problem. Her whole family was thin.

He slept the first month down at her place, but by the end of January, when she suggested he start spending some nights up on Ninety-eighth, he resisted. She pressed him on it and finally he told her about the mist, and that he was sometimes a little concerned it might be up there waiting.

Once she knew that, she forced him to try. Because you had to face things eventually, and Chub started going back home some evenings, and if the mist was there, he'd talk to her on the phone, for hours sometimes, until he was alone and could sleep.

She liked being alone at night sometimes because often she worked then, jotted notes. Chub pressed her and finally she told him that the clusters often came at night and it humiliated her for him to be around then.

She *never* came to Ninety-eighth Street—never would again, that once was it for her. Why? She tried to phrase it carefully. "I don't want to know the guy who lives there."

Chub understood. It was a dungeon. He promised her he'd move soon. She accepted that. What he didn't tell her was that he'd been making himself the same promise for years.

He met some of her modeling friends, she met the Kitchels and the Baylors. But mostly they spent their evenings alone. The contact meant that much. They needed their time together. Sometimes they were quiet. More often they argued. She gave him her screenplay, *Skeletons* (eleven corpses with the last third yet to come). He told her it was gripping. He screwed up his courage and gave her a hardcover copy of his book. She thanked him profusely, saw it was fiction, told him she never read fiction. "I read your screenplay and it was fiction," Chub said, stung. "It was not, it was not fiction, it was *Trash.* God you piss me off sometimes."

He got back at her the next week when they went to the Garden to see André the Giant beat two bearded guys at once by knocking their heads together. The Bone urged André on at the top of her lungs throughout the match and when it was over Chub said that the other two guys weren't trying and, more than that, either one of them could have mopped up on a slob like André by themselves.

She belted him with her program, which was fortunately thin.

They watched endless Hitchcocks on the tube and the others that she owned on her Betamax. They went to splatter revivals, where The Bone tried explaining between the audiences' screams that *The Texas Chainsaw Massacre* was great Trash while *The Shining* wasn't Trash at all since there was an attempt at mentality behind it. Besides, too many of the good guys lived.

Chub sent off for actual Xeroxes of old papers detailing The Cherry Sisters, their various tours, their attempts to conquer Iowa society, their comebacks. He was touched the night of April fifteenth when she set a special place for dinner because in the papers that day it had been reported that none other than Norbert Pearlroth had died, Pearlroth being perhaps the greatest researcher, the man who for fifty-two years spent his life at Forty-second and Fifth and was really responsible for finding out the facts used in *Ripley's Believe It or Not!* Chub responded by clipping out all the Kafka meetings that were scheduled in the ensuing weeks in New York, 1983 being the hundredth anniversary of his birth, and he knew The Bone would want to crash them and ask questions.

All this and more they did for and to each other, and always unspoken was the fact that what they really were were survivors of Bataan, and they were lockstepping back to strength. Chub knew he was not just recovering but that he was all the way back. He weighed 160 again, the mist had left him alone. And so he called her from a phone booth one May afternoon from Columbia, to see what was on for the evening and how was the Kafka convention she had been to that day and when she asked, "Do you know who spoke, a guy named Andrew Cheyney," and Chub replied yes, he had known Cheyney from Oberlin, then The Bone said, "I figured that, so I went up and asked if he remembered you and you know what he told me? 'Remember him? Of course I remember him. He's our greatest failure,' and then he said—"

—but Chub didn't want to know what Cheyney said next, the last thing he wanted to hear was that, so he slammed down the phone and for a moment he felt like a giant gem that someone had touched at just the right spot for the stone to break apart and Chub, not sure he could move, took a breath and did, first slowly, then faster, then fast, and all he could think was this: Yes, he was the greatest failure—was there ever a day in the last decade when he didn't realize he was the greatest failure?— but—but Jesus, *she didn't have to tell me.*

Late on a late spring afternoon, Chub, fleeing across the Columbia campus, was astonished, in a passing classroom window, to see himself burst into tears.

CHAPTER 2

At Four A.M.,
the Phone Rang
Softly. . . .

Then, at four A.M., the phone rang softly.

(At least Chub thought it sounded that way, but he had been so out of it when he went to sleep, there really wasn't a lot he could be sure of.

(After he had seen his face in the classroom window he had rushed inside the nearest building, found an empty corridor, stood in the corner—like a bad schoolboy, Jesus God—until he hoped he looked presentable, the tears dry, his first tears in half a lifetime, since his father's pulse beat steady and strong on the emergency-room table but no one would listen to him as they dragged him away.

(Why had he lost it that way? He left the building, trying to figure it. Probably because he had been so unprepared. The Bone had wounded him before—and he had snapped at her—but usually there had been a build preceding. That was one reason. And that Cheyney had said it, that was another—Cheyney didn't like him but Cheyney didn't lie, and if he had given his appraisal to a stranger like The Bone, surely he had not been reticent with those he knew. The word, Cheyney's word, must have been all over, and that was another reason.

(But overriding these was the fact that he had overrated himself, had assumed recovery. Wrong. So wrong. He was still, still fragile. And the mist would surely be curled and waiting in a corner of his rooms on Ninety-eighth Street.)

Chub put off returning. There was a film *noir* double feature at the Thalia, lots of bang-bang action assured, that was good. He bought himself a pint of Hunan lamb at a takeout dump near the theatre, ignored their look as he asked for a plastic fork—he could never, no matter how often he ate with the Baylors, master chopsticks. He took the food into the theatre, sat alone in the farthest seat on the left, ate as much as he could stomach, concentrated on the flickering black-and-white images.

It was dark when he left and he headed toward Riverside Park, moving down to the Hudson—the moon blessed the water, you couldn't see the shit floating on the surface. Chub never jogged but now he did, running down the river walk to the boat basin. He was exhausted when he got there but that was good. He paused only briefly before turning, jogging back to the exit near his place. A liquor shop was open so he bought a quart of Wild Turkey, opened it on the street, took a few swallows, closed it, made his slow way—his legs ached—to his street and then up the ninety-seven steps to where Isaac Singer might have lived.

Inside, he could feel his skin beginning to react, could see the third wave coming, and coming, and coming again, and his hands trembled while he rolled a joint. It was wonderful stuff—Baylor hadn't lied—the police confiscated nothing but the best. He took most of the joint in deep quick inhales, punctuated only by his swilling of the whiskey. He undressed, carried the bottle to bed, kept at the booze, stopping only when he thought he might get sick, and finally, well after midnight, the mist was weaker and he slept.

Then the phone. After he wasn't sure how many rings, he rolled over in bed, grabbed the receiver, anything to stop the sound. "Yuh?"

"Is this Charles Fuller?" Even in his stupor Chub knew it was no voice he had ever heard before. Young, maybe twenty or so, female.

"Yuh."

"The writer?"

Dazed, Chub held the receiver, trying to figure how best to answer that.

"Is this the Charles Fuller that wrote *Under the Weather?*"

"I did," Chub said.

"Aw, shit," the girl said then, and then burst into tears.

Chub sat up by his bed, blinking, listening to the sobs, and he wondered if this was the day for crying, all over the world. He had seen a kissing day once, three, four years ago, five, and he'd been taking a cab down through Central Park, delivering a rush research job, and it was a warm summer day, and while he rode he went over his work, making sure it was in order, and once, maybe around Ninetieth, he glanced out and there in the grass a young couple was intertwined, their mouths touching, and he'd watched them till they were gone, then returned to his work, and perhaps twenty blocks later when he looked out at the park, there was another couple, different, but locked, and Chub watched them too. The third time he looked out, it was incredible but it was true, the closest thing maybe to a surrealistic experience he'd ever had, but there was a third couple doing what the other two had done and Chub wondered as he watched if the whole world was embracing on this day, if he alone had been left out. That had been a day for kissing, perhaps today was the day for tears.

". . . sorry . . ."

"Don't worry about it."

"I musta woke you."

"Don't worry about that either."

"I dunno how to explain. I just hadda talk. I called all the Charles Fullers in New York till I found you."

"Well, you have me, what's the matter?" Chub could sense her starting to lose control again. "Take your time."

"Well . . ." she began. "I got a boyfriend. An' I think he wants to get engaged and all."

"Wonderful."

"No—no, see—" And now came the burst. "He says his name is Charles Fuller—he says he wrote *Under the Weather*, he says he's you, an', an' I just found out today that he isn't *and I'm scared*."

Stunned, Chub listened as the tears had her again. He excused himself, made his way to the sink, ran the cold water, stuck his face under the spigot, letting the chill massage his eyes. When he got back to the phone he was surprised to find his hands shaking when he reached for the receiver. Maybe the Wild Turkey. Then again, maybe not. "Can you talk?"

"I . . . can try."

"Try and tell me."

"Couple weeks ago I was reading it in the park, the paperback, that's all I own, and this man came up and asked did I like the book and I told him the truth, that I'd read it over and over, and he smiled and said I'd made him very happy because he wrote it. I'm dumb but I'm not that dumb and I said you're bullshitting me and he asked me to ask him anything about the book, so I did, and he knew it all, no matter how tiny a thing I asked, and then he showed me his driver's license with his name and all, and he told me how he was brought up in Athens and went to Oberlin and we went for coffee and I'd never met anybody famous before, especially anybody I was crazy about before I ever met him and he was kind, real kind and shy like writers are all supposed to be and he asked me out and what could I say except yes and he was busy, he was writing, so he couldn't see me a lot but when we did—it was wonderful."

Chub held the receiver tightly pressed against his ear. It was crazy but he knew as he listened to this girl with the middle western accent that she was telling her truth. "How did you find out he was lying?"

"Late today, I was in Chicago and there was a bookstore open late, used stuff, and I just thought wouldn't it be wonderful if I could get a real copy, the hard kind, and he could say something wonderful in it to me, so I asked and they had it and I looked at it and then I turned it over and—and the picture on the back wasn't him. I just put the book down and ran."

Chub rubbed his eyes and said, "Jesus."

"*I didn't tell him.* I just sat here alone going crazy until I remembered the hard book said Charles Fuller lived in New York so awhile ago I got up the guts and started calling. I don't know what to do. You gotta tell me."

"I'm not in any position to do that. I'm hung over and I'm whipped and it's your life."

"*Please.*"

"I'm not a doctor."

"Please! I need you!"

Chub could sense her starting to go again, so he said quietly, "Look, anyone can be sure of this: You're involved with a compulsive liar, he's not playing with a full deck, it could get ugly, don't see him anymore."

"I got a date today with him."

"Break it."

"He'll want to know why."

"Don't tell him."

"He scares me sometimes, he'll make me."

Chub rubbed his eyes again. "Look, I'm almost as surprised as you are. All I can do is wish you the best and tell you to end it before something happens. And if you can't do that, get away."

There was a long pause. Then she said, "You don't wanna hear me sob anymore, I'm sorry, I'm sorry for bugging you, but ... it was good ... just talking was good ... thanks ... thanks."

After she hung up Chub lay back and stared around his pit. He was almost awake now so he got up and went to the big window in the other room and stared out at the night, and while he stared there was only one thought in his mind: Why in the world would anybody want to be me?

The wire from The Bone arrived the next day:

CHUB CHUB. I GOT IT BACKWARDS. THE CHEYNEY THING. I
DIDN'T CALL BECAUSE I KNEW THE LAST THING YOU NEEDED
WAS MY VOICE. BUT WHY WOULD I HURT YOU? I WOULDN'T. I
WOULDN'T. WHY WOULD I WHEN I CARE SO. PLEASE CALL.
PLEASE. I NEED FOR YOU TO.

They did not get down to cases until after dinner. The
Bone seemed incredibly nervous, and Chub wondered if
she was in the midst of a cluster series—they came that
way, nothing for months, then, inexplicably, days or
weeks of the hot poker forcing its way through your
eyeball into your brain.

Naw, she said, though this was one of the bad months
for her sometimes, May. It was that she'd never made
this particular main course before and she was worried
she'd louse things. The appetizer was a specialty of hers,
seviche, and the dessert another, *crème brûlée.* The main
course, it turned out, was crown rack of lamb, which
Chub remembered from his first night in New York, at
the Kitchels, with the white ruffles on them. The version
The Bone served, very nervous, was without the orna-
ments. As she cut it she said, "Betcha don't know what
this is called," and Chub said he had no idea. "I knew it,"
she said, "I never had it, either, too well done?"

Perfect, Chub said, as she handed him his plate, and it
was true. After the Chablis and after the Gloria, when
they were settled on the couch, drinking port, she was
quiet and Chub knew she was getting ready and she was.

"The bastard, see, he took me so by surprise when he
said that and I couldn't get organized until he went on
about some review he'd written about you that didn't do
a lot for his reputation and by then I was ready and I
said, 'What fucking reputation? Do you know what I
heard them saying about you when you got up to bore the
shit out of us?—here comes the old queen, it's sleepy time
down south.' " She looked at Chub. "I made that up,

none of the other Kafka nuts said it, but pretty good, huh?"

"Very inventive," Chub said.

"And then I really got heated up. 'Do you know what a failure is? Every time you look in the mirror, that's what a failure is,' and he started to turn away but I jumped smack in his way and said, 'What counts in this world, asshole, is being decent, being kind, and that's Chub Fuller, being *there, there* when there's pain to be dealt with,' and by now a crowd had gathered and some English whacko with a stutter was going, 'G-g-good show, b-b-better than the t-t-talk,' and Cheyney was cornered, see, the crowd was tightening up and I took off on him, how he was a phony and a fart and finally—you would have loved this—he *ran*. He couldn't think of anything else to do, just finally when I'd nailed him and nailed him he ducked his head and pushed his way past everybody and took the hell off like a coward. You'd have loved that, I wished you'd been there."

Chub made a nod.

"It's my goddamn backwards thing, I never should have started with what he said, I should have started with me, me humiliating the bastard, d'ya see? D'ya understand? You're not upset now, right?"

"I can never stay upset with you." He looked at her carefully. She was still nervous. "I'm not upset, it's history."

"Good, that's good, everything's good." They sat quietly then, with her "sss—sss" the only sound, except for the three cats clawing at the sofa. Chub sipped his port, watched her chain-smoke the English Ovals. Usually she took some pleasure in killing each cigarette in an ashtray or crushing it under her shoe if they were outside. Now she just lit the one off the other.

"I suspect everything isn't good," he said finally.

She waved him away.

"I thought I was always *there* when you needed me; I heard that bruited someplace."

The Bone jammed out a cigarette. "It's The Cherry Sisters," she said.

"Trouble with the writing?"

"No, shit no, the writing's great like always it's just"—she lit another English Oval—"I sent it out to some publishers—"

"—you never said you'd finished."

"I'm not, but I got a hundred fifty pages perfect and an outline for the rest and I wanted to do it on my own, I didn't want to use you and Kitchel, so I sent a dozen copies to a dozen houses—and every goddamn one sent it back. I figured with a hundred fifty great pages and a great outline I'd get an advance, use it to finish—I hate goddamn catalog work—and I didn't even get a *letter*—just standard rejection crap."

"I wish you'd told me—there's a reason for that—unsolicited stuff lands in the slush pile where all these genius Ivy Leaguers are trained to send things back. Probably most of them didn't even read it. Give me a copy, I'll get it to Kitchel."

"Will he read it himself, do you think?"

"I guarantee it."

"And will he be honest?"

"I promise."

She lit another English Oval, went "sss—sss." "Do you think people will think less of me, getting published through contacts?"

Chub had to smile. "Happens in the best of families."

They drank some more, and when it was late Chub stood, except she asked him if he wouldn't mind spending the night there. He was a little surprised—he hadn't done that in weeks—but he said he would, and they got ready for sleep, turned out the lights, shooed the cats off the bed.

Then The Bone asked if anything was new with him. It was the first time she'd enquired and while he held her he told her about the call from the girl in Chicago.

When he was done The Bone said, "Christ, there are

some weird people out there." Then she said, after a moment: "Why would anybody want to be you?—oh, shit, I'm sorry, I did that backwards again."

Chub held her. "No, no you didn't. You're dead on the money." They embraced a little longer, and then slept.

The next day was Sunday, the twenty-second, and it started badly, then got worse. Chub and The Bone decided to head for a late *dim sum* breakfast in Chinatown before they split, except the lines were too long to wait outside because a light rain had already begun. It was the tenth Sunday in a row (with maybe one exception) when it had pissed down all day, so The Bone went back to Prince Street while Chub, a copy of her Cherry Sisters material underneath his Windbreaker, headed for the subway.

Home, he made himself a tuna club, munched it while he glanced through The Bone's stuff, quickly read the outline to see if it all made sense. It did, and it was all beautifully typed and Chub lay down in bed for a while, listening to the rain.

Finally he called Two-Brew. "Huge favor?"

"For you? Under no conditions."

"The Bone's into a book and I need a quick read."

"How long is it?"

Chub told him.

"Heaven," Two-Brew said. "I'll read it today."

"It doesn't have to be that quick."

"I *want* to read today; if I don't, I'll have to talk to the fair Lydia."

"I'm sorry."

"I'm the one that's sorry, chubbycheeks. Get it over to me. We can talk about it tomorrow—stop by for lunch, we'll have yogurt in the office, I'll spring."

"Deal."

"Fiction?"

"No."

"Good?"

"Don't try and sucker me—if I say it's good you'll only say I'm an ignorant asshole."

"True. But then you are."

"I'll tell you this much, just to tease you along: It's great material."

"That sound you hear," Two-Brew said, "is me panting."

They hung up. The rain was harder now, so Chub carefully wrapped The Bone's work in layers of newspaper, then that into several plastic bags. It took him an hour to make the delivery and by the time he was home he was soaked, which irritated him but not as much as the fact that within five minutes, the rain had stopped. At least for a while. Probably until he had to go outside again.

And the night was going to be a bitch. A lady acquaintance of Elliott Carter's who lived in Syracuse was a new client. Usually she wrote household hint books but a month ago her husband had left her for their laundress and now she was filled with questions about how an innocent housewife might successfully do away with her husband. Ordinarily, this would have been fine—an interview with Baylor, answering all her questions, then just mail off the tape. Only the lady didn't want the tape, she didn't want to do the transcribing, Chub had to do that. It would mean hours of typing, and the money was fine, but lately Chub had come to loathe transcription work. It was just so goddamn dull.

The only thing he was looking forward to was seeing Baylor, who was due at seven, sitting around, BS-ing, talking about how law school was coming and was Maya going to get wise and come live with Chub. They would sit around and manhandle a six-pack and the time always went so pleasantly.

At six-fifteen two things happened: The rain resumed, *hard,* just as Chub checked the icebox and found he was totally out of beer. "I just goddamn *knew* it," he told himself, grabbing his raincoat, running down the ninety-seven steps and then off to Broadway, where the nearest deli was several blocks down. He made it back in time to dry off again and put the beer in the icebox before Baylor appeared.

The black policeman that walked into his apartment was a different human being than Chub had known over their years together. He was half an hour late—Baylor was compulsively prompt—and without apology or explanation. And he didn't want beer, he wanted a drink. Chub poured some Wild Turkey into the glass and before he was halfway back to Baylor seated by the large window Baylor said, "A drink, for Chrissakes, fill the goddamn thing." (Chub didn't know till later, when Rory was drunk, that Maya had not been rehired by the fancy school in Riverdale, and the job market sucked and she had no secretarial skills, so what it all meant was less money, a lot less money. Which meant he couldn't attend law school in the near future. Which meant at least three more years of police work. Which he had come to hate.)

Chub made sure his tape was working, got out his client's list, started asking. In real life, how hard was it to fool the police, because you never could on television. Rory emptied half his glass, glaring at Chub before he spoke. Cops were like lawyers. Lawyers didn't care about truth or justice, they cared about closing cases so they could get their fee. Same with cops, except there was no fee. If they were experienced cops, they could give less of a shit about truth or justice, they just wanted the damn case *closed, closed fast,* because they had fifty other cases that needed immediate tending, that was their life. "You don't need me for this kind of crap," Baylor said then. "I've told you this a hundred times before."

"She's entitled to her money's worth, just like you are when we're done, I'm sorry, I'll go fast. Is there a best time?"

"To commit a crime, no; to get away with it?" He nodded and gestured outside.

"The rain?"

"When the weather starts to warm—like now—people

go crazy when there's heat." He swigged the rest of his liquor, Chub got up, refilled his glass, this time all the way.

"The values of an education," Baylor said. "Pick things up fast," and Chub thought he might smile till he asked about how an ordinary person might go about getting a gun and Baylor said, you mean a hunting rifle, something fine, and Chub said no, just a gun, a Saturday Night Special or—

Baylor stood up suddenly and pointed to the door. "You find that out yourself—take your raincoat and head for the corner—right now—there was half a dozen transvestites under the awning when I came, they're always there, you know them, you probably bought shit from them, they've seen you, so you just go out and say something like a friend of yours is in the market for a Special and money don't matter and see what the answer is."

"You serious?"

He was. *"You just move your ass."*

Chub went and came back inside fifteen minutes, stared at Baylor. "Jesus Christ," he said. "Two guys had them. *With* them. I could have made a buy. Sixty bucks."

Baylor held out his empty glass. "You're a dumb bastard—you could have had one for twenty." He stood, stared blackly out at the rain. "See how easy it is keeping 'law and order'? Closing cases, man, that's the name of this game—'cause there're always millions more than you can handle."

Rory was drunk by eight and they were done by then; Chub paid him for his time, Chub thanked him, and then Baylor sat by the big window and started to talk about what had happened, Maya, the job, the rest. Chub was surprised, sorry, the rest, said so. Baylor nodded. Chub told him he'd feel better soon. Rory shook his head, promised only that things were going to get worse before they got better. . . .

It was after nine before he could force himself to begin to sit at his desk and start transcribing. It would be at least one before he was finished, assuming he didn't make too many stupid mistakes. At ten he broke, called The Bone, told her of his talk with Kitchel, wished her happy dreams. The rain was pounding now, but at least he was inside, inside with nothing better to do, so he didn't break again till eleven-thirty, checked the remainder of the tape, saw that he had a good shot at closing up shop in an hour, which gave him the will to go on. He allowed himself a beer at midnight, another while he put the finished job in order, was into a third when he heard his name called outside the door.

"Who is it?"

"Sandy. Sandy Smith."

Chub rubbed his eyes—where the hell had he met a girl named Sandy Smith if he'd ever met a girl named Sandy Smith? The voice didn't sound menacing, just tired, so he was halfway across the room before he realized he had no way of knowing if she was alone, so he stopped by the sink, grabbed a sharp small knife, opened the door a little, looked out.

The creature standing outside was small, five two maybe, and soaked—water dripped from all parts of her, forming a growing puddle on the corridor outside. She wore a large-brimmed, bedraggled rain hat tight at the throat, an old red slicker. Her jeans were sticking to her legs and her loafers were tearing along the seams where they had been beaten by the rain. Chub couldn't see her clearly, the hat hid her face, preventing that, but he was sure she was not some secret from his past.

She stared up at him for a long time. Then she said, very quietly, "Yeah, you're you," and Chub realized that she was from his past, he had spoken to her two nights before, only then she had phoned from Chicago.

"The downstairs door was kind of open so I just came on up," she said.

"Doormen must have been changing shifts," Chub answered, not knowing what the hell else to say.

"You've got real doormen?"

"Bad joke."

"I didn't mean to scare you." The door was open wide enough now for her to see the knife.

"No, nothing like that," Chub laughed. "I was about to make a midnight snack when you knocked."

The puddle around her would not stop growing.

"Could we talk?"

"Scrooge couldn't leave you standing out there like that," Chub said, opening the door. "What in the name of God are you doing here?"

"That's kind of what I want to talk about."

"Sure, sure, c'mon in, take off your stuff if you want, get dry."

He closed the door and she untied her large rain hat, pulled it off, shook her head, and when Chub saw her he was seeing, he knew, a perfect cheerleader's face, round, pouty, Ann-Margret, Sandra Dee, the kind of creature who was always the most sought after in high school, the one you fantasized over before sleep.

Then she took off her slicker. She wore a T-shirt, white, and tucked into her jeans, no bra, her breasts were big but she was young, could still survive very happily without the assistance, and Chub, staring now, was back twenty years, waiting at the airport with his father when the girl appeared to them, rising up the escalator, and he saw, for the first time, the sure knowledge that his father could kill.

She had no luggage, just a small imitation-leather purse held tightly in her hands. Chub took her hat and slicker, tossed them over the shower rod in the bathroom. When he returned she was sitting on the sill of the large central window, her jeans and loafers already forming a new puddle. "Go ahead with your midnight snack. I'm not hungry."

Chub, the small sharp knife still in his hands, said, "Sure? I was just going to make a tuna club."

"How ever do you open tuna cans with a knife?" She sounded very impressed.

Chub put the weapon down in the sink. "The knife was for the tomato. But I don't have to eat, I'm not hungry either."

"I fibbed," she said. "I am. And I'd love some milk too."

"Two tuna clubs coming up." He got out the can opener, the tomatoes and bread, the other essentials, started to work. When he looked back at her, the puddle was bigger. "Look—I've got a robe in the bathroom—there's a radiator in there too. You might get dry a lot faster if you changed. And that's not a line."

"I've heard enough of them to know."

Chub watched her as she crossed the room, disappeared. She had the kind of face that probably wouldn't last and who knew what would happen to her figure—Lydia Kitchel had been voluptuous once, too—but as she moved, Chub never doubted for a moment that on a summer day, dressed as she was dressed now, traffic undoubtedly stopped more often than not. He could hear her singing softly in the bathroom, a pretty song, he couldn't get the words—something about a wheel.

She modeled the robe for him as she came out barefooted, pivoting. "You know that movie? Where the girl has the cripple leg and a gentleman caller comes? It looks like you've got a lady caller now."

Chub nodded. "Tennessee Williams, he just died."

"Oh, no, he couldn't have," she said, suddenly upset. "I just love the way he sang '16 Tons.' "

Chub decided there was no point to furthering that particular subject. "Must be I'm wrong. And it is a great movie."

She went back to the windowsill, waited till he was done. He put the sandwiches on plates, carried them over along with a beer and some half-and-half, the closest he ever came to having milk. She wolfed her sandwich before he was halfway done with his. When he offered her his other half, she said no, she was full. Then she said, "I fibbed again, are you sure?"

Chub, who had had no intention of eating at all, raised his right hand.

She wolfed that, too, finished the half-and-half, then started explaining how depressed she was back in Portland, all the others getting ready for college while she was barely scraping through for her high school diploma and feeling blue, in the dumps, down, she wandered into a department store to look at the perfumes and then the lingerie and next to that was the book section and there, right there, was this paperback with a title that said her mood so well, *Under the Weather,* so she bought it, never really sure if she would read it or not, but that night she was alone, it was the late night at the store her mother worked at as bookkeeper, so she opened it—

—and it was *her* story.

Sure, it was about a boy but to heck with that, except for that, it was the same. Her father—an Army man who never rose above the rank of captain—was forced to get out by her mother, who was the real boss. And he was a drinker. And he died of it. And she had a real older brother—three years older—who was killed crossing the street—which her parents, for reasons of their own, blamed her for.

And on.

"I finished the whole book in three days and when you married that girl at the end, I just cried so, I wanted you to marry me. Was she real? What happened to her?"

"I married her," Chub said.

"She wasn't near good enough for you. I'll bet you divorced her."

"She divorced me."

"Some people don't know what they have when they have it."

Chub shrugged, said nothing.

"As soon as I got done crying, I started the book all over again, from the very beginning. I only did that once before—there's only one writer as great as you."

Chub looked at the creature who sat before him now,

wearing his robe, her stomach full of tuna clubs, her mind full of God only knew. He asked, as Hemingway would, who he was in the ring with, Cervantes or Tolstoi?

She looked blank. "Carolyn Keene."

"I must have missed her."

"You never read the Nancy Drew books? Oh, you must, they got me through school practically." She paused. " 'Course I was younger, maybe you're too old for her now, what do I know, I'm not what you call a great reader."

Chub said nothing, didn't smile, just waited.

After Sandy split with her mother she tried Seattle. She was used to moving around, she'd been an Army brat, but Seattle was rainy all the time. Next came Chicago where she changed the spelling of her name: "Growing up I was Sand*i,* with the 'i,' but that was too small town for a place like Chicago." She had a bunch of dumb jobs, none of them lasting, and she was sitting in the park less than a month ago, reading *Under the Weather* for the umpty-umpth time—it always made her feel better, even with the sad ending—when she met Charley.

"Charley?"

Once they started dating he liked for her to call him that: "Charley." Charles was for when you didn't know somebody well. She couldn't believe someone like him would be interested in someone like her. But he was so nice. He drove her out to Athens, showed her where he'd gone to school, where he'd lived. "You remember that story *The Arbor Day Tree?*—the one about the tree you planted and how your father tried to cut it down when it got taller than he was? Charley stopped the car and pointed it out, the tree, and then he walked me to it and lifted me up and set me in the branches. I wanted a picture so bad, only we didn't have a camera along."

Chub just stared at her, trying to think. "You don't remember the street, do you?"

" 'Course I do—it had a tree name—Linden—it was the second house in from the corner."

"That was the house," Chub managed. "How the hell did he know?"

She shook her head.

"He talked about Oberlin?"

"Oh, yes, and how he got his early stories into magazines, and coming to New York to work on *The Dead Pile*—"

"Jesus," Chub said.

"—and how he left New York two years back, he needed to be nearer his roots, so he came to Chicago."

"Where in Chicago?"

"The Near North, I think."

"What do you mean you 'think'?"

"He lived and he worked alone and he didn't want anybody pestering him, that's why he didn't have a phone."

"Hold it—and you believed all this?"

"Yes. Yes! *Every word.*" It was the first time she'd raised her voice, the first time she showed the upset underneath.

Chub waited, staring out at the rain.

"A lot of people don't have phones—I almost never had one since I left Portland. The only reason I could call you from inside the other night was because Becky—"

"—Becky?"

"I was out of a job and my girl friend had a girl friend named Becky who was going on vacation and said it was okay to live in her place till she got back."

"What happened after you called the other night?"

"Just what I knew would. Charley called me later and said he was coming over and I said not to and he said why and I said no reason and he said fine, then in ten minutes he was at the door and . . ." She drifted.

"And you told him you knew?"

"He made me."

"And?"

And now the drifting returned to her speech. But it got, well, bad. And he got, he got physical. Because she was . . . she lied, she wasn't all there, and if she didn't watch it, she was going to be in big trouble, lying about people, there were lawyers who took care of people who lied about people, crazy people who lied.

"Did you say we'd talked?"

"No. Just that I saw the book picture. But what was so hard . . . see . . . he's so smart and I never been that way and I got so frightened 'cause . . . when he was done, I didn't mind that he hurt me, but he was so sure I was lying that by the time he left I thought maybe he was right, maybe I was crazy and he was Charley Fuller all the time." She looked at Chub. "So I did what you told me."

"What did I tell you?"

"To get away, to come see you—"

"—I just said to get away, period."

She was silent for a long time. "I know. I fibbed. It's just, well, I been through a shitload lately and I had to see your face was all."

"You've sure been through a shitload," Chub said.

"He left after midnight—it was raining in Chicago, too—then I thought he was going to come back maybe, come back with *proof* it was me who was wrong, crazy, and I just took off out the door. I been on the road since last night." She stood then, moved to Chub, put her small hands on his cheeks. "You look like yourself, y'know?"

Chub looked up at the young face, exhausted from travel, drained from days of panic. "One of my major achievements."

She dropped her hands. "I'll get dressed now."

"Where will you go?"

She gestured toward the rain.

"You know New York?"

"A city's a city."

"You've got money?"

She nodded.

"Let me see your purse."

She hesitated.

"Give it to me."

Chub opened it. It was not exactly crammed with

American Express Gold Cards. There was one piece of plastic, which identified Ruth Rogelski as an employee at Marshall Field. "Is this Ruth the friend of Becky's?"

She shook her head. "It's a phony ID I bought in the Loop one night. I get carded a lot at bars and discos, on account of people sometimes think I don't look twenty-one. That card's just a hassle-saver is all."

The purse also contained a five-dollar bill, three crumpled singles, close to a dollar in change, and a dog-eared paperback of *Under the Weather,* with many of the pages loose.

"I had more dough when I left, but when I couldn't thumb, I took some buses."

Chub stood, gave her back the purse. "You'll spend the night here; anything else is not only stupid but dangerous."

"I caused enough trouble."

"Sandy," Chub said, "with your face and your figure, you are going to cause a lot more havoc before you pack it in, and that's not a line either." He moved to get her some pajamas. "You take the bed, I'll sleep there," and he pointed to a large upholstered chair near the windows. Before she could object he said, "Just shut up, all right, it's no big deal, I fall asleep in the chair all the time when I take breaks." Not exactly true. He hated the chair. Like all the other Salvation Army shit that was growing old along with him.

He led her into the bedroom when she stopped dead in the doorway, suddenly a look of wonder on her face, as she stared at the television set. "It's just gigantic." She hopped on the bed, began fiddling with the controls. "How does it go on, though?"

Chub took the clicker from his bedside table, pushed a button. In a moment they were watching the end of a commercial for the Mormon Church, which was quickly followed by another commercial, this one for what looked like ski clothes, all kinds of coats thick with down, except it turned out to be a plug for bulletproof clothing.

He felt suddenly irritated with something, tossed her

the clicker and got ready for bed. Or, more accurately, got ready for chair.

She was sitting on the bed, playing with the clicker while Chub got a pillow and blanket from a closet. "It's my first clicker," she said. Then she flicked it off, lay back in bed. Chub turned out the light, went to the other room, flicked out that light, too, groped to the chair without incident. As he settled himself, he could hear her singing again, the "wheel" song.

"What is that?" he called.

"I'm writing it," she said.

"I didn't know you did that."

"I shoulda said I've been writing it for three years—I started in Vegas and this is as far as I've got. I do it every night before I go to sleep."

"Do it for me."

From the next dark room, there was silence, then an intake of breath, then a small tired voice began to sing.

> *Oh, the wheel is always in spin.*
> *No matter how bad it's been where I been.*
> *No matter how sad the troubles I'm in.*
> *Thank God that the wheel,*
>   *it's always in spin.*

"Thank you," Chub said. "It's very pretty and very sad." Just like you, he didn't add. " 'Night."

"Same."

In a moment he could hear her breathing start to even out. He shifted positions in the chair. His neck was tilted. He shifted again. Now he could feel his back start to stiffen. He tried several more shifts, then quietly stood, put the pillow and the blanket on the floor, lay down.

A moment later, the bedroom light was on and she stood in the doorway. "Comfy?"

"Fine."

"Do you fall asleep on the floor a lot too when you take breaks?"

Chub fluffed the pillow.

"It's a big bed."

Chub lay there a moment longer before deciding he was acting as stupidly as he had of late, so he got up, and the two of them lay on opposite sides of the bed from each other. Chub reached out for the bed light and they were in darkness.

"Why did you stop?" she asked after a moment.

"Stop?"

"You know, writing."

"I didn't—I just started researching instead."

"I would never have stopped—not if I was brilliant like you."

"Oh, knock it off."

She did. For at least a minute. Then she said, "Do you want to go to bed with me?"

"I'm *in* bed with you."

"I meant the other."

"I figured."

"It's the one thing in the world I'm good at."

"I believe you."

"Well?"

The answer was a resounding yes. He was already half erect. For the first time since B.J. Peacock danced for him in her apartment bedroom, the half-slip covering her body, he wanted a woman. But something about it made him feel like a charity case, so he said, "I'm involved."

"She'll never know."

"*I'll* know."

She just looked at him.

"Suppose I don't want to disappoint you," Chub said.

"You couldn't, I wouldn't let you, I'm good enough for both of us."

"Maybe in the morning, all right?"

"Not during the game shows."

Chub let that echo for a moment. She *meant* that. He lay still, cursing his sense of whatever it was: "Goodness" with all of its negative ramifications. His penis grew small again. Probably it would serve him right if it froze permanently like that.

Now she was breathing evenly, sleep overtaking her. In a whisper she asked, "Was I wrong? Coming here?"

"No."

"Oh, good . . . I just hate it so being wrong . . . when I make a . . . a fooh-pah, it just upsets me so. . . ."

Chub smiled in the darkness. Later, asleep, she rolled into his arms. He stayed awake as long as he could, wondering just what it was he was holding.

Monday morning the rain had stopped, but the clouds were dark, the air heavy with moist promise. Chub overslept, forced himself to the kitchen, started brewing coffee, making eggs. Sandy sat up in bed, the clicker in her hands, watching the tube. He took the food, carried it to his tiny kitchen table. Then he called her to eat.

She stayed glued to the set.

Chub went to the doorway. "Breakfast."

"But it's the *$25,000 Pyramid.* It'll be over in ten minutes."

"Your food will be cold."

She continued watching the program. "I hate breakfast anyway."

Chub ate alone, left her plate covered in case she changed her mind, showered, shaved, dressed. Then he went back to the bedroom. Her position was unchanged. "I'm going."

She nodded.

"We have to talk, Sandy."

"This is *Sale of the Century.*"

"Turn it off," Chub said.

She looked at him. "I can hear fine."

"Well, I can't," Chub said. "Now, come on out here."

Reluctantly, she followed.

Chub sat her down in the overstuffed chair. "We both have to be going," he said.

"Going? I don't want to go anywhere."

"Well, you have to."

"But why?—nobody knows I'm here—nobody saw me come—I'll just stay here all quiet—I won't answer the phone, I promise. I can be your secret."

"Sandy, last night you were anxious to go."

"But that's only because I knew you wouldn't let me. If you'd said okay, you'd have had some fight on your hands."

"Well, I don't want one on my hands now. I've got my life to lead and you have yours. You can't stay here. I told you I'm involved." He took out his wallet. "Here's eighty bucks—I'm sorry it isn't more but it's all I've got and it's enough to get you started somewhere or on something or whatever you want. Now, please tell me you see I'm right."

She gnawed on her lip awhile, then nodded. "This minute?"

"No—no hurry. Take your time."

"When will you be back?"

"I'm having dinner with the woman I'm involved with."

"What's her name?"

"Bonita Kraus."

"It's an ugly name, the lucky bitch."

Chub glanced outside. The clouds were darker. He went to the closet, took out his umbrella.

"Charley?"

Chub turned. "Chub."

"Chub? Is that what people call you?"

"People I like."

"Will you do me a favor, Chub?"

He nodded.

She got up, scrambled for her purse, came back with her tattered copy of *Under the Weather*. "Sign it?"

Chub almost changed his mind then, almost asked her to stay, be his secret. Quickly he turned to the title page, grabbed a pen. "Which spelling, the 'y' or the 'i'?"

" 'y.' This is a big city."

Chub wrote her name, then added, "who will have much joy. I wish her all of mine." He signed it, handed it back.

"I'll look at it when you're gone."

Chub stood.

"I owe you. And I won't be here when you get back from dinner—I hope she burns it."

Chub smiled, they hugged, he headed for the door. "Sandy? Were you ever a cheerleader?"

"In Hawaii once when I was a freshman."

"I'll bet you were good."

"You want the truth? I was clumsy as hell, but the boys didn't seem to mind."

Chub left her then, closing the door behind him. For a moment he stood motionless, clutching his umbrella. He had done the right thing, the only thing really. So why did he feel so sour?

Nothing much in the immediate future improved matters. Along with his umbrella he had grabbed his typed copy of the Baylor interview for the new lady client in Syracuse who was fictionalizing a little revenge on her hubby. He Express Mailed it up to her so she'd have it the next day, Tuesday, but that meant waiting forever in the post office line.

In the beginning those waits used to infuriate him, but now he was always fortified with the morning *Times,* which he could sometimes get halfway through before reaching the postal clerk. Two articles this day caught his particular attention, the first headlined "Era Ends in Book Row for Hunters of Bargains." It detailed the imminent closing of Dauber & Pine, the great old bargain store in the Village. Fifty plus years and now over. Chub had spent hundreds of hours in the glorious disarray of the place; he had bought a lot of books for a lot of clients at Dauber & Pine. If you had to do research, you knew when you entered you were among friends.

It'll all be computers someday, Chub thought, along with the wish that whoever first invented those goddamn machines be permanently denied entrance into Heaven. The fuckers.

The second article was datelined Poughkeepsie, NY, and its headline read "Miss Streep Urges Graduates to Try for Excellence." Meryl Streep had given the commencement address at her alma mater, Vassar, before one of the largest such gatherings in the college's history, and she was given a standing ovation. She—

—Chub folded the paper, dealt with the postal clerk, paid her, headed for the subway that would take him to the main library—

He pitched the *Times* into an overflowing garbage basket. He wasn't half done but he didn't want the thing. Which gave him time to stare at all the other undergrounders as the train bumped along. And to think. What did he have against Meryl Streep, for Chrissakes, she could *act*. Nothing much really, except maybe the little phrase that gave the year she entered Vassar, which was the same year he'd started Oberlin.

None of the books he requested was available at the library. Not goddamn one. That had happened before, on various occasions, but before he'd done nothing, just waited quietly until he could get what he needed, or shifted to some other work that needed doing. This time he chose to argue with the librarian, a guy who had been helpful in the past. Chub told him either that (a) the guy was having a personal vendetta, withholding information, or (b) the whole place was going straight over the cliff.

He stormed out of the card room, wasted an hour scowling at passersby until it was time for lunch with Kitchel. He went outside—

—and it was *sunny*. Here he was, on what had turned into a beautiful spring day, carrying a stupid umbrella. He hated it when that happened. You felt like such a jerk when that happened. A Milquetoast, carrying your rain gear while everyone else walked along, the men in their suits and ties, the women in blouses and skirts, their bodies coming out from beneath the long winter's nap. It was hot as he walked along, and he was sweating. Better and better.

At least Kitchel's office was air-conditioned. He sat at his desk with four yogurts in a line, four plastic spoons, The Bone's manuscript off to one side. Two-Brew put a finger above each container. "Coffee, strawberry, vanilla or plain—since you're my guest, I give you freedom of choice, if that's not too great a task for what's left of your brain."

"Not hungry; you can have a pig-out."

"Period come early?"

Chub said nothing.

Kitchel lifted a container, opened it. "I was afraid you were going to select the coffee. I have a passion for it." He took a dainty nibble from his plastic spoon. "Ambrosia."

Chub gave him the finger.

"That's some improvement," Two-Brew said, digging more deeply into the container now. "You were right," he said then. "It is great material. I assume it's true."

"All verifiable."

Kitchel put the container down then and looked across his desk. "Chub, it's unpublishable. It's just amateurish. It's crazy."

Chub nodded. "I looked at it yesterday."

"I mean maybe deVries or Buchwald—or Russell Baker best of all—they might be able to come up with something. It's funny stuff but Jesus, she treats it like the Gideon Bible."

"I know. She *believes* in it that way."

"I'm sorry, Chubbo—truly—I wanted to like it. God's truth. Has she tried anyplace else, I could be wrong—if I remember correctly I was wrong once in the winter of '79."

"She's been shot down a dozen times so far." He got up, looked out Kitchel's window at the sunlit city. "Just shit, that's all. She *knew* you were going to take it. She was worried people might think you did it out of friendship for me."

"I could fake a couple of decent reader's reports and send them along with the manuscript. You know, 'Sorry, not for us but good luck.' I could put a note in along with it telling her please to show me the completed manuscript but not to get her hopes up because we've taken a bath on show-business biographies lately." He opened the vanilla yogurt. "Which is true. You want twenty-five thousand copies of the life of Deanna Durbin? I happen to have a warehouse full of them."

"Would you mind calling her?" Chub said. "Say no if you do, but I think it'd give her a boost, hearing from you. Don't get her hopes up—tell her you probably won't publish it because there's no market, but you'd love to see the next book she writes. I'm seeing her later—it would' make the evening pass more happily."

"You got it," Two-Brew said.

"You're a good man," Chub said. Then he said, "No, actually you're a fart, but you occasionally do good things." He picked up his lousy umbrella, started for the door.

Two-Brew was watching him closely. "Everything okay with you?"

Chub turned. "Everything okay with Lydia?"

"Touché." Kitchel waved and as Chub exited he called out, "Listen, I've got a raincoat in the closet if you want to borrow it—looks like a monsoon's coming outside."

"Touché," Chub said, laughing for the first time that day. Then he was out the door and headed back to face the librarian he'd been arguing with. This time the books he needed had been returned and were available and he worked the next hours.

On the subject of magic suits. One of his clients wanted to know all about those tuxedos magicians wear, the garment they pin their crucial paraphernalia inside. How did you make such a garment? With what material? Was there a special kind of stitching needed?

Chub buried his head in his hands, wondering who could care about such a thing, were there actually creatures extant who gave a shit about magic suits and hiding doves? And while he was in that position, his eyes shut tight, he remembered the two commercials that had made him irritated with something, the bulletproof clothing following the Mormon Church.

And it wasn't some*thing* that irritated him, it was some*one* and that person was himself. Because those two commercials, one coming hard upon the other, they were *material.* Material for God only knew what, but once upon a time he would have rushed to his Journal and made a note of it, because you never knew when material would come in handy. It would have made an instant conscious connection once. Now there was nothing conscious, just a feeling or irritation, and it took half a day and more before he was able to come up with the connection now.

He tried to concentrate on the magic suits again, but he couldn't. He brought the book back, Xeroxed nothing, started out, returned, muttered something to the librarian that he hoped would be taken as apology because that's what he meant, and left.

Outside, the sunshine taunted him. He was early for The Bone's and he stood on the library steps between the lions, wondering what the hell to do for an hour. He went to a garbage basket, raised his umbrella, was about to pitch the goddamn thing, decided the way his day was going, if he did pitch it, a monsoon *would* come up, so he kept it, told himself it wasn't really an umbrella but a walking stick, and began the long trek down toward SoHo.

He was tired when he got there but she had energy for both. "Kitchel called," she said.

"Has he read it? Jesus, I just gave it to him yesterday."

She held up a piece of paper. "I took notes. There's good news and there's bad news, which way shall we swing, baby?"

"I've spent the afternoon hot on the trail of magic suits, hit me with the good."

"Well. First of all, it's great material, as far as he knows, you should pardon the expression, virgin. He asked was it true, for Chrissakes, did people actually throw things."

"I hope you told him you've had the assistance of an impeccable researcher on occasion."

"Shut up, listen to what else: He wants to see whatever I write next. And I don't need 'some asshole'—that's a direct quote—delivering it, I can bring it straight to him the second I'm done." Now she started to read: "Answer me this: What do Ava Gardner, Ralph Richardson, Mike Todd, John Wayne, Lana Turner and Lana Turner have in common?"

"All performers? Not Mike Todd but the rest."

"They're all in show business and they've all had books written about them lately—*two* about Lana—and they've all stiffed. Show business bios are out, he said; he got killed on a Deanna Durbin himself and he doesn't see that he can publish subject matter like this."

"Maybe it'll change by the time you're done," Chub said. "And even if it doesn't, the fact that your subject matter isn't commercial isn't such bad news."

"That's not the bad news," The Bone said then—"*The bad news is he was bullshitting me.* The whole fucking phone call was bullshit—he's never called me before in his life, why would he call me now?"

"Because he knows about us."

"*Wrong!*—I know you, buster, and I know he never would have thought of calling if you hadn't put him up to it. Now, what did he really think?"

"What are you asking like this for—are you getting a cluster?—well, I'm sorry if you are, God knows, but don't take it out on me."

"Liar."

"Bonita—"

"—I know what you thought—that I couldn't take it—well, I can take anything except liars, *now you answer me.*"

"I haven't talked to him today."

"He told me you were there for lunch, goddamnit!"

Chub sat on the couch, thinking of the vision that rose

up in front of his eyes on an escalator except this vision
had been in his bed last night, for one magical night, and
what had he said? "I'm involved." And now the vision
was gone, eighty dollars away, and Chub rubbed his eyes,
wishing he could dear God just once have last night over
again.

"Oh, so weary," The Bone said. "Such a sweet fellow,
so put upon by the mean old world."

"I don't want to hurt anybody, maybe most of all you,
please."

"Five months we've been seeing each other, and I
thought helping each other, but now it turns out you
don't think I'm any better than when you shot me down
in the coffee shop. Now, you tell me what he said—every
goddamn word he said—I'm not quitting on this, you
know I'm not a quitter when I've got my mind made up
and it's made up, *so tell me.*"

Chub took a deep breath. " 'Amateurish and unpublishable,' I'm not sure of the order. You want the rest?"

"*Everything.*"

"It's funny subject matter, but you treat it like gospel,
and that's crazy." He looked at her. "Now you happy?"

"Happi*er.*" She ground out an English Oval, lit another. ("Sss—sss—sss") " 'Cause he's *wrong. The Naked
and the Dead* got shot down by twenty-five asshole publishers like him. *War and Peace* was rejected by some
asshole publisher like him. Now, why did you go through
this whole goddamn charade?"

"To spare you."

"Bull*shit.*" She was advancing on him now, holding
the page of notes in her hand. "It's because you didn't
have faith in me. 'Cause you thought I'd go all to pieces
like some fucking Barbie doll. Well, I can take anything
this world wants to dish out—except I was wrong before
when I said it was only liars I can't take. I can't take *you*
either, in fact I'm sick of you just now. . . ."

"I believe you."

"Dinner will not be served tonight—now, why don't
you just get the hell out of here?"

Chub got out, quietly, headed for the subway. It was after seven before he reached the corner of Ninety-sixth and Broadway. He started into a Chinese restaurant, sat by himself at a table until a waiter brought him a menu. Then he stood and left because he didn't want to stare at all the faces. Or have all the faces staring at him. He went into a Chinese takeout, started to give an order, changed his mind; he was sick of fucking Chinese food. He started toward the deli for a sandwich, changed his mind. Finally he stood on the corner, clutching the umbrella as the light dimmed, turned in circles. Finally he crossed the street, ordered a small pizza to go, waited till they got it ready, took it to his building, made his slow way up the ninety-seven stairs. He opened his door, threw the umbrella down, was heading for the kitchen area with the pizza box in his hands when the words "Now *I* got a gentleman caller" came to him from the bedroom.

Sandy was seated on his bed, in his robe, the clicker in her hands. "I fibbed," she said, "about going. You mad?"

Chub shook his head.

She stood, put the clicker down. "You glad, even a little?"

"Oh, Jesus God, yes."

She came at him like an avalanche. She was naked beneath the robe and in a few moments, he was naked, too, and they were on the bed. Chub had not been a virgin, not for many years, and he never knew how he rated with the women he had slept with, all he did know was that he had tried, always tried, to give them pleasure if he could.

But this one now was different—she didn't want him to work at all; if there was to be pleasure, she only wanted to be the one to give it. They embraced at first, and his tongue went into her mouth with all the force he had but she pulled back and whispered, "You just take it easy," and then her hands caressed his cheeks and her tongue darted into his ear and Chub knew as her fingertips touched his nipples that this was no virgin arousing him now, this one understood more about bed than he

would know ever, and he began to relax more until she
suddenly bit his nipples and he could feel that all the way
down to his groin. Then her fingertips moved down his
body, down toward his penis, where they stopped and she
circled around that area, beginning to move slowly up
and down the insides of his thighs. He closed his eyes,
went with the sensation, feeling himself begin to harden,
and then her fingertips were there, helping him swell, and
a moment later her lips replaced her fingertips and her
tongue was moving along the underside of his shaft and
he knew he couldn't hold back, not a moment longer. But
somehow she knew it, too, because she lifted her head,
moved up alongside him, let him hold her, kiss her
mouth. She shifted up again until her breasts were by his
face and she moved so slowly, letting her extended nipples move around and around his mouth before allowing
him to have them.

He tongued them, they were so firm he moved his
mouth from one to the other, faster, until she pulled
slightly away and whispered, "Now there *is* no fire," and
when she gave them back to him he went more slowly.
While he kissed them she took one of his hands and
guided it down to her clitoris, got him into a gentle up-
and-down motion, and then, when he was doing it the
way she had guided him, she took her hand away and
began to masturbate him. When he was hard again she
sat, slowly, moved down, straddled his body, took his
penis, placed it slowly inside her as she sat above him,
letting him thrust up into her as deeply as he wanted. He
was breathing fast now, fast and now faster and then she
lifted her body away, letting him subside again, bringing
her breasts back for his mouth to suckle.

Chub was heaving now and he took his mouth away,
found hers, brought his arms around her and held her,
just held her, making sure she was there. She pulled away
slowly a little later, and kissed his nipples again while her
fingers got him hard for the third time, the last time,
because now her lips took him and went slowly all the

way down his cock, taking it all, then slowly moving up until her tongue could circle his tip, and then her tongue went down the underside and he was losing control and this time she let it happen, put her mouth around him again, moving quickly up and down his cock, and a moment later he was biting his own forearm to keep from shrieking out loud as he thrust up, a final movement, before he came and came and came in her perfect cheerleader's mouth.

"What are you, dead?" Sandy asked after five minutes, during which Chub had just held her naked body next to his.

He kept his eyes closed. "Try 'appreciative.'" Now he looked at her. "I thought you said you were good at bed."

She smiled, stretched. "I ought to be, I've had enough practice—it bother you when I say that?"

"Sandy, considering the rescue job you've just accomplished, I can think of nothing you might say that would bother me."

"I'll tell you the truth, this was one of my best efforts. I really enjoyed it."

"Well, I'm glad one of us did," Chub said.

She swatted him on the ass, and then they got up, put on pajamas, and attacked the pizza, which was not exactly bubbling hot, but no one seemed to mind.

Ten minutes later, she went to his desk, took out his Journal, and started flipping through.

"Where the hell did you get that?"

"When I was gonna leave I was looking around for something to write a good-bye note with and I found it in the drawer."

"Doubtful," Chub said, indicating the paper and pens on the top of his desk.

"Okay, I fibbed—I never meant to write a note—I don't write anything if I can help it on account of people always laugh at my spelling. The truth is, I was so pissed at you I was looking around for something important to steal so you'd know what a shit you were making me go. And I found it."

"Have you ever stolen anything?"

"Don't ask. The truth is, I'm snoopy." And now her voice was building. "And then when I came across the Journal, it was like the top of my head came off. You gotta explain some of this: Like what does this mean— 'story—death fight in florist shop.' "

Chub sat by the open window, looked outside. The night was cool now. For years the building had been promising to get the place ready for air conditioning but it had never happened. The apartment was at its most bearable when the nights were cool. Chub shook his head. "I don't remember."

"Well, you got to. You can't just forget something like that."

"Sure I can. I put that down years ago."

She turned the page. "Well, this one I've got to know about: 'story—the end of the rain.' "

"No clue."

"Well, I'm gonna make you remember—I'm gonna pester you until you do."

"Don't pester me, okay? It won't do any good."

"Well, shit."

Chub stood. "I'm going to lie down."

"Ho-ho-ho, and that's supposed to get rid of me? —fat chance." She followed him to the bed, dragging the Journal along. Chub lay down. She turned on the bed lamp. "This is the last one in the book—'material—when the leopard kills, a blessing.' "

Chub put his arm across his eyes. "It must be five years ago."

"What does it mean?"

"It was a newspaper article. Some scientists were doing a study, I don't know where, probably Africa, maybe Ceylon, and they took a census of the animals and the leopards were killing lots of the others. Eating them.

Everybody hates the leopard because of that. But then the scientists discovered that it was a good thing, because if the leopards didn't kill, all the other animals would die—overpopulation, there wouldn't be enough food. See, the prey needs the predator as much as the predator needs the prey."

She made a face at him. "*That* you had to remember. I think it's creepy." She was turning back toward the center of the Journal when the phone rang. Chub reached across her, answered.

"You were right," The Bone said. "I did have a cluster coming on. I never would have behaved like that otherwise."

"I'm sorry."

"Don't *you* be sorry, putz—that's my rule. You were just being a support and I was too out of my skull to accept it."

"It's history."

Sandy put the Journal down now, listened.

"Tell me what you think of this—maybe I got too close to The Cherry Sisters—maybe I ought to go back and finish my screenplay. You know, *Skeletons?*"

"Good idea."

"Are we on for dinner?"

Chub looked at Sandy a moment, then said, "I'm due up in Connecticut tomorrow night—there's an expert on tinnitus I'm supposed to tape."

"I'd really like to see you, Chub. Honest to God."

Chub closed his eyes a moment. She sounded so whipped. He opened his eyes when he felt Sandy biting his nipple. He moved out of range. "I've got to do some stuff in TriBeCa. I'll stop over when I'm done, you can buy me lunch."

"I'd like that. And I'm really really sorry."

"For no reason," Chub told her, and then they hung up.

"Was that the bitch?" Sandy wanted to know.

"Don't call her that."

"It didn't sound like such a red-hot love affair to me."

"I just said we were 'involved.' "

"Oh, I hope I never get 'involved,' then." She began flipping through the Journal again.

"Turn out the light," Chub said.

"Why?"

"Because I want to touch you."

"Sorry, buddy, you're involved. And knowing men, you'd probably want sex and that's out—you might have herpes."

Chub laughed. "Sandy, if I do, after what we've done already, I'm sure you've got it too."

"Oh, I got it already," she said. Then, "Fibbing, fibbing."

They undressed each other after she turned out the light. "I wonder sometimes if my folks ever screwed for pleasure. God, if my sainted mother back in Portland could be here now, I wonder what she'd say, what would your mother say?"

"I don't know."

"How can you not know, is she dead?"

"I don't know."

"Well, we don't go one step further till you make sense out of *that.*"

"It's crazy, but a long time ago my grandmother called from Florida and said, 'Well, we buried Gretchen yesterday,' and I remember thinking, 'She *died* and you didn't tell me?' Then I realized that was what my mother wanted—me out of her life. Then, after we hung up I got to thinking maybe she wasn't dead at all, maybe she just had me told that so she could go her own way without me bugging her, she could travel the world all she wanted, maybe looking for my brother. Sometimes I think he's not dead, either, but just out there, waiting for her to come to him."

"You must write that," Sandy said. "That's just so goddamn sad."

"Nothing is sad," he whispered as he ran his hands

across her perfect body. "How could anything be sad now?"

He awoke suddenly. Dark out. Four. And his head—there was noise in his head. Chub lay still. The noise began to clarify. Then the location of the noise began to clarify. He was in a florist's shop. In Athens. With Mike and Gretchen, only he called them "Mommy" and "Daddy" then. His aunt, the one who had worked in the library, the one who had been so patient with him, showing him where this was, where that was, Aunt Audrey wasn't with them. She was in the hospital. She had been there a long time. Mike and Gretchen were moving around the shop, looking at the flowers, then asking the owner, "How much?" "How much?" and he answered. It smelled nice in the shop. Chub wandered alone, looking at the colors. Then their voices, Mike's and Gretchen's voices, began to escalate so Chub went to the farthest corner he could find and concentrated on the colors. But he could still hear them. They were arguing about how much to spend and they were angry now and Mike said, "Oh, for Chrissakes, do what you goddamn please," and Gretchen said, "I will," and Mike said, "Sure, what the hell, all I do is earn it," and Gretchen said, "She's my sister," and then Mike exploded and said, "Just tell me what sense it makes, spending a fortune on flowers when we both know she's going to be dead by morning," and Gretchen said, "You're right, it is silly," and they bought some cheap flowers and on the way out Chub said, "We love Aunt Audrey," and Gretchen said, "Of course we do, why do you think we're bringing her flowers?"

Chub lay very still, remembering the scene more and more clearly because he didn't know it then, couldn't articulate it, but it was probably the first time he realized the true infrequency of love.

After a while, four-twenty, he had to move, because for the first time in he didn't want to think how many years, the impulse was in him, not like it had been back in

school, not that strong, but it was there, so he crept out
of bed, leaving Sandy sleeping curled, holding a pillow,
and he left the room, closing the door. He went to his
desk, turned on the light, got out paper and carbon,
began to type.

He called it "Flores para los Muertos"—"Flowers for
the Dead," a line a Mexican woman kept repeating to
Blanche in *Streetcar*, and whenever the Mexican woman
appeared, trying to sell her wares, it frightened Blanche,
just as Chub had been frightened, hiding in the corner of
the florist's shop, trying so hard to think only of the
colors.

He finished it at nine and for the last hour he wasn't
alone. Sandy sat in the overstuffed chair, wearing her T-
shirt and jeans, sitting cross-legged, watching him, not
saying a word. When he was done he got up. He should
have been tired but he was the reverse. He asked Sandy if
she wanted breakfast but she just shook her head. So he
started making a pot of coffee and while it was brewing,
took a quick shower.

When he returned, Sandy was sitting at his desk,
reading the story. It was seven pages long and when she
finished it she didn't say a word, just started from the top
again. She was not a very fast reader—it took her forty-
five minutes to go through it twice. Chub was lying down
by then.

"It's just the most wonderful thing," she said. "It
made me want to cry. Why does everything you write
make me want to do that?"

Chub shook his head, thanked her dearly for her opinion.

"Not opinion—it's a *fact*."

Chub smiled. There was no question of her sincerity—
she had missed all of *Tic Tac Dough* and half of *The
Joker's Wild* to read the story twice.

She asked if he minded if she watched the TV while he
lay there. He said he didn't. And when the tube came on,
he wasn't much aware. Because all that was in his head
was this: Was the story any good at all? He could have

written *The quick brown fox* ... five hundred times and probably she would have thought it was "just the most wonderful thing."

But was it? Was it anything? Did it have any quality at all? He wanted so desperately to find out, find out *now*, and Kitchel was a possibility but if it wasn't, he could not bring himself to face Kitchel's "praise."

He decided to give it to The Bone. She was smart and she was fiercely honest and he was going to be seeing her in a couple of hours. But there was no way he felt strong enough to tell her it was new—"Huh?—this is the crap you turn out at your age?—kiddie reminiscences?" What he would do would shitkick a little, tell her, believe it or not, he was cleaning out his zoo and he found this thing he'd written back in school and maybe it would give her a laugh. He couldn't hand her the original, it looked too new, but the carbon, if he rumpled it, would pass.

Her reaction, when she read it before lunch, startled him. "Why didn't you stick this in your book?" she said, lying on her couch, swatting her cats away.

"Huh?"

"It would have fit perfect in *Under the Weather*. Right after the kid breaks the window with the yo-yo, that story, and that Bethlehem scene thing."

"I didn't know you read my book—when did you?"

"When you gave it to me, *schmuck*."

"That was back before the sixteenth century—why the hell didn't you tell me?"

"I just couldn't."

Chub sat beside her on the couch. "Quit eating that goddamn cigarette and explain."

Very softly she said, "Because it was so goddamn good it pissed me off—it was good and it wasn't Trash and I didn't want to deal with that. I was afraid you'd do a number on me." She put the carbon on the coffee table by the couch. "This should have gone in, Chub—it's probably better than anything you've done."

Chub suddenly hugged her.

"What's that about?"

"It's new—I just wrote it."

"Then why the song and dance?"

"I was worried about what you might say. I wanted it to be good but I didn't know, so I protected myself. I guess I was afraid you'd do a number on me."

"Christ, are we ever some team." And now her arms were around him.

Chub was about to release her when he realized she didn't want him to. The pressure of her arms was different and it crossed his mind that she wanted him, but what if he made a move and she didn't. He risked it—he was so thrilled with what she'd said about "Flores para los Muertos" that what the hell. And she did want him.

But she was awkward, insecure, all edges and elbows, and he calmed her, whispered, "Now there *is* no fire," and in a moment he lifted her, took her to the bed, undressed her slowly, and when he was naked, too, he began to massage her long body, making sure this time she would be wet and ready, and when she was, with pride, he brought her to orgasm.

In the next days Chub came to realize three remarkable things.

First: Sandy was genuinely *weird* when it came to television. Not *all* television—primarily the game shows and the soaps, the first because she said it made her happy when people had their wishes come true, the soaps because you were always on edge, never knowing what was going to happen next.

Chub watched *The Price Is Right* with her once, and she was a demon at knowing what brand names cost. When a pair of Elgin quartz watches came up for bid, she screamed, "Six hundred seventy, six hundred seventy," and then "No— No— No— No" as the four contestants gave their guesses. Needless to say, six hundred and seventy was the answer. She was just as deadly on Whirlpool washers, 1.5-litre Mazda hatchbacks, any item at all. There were twelve game shows on the air, and she had never enjoyed them as much, because now, with the clicker, she could scoot from one station to another during commercial breaks and not miss anything.

It wasn't just the prices though. It was much more. As far as Chub could calculate, every bit of her knowledge she had gleaned from game show questions. He realized this first when he returned with his story from The Bone's, and was opening his mail when he walked into his apartment. A couple of checks, a request for some research, a pile of junk mail. Sandy watched him as he went through it and then she said, "I wonder, if you averaged all the mail sent out each year, how much would each person get?" Chub told her he hadn't any idea.

"Probably about sixty-one pounds," Sandy said. With pride.

It was that particular tone she used that was the key. Later she said, "You know, a lot of people still have it in for Richard Nixon and his wife, Thelma."

"Pat, I think," Chub said.

"People call her Pat," Sandy said. "But her real name is Thelma."

Sometimes she just came out with information; that night, before sex, she said, "Did you know the average American woman's favorite recreation is reading a book?" She bit his lip. "It sure isn't mine."

Sometimes she tried to ease her knowledge into the conversation. When Chub was reading an article in the *Times* about the latest outbreak in Lebanon, Sandy said, peering over his shoulder, "I just hate war so."

"There's nothing worse."

"My father, he fought a lot. He was in England and he told me how in London, everyplace you saw a new building, that meant the old one had been killed in the war. They suffered terrible times in London."

"They did indeed."

"They never knocked down Big Ben, though, the Germans."

Chub could tell from her tone now that a quiz answer was on the horizon.

"Do you know, during the war, what it meant when Big Ben struck four?"

"All clear?"

"Nope—it meant it was four o'clock, that's all." And then she walked back into the bedroom, turned on the TV.

It was from Sandy that Chub found that mosquitoes heard and smelled from the same part of their body, that a lock of George Washington's hair was worth more than a million dollars, that Teddy Roosevelt fought San Juan Hill on foot because the horses missed their boat. He learned a lot, no question.

But the soaps were beyond him. She tried to keep him up with things, but he could never get the names straight. Were Phoebe and Brooke on *All My Children* or *Capitol?* And which show was Erica being diabolical on? Or was it Erica that was diabolical? Maybe it was Burke. And were Raven and Ian in love or trying to kill each other?

Had there ever been a Herschel or an Alvin on a soap, Chub wondered. Or a Frieda? Probably it would be against the Public Broadcasting Code.

Sandy never minded his ineptness. She told him it took her awhile, too, but she just knew he'd get the hang of it, like she had.

As a matter of fact, Sandy never minded anything as long as the TV was on. As long as she could have her soap opera thrills to watch, as long as she could see couples cry when they won their dream houses or trips to Hawaii, nothing was wrong with the world. . . .

The second thing Chub learned was this: Sandy was genuinely weird, *period.* Perhaps dangerously so.

That came clear to him on Tuesday night, the same night The Bone had given him such high marks on "Flores para los Muertos." He and Sandy had·finished dinner—Kentucky Fried. Sandy really only liked junk food, which was fine with Chub, because he had come to hate his stove—it burned him when he wasn't looking, sometimes when he was. They went to bed early; he was tired. And with reason. Not only had he spent the night before writing, but he had slept three times with two women in a day and a half, not that anyone was counting, Mrs. Ginsberg.

She was poring over his Journal when he remembered what "the end of the rain" was about. She put the Journal down while he told her, haltingly, trying to get the specifics straight.

It had all centered on his father's passion for stuffed goose. Except they were illegal in Illinois then, maybe they still were. It involved force-feeding the dumb beasts, constantly stuffing large food pellets down their throats until they were particularly fat, which, his father said, made them particularly delicious when you cooked them.

So Mike and Gretchen and Chub got in their car— Chub must have been six, seven, that region—and drove to Wisconsin. Stuffed geese were illegal there, too, but his father had gotten some tips on some farmers who did it on the sly. Chub sat in the back as they stopped at one farmhouse after another, until finally, for whatever reason, a farmer trusted Mike and the family trooped to the barn in the back where some men were stuffing pellets down the birds' mouths. Mike picked one, paid, the animal was slaughtered and wrapped and stuck in the trunk and they began the drive down to Illinois.

Uneventful drive. Little talk. Rain falling. The main sound the windshield wipers.

And then it happened—the car was in sunshine. Chub looked back—and it was still raining. He begged his father to stop, please, please, and Mike, happy with his stuffed goose safely in the trunk, stopped. Now back up, please, *please*. Mike humored him. There was no traffic on the quiet country road. He backed up until the front half of the car was in sun, the rear in rain.

Chub had to get out and they let him. He stood in the sunshine, stared at the rain. Until that moment, he had always thought when it was raining on him it was raining on everyone. Then he ran to the back of the car, let the rain fall on him. And then he cried, "I command sunshine," and he ran to the front and when he was at the front he cried, "I command rain," and he circled around to where it was wet.

Then he began to run, laughing and churning his short legs, racing around and around the stationary vehicle, while his parents watched silently from inside. He ran till he was exhausted and when they told him to get in, he ran just a few more times, begging them to let him do it just once more, just once more, and they let him until their patience was gone.

Chub lay in the backseat as the car began to make its way south. He kind of dozed, pondering what had just happened. What he thought then was that it was probably the happiest, certainly the most wondrous moment, of his life. What he came to realize later was that it was the first time (and alas the last) that he actually believed in God.

Chub lay beside her when he was done, the impulse to write faint but there. "You better get right to work," she said.

He shook his head. "Too whipped, I'd screw it up." But he did go to his desk, took enough notes so that in the morning he would know everything he had just spoken aloud.

He awoke at three. Felt for her. The other side of the bed was empty. But he could hear her. Faintly. From the next room, doing her wheel song.

Oh, the wheel is always in spin
No matter how bad it's been where I been,
No matter how sad the troubles I'm in.

"What troubles," Chub asked, standing in the dark doorway separating the two rooms. In a moment he could make her out clearly. By the large open window. Only she wasn't sitting in a chair beside it and she wasn't sitting on the sill—she was lying hunched up across the sill, her body balanced precariously, one of her legs dangling in space.

Her back to him, she stayed motionless, staring out.

"Go back to sleep, you need your sleep for when you're writing."

"I've discovered this wonderful new sedative, I'm helpless without it, and right now it's staring out the window. Come." He began moving in the darkness toward her.

"You never would have remembered about running around in the rain without me."

"You don't know how right you are."

"I do you good."

"You haven't made too many mistakes so far—now, come away from there."

"Why?"

"Because it's dangerous."

She still was frozen, lying on the sill. "So?"

"You're being silly, come on."

She was quiet for a while. He was beside her now, able to reach her. "Sometimes . . ." she said, but that was all.

Chub waited. Her voice was dreamy.

Now she pointed to the night. "Sometimes I think I'd like to go out there."

"For a walk?"

"No—out *there*—" and this time she pointed down. "Just go out the window and fly a few seconds and then it would all be over."

"Shut up with that kind of talk."

"I fucked up my life."

"You haven't *begun* your life, for Chrissakes—what are you, twenty? As ancient as twenty-two?"

"How much do you care for me?—really really way deep down?"

"What is this, you've been here three nights and you're proposing?"

"*Way deep down,* I asked."

"I was married once, Sandy—it turns out I wasn't good at it."

"Very impressive. Well, I been married twice, to two shits—they humped me and dumped me. The second time I took all the Valium my mother had and when I woke up alive the next morning I cried all day. After that

I left Portland. And now I find you, only you don't care beans and you never will, not deep down."

Chub grabbed her then, began to pull her.

She resisted.

"Get the fuck away from there," Chub said, and this time, perhaps because of his tone, perhaps because he used more of his strength, she walked with him to the bedroom. But he could not help noticing the way she kept glancing back toward the large open window. And he wasn't too pleased about the look in her eyes. . . .

The third thing Chub discovered was perhaps, when he realized it, the weirdest of all: He *loved* his situation.

Part of the reason, obviously, was the sex. No one, not even B.J., had aroused him as Sandy did, had enjoyed his body, had brought him to such climax. And part of that was probably the illicit nature of their relationship. She was indeed his secret. This glorious confection that had appeared in the storm, wanted nothing from him except the use of his clicker and the right to sit there silently, in her T-shirt and jeans, while he pounded away at his old Olympia.

The Bone helped, unknowingly, by not making him feel guilty, since she was flying herself. She had lucked into a catalog job she was getting a raping amount of money for, and when she wasn't doing that, she was "knocking the crap" out of *Skeletons,* she hoped to be done in a week, and a photographer buddy of hers knew a schlock producer in Hollywood who was more than anxious to read it when it was done. So Chub didn't have to see her, instead kept in contact by phone and more often than not, it was The Bone who needed to get off and get chugging.

But the main reason, the crucial reason, for Chub's era of good feelings was simple: His impulse was back. He was—stand back, world—writing again.

It was Thursday morning when he realized that Sandy was actually a modern-day Kitchel, more splendid to look upon, surely, but their functions were the same. (He would never have written "The Girl(s) of My Dreams" if

Kitchel had not come bursting in on him after he'd quit the Cheyney class and called him a fool, because he had a voice—Chub could still hear Two-Brew saying that he knew Chub wasn't alone in the graffiti-covered men's room—and then, "That was your father in there with you.")

Kitchel of course was brilliant, while it was doubtful that Sandy would ever qualify for a Rhodes scholarship, but none the less, their functions were the same: They *believed*. More than that, they *knew*. That as much as he might try and argue, kick and struggle, he had more than his share of it, talent. And evidently, more than he had ever dreamed, he needed that unchanging and unchallengeable belief.

Those days, for the first time in he didn't want to count how many years, Chub was happy.

His schedule was constant: wake, touch, coffee, embrace, chat, click—as soon as *Tic Tac Dough* came on, he took off. He would have preferred to remain but Elliott Carter had a large and detailed piece of research that needed doing that week, and Chub could never refuse him. Anyway, until the soaps were over, he was vestigial.

He would work, beep in for messages, skip lunch, work some more, try and get his calls to The Bone completed before he returned home late afternoon carrying a bag from McDonald's (she *devoured* the fries) or a pizza.

After food, bed, and after bed, the Olympia. "The End of the Rain" ran ten pages. Sandy was not disappointed: It made her want to cry even more than the other one.

On Thursday, he told her he would write a story that not only wouldn't make her want to cry, it was to be especially for her. It was to be called "The Cracker Barrel" and it was about an old widow who lived alone in the suburbs and whose main joy in life was soap operas, especially *The Cracker Barrel,* which had kept her company for twenty years. Then one day she learned from a friend that the writer was going to kill off her favorite character, so she took her husband's old pistol, rode on the train into New York, went to the writer's apartment, killed *him* off, then hurried to the train station, getting home just in time to catch the afternoon episode of *The Cracker Barrel.*

"Serves him right," Sandy said after he told her. Then she came into his lap. "Could you call the lady Sandra?" she asked.

"Sandra it shall be," Chub promised, and he started the story, got a few pages done before showering, singing "The Wheel" as he lathered, dried off, turned out the lights, moved through the dark apartment to where she waited. The idea that he was actually writing a story for her made her particularly inventive.

Not a bad life.

With only occasional clouds. On Friday morning, when he delivered his research to Carter, the old man was not happy. Chub had done some sloppy work, not as complete as needed, perhaps not as accurate as desired. Chub, impressed that he had been able to do *any* work at all considering where his mind was, apologized, promised to make everything right next week.

And then there was the new client, the lady from Syracuse whose husband had left her for the laundress. She phoned because she simply wasn't happy at all. Chub, used to new clients' occasional disappointments and knowing the job was competent, stood by what he'd mailed her.

She wanted more questions answered, and more completely. And she wanted them now. The best thing, Chub told her, was if she talked directly to the expert himself and asked him.

Fine, when?

Chub knew that Rory in the past had not minded talking on the phone during his lunch break, money was money. He told the Syracuse lady that if he didn't call her back, she would receive a collect call from the expert Friday between twelve and one. (He checked later with Rory, the time was fine.) Then Chub explained that the interview would cost her.

She got angry; she had already paid.

And you got what you paid for.

Pause. Finally she said all right, but Chub suspected there was going to be trouble when Rory told her where to send him her check for his services and time.

So, Friday afternoon, as soon as he was sure their interview would be done, Chub called Rory at the precinct house, got right through and was not surprised that Baylor wanted to have some conversation. "I left a message for you on your machine, I want to talk now, how 'bout if I come over to your place?"

Chub, thinking of Sandy, said, "You won't believe this but I'm being painted this week and the fumes would stagger Bruno Sammartino."

"Okay. How 'bout if you come here?"

"When?"

"I'm waiting."

Chub went straight to the precinct house from the main-library pay phone. It was four when he sat down at Rory's desk in the squad room. The place was noisy, phones ringing off the wall, men moving up aisles, down, shouting to each other, sometimes questions, sometimes vulgarities.

Rory looked angry. Or whipped. Maybe both. Before Chub could apologize about the goddamn lady in Syracuse, before he could begin to explain that it would all get straightened out, the money, Baylor said, "We've done each other a lot of favors over the years."

"I'm way behind," Chub said.

"If you want to think of it that way, fine, I don't, but that doesn't matter. I want you to do a favor for me now," and he handed Chub several large photographs of the corpse of Sandy Smith, lying sprawled on the cement that Chub knew so well, he had looked down at it for years, the cement "garden" in the rear of his building, below his large window, ninety-seven steps below. He raised the pictures up to his face, blotting Rory out, pretending to study them. And while he looked—there was surprisingly little blood, almost none—Rory explained in a weary monotonous voice that the body of the unidentified female was heard landing at approximately noon, that the general consensus was she had leapt from either the roof of his building or the neighboring one, the angle made it difficult to ascertain, that both roofs were full of footprints so it was impossible to identify anything with precision, but some of them must have been made by said unidentified female, that he, Rory, had been spending the last hours contacting the inhabitants of both buildings, that he had called Chub not much after two, that he had reached all but three, that no one knew her or had ever seen her, that the thesis of the crime unit that took the pictures was simply that she had entered one of the two buildings, there was no problem gaining entrance, had walked to the roof and leapt off and—

—and while he went on and on, Chub stared at the photos, knowing that Sandy had not leapt from the roof but from his window, something she had almost done a few nights before, maybe would have if he hadn't awakened in time. And if he told Rory that, what would be gained? Sandy was dead. When he felt he was able to talk calmly, he put the photos back on Rory's desk. "Why do you think it was suicide?"

"Because there are no other indications, but that's secondary—I want it to be. It's my case and I want it closed." He gestured to his desk, which was piled with official-looking material. "I got plenty to do. And this is the start of the season for leapers. Yesterday a fifteen-year-old Spanish girl went off her roof—good student, no drug history. You know why? The last thing her mother remembers is the kid got hysterical because she thought she looked fat in last year's bathing suit."

"At fifteen?" Chub asked, not caring but needing time to figure—if he told Rory what he knew, would that mean more questions? He didn't mind more questions but what if The Bone found out? Bad, bad, bad.

"Tell me you don't know her. That's my favor."

"You got it," Chub said.

Rory almost smiled. "Now I only got two more people to go. Thanks for getting up here."

"*De nada,*" Chub said, rising quickly now, getting the hell out before Rory or anyone else saw how his hands were shaking. He left the precinct house, got out of sight around the corner, then leaned against a building for support. What if he'd told Sandy over and over what she was doing for him? What if, that night by the open window, he had said *maybe* he might marry again, what if—

—enough "what if"s. She was dead. Just another leaper. And this was the start of the season—

—enough "start of the season" bullshit. He had failed. That was the bottom line. Failed again. Even when someone adored him, he couldn't keep them alive.

He had never bought a pack of cigarettes in his life, but he had to do something with his hands, so he paid for a pack of English Ovals, lit one, inhaled, coughed, inhaled again. The stationery guy had an odd look, so Chub bought a copy of the *Times,* just to prove he had nothing to hide. But even though he had committed no crime— no jailable crime—he was suddenly in a glass world, every man on the street was looking through him, every woman, every child, and he broke into a run to make them stop, ran till he reached his building, ran up the cursed ninety-seven stairs even though his legs were starting to cramp. It was only when he was inside his silent apartment that he stopped running, leaning against the door, gasping.

And just as his world had bucked beneath him in the squad room, now it jolted him again. Because the apartment wasn't silent.

The TV was on.

The TV was on.

Chub ran to the bedroom, stared at the picture of some asshole situation-comedy rerun, listened to the rancid canned laughter. Then he spun out of the room, went to

the deadly open window. What was it Rory had said?
The body landed around noon. Noon was game shows or
soap operas—noon was one or the other—

—*and she would never have gone out the window then,
she was happy then!*

No. He was wrong. She *had* gone out the window. But
not unaided. Some final gentleman caller had come and
sent her on her way, had made deadly sure that for Sandy
Smith, the wheel was no longer in spin.

CHAPTER 3

Material

"Lied about what?" Baylor said as he barged into Chub's apartment.

(It was twenty minutes later and Chub had called the precinct house as soon as he'd made his discovery, had said that Baylor better get over and when Rory said he was not totally unoccupied at the moment, Chub shouted, "Get your ass over here right now, you son of a bitch, I *lied*," and then he slammed down the receiver. Sometimes you had to be overdramatic to get Rory's attention.

(He went back into the bedroom then, stared at the TV picture, the clicker, but that was not a place of joy for him just then, so he went back to the other room, kept away from the window, grabbed the *Times* he'd just bought because he hadn't had much of a shot at it this morning, what with all the rushing around to deliver to Elliott Carter, and the *Times* would keep him quietly occupied till Rory got there.

(Clark Gable's widow, Kay, had died at sixty-six.

(Chub thought of his fight on the playground about whether or not Gable's teeth were real and then he thought that what if Gretchen was out there now, reading this news, would it please her, would it make her go to California because maybe Gable was alive, too, and this would be her greatest chance to at last nab him and find true happiness—

(—are you crazy, they're dead, Chub thought, ripping his eyes from the obituary page—they're all dead, Kay

361

and Clark and yes, Gretchen, too, and yes, yes, most recently, Sandy, *what's the matter with you?*

(He pitched the "B" section into the wastebasket, concentrated on getting another English Oval lit but his hands still weren't all that much under his control, so it took three matches. He pulled out the fat Friday entertainment section and started flipping through, because if anything could take his mind away, that would be it. The movie reviews—what the fuck was *Blue Thunder?*—and the theatre gossip and those ads with their quotes that made every attraction seem like Shakespeare had arisen. And Mimi Sheraton pasting some restaurant because the waiters didn't give the prices on the specials, and then a headline caught his eye: "Publishing: Time Out for Writers' Conferences." Chub wanted to continue on but he was caught, and his eyes scanned the article.

(". . . there are more than any single author, editor, or aspiring writer could possibly attend. 'If I wanted to, I could go from one to another all summer long,' said Galway Kinnell, the 1983 Pulitzer Prizewinning poet, who is limiting his participation this summer to two conferences."

(The word "limiting" almost made him rip the section to pieces but Chub read on. They were going on all over the country, the goddamn conferences. There was even going to be one on the *Queen Elizabeth II.* And just about everybody was going to show up somewhere or another: Bernard Malamud, Ralph Ellison, Paule Marshall, Budd Schulberg, Robert Stone, John Irving.

(Chub lit another cigarette. Two matches this time. Every day in every way I am getting better and better. He inhaled, stared out the late sunlit afternoon. ". . . Charles Fuller, the 1984 Pulitzer Prizewinner for fiction, is limiting his appearances this summer to but one—an ocean crossing on the *Queen Elizabeth II.* Such is the interest in Mr. Fuller's work, that the entire liner has been totally sold out for the past months, and the waiting list is now over a thousand. Mr. Fuller, when reached by phone, was his usual quiet, modest self, said that he hoped he would be of at least some aid to his aspiring fans, but that they should not raise their hopes overly high: He was, after all, a simple worker at his craft, no matter how extravagant the claims of his many reviewers and the fact that he was the first artist since Bruce Springsteen to appear simultaneously on the covers of both *Time* and *Newsweek,* although certainly flattering—"

(—*Time* and *Newsweek?*—are you crazy?—you've written maybe two decent stories in ten years and the only reason you were able to do that is gone, dead, *what's the matter with you?*)

"I lied about everything," Chub said then as he let Baylor into the room.

Baylor looked at him a moment. "You fooled me. Or maybe I wanted you to."

"Don't flatter yourself—I'm good at lying—I didn't used to be, but I sure am now." He reached for another cigarette.

"When'd you start smoking?"

Chub exploded—"What the hell difference does that make? I lied, don't you get that? I knew the girl. And she didn't commit suicide, it was murder."

Baylor studied him a moment in silence.

"Jesus, Rory, didn't you hear me—she was thrown out the window—I can prove it, you want me to prove it, goddamn it, come along," and he led the cop into the bedroom, pointing.

"I don't get it," Rory said.

"Well, look—use your eyes, can't you see? The television's on!"

Rory got out a notebook and pen. "Let's go slow, shall we? Let's go back and sit down and you tell me everything. Nice and easy."

"How the fuck can I be 'nice and easy' when a murder's been committed in my apartment?"

"It's hard—but you've got to try—all right?"

Chub sat at his desk, Baylor in the overstuffed chair. "Name of the deceased?" Baylor said.

"*Victim,* you mean. Name of the victim."

"Okay, victim."

"Sandy Smith."

"Spelled?"

"Whatsa matter, you can't spell 'Smith'?"

Baylor put his notebook down and took a breath. "Chub," he said, "I do not like the way you're acting—it's like we're back at Christmas and you lost it. When I said 'nice and easy,' I meant 'nice' and I also meant 'easy.' Now, you get your shit together, and while you're doing that I'm telling you that yes, probably I can spell 'Smith,' it was the first cognomen I was enquiring after, and yes, I can spell 'cognomen.' "

Chub stamped out his cigarette. "I'm sorry, Rory, it's not like this is my average day."

"We'll get to everything, I promise. Now go."

"It's gonna sound a little weird, but in little places she ended with an 'i' but when she was in big cities, she said the 'i' sounded too small-town so she used the 'y.' "

"Can we compromise on Sandra?" Baylor asked.

Chub nodded.

"Address?"

"Here, with me, since last Sunday night. We did our interview with the lady from Syracuse, remember?—you sent me out in the rain to try and see how easy it was to buy a gun? I'd just finished typing up the transcript when she came." Six days. Had it only been six days? It wasn't even that—it wouldn't be that till after midnight. "She was like a blessing, Rory—she was my secret—no one saw her come, she never left, she was . . . she meant a lot to me."

"I'm sure. What I meant by 'address' was her home."

"Chicago."

"Where in Chicago?"

"She was staying with a girl friend named Becky—no—she was staying with a girl friend *of* Becky's."

"Becky who?"

Chub shook his head.

"No known address," Baylor said, and wrote in his notebook. "Any articles of identification?"

"Raincoat, hat, purse."

"May I see them?"

Chub got up, went to the closet for the clothes, the bed table for the purse, handed them over. Baylor examined the clothes briefly, opened the purse. "Ruth Rogelski?" he asked, holding up a plastic card. "Friend?"

Chub shook his head. "Phony ID. So she wouldn't get carded in discos or bars—you know from her photos how young she looked."

Baylor looked at the purse a moment more, then clicked it shut. "Chub—think now—do you know the least fucking thing about this girl?"

"I know she was murdered."

"We'll get to that—I mean anything about the specifics of her life?"

"I know *everything* about the specifics of her life, 'officer.' She was an Army brat. Father was a captain. She was a cheerleader in Hawaii her freshman year of high school. She lived in Portland with her mother until she moved to Seattle and then Chicago. And she was married twice, both times to shits."

Baylor sighed, held out his hands. "Give me one of those goddamn things." He pointed toward the cigarette.

"Since when did you start smoking?"

"Don't tell Maya, okay?"

Chub handed him the pack of English Ovals. Baylor lit one. First match. "Were there any signs of a struggle when you got here?"

"I didn't touch a thing."

"From my cursory observations, I would say I saw no signs of a struggle, would you agree?"

After a moment Chub made a nod.

"Motive?"

"I don't know—you're the one said people go crazy when the weather starts heating up. Robbery, maybe."

Baylor inhaled deeply. "Chub, how long you lived here?"

" '72."

"And I'll bet you've never been robbed, am I right?"

"That doesn't mean there couldn't be a first time."

"Correct. But let me tell you two things about thieves, the first pertaining to the ones that bloom in our area, and second to the species in general. Our local varieties are after one thing and one thing only—anything that has immediate street resale value so they can get their drugs. That means TV sets, stereos, et cetera."

"So?"

"The second point is this: Every one of those mothers shares a trait and it's this: They're lazy. They don't want to mug Bronko Nagurski, they want an old lady alone hobbling along on a cane. And no thief yet born is going to climb—how many steps did you tell me?—"

"—ninety-seven."

"Ain't none of 'em gonna hike this high to grab something that's heavy because he's then got to carry it all the way *down.* It could be a robbery—but my experience tells me the odds are inconceivable to one." He put out the cigarette. "Now tell me about the TV being on."

"Believe this, promise?"

"If you'll give me another cigarette."

They both lit up. "She was an absolute nut about the tube. Not all of it, naturally, but the game shows and the soaps, she was in hog heaven when they were on. She was *happy* when they were on, Rory. She'd just sit there with the clicker and you never saw anyone happier, every second."

"I don't watch much television, when are these shows on?"

"They start at nine in the morning—I left her today at nine in the morning and she was glued to the set—and they last till maybe four in the afternoon."

Baylor studied his notebook a moment then before looking at Chub. "And she died around noon. And her programs were on around noon. And so she would have been happy at noon. And she never would have gone out the window at noon, not when she was happy. Not without some guy doing the work."

"Well, Jesus Christ, hallelujah."

Baylor got up then, went briefly into the bedroom, looked at the television set, then returned, looked at the large wide-open window. "I am never going to be confused with Sherlock Holmes," he said.

"I'll say." Chub lit two cigarettes, handed one to Rory.

"Or Mr. Poirot either—" Baylor inhaled. "But I like to think I am not totally ignorant when it comes to human psychology—"

"—nobody's *totally* ignorant, don't feel bad." Chub smiled.

"And it's my firm belief—listen, now—I know you, I know you pretty well—and it's my belief that the only reason you were able to get away with lying to me earlier was because *you were not totally surprised that she went out the window—now, am I right?*"

Chub, stunned, stared at the black man. "What the fuck are you talking about—*she was happy.*"

"Am I right, goddamnit, answer me."

"You mean did she giggle twenty-four hours a day? Of course not."

"Was she moody?"

"Aren't you sometimes?"

"I am right now."

"I know what you're trying to do—" Chub shoved his desk chair back, stood. "You're so goddamn anxious to close the case you won't listen to reason."

"*You're* who's not being reasonable. Yes, I want to close the case but I also would like to have a solved murder on my record even more—but I am not going to go to the assholes above me and tell them that my proof is that *To Tell the fucking Truth* was on the air. Now, quit dodging—was she *moody.*"

"Maybe a little."

"You're still dodging—how little?"

"She'd had a couple bad marriages, that's bound to have an effect."

"Had she ever tried it before?"

"Go fuck yourself."

"Once?—twice?—how many times?"

"She mentioned something I think about Valium."

"And that's all?—you don't sound like that's all."

"Rory—please—don't do this to me—I'm right—you've got to believe me—I know in my heart because I knew her and—and quit looking at me!"

Quietly, Rory said, "We've been through too much to go on like this. Let's finish it off."

Quietly, Chub said, "The Valium once and she talked about maybe going out the window. But at night. We all get weird thoughts at night. Never when the TV was on. She was crazy about me, Rory—she would never have left me this way."

"She did, Chub. You better start to consider that. Unless you can bring me proof and I'm afraid we're back to inconceivable-to-one odds again."

"You're just finished, is that it?"

"I didn't say that—because it's you, I'll have prints lifted—do it myself right now. I'll go to the precinct and get the equipment and I'll dust anyplace you want. I'll take your prints because you live here and we've got hers on record—"

"—you'll find another man, Rory. I promise you. There'll be another guy's prints on the window."

"I would like that. I like you. None of what we've said goes outside this room because nothing affects my job—I don't care where she leapt from."

Chub slumped back in the chair. "I want one big fucking apology from you when you find that other guy's prints."

"Gladly given—and by the way, where were you around noon?"

Chub looked up at him. "At the main library with fifty witnesses."

"Well, I was on the phone with your bitch up in Syracuse, so I guess we're innocent." He touched Chub's shoulder. "I was trying to lighten things."

Chub said nothing, concentrated on the darkening sky.

Baylor was back and done not much past seven-thirty. They didn't talk much. When Rory was ready to leave, he promised Chub he'd get right on it.

Chub nodded.

"Maya would love some company."

"Thanks. I'm fine."

"Then I don't ever want to be fine," Rory said.

Chub made no reply, sat totally still till he was alone. Staring now at the night. He looked very tranquil but the truth was this: For the first time in his life he genuinely wanted to kill somebody, he just didn't know who. . . .

Wild anger, wrath, call it what you will, was something Chub had never dealt with much—not overtly anyway. He was far too closed in for that. Now he wondered how he would react.

Same song, second verse.

He sat, he smoked, he stared. Once he got up, made himself a tuna club, took a bite, spit it out, went back to his desk, sat and smoked some more.

At eight, he thought he ought to check in with The Bone, just be heard from. He hadn't called her before he reached home, so he was due—if he didn't, she'd probably call him and he wanted to be in charge of things. Besides, maybe she was out.

At eight-fifteen he dialed and she was in but she was happy, another scene in her screenplay had just gone well. Chub kept his voice level, told her she could support him in their old age. He could sense she wanted to get back to her writing, so he signed off, his voice clearly level, she didn't ask if anything was wrong.

As he hung up he saw he had two messages on his machine. Ordinarily, these last days, Sandy would have told him that the phone rang three times, or five times, or once, but she couldn't handle that chore now. And ordinarily he would have looked at his machine before this, except when he got home he had other things on his mind. He still had other things on his mind. Screw the messages, he knew what they were: The first would be Baylor calling—Baylor had told him in the precinct house he'd left a message. And the other would be the woman from Syracuse bitching that she wasn't going to pay extra.

He didn't need to hear that, not now.

He sat and smoked some more. Goddamn crazy women with their goddamn research needs. Not just the women—goddamn them all, with their requests for magic suits and the size of Rasputin's cock and what really happened—with maps, please—during the Peloponnesian War.

At eight-thirty he realized what he needed most was to hear the bitching from Syracuse. He hoped she was really hostile because then he could dial her long distance and blast her out of her seat, just sit at his desk and tell her where she could please go and quickly. He turned on his machine, and the second message was indeed Baylor, saying it was two and give him a buzz at his desk. The first message had no time and it was not from the lady in Syracuse. It was very short and the voice low and slow and familiar:

> Hey, pal . . . I'm happy. . . . Are you
> happy? . . . I'll bet I'm happier
> than you are. . . .

Click.

Chub played it again and again and again, searing the sound of Peter Hungerford into his brain. The message could have come at any time between nine and two. Baylor had called at two and Sandy was dead then. Chub had left at nine and Sandy was smiling.

> Hey, pal . . . I'm happy. . . . Are you
> happy? . . . I'll bet I'm happier
> than you are. . . .

Click.

> Hey, pal . . . I'm happy. . . . Are you
> happy? . . . I'll bet I'm happier
> than you are. . . .

Click.

Something went "click" in Chub's brain, too: He was amazed at the sense of calm that descended. He knew so much. Chub knew who the murderer was and he knew *where* the murderer was: Frost had said it. Home was when you had to go there, they had to take you in.

So Peter would be hiding with his parents, either across the park in the town house or out at the place in the Hamptons. It didn't matter which. It didn't even matter if Hungerford was someplace else. Chub would find him. He had time.

What he didn't have was a weapon, so he slipped on his Windbreaker, went outside to the transvestite group standing in the permanent gathering on the corner, repeated what Rory had told him to say just last Sunday. (Rory wanted proof, proof he would have, breathing or not.)

In five minutes, for fifty dollars, he had a Saturday Night Special in his Windbreaker pocket. The transvestites were laughing nervously. Chub looked at their painted faces, going from one to the next.

The laughter stopped.

It started again when he left them to look for a cab, but that was all right with him: When he needed to silence them, he had the power.

At ten after nine Chub got out of the cab in the East Sixties, paid calmly, walked calmly into the expensive block of town houses where the Hungerfords resided. He moved easily on the other side of the street from their place. Most of the houses were dark.

Not the Hungerfords'. Standing silhouetted in the second-floor window was the father. And the mother. And between them, enormous and staring, was the son. Chub started to reach into his Windbreaker pocket but stopped before the motion was half completed. He was not expert with firearms. And there was no point in hurting the innocent, not when the guilty was there, waiting.

For a moment, Chub studied the family portrait. The parents close to the child. Mrs. Hungerford had her arms around his waist, the father an arm around Peter's shoulders. They were almost frozen, as if waiting for a photographer. Who did all the rich people? The Bone would know. Bachrach? Something like that. Bachrach should take them now. "The Hungerfords at Home."

Chub crossed to the home now, pressed calmly on the buzzer, waiting for some servant to answer. The door was not opened by a servant, which surprised Chub, but that was not the reason for his ensuing silence. Rather it was that his life seemed to be folding back in on him in some bizarre way: A couple of hours ago he was reading about Gable's widow and Gretchen finally having her shot. Now the man he was staring at reminded him of Mike's friend, the guy who ran the dimestore back in Athens and let Mike work there on and off, until that last day when Mike dumped all the drawers because he wasn't even able to locate a tailor's thimble. Finally Chub said, "I'm here for Peter Hungerford."

The old guy in the doorway—he was armed and wearing a uniform with a patch on the right shoulder that read "Wellspring"—made no reply.

"I know he's here, don't bother telling me he isn't, I just saw him in the upstairs window."

"Nobody said he wasn't here, son. You a friend?"

Chub shook his head. "He tried to kill me a couple of years ago. Today he did kill somebody."

The guard nodded. "I know."

Chub blinked. "How did you find out?"

"That doesn't matter much now."

Chub stepped into the foyer. "It fucking matters, mister. And don't try humoring me—I've got a gun."

"We all have guns," the old guard said wearily, and he glanced behind him.

Chub followed his look. Two more armed men in uniform were stationed on the stairs. "You don't scare me, any of you. Peter Hungerford escaped from Wellspring today, he called me on the phone. He left a message. I know what it meant—it meant he killed the girl I was living with."

"Was her name Edward Streeter?"

"Huh?"

"That was who he killed."

"No. You're lying."

The old guard sighed. "Son—I've had a long and a genuine bitch of a day, and I don't much feel pleased being called a liar. I run security at Wellspring and nothing like this has ever happened before; now, if Peter tried to kill you, and I believe he did—I think that's why he was transferred down to us, some kind of attempt on somebody—then you deserve an explanation and I'll give it to you, but then you're gone, do you understand that? If you make trouble, fine, I'm in a mood for making trouble too."

"Get on with it," Chub said.

The guard glanced back to the men on the stairs. "Everything quiet?"

Nods.

He turned to Chub now. "He escaped once before, for only a few minutes, we caught him waiting for a train."

"I know all that."

"Today, when he got out, when he overpowered two people and changed clothes and took off, it was very early, not much past dawn. Only this time he didn't wait for a train, he thumbed, and the first car that stopped was two men driving to Boston. He sat in the back, didn't say much. They stopped along the way for breakfast. Peter paid. Out of gratitude he told them. A couple of hours later, close to eleven, they were on the outskirts of Boston and one of the guys had to take a leak, and while he was gone, Peter broke the neck of the driver—Edward Streeter—shoved him over, went through his pockets, took his valuables, then drove on to the airport."

"What time did he get there?"

"Just before eleven."

"And he shuttled to New York—it all times out."

"*I'll* tell you what times out, all right?"

"Just don't try bullshitting me, because I know."

"We had an all-points out by now but it wasn't much use—then the guy who took the leak called the cops. At first, he said he thought Streeter was pulling a joke—he loved jokes, evidently, but he's not going to pull any more. Streeter's friend told the cops that Streeter and he had tickets for Chicago—and he described Peter, that wasn't hard. But by the time we put it all together, the plane had taken off. I took the next available flight. The cops in Chicago didn't have any trouble recognizing Peter. He was walking around the exit area, telling everybody how he hoped they were happy."

"No! You're dead dead wrong about all this. He took the shuttle to New York and shoved my girl out the window."

The old guard shook his head.

"He was *violent,* for Chrissakes."

"Yes, he was, that's why we had him in an isolation room. And I'm no shrink but Peter was getting worse and worse and what I think is when he finally killed Streeter, some part of him knew it was over. I shackled him and brought him back and he didn't say much. I called the Hungerfords when I got to the airport and they said please, could they see him one more time and they're very important people and we had plenty of guards so I said yes but not for long."

"See him one more time?" Chub needed the wall now.

"We can't hold him—an isolation room is the best we've got and it wasn't good enough. After the trial, if there's a trial, and maybe it can be avoided, there's no point, we all know what's going to happen, Peter's going to spend his life in a facility for the criminally insane."

"He killed Sandy," Chub said. "I *know* that, don't you understand?"

"When did she die?"

"Today—a little after noon."

"Here." The old guard handed him some paper.

Chub tried to focus. Finally he saw it was a ticket, an airplane ticket for Edward Streeter. "I hope that's proof enough, son. When your girl died, Peter Hungerford was thirty-five thousand feet up in the air, flying to Chicago."

Chub stared at the ticket. He couldn't make out the words now, but he stared.

"Okay," one of the guards called.

"Now you know, now you leave," the old guard said, and he put his hand on the door.

Chub could hear voices, coming closer. One voice really, out of sight, from the top of the stairs, Peter Hungerford's saying over and over, "I'm happy, Mommy. . . . Are you happy? . . . I'll bet I'm happier than you are. . . ."

Spinning. Chub stood on the corner of Third in the Sixties and that was his chief sensation—that somehow, gradually but now more and more, the world was going to spin him off it, gravity would desert him and he would be hurled into the frozen atmosphere.

Hungerford didn't do it—he had to have done it but he didn't—which left how many men to choose from? A billion? What were those odds? He remembered Rory's phrase, "inconceivable to one." Maxwell's Plum was just there, so Chub went in, ordered a double Wild Turkey, looked at the Friday-night crowd. Maybe it was early or maybe it was a combination of AIDS and herpes but it didn't seem as jammed as he thought. He heard Sandy then: "I got herpes—fibbing, fibbing," so he downed the drink fast, paid, got the hell out, hailed a cab.

Then he was trudging up the ninety-seven stairs. Then he was in his room. He tossed off his Windbreaker and it made a clunk when it landed. The gun. Oh, what a sage purchase that had been. Jack Armstrong on the trail.

Chub poured himself another double of Wild Turkey, went to the window and sat, didn't like it there, went to his bed and lay down, didn't like it there, the television was not the companion he needed, so he moved to his desk, looked at the two neatly typed title pages, "Flores para los Muertos" and "The End of the Rain." He picked up the latter, thumbed through it. The little boy who believed in God that afternoon was not in the vicinity.

A mistake, probably, because the phone rang at ten-forty-five and a male voice said, "We have to talk."

"Who is this—who do you want?"

"I want Charles Fuller, and I believe this is he." Ordinary voice. Nothing unusual.

So why was Chub's heart beginning to quicken?

"I'd like to meet—and chat—now—someplace where we can be very much alone—"

"What do you want to talk about?"

A long pause. " 'The Sad Life of Sandy Smith'—you're a writer, that's not a bad title, wouldn't you agree, nice use of alliteration?"

"Who *is* this?" Chub said, though he already knew.

"Charley Fuller."

They talked briefly, arranging an assignation, but all the while, Chub's eyes were focused on his Windbreaker. He had been smart to buy the gun after all. . . .

At eleven-fifteen, alone and chill, Chub waited inside the entrance to Central Park at Eighty-sixth Street. A few people wandered by. Chub looked at them, none of them looked back. It was probably in the fifties now, and a wind was rising.

Then a guy his own age was watching him. Not as big as Chub had imagined, not as handsome. Like his voice, ordinary. Then the guy started coming toward him, saying, "This is a pleasure, I suppose you know I'm a true fan of yours."

And then he held out his hand.

"I don't want to shake with you, for Chrissakes!" Chub said.

"Understood," the guy said, and with that, they began to walk into the park.

"Why did you do it?" Chub said.

"Since *I* am the one who initiated calling this meeting to order, I am also going to be in charge of parliamentary procedures, I hope you have no problem comprehending that."

Chub said nothing at first. The guy spoke distinctly, and he clearly enjoyed the sound of his own voice, the use of a longer word when a shorter one would have sufficed. "What's your real name?"

"I can't imagine any reason for further functioning in secrecy. Ben. Ben Werner. German. Ugly. I've always loathed it, and there was a time when I actually contemplated going to court and having it altered, perhaps to something mellifluous like—"

"—I don't give a shit," Chub cut in.

"Understood."

They walked slowly deeper into the park. There were still passersby, but they were becoming fewer in number. Chub kept his hands in his pockets now, the right one on the metal.

"A man of action, is that the kind of fellow you are? Get right to cases. A bottom liner."

"If 'parliamentary procedure' is your way of saying 'diarrhea of the mouth,' you can get off it."

Ben Werner looked at Chub, smiled. "All right, down to cases. I've been being you for years. Not compulsively—no fetish involved. But I should guess I began around '78."

"Why, for God's sake?"

"I was getting my master's when your book came out in paper. I wanted desperately to be a writer. I was entranced with your skill. Now, I won't deny I hated you for being so young with all that gift, but on the whole, I was, as I say, entranced. But not nearly as entranced as the way people talked about it. It and you. There was a genuine fad." Ben Werner paused. "Christ, I wanted that." He looked at Chub. "In your dreams you cannot imagine how much. And in my dreams there was no doubt I was going to have it."

"You're a writer, then?"

"I teach German in a public high school in Chicago.

That was not, may I add, where I thought I would spend my life, not when your book came out. Several events altered my course. One: It turned out I lacked talent. Two: It turned out the girl I was dating was pregnant. Three: She was deeply Catholic. Pressure was applied. We now have been together for a decade, we have five children, ours is not as blissful a ménage as, say, the Partridge Family."

"Get to me, all right?"

"Ah, yes, you, the sainted Charles Fuller. In point of fact, you appeared quite by accident. I'd stopped in a bar—I needed a bracer or two before I could face the home front—different bars, always, not good for a teacher to be seen imbibing, you understand, I'm sure."

Chub glanced around. There was no one around now. He took out his cigarettes, lit an English Oval, put it in his left, put his right back in his Windbreaker pocket.

"The barfly on the next stool was reading and we got to talking and he asked what I did and for no reason I can remember, I said I was a writer. He said he read a lot, who was I. I chanced it, said Charley Fuller. He hadn't heard of me but he didn't care—he'd never met a writer before. He began peppering me with questions and then called the bartender over to buy me a free drink and I was gracious and accepted, and when the barfly asked if I knew Norman Mailer I thought, in for a penny, why not. Yes, I knew Norman. Not intimately, but we occasionally corresponded. I'd gotten drunk with him at Elaine's. We'd butted heads, so I knew he liked me." He stopped. "That is right, isn't it? Doesn't Mailer butt heads with people when he likes them? I'm sure I read that someplace."

"I don't know, I've never met Norman Mailer."

"I'm amazed," Ben Werner said. "I thought you all knew each other."

"Maybe they do, I don't, go on."

"Well, I had a *wonderful* time in that bar. And that was the beginning. I kept on doing it. Once when I took a short vacation alone, I was you for three entire days. That was the first time I slept with a girl because of it. She had, as she elegantly put it, 'a thing' for guys with words."

Chub shook his head—it sounded like the guy had had a better time being him than he had.

"Of course I was always worried about being discovered. So I went to school on you. I drove out to Athens—you haven't been back since high school, I know, but you're quite the figure there. The librarian knew all about you, where you'd lived, gone to school. You'd even spent time in the library when you were a kid when your aunt worked there. Ummm . . . Aunt—"

"—Audrey."

"Thank you, but I would have gotten it, I promise you. And I had some false identification made up, driver's license, that sort of handy paraphernalia, in case anyone thought I might be lying. Which brings us up to Sandy, shall we sit?" He pointed to a bench. They were totally alone now.

Chub let him sit first, then carefully sat on Werner's right. So his own right hand could move unencumbered.

"Poor poor sad Sandy Smith. Sitting alone, reading your book. You must understand that had never happened before. Not since my impersonations began—actually *seeing* someone with that book in her hands. Seeing someone as sensual as that, reading your book, while at home I had—well, five children can change a woman, especially if she was not particularly fair to look upon in her prime. Sandy was, when she came to believe in me, a blessing. Of course I couldn't tell her how to get in touch with me and bless her for not questioning when I told her I had no phone, wanted no interruptions, not when I was writing. And then, of course, she discovered the truth."

"*Now* you can answer me: *Why did you do it?*"

"I was so frightened—afraid everything would be discovered and *ruined*—so I called her bad things, hurt her, threatened her and hurt her some more—and then these last days I realized something—it didn't matter if what I had was ruined, it was all ruined anyway, so I left my wife and I left my children and I left my job and I've come to you because I know she would have come to you—you would never be here now if she hadn't—and I want you to go to her and tell her I need her back, that the lies are done, that I'll do anything to make her happy, anything, I love her, I've never been happy except when I was with her, *you must help me!*" And he grabbed for Chub, begging, "I'm nothing if I can't have her back, you can do it for me, *please.*"

"She's dead," Chub said, stunned. "She died today—you knew that."

But in a moment, Chub realized a different truth: Because as he stared, Ben Werner's face came apart. It wasn't just the tears, it was the agony that forced them out, and his body stiffened, and that went on, the tears and the crying out, the body almost flopping in the darkness, and then the man Chub had brought the gun for was reaching for him, holding him, his face buried in Chub's neck, the tears trickling down Chub's skin.

Chub walked home very much alone. It was cold, but he didn't care. His body shivered, but he didn't care. It was over. He had been wrong. Hungerford hadn't done it and Werner hadn't done it, no one had done it but Sandy all by her lonesome, she had decided to fly a few seconds and then it would be over, and so it was.

A piece of paper was shoved into his mail slot. From Baylor.

Chub:

I have spent the night at the lab. When you said I'd find the prints of another man, you were right—they were *mine,* asshole. I sat on that fucking sill last Sunday when we recorded the interview. (The bitch won't pay me, but right now that is not high on my list of priorities.)

It just was swell at the lab, and I really had a fun time, thanks to you. And as far as I'm concerned, since *we* both have alibis, *the case is closed.*

Maya will forgive you I'm sure, but it's going to take me awhile. You're invited for dinner, Sunday—just don't expect me to talk to you.

Rory

Chub tried to make it up the stairs without stopping, but he couldn't. Each flight took more out of him. Higher and higher the steps took him, and to where? A despised cage where Isaac Singer might have once, long ago, breathed.

He made it eventually, and he leaned against the door, catching his breath, and then he took off his Windbreaker and there was the "clunk" sound again. Chub reached into the right pocket, took out the weapon, closed his eyes.

All his life, all he had ever tried to do was please. Be good, be better, be the bestest good boy in all the land.

And now Sandy was dead and dear Jesse was dead and his father was dead and his mother, if she was dead, didn't even want him at her funeral, and always in the air now, always a step and a year ahead of him, always laughing and triumphant, was his perfect brother with his perfect blue eyes.

And a rage of such power broke over Chub, because there was an element left out of his life's equation: There was a secret to living and no one had seen fit to tell him—there was a trick to surviving the days but no one had let him in on the solution, much less that the trick existed at all.

And while the rage had him he raced to the window, raised the gun, fired six shots at the night—

—only the gun didn't work.

It jammed before he could finish pulling the trigger. That was why the transvestites were laughing: They had stuck a sucker with a busted piece.

Now Chub, looking at the useless metal, had to laugh, too—it was so perfect, so symbolic of it all, and as he stood there by the open window he knew what his epitaph should be:

Here lies Charles Fuller
He couldn't hurt a fly—
But he could sure hurt people.

Not bad. Not poetry, but it had the ring of truth. He made himself a drink, rolled a piece of paper into his Olympia, wrote down the epitaph because at least now he remembered it and by the time the mist was done with him that night, and he had no doubt that it was on the stairway now, the thought would be gone.

He sat, sipped the Wild Turkey, waited. He got up, crossed to the windowsill where he had dropped the gun, brought it back, stuck it on his desk for all to see. As a reminder of how wrong he was, always, always, now and forever. Besides, it would make a great paperweight.

Chub took another sip, began to fiddle with his Olympia.

```
somewhere there is someone who is always
   right, and boy do I envy that mother.

(ah, the glories of self-pity.)

but there's supposed to be something
   called the law of averages.

        --wait wait wait--

what if--
what if--

WHAT IF THIS TIME, JUST THIS ONE TIME,
   I WASN'T WRONG--and ten years from
   now some guy admits killing Sandy.

--wait--
--wait--
```

WHAT IF IT DIDN'T HAPPEN IN TEN YEARS--
WHAT IF HE ADMITTED IT NOW.

AND WHAT IF I MADE IT HAPPEN?
How, though?

Chub got up, went to his icebox, brought back some cubes, dumped them into his Wild Turkey, fiddled some more.

How in the hell could I make it happen?

welllll

hmmmmmm

shit--

--no--look--what if I became obsessed--
(boy do I understand that)
--and what if I went to Chicago or Portland
  or any damn place and met somebody somehow--
  Sandy's mother maybe, I don't care who--
    JUST SOMEONE WHO KNEW SOMETHING.

Maybe her friend Becky.

Just enough for a lead clue.

And off to Chicago and WHAMMO--

I CAPTURE THE KILLER!

Might make a story. (Might not too.)

Forget that, who would the ''I'' be?

hmmmmm.

fug.

--no no no, genius notion--

WHAT IF THE ''I'' WAS ME?

And what if I wrote about me?
  Give the hero my background.

It's my life, after all, it's my material.

Chub pushed himself away from his desk, wondered if there was any of the tuna club left. There wasn't. He lit an English Oval, went and lay down.

Because there was a problem—a big problem and it was this: There was too much material for a story, it wouldn't work as a story, too skeletal, the motivations would be too thin, nothing to buttress them, make them hold, it couldn't be a story—

—but it could be a book.

He sat up with the thought, left the bedroom, began to pace around, from the window to the desk to the window and yes, it was his material but it was more than that because chasing after the unknown—he'd been doing that half his life damn near, chasing the perfection of the blue-eyed boy who never wet his bed, never caused trouble, was always so perfect.

Chub began to move faster because if it was a book it had all the elements—surprise, subtext, suspense, death—it could really be something, big, a huge success—

"Asshole," he said out loud. "You goddamn fucking asshole." Because the truth was this: If he could only *write* it, if he could only get it down—*that act would make it a success.*

Chub stood still, unaware of so many things. (That he would fiddle for two hours, he didn't know that. That he would write a ten-page outline and finish before dawn and shove it in Kitchel's surprised face—he didn't know that either.) All he did know was this: For the first time in a decade when he was alone, the impulse was on him. And strong.

He went to his typewriter, rubbed his eyes, took a sip of the diluted Wild Turkey, lit an English Oval, let his fingers fly.

book in parts, yes? yes.

part one could be me growing up--

--NO. WRONG. WRITTEN THAT.
 NO MORE GROWING-UP SHIT!

BEGIN WITH HERE. NEW YORK. YOUNG WRITER.
 contract--a star is born--
 ''Hello, everybody, this is Mrs. Norman maine.''

WAIT WAIT WAIT

it falls into <u>four</u> parts.

the success part--up until maybe first great
 children of alcoholics meeting--elephant
 in the living room--

and second part opens with next alcoholics
 meeting ONLY SURPRISE KICKER--years have
 passed--I'm not writing anymore.

anyway, second part is downhill--
 ''the greatest failure''--fuck you, cheyney--
 impulse gone--research--hates it--

then the mist and saved by the bone.

CAN'T CALL HER BONE.
 let her keep her english ovals and fierceness
 and love of hitchcock--
 but make her fat--like lydia (not bad)
THE TUB. That could be her name.

anyway, part two ends with me at bottom--
 breaking into tears--

HOLD IT HOLD IT--I got names for the parts.

 PART I (SUCCESS)   ON THE COME
 PART II (FAILURE)   ON THE SKIDS
 PART III (AFFAIR)   ON THE SPOT
 PART IV (AFTER KILLER)   ON THE TRAIL

part three is Sandy--
 call her ''the cheerleader'' for now--
 she comes, wild, adoring, all secret--
 the impulse comes back--

for affair to have greater pressure,
  I must be married to the tub--

and maybe the tub realizes she's losing me.

Cheerleader dies, same as sandy, case closed--
  only charley fuller doesn't come after me--

I GO AFTER CHARLEY FULLER. (THAT'S PART FOUR)
  where?
    where?
got to be a locale where a writer sticks out--not a
city--
  --and remember, there's been a murder--okay, a locale where violence isn't unknown--small town, ru-
ral--
    where?
      where?

OH SHIT--GREAT--<u>TEXAS</u>.

okay, I go to my fat hitchcock-loving wife--
  and lie--''got to go to texas for a little,
  big research job, see you.''

AND OFF I GO TO FIND THE GUY WHO'S BEEN LIVING
MY LIFE AND HAVING A BETTER TIME OF IT THAN
I HAVE.

--wait--wait--mistake--
--NEEDS MORE TENSION--

--got it, GOT IT--

SECOND DAY IN TEXAS, the tub waltzes in.
''Surprise.''

why would she come? maybe she's in rocky shape.
    (I can write that)
she can't take the being alone.

she knows their marriage slip-sliding away--
  maybe in their time together in texas,
  whatever they once had, they get it back.

SO: it's not just a novel of <u>obsession</u>--
    it's also a novel of <u>redemption</u>.
    DOUBLE REDEMPTION MAYBE
    --I'm vindicated, write the story
    of our adventures and victory--
    --and along the way, <u>we're</u> redeemed.

(easy money at the brick factory)

Chub stopped, closed his eyes. He stood, wondered if
there was any tuna club left, went to look, remembered
he'd done that already, ran back to his machine.

Jesus, when I come to town, that's got to
    shake the phony ''me'' at least a little--
    he's got to know I'm not there by accident,

So then?
What?

Maybe time passes, frustrating, no clues--

The tub's got to wonder what's going on so
    maybe I tell half the truth--that the cheer-
    leader visited and I'm tracking her because
    it's good material, maybe I could write it--

And the tub is in ecstasy--it's a <u>mystery</u>--
    like hitchcock--and maybe she gets all
    revved up--''what would hitch do, where
    would hitch go?''--

JESUS CHRIST WAIT

WHAT IF THE VILLAIN CAPTURES THE WIFE?
    (she's stumbled too close to the truth)

I'm in our motel room, the tub calls--scared--
    then man's voice--''you want her back,
    come get her.'' Gives address. ''Alone.''

So I go alone--terrible night--winds outside--
    deserted place--
    farmhouse maybe--

I go in--she's there--villain too--armed--
  and now he's got us both--

KICKER--fucking tornado hits (remember how
  it came from nowhere so fast?)

--darkness now--I yell for tub to run--
  fight--he's too strong--

WAIT WAIT--VILLAIN COULD BE
HUGE CRAZY GUY--PETER HUNGERFORD

fight no contest--hungerford's way too strong--

--zap--the tub returns, creams hungerford
  with poker, I don't give a shit what--but
  he crumples--

--and we embrace--

kicker--hungerford's dead.

We're murderers now.

Outside the weather is screaming--then
  sudden silence--it's moved on.

And in that silence I say I'll take the rap--
  I'll say I hit him--and now I
  tell total truth of cheerleader, affair,
  how she got me writing, how no one would
  believe it murder, how I had to prove to
  the world I wasn't wrong again--
  I finish talking--

silence--sss--sss--she smokes, she's
  been lied to, I've had affair and--

kicker--great reaction--she says, ''I'M NOT
LOSING YOU OVER THIS ASSHOLE.''

She walks around muttering, ''what would hitch
  do with the body?'' and I just stand there
  and she whirls on me and says, ''for chrissakes,
  you're a researcher, don't you know anything?''

And maybe I mumble about
  once seeing quicksand in texas--

--and suddenly she's a dervish--''It's better
than <u>psycho</u> when tony put janet in the lake--
we'll put this bastard in his car--there's
been a tornado, no one will suspect squat--
we'll put him at the wheel of his car and
find some quicksand and dump his ass.''

So off we go in the night, me driving the
corpse, the tub in our rented car--
and of course it's impossible, you just
don't find quicksand--

ONLY--ONLY--GOD'S ON OUR SIDE--
We <u>find</u> some--deep and ugly--and it's
a bitch but we make it.

THE CAR AND THE KILLER SLOWLY BUBBLE DOWN
DOWN
  DOWN

And we take off, crazy and happy and safe and
we make love in our motel and the next
morning--

THE NEXT MORNING--FANTASTIC KICKER--

We've <u>made</u> <u>a</u> <u>mistake</u>--

"Holy shit, they killed the wrong guy?" Kitchel said
the following dawn, halfway through reading Chub's
outline. "They put the wrong fucker in the quicksand?"

"Just finish it, then we'll talk," Chub said, pacing
around Kitchel's living room. He hadn't slept in a day,
had worked all night, but still had too much energy to
land anyplace.

It was after seven when Two-Brew put the outline
down, sat back in his desk chair, spoke not a syllable for
a while.

Chub paced, trying not to watch him, just kept moving
and praying to hear the four magic words.

"On to the next," Kitchel said finally.

Chub nodded.

Kitchel rose then. "I am almost thirty-three, it is time

I committed my first sentimental gesture." And he did something Chub had never seen before—he moved around his desk, not using his crutches for support but just his arms, and when he was near to Chub he reached out, grabbed him, held him tight.

Chub, thrilled by the reaction but embarrassed a little, too, said quickly, "I take it this means I've risen above putrescent."

"Oh, fuck you, you have no soul," Kitchel said, letting go, fulcruming himself back to his desk chair, flopping down. He picked up the outline again, looked at the last pages.

"You know a choice you lucked into I really like—I'm sure you didn't mean it, considering your feeble mentality, but at the end—when the hero and the *real* killer finally meet and the killer gets zapped—the hero feels sad."

"That's why the working title is *The Predator and the Prey.* Without the killer, the hero would never have been able to come back. They needed each other—I read an article about leopards once."

"I'm sure you'll screw it up, but you know what this is? It's kind of like early Graham Greene out of Kafka."

Chub smiled. The Bone would like the Kafka part.

"When will you be able to Crayola me a first draft? This is late May, I would like it before Christmas. Bring it out early the following fall, that's best for getting critical attention."

"Don't pressure me."

"I always used to, I can now."

"I want to go to Texas a little before I start—I want The Bone to come along—I think she'll be funny in those little Texas towns. And useful." He paused. "Okay. Christmas."

Kitchel closed his eyes and started talking quietly. "You know, if I hadn't gotten you going on *The Dead Pile* . . . a lot of what's happened is on my head."

"Oh, bullshit. It's still good stuff. I just wasn't ready to write it, I'm still not, I may never be. I tell you what I've come to think: Life is material, everything is material—you just have to be able to live long enough to see how to use it."

Kitchel held up the outline. "And this happened why?"

"Don't know—maybe because I kept hitting bottom. Except when I did, I fell through the floor each time. Last night I guess there were no more floors to fall through."

"Please leave that last prepubescent piece of trivia *out* of the manuscript."

"Promise."

Kitchel smiled. "I envy you, you turd. I remember once, back in a snowstorm at Oberlin, I told you that I was going to be your Maxwell Perkins and you were going to be my star. Some Maxwell Perkins—I don't edit, I spend my days making deals with agents and fighting with lawyers and overpaying writers. But you—you can still make it happen."

Chub shook his head. "I was kind of a starlet once, that blink when the book took off in paper. I don't want that. I just want to write my ass off."

"Well, I have confidence—if anyone can create something as fine as 'Dick, see Dick run'—Chubbo, you're the man."

Chub smiled, got ready to go.

Kitchel indicated the outline—"May I keep this?"

Chub nodded. "I've got the carbon."

Two-Brew reached for his crutches, positioned them under his arms, accompanied Chub to the door. They shook hands. "Young Fuller has returned," Kitchel said.

"Not so young anymore." Chub thought a moment before he said it: "But he's back."

He taxied down to SoHo, let himself quietly into The Bone's place. She lay drained on her bed, her right eye bloodshot, the blood vessels in her right temple visible. A cluster was either coming or going.

Chub took her hand gently, whispered, "Bonita Kraus, she's got the prettiest eyes."

She managed a smile. "It's okay—I think this was the last one for the night."

"I have to talk to you," Chub said. "It won't take long but it's important, so tell me when you're able to listen."

"... I can listen. ..."

"Sure?"

She nodded.

Chub looked at her a moment. A wonderful, strange creature, fierce and wounding, but never never dull. Bright and getting brighter. Perhaps even talented. But there was no "perhaps" about this: When he had needed her, and he had needed her, she had been there for him.

"I hate my apartment," Chub said. "I want to get out of it."

"... Singer never lived there. ..."

"Huh?"

"I met a Singer freak once ... when I crashed a publishing party ... not long ago.... I asked him if Singer ever lived on Ninety-eighth Street. He didn't."

"Why didn't you tell me?"

"I don't know ... maybe when I found out I figured you didn't need any more bad news."

Chub kissed her temple, but just grazed it with his lips. She didn't need any more pain. "Okay. I want to move out of there and in here with you. I want to live with you. I'm going to write a novel and that may be a problem, two of us hacking away, but it if is, I'll find an office close by."

She reached out, took him in her arms. "It won't be a problem. You stay right here ... can I still yell at you?"

"Daily."

"I would like that."

"Well, you may not like this, but I don't want anything secret between us, so I've got to tell you. That girl I told you about? The one who thought her boyfriend was me? She came to my place on Sunday. She stayed with me and yes, we slept together."

"If she's moving in here, too ... the deal is off."

"She committed suicide yesterday. That's what my

book's about. About a guy like me who gets obsessed that it wasn't suicide, even though the cops have shut the books on the case. In the book, I go on this lunatic hunt to find the guy who was me." He paused. The blood vessels in her temple were subsiding, but very slowly. "Would an icebag help you feel better?" He touched her temple. "There?"

"Oh, yes." She closed her eyes.

Chub stood up.

"Why does the guy get obsessed? Is he crazy or something?"

"Same reason I did," Chub said, as he headed for the refrigerator in the kitchen area. "The girl was a TV freak—she was always happy when there was TV."

"Oh, that's right," The Bone said. "The TV was on."

In the kitchen, Chub clung to the wall, made no sound whatsoever, but his mouth opened and closed, opened and closed, as he told himself, kept telling himself, that life was material, everything was material—you just had to live long enough to see how to use it.

February 21–Memorial Day, 1983
New York City